Book Three of the Cairnmor Trilogy

When Anna Stewart begins a relationship with journalist Marcus Kendrick, the ramifications are felt from New York all the way across the Atlantic to the remote and beautiful Scottish island of Cairnmor, where her family live. Yet even as she and Marcus draw closer, Anna cannot forget her estranged husband whom she has not seen for many years.

When tragedy strikes, for some, Cairnmor becomes a refuge, a place of solace to ease the troubled spirit and an escape from painful reality; for others, it becomes a place of enterprise and adventure – a place in which to dream of an unfettered future.

This third book in the Cairnmor Trilogy, takes the action forward into the late nineteen-sixties as well as recalling familiar characters' lives from the intervening years. Where Gloom and Brightness Meet is a story of heartbreak and redemptive love; of long-dead passion remembered and retained in isolation; of unfaltering loyalty and steadfast devotion. It is a story that juxtaposes the old and the new; a story that reflects the conflicting attitudes, problems and joys of a liberating era.

Sally Aviss

Where Gloom and Brightness Meet

Ōzaru
Books

Published by Ōzaru Books, an imprint of BJ Translations Ltd
Street Acre, Shuart Lane, St Nicholas-at-Wade,
BIRCHINGTON, CT7 0NG, U.K.
www.ozaru.net

First edition published 20 November 2015
Printed by Lightning Source
ISBN: 978-0-9931587-1-1

For my family
with my love

Acknowledgements

I am, as ever, indebted to my family: Peter, Tim and Elizabeth Aviss; to my reading panel Christine Lord, Annette Vidler and Katie Boughton and to Ben Jones of Ozaru Books for all their continuing support.

Idyll

In the grey summer garden I shall find you

With day-break and the morning hills behind you.

There will be rain-wet roses; stir of wings;

And down the wood a thrush that wakes and sings.

Not from the past you'll come, but from that deep

Where beauty murmurs to the soul asleep:

And I shall know the sense of life re-born

From dreams into the mystery of noon

Where gloom and brightness meet. And standing there

Till that calm song is done, at last we'll share

The league spread, quiring symphonies that are

Joy in the world, and peace, and dawn's one star.

Siegfried Sassoon, 1919

Contents

PART ONE

October 1968 – April 1969

CHAPTER 1

New York
Anna

"Jack, where are you? I need you. Jack!"

She was calling, calling, but no sound came from her lips. She tried again and again but it was always the same. She reached out to him but he kept disappearing, slipping through her fingers, obscured by mist and darkness.

She needed him. He had always come to her when she needed him. Why wasn't he here? Why didn't he come to her?

Anna Stewart woke up with a start; sweating, anxious, afraid in the darkness. She looked at the man sleeping beside her: someone she barely knew; someone she didn't particularly want to see again. Why had she gone to bed with him?

Her head throbbed. Oh yes. She'd had too much to drink at the opening-night party after the play, her first time on a Broadway stage. She wasn't the lead or anything but it was a good role, a showy role and she thought she'd done well in it. Many people had come backstage to congratulate her, including this man. He'd hung around afterwards and they'd gone to the party together. They all said the play was good enough to run and run but the early morning reviews had been mixed, and everyone had gone home feeling slightly deflated. He'd offered to take her home to her apartment and she'd invited him in.

The man stirred and turned towards her. He was a journalist or something. Quite high up and respected, apparently. Marcus Kendrick. She'd vaguely heard of him. She wondered if he was married. Probably. The nicest ones usually were.

Her mouth felt like sandpaper. She clambered out of bed, disentangling herself from the covers, pulled on her robe and went into the kitchen where she gulped down a glass of water and a couple of aspirin. She looked at the clock. She had time for more sleep before the rehearsal at ten, but the picture of Jack Rutherford kept going round and round in her mind.

Why should she dream so vividly of him? Why now? She hadn't had any contact with him in years, not since he'd walked out on her that day. What had she done to make him so angry and upset? Anna couldn't remember. No, that was stupid. Of course she could remember. How could she ever forget? But right now her head hurt.

Later, when she came back from rehearsal, the journalist was still there. He'd made himself at home and had prepared sandwiches for them both.

"Don't you have a home to go to?" she asked, not ungratefully. All she wanted to do was eat and sleep.

"Yes, but my wife's abroad. So I'm at a loose end."

"Ah." Anna didn't like being described as a loose end but maybe that's what she was in her private life; what she had finally become.

He pulled her into his arms and took her into bed with him again. Now that she wasn't drunk, she found it very pleasant; in fact she almost enjoyed herself.

2

Afterwards, she fell asleep immediately and when she woke up a few hours later, he brought her the lunch he had prepared earlier but which neither of them had eaten. Fully dressed, he sat on the bed and watched her while she ate.

"Who's Jack?"

The question caught Anna by surprise. "How do you know about Jack?"

"You kept calling his name in your sleep."

She viewed him suspiciously. "Is this professional curiosity or genuine interest?"

He laughed. "Both."

"I don't believe you."

"It's true." He came to sit beside her, leaning back against the headboard, his legs stretched out on the bed. "What time do you have to leave for the theatre?"

"Six."

He looked at the clock. "Then there's plenty of time."

"For what?" She raised an eyebrow at him.

"For you to tell me all about Jack."

Her body experienced disappointment but her mind was engaged. "Why?"

"Because I find it intriguing." There might be copy here but he liked this woman. Very much. He wanted to see more of her. He wanted to know all about her for herself. Not the actress on the stage; not as some potential for an article.

"Oh. Where shall I start?"

"At the beginning?"

It was as good a place as any.

She thought for a moment. "I suppose my first clear memory of Jack was when I was about eight years old. The war had just ended and we went to stay on Cairnmor for the holidays."

"Who's we?"

"My mother, my twin brother Rupert and I."

"Your twin brother?"

"Yes."

"Where's Cairnmor?"

"Off the west coast of Scotland. It's an island. Look, if you're going to keep asking me questions, then we'll never get anywhere."

The journalist laughed again and put his arm round her.

This man has a musical laugh, thought Anna. *He's quite good looking too and his face has character. But he's not as handsome as Jack. No one could ever be as handsome as Jack.*

Unbidden to her mind came a vivid picture of him walking towards her along the white-gold sands of Cairnmor, a broad smile lighting his face; his naval officer's cap at a rakish angle, the sleeves of his white polo-neck jumper rolled up and his manner relaxed. The moment he saw her running along the seashore to greet him, he had held out his arms for her, gathering her to him with absolute joy, holding her tightly, kissing her face and her lips. Her body tingled at the memory and tears pricked her eyes.

But that was later, much later. First things first. She took a deep breath.

"Jack Rutherford served with my grandfather during the second world war in the R.N.V.R."

"What's the R.N.V.R.?"

"There you go again."

"What?"

"Asking questions."

"I'm a journalist. It's my nature."

"I suppose you're going to put everything I say in the newspaper you work for. And my private life will become public property yet again."

"Not necessarily. And I don't work for a newspaper. I work for *Chronicle* magazine."

"Oh. Very intellectual and upmarket."

"I guess so. And I don't do shock journalism either, nor do I pry into people's personal lives for the sake of it or for monetary gain."

"A journalist with scruples, huh? A rare beast indeed. Then why do you want to know about Jack?"

"Because I'm interested in you." He was taking a risk here – it was too soon: they didn't know each other; she didn't know *him*.

"*Me*?" She expressed surprise and subtly withdrew from him.

"Yes," he said quickly, sensing her distance. "Not the actress. Not for an article. You." He took the ends of her hair between his fingers, playing with it; holding her attention, not giving her the chance to retreat completely. "Now, what's the R.N.V.R.?"

"Royal Naval Voluntary Reserve. Although after the war, Jack signed up as a regular in the Royal Navy."

"Go on."

So she did.

When Anna was eight years old, in 1946, her mother Katherine had had a baby. A little girl. She and Alastair called her Grace. She was their child, a love child, born before they were married. A sort of three-quarters sister for Anna and Rupert.

Alastair, whom she had grown up thinking of as her father, was in fact her grandfather. She made the discovery quite by chance when she was fourteen and the news had so shocked Anna that it changed her life. Already wilful in the eyes of her family, she became even more disobedient and headstrong, doing everything she could to scandalize and hurt her parents; well, her mother and grandfather. How could they have allowed her to believe Alastair was her father when all the time her real, biological father was living in Australia?

He was Alastair's son and Katherine's former husband. They had been told he had been killed in the war but Alex (that was his name) turned out to be alive after all. He'd suffered head injuries while serving in the Far East which had resulted in a complete loss of memory. For years he had been living in Melbourne with Rachel Curtis, the doctor who had saved his life in Malaya and who later restored him to health.

Believing Alex to be dead, and because they had always been very close, it was only natural that Katherine and Alastair should fall in love and want to be together, they told her.

4

Anna had been horrified. *Natural*? Unnatural. Her mother and her grandfather. Together. Ugh. Disgusting. She felt betrayed, let down.

Everyone else seemed to know and not be concerned about it – her other grandparents, newly-arrived from Canada, as well as Mary and Michael. Even Aunt Lily and Uncle Phillippe in France. She hated all of them after that but especially her mother.

Upset by her immediate reaction, they said they had been waiting to tell her and Rupert once they were old enough to understand. Alex had never shown any interest in her or her brother, they said, therefore it became less and less important that she and Rupert should know.

Her brother took it all in his stride. He tried to make her see that Alastair had brought them up, had provided for them since they were babies; had loved them, helped them and would do anything for them. He was indeed their real father – the person who had always cared for them. He was the best and kindest father anyone could possibly have. This Alex person in Australia obviously didn't care a fig about them and therefore, was not worth their time.

Rupert had gone to Mary and Michael and asked them about it all. They'd told him honestly and openly and he came away satisfied and philosophical; his relationship towards Alastair and Katherine unchanged, his regard and love for them intact.

But for Anna, it was different.

"Have you never come to terms with it?" asked Marcus, curious and concerned.

"No."

"Have you ever spoken about this to anyone before?"

Anna was silent for a moment. "No," she said quietly.

Perhaps she could talk to him because he was a stranger; well not a complete stranger. They had been intimate with each other. Twice. But even so, she didn't know him as a person. Well, that wasn't strictly true either. He'd been very considerate towards her in bed and seemed genuine in his manner. He didn't appear to be some kind of hack trying to get a story, either.

"Why not?"

"There you go, asking questions again." She avoided giving him a direct answer. She was supposed to be talking about Jack Rutherford.

"Before all this happened, during that Easter holiday in 1946, Jack came to visit Alastair and stayed with us. They'd served together at Dunkirk and in the Mediterranean and then at the Admiralty. He was twenty-four and had just taken up his commission as a career officer in the Royal Navy. Alastair was very proud and pleased for him. They were good friends and spent many hours talking about the service which my grandfather loved so much and had just retired from.

"Jack had brought some sort of heavy book with him and asked Alastair if he would keep it safe and look after it for him while he was away at sea. It was one of his most prized possessions, he said, and only someone who knew about it would understand. Alastair was only too happy to oblige.

"When I asked what it was about, Jack showed me some pictures – 'Mickey Mouse' diagrams he said they were – but I remember being very disappointed as I couldn't see any Mickey Mouses in there, only tiny diagrams of ships going from England to France."

Anna smiled at the recollection and observing her quietly, Marcus thought how beautiful she was.

"Anyway, Jack stayed for two weeks. He made a great fuss of little Grace who, I have to admit, was a very sweet baby, and as Rupert was off playing with Rose every day..."

"Who's Rose?"

"Michael and Mary's daughter."

"And they are...?"

"Alastair and Katherine's best friends."

"Go on."

"I'm trying, Marcus."

"Very trying." He smiled and touched her cheek.

"As Rupert was off playing with Rose every day, I took it upon myself to show Jack over the island..."

"Cairnmor?"

"Marcus!" Anna smiled this time. "Stop interrupting." But her admonishment was good natured.

"I want to know; to understand."

"Yes. Cairnmor."

"What sort of island is it?"

Anna became wistful. "Beautiful, spectacular. High mountains and deep valleys. Has the most amazing pale gold sands. Secret coves, magical hidden places. Bogs. Huge storms. And the wind! Sometimes the wind is so fierce you can't stand upright. My mother lived there until she met Alex and they got married."

"What did she do during the war?"

"She was in the Wrens." Pre-empting the inevitable question, Anna explained, "Women's Royal Naval Service. I think she and Alastair worked together on the staff of the admiral who planned the amphibious landings for the invasion of Normandy. Or something like that, anyway."

"Wow! Was the book that Jack brought anything to do with this?"

"Yes. It contained the operational orders for the allied navies on D-Day."

"Some document!" Marcus was impressed. "Now, where were we? You were showing Jack over the island."

"Yes. We walked for miles that first visit and on subsequent ones. Then I would spend hours sitting beside him while he sketched or painted. He was an accomplished artist."

"Did he ever do any drawings of you?"

"Some, but not that many, I'm afraid. I used to get restless after a while and wander off. I keep them in a box somewhere."

She seemed casual, careless almost in her attitude, but Marcus sensed an underlying admiration for Jack's talent. He assumed it meant a great deal to her.

"He was also very knowledgeable about plants and mosses and such like and enjoyed talking about them. He was a lovely man. Kind, thoughtful. And handsome. Boy, was he handsome!"

And watching her expression, Marcus began to feel the first stirrings of jealousy towards this apparent paragon.

"Anyway," continued Anna, oblivious to her companion's discomfort, "after that first time, he would come and see us during every leave, usually spending a week or a fortnight; sometimes on Cairnmor, if it was during the school holidays, sometimes at our country house in Oxfordshire or the house in London during term-time. We saw a lot of him."

Marcus concluded that Anna's family must be very wealthy. Perhaps that would explain this apartment on the swanky Upper East Side. She couldn't afford it on her salary from the play or her TV work, that much was obvious. "So, he saw you grow up."

"Yes." Anna was silent for a moment. Then she glanced at the clock. "Goodness! That can't be the time! I must shower and dress. I have to be at the theatre in just under an hour."

She fussed around finding clothes and make-up. The last thing she wanted was to arrive in a panic for the performance that evening.

Marcus lay back against the pillows, his hands behind his head and waited for her to come back into the bedroom.

"Are you coming to see the play again tonight?" she called out from the bathroom.

"Would you like me to?"

The words slipped out before he could stop them. It was common knowledge that in her personal life, Anna Stewart was renowned for fighting shy from any pressure or lasting commitment in her relationships. Many lovers had tried and failed, usually in a blaze of intrusive publicity. She was, however, totally professional when it came to her work ethic and career.

She was a reasonably well known actress, and although her range was unremarkable, Marcus admired her abilities on the small screen. It was a medium that suited her. His appearance at yesterday's première had not been exactly spontaneous nor was it anything to do with his work as he rarely contributed to the review section of the magazine. He had wanted to see her live on stage; in the flesh, so to speak, rather than just as a black and white image on television. He'd pulled all sorts of strings to get himself a ticket for the opening night.

From the moment that she walked out on stage, he'd been captivated by her, unable to take his eyes away from her. He knew he had to meet her after the performance and it had turned out far better than he could have ever anticipated.

Her offer of bed had been totally unexpected: a wonderful bonus, a gift, one he couldn't refuse. He smiled to himself. He really had seen her in the flesh.

"Yes," she called out. "Yes, I'd like you to come tonight. As my guest."

Taken completely unawares by her reply, Marcus leapt off the bed. He couldn't believe his luck.

CHAPTER 2

Marcus

Having dropped Anna off at the theatre, Marcus hailed a cab and went back to his apartment. He just had time for a shower and shave and to change his clothes before the performance. They had arranged that a complimentary ticket should be left for him at the box office but even so, he would have to hurry as there wasn't much time.

As he opened the door of his apartment, he felt the involuntary, habitual twin responses of vigilance and dread tighten his stomach muscles but he took several deep calming breaths and reminded himself that there was nothing to be anxious about. The rooms were deserted; his wife was away.

The apartment always struck him as cold and soulless but it was where he and Virginia lived or, more accurately, where they existed.

Guilt played around the edges of his conscience. He was not in the habit of being unfaithful, even though their marriage was strained and difficult, but the ease with which he had accepted the offer to spend that first night with Anna had caught him off-guard. Marcus sensed emotional danger here. He knew he would have to be careful; very careful indeed. He understood only too well what was at stake.

Virginia had seemed an attractive yet vulnerable young woman when he had asked her out and after only a matter of weeks, overwhelmed by her charm and persuasiveness, he had stupidly proposed to her. At the start, their marriage seemed happy but within a few short months, it had deteriorated to such an extent that now there was nothing left. Marcus had mourned its passing a long time ago and only stayed with her out of a strong sense of duty to try and save her from herself. She had no one else to turn to for help.

For most of the time and despite his best efforts, Virginia was out of it: either hitting the streets or ranting and raving in rehab.

With the latter, he could do nothing for her except allow the treatment to take its course and visit her from time to time. At the end of each stay, she would come home and things would be relatively calm for a while but soon the whole cycle would begin again, no matter how careful he was to keep alcohol out of the house and Virginia away from the bars and the drugs. It was impossible for him to be with her twenty-four hours a day, seven days a week. He had to earn the money to pay the bills and enough to pay for her treatment.

When she was tucked away in the sanatorium, he always said to people that she was abroad. It was easier that way and avoided embarrassing questions.

Quickly, Marcus completed his tasks and hailed another cab, arriving at the theatre with just enough time to collect his ticket and take his seat as the curtain was going up. When Anna made her entrance, he was riveted by her physical movements: her stage presence rendered more powerful for him by his intimate knowledge of her.

Without either of them saying a word, they left the post-performance party early, where Marcus ensured that Anna drank only one glass of wine, and went back to her apartment. As soon as they walked in the door, they headed straight for the bedroom. Afterwards, exhausted, they both fell deeply asleep just as the outside world was stirring; their arms round each other.

Later that morning, he made breakfast, taking it to her and watching her as she stretched luxuriously.

"Hello," she said, opening her eyes and smiling.

"Hello," he replied, placing the tray on her lap as she sat up.

"Breakfast! What a treat!" She reached out and he took her hand. "That was quite something last night."

He grinned broadly at her. "Yes."

"Even I was satisfied." She looked at him with admiration. "And that's saying something. No one since Jack has been capable of that."

Swallowing his resentment of Jack, and acting upon this unexpected compliment of his own prowess, Marcus removed the tray from her lap and slipped into bed beside her. She welcomed him into her arms and embraced him with such passion and desire, that he responded to her with an energy and ease that surprised even him, considering their adventures of the previous night.

Later, in satiated silence, they shared the breakfast he had made for them which, unlike their ardour, was somewhat cooler than he intended.

Unfortunately, there was no time to linger, as she had to be at the theatre for some scene changes and he at the office to collect his assignment.

"How old are you, Marcus?" asked Anna, later that afternoon as they walked hand in hand through Central Park. Earlier, they had eaten lunch at Luigi's, a chic, much sought after Italian restaurant situated round the corner from the theatre.

"Thirty-four. And you?"

"Twenty-nine. I'm thirty next July. Getting old."

Marcus laughed. "Hardly," he replied, taking in her flawless complexion and graceful movements. "I would have estimated your age to be…" He scrutinized her, rubbing his chin in contemplation. "Ninety-eight at least," he concluded.

Anna threw her head back and laughed. Companionably, they walked on, enjoying the quiet warmth of the afternoon; the incessant traffic's roar a distant undertone.

"Tell me about your wife," asked Anna, as they found a vacant bench and sat down.

Marcus hesitated and took an involuntary inward breath. "My wife is an alcoholic," he said at length.

Having spoken the words out loud, he felt as though he was the one attending an AA meeting, courageously making his first fateful statement. He had accompanied Virginia to many such meetings, all to no avail. She still didn't believe she was addicted. Even after all these years, she was in denial.

Anna regarded him sympathetically. "That must be difficult for you."

He laughed: a harsh sound that caught the back of his throat. "That's an understatement."

Anna thought about her own frequent excesses. Fortunately, she could take it or leave it. She would take it more often than not though. She had to admit that it had been good waking up with a clear head that morning rather than having to fight a full-blown hangover or a vague disorientating headache. She felt better too; more alert.

She recalled the party they had been to the previous night, realizing now that Marcus had subtly steered her away from the gin and the vodka. She had consumed just one glass of wine. *Unheard of*. He had had nothing at all, just a tonic water.

She studied him; not with wonder exactly, but certainly with respect. Could it be that this man was a good influence on her without her realizing it? She'd known him such a short time. Was it possible? Her performance last night on stage had been something else. For the first time she really felt as though she had nailed her character. And as for the apartment afterwards…

"Where is she at the moment?" Anna asked.

"In rehab. Again."

"Expensive?"

"*Very*."

"How long is she in there for?"

"As long as it takes. You see, it's not just the alcohol; it's uppers and downers as well. She experiments too: LSD, hash."

"Oh Marcus. Why?"

"I've no idea. She has an uncle who drinks too much. Perhaps addictive personalities run in the family."

"Why did you marry her?"

Again, Marcus drew in a very deep breath. "Because I was in love with her; because I thought she was the most enchanting creature I'd ever met. I thought she loved me too."

"But she didn't?"

"No. She saw me as a prop; someone who could pick up the pieces when she'd had too much and put her back together. Someone who she hoped would give her money to fuel her habits. But I refused to do that."

"When did she become addicted?"

He hesitated and said quietly, "She was already using when we met."

"And you didn't realize?"

"I gave her the benefit of the doubt. Foolishly, I closed my mind to reality."

"Have you ever thought of leaving her?"

"Many times. Every day. Twice a day. But I can't."

"Why not?"

"She has no one else."

"No family?"

"None to speak of; who would be of any use to her, that is."

"Then we must make the most of the time we have together."

Anna's words caught him off balance. Knowing her reputation, he had not expected her to risk a response of such warmth. Gratefully, he took her in his arms and kissed her just as they heard the tell-tale click, click, click of a camera.

"Damn." Quickly, Marcus turned round and confronted the photographer. He was livid. "What the hell do you think you're doing?"

"What's it look like?"

"This is none of your damn business."

"The readers'll love it, though." The man was scornful.

"Which filthy rag do you work for?"

Scornfully, and without making any attempt to keep its identity secret, the photographer gave the name of a disreputable newspaper. Marcus knew someone who knew the editor. He'd have those pictures squashed. But he'd have to work fast. He tried again: his voice stern, his manner authoritative.

"Hand over that film buddy."

The man refused. Marcus tried to grab the camera but the photographer sidestepped him neatly and ran off.

"Don't worry about it," said Anna resignedly. "There's nothing we can do."

"I can make sure those pictures are not printed. It's a gross invasion of our privacy."

"Yes, but if you make a fuss, it'll only make things worse. Please believe me. But it's sweet of you to try."

Marcus was still angry. She wasn't the one who was married. He was. And therefore it put both his and Anna's reputations on the line.

"Why don't we go back to the apartment? Then we can be alone. I need to rest anyway before the performance tonight." Anna tucked her arm through his. She could see he was still very upset.

For some obscure reason, the photos were not published in the paper the following day or the one after that. Greatly relieved, they took the decision that even so, it would perhaps be judicious if Marcus didn't come to the theatre for a few nights. The hacks would have nothing to work on if he laid low for a bit.

That evening, once Anna had left for the theatre, he set to work on his assignment for the week: the political implications of the war in Vietnam. It was a grim and difficult subject and after failing to find any inspiration at all, he took a cab to his apartment and packed clean clothes, his wash things and a typewriter.

He selected several books that might be of current relevance and as he was boxing them up, Marcus decided on the spur of the moment to phone his friend about the photographer. In his reply, his friend felt Anna had been correct in her assumption that it would only inflame things further if they made an issue out of the whole incident. Even though no photographs had been printed, he agreed it would be best if Marcus were to lay low for a while. Without anything to feed off, any potential story would die a natural death.

He had no option but to acquiesce and returned to Anna's apartment without being recognized; yet feeling all the while like a hunted criminal. However, his mood lifted when she returned on a high after a successful performance, having come straight from the theatre, unusually eschewing any party that was on offer. Glad to see her, he immediately took her into his arms.

They awoke early the next morning and turning towards her, Marcus said, "Tell me more about Jack."

Did he really want to know? Could he bear it? Yes. He was curious. He wanted to know what had happened next; wanted to know and understand more about Anna.

Did he see Jack as a rival for her affections? Yes. However, Marcus reasoned, there was no need to feel this as her ex-husband had disappeared out of her life many years ago. But for some reason, Anna needed to talk about Jack; that much he sensed. She had obviously been suppressing her memories for a long time.

Anna was thoughtful before replying. "He was very good to me after I found out about Katherine and Alastair. I threw a real wobbly and was horrid to absolutely everyone, especially Grace."

"Why Grace?"

"Because she was *their* child. She had both her real parents, whereas I only had one of mine. And felt rejected by the other whom I didn't know. She didn't have to deal with her whole world being turned upside down."

"But Alastair was a good father, judging from what you've already told me."

"Yes. He was wonderful to Rupert and me. He's a very special man," she added quietly.

"Have you ever told him that?"

"What, since I found out?"

Marcus nodded.

"No."

"How old is he?"

"He must be nearly eighty."

"Don't you think you ought to?"

"You mean before he snuffs it?"

Marcus winced at the crude expression. But it was what he had been thinking of in essence.

"Perhaps," she continued. "But he's as sprightly as they come. At least he was the last time I saw him. When he was seventy, he looked about fifty and had the energy to match. Has the secret of eternal youth does Alastair."

Guilt pricked her conscience. She had not contacted her mother and grandfather apart from a letter informing them she had moved to the States and enclosing the name and address of her American agent. That was nearly ten years ago. Perhaps she ought to write soon. Anxiety rose in her throat. She'd left it too long. It was all too difficult.

"What did you do to poor Grace?" Gently, Marcus brought her back from wherever she had been in her mind.

"I teased her, slapped her, pushed her over and made fun of her. Broke some of her favourite toys."

"How old was she?"

"She was six. She hated me."

Marcus grimaced. "I'm not surprised," he said.

Anna's expression was rueful. "Nor am I. I behaved like a perfect bitch. Anyway, Jack took me in hand and kept me out of the house as much as he could. Fortunately, we were on Cairnmor when it happened and there were plenty of places to go. He took me on such long rambles that I was tired out by the time we got home and I fell into bed and was fast asleep before I could cause any more trouble. One day,

Jack and I were resting after a particularly difficult climb in a remote part of the island, when I kissed him. Full on the lips. Just like that."

"Goodness! How old were you?"

"Fourteen."

"What about him?"

"Thirty."

This was unexpected; well perhaps not, knowing Anna's libido. "How did he react?"

"Incredulously. He was shocked and angry and pushed me away from him. I was disappointed and upset because when I'd kissed him, for a split second, I thought that he was going to respond. But he didn't. Too honourable, I guess. Anyway, keeping me at arm's length, he looked at me with that amazingly direct expression he has and said very quietly, but censoriously, "Don't ever do that again to any man, at least not until you're of age and going out with someone you can trust. Otherwise, you'll get more than you bargained for, young lady. Just be grateful it was me this time.""

"Humiliated and with my cheeks burning with embarrassment, I slapped his face and walked home by myself. He let me go, knowing I'd be perfectly safe as I knew the island like the back of my hand. I never heard him come home. He must have been very late."

Marcus threw back his head and laughed. Good for Jack. But what must have been going through his mind after she had left?

"What happened then?"

"I behaved much better after that. I was very polite to him. I realized I'd been stupid. I knew I'd upset him and that upset me because we were such good friends and I cared about him. When he left on the steamer, I went to see him off and he looked at me and said meaningfully, tapping my nose, "Be good, young lady." I promised I would. I didn't see him again for another two years."

"Why did you kiss him? Did you have some kind of crush on him?"

"Not exactly; well sort of. I'm not sure really. I think it was more that I wanted to see what it was like to kiss a man who might respond passionately and not just some spotty youth. He was the only one I knew who I was close enough to do that to and he was my friend."

Marcus smiled again and kissed her. Passionately, until she was breathless. "I hope you're not going to slap my face," he said.

Anna laughed. "Never," she said.

"I'll keep you to that," he replied, holding her close. "So, what happened next with Jack?"

"He didn't come to visit us for two years. When I next saw him, I had just turned sixteen and I set out to seduce him."

"You did what?!" He looked at her, shocked.

Anna smiled enigmatically, suddenly feeling free to say anything. "Fortunately, he saw through me and refused to let anything happen. He said if we were going to go down that particular road, we'd have to be married first and that once we were husband and wife, I could seduce him as much as I liked and that he'd look forward to it!"

Anna recalled the humour and warmth in Jack's eyes; his desire for her that suffused his whole being as they lay together on the grass in her mother's secluded rose garden, the place where she had planned that the seduction scene should take place.

"Then he actually proposed. He said he hadn't been able to think about anyone else except me for the past two years. That I should never have kissed him as I did that time. That because I was so young, he had stayed away as long as he could."

Marcus smiled to himself. He was glad that Jack Rutherford was turning out to be a decent man.

"What did you say to his proposal?"

"Yes, of course. I thought I had fallen head over heels in love with a handsome, mature man who I could see adored and wanted me."

But married? At sixteen? "What did Katherine and Alastair say?"

"They were surprised, shocked and said no, that I was far too young; that I had my whole career in front of me; that I'd just won a scholarship to study at the Guildhall School of Music and Drama."

"Isn't the Guildhall one of the top places in London for dramatic training?"

"Yes, but I didn't do drama," failing to add 'at that time', preferring to keep that fact to herself for the moment. "I'd won a scholarship to study music."

Marcus shifted position, propping himself up on one elbow. "I had no idea you were a musician as well as an actress."

"Do you just do journalism?"

"No, I write novels and historical non-fiction." They smiled at each other. "Which instrument?"

"Piano."

"But to be accepted at sixteen at a conservatoire?! You must have been good."

"I was." There was pride in her reply; a simple acknowledgement of ability. "I wanted to be a concert pianist."

"I'd love to hear you play one day."

"Perhaps." She hadn't touched the instrument since Jack left.

"What happened then?"

"Jack had a very frank conversation with Alastair and said that I ought to be married, and quickly, to someone who understood me and who would look after me properly while I was in London. He felt I wouldn't be able to keep my sex drive under control if I was on my own and that I'd get myself in trouble. It was better that I should be with him." Anna laughed. "Jack was quite right of course. He knew me very well. Also, he'd just got a staff posting at the Admiralty and would be in London for the next two years at least, so it was perfect."

Marcus was silent. What could he say?

"Alastair and Katherine knew how I felt about him and had done since I was fourteen."

"So your impromptu kiss had an unanticipated effect on you as well?"

"Yes. I was already a physically mature fourteen-year old and something about that kiss woke me up sexually. Afterwards, I wanted more of the same. From him. But that wasn't all. My mother and grandfather found out from Rupert that I'd gained quite a reputation at boarding school for bunking off lessons and staying out late. In fact, I was almost expelled but managed to persuade the headmistress not to tell anyone at home by promising to behave myself."

"You were lucky." Either that or the principal had been negligent.

"What Rupert or they didn't realize was that I had been secretly getting as much experience as I could in order to seduce Jack. I wanted him to be the first to make love to me but I needed to know certain things. So in the end, against their better judgement, Katherine and Alastair said yes."

"And...?"

"Jack spent the whole of his leave on Cairnmor, apart from taking me to meet his parents, and for the rest of that time, we were inseparable. He made it the most romantic, special time I've ever known. Then, at the end of August, just before my first term at Guildhall, we were married."

"So did you seduce him?" Marcus had to ask.

"We seduced each other. And how!" Anna blushed at the memory "It was erotic, sensuous, passionate. He..." She stopped, suddenly realizing that she had probably said enough for the man currently sharing her bed to cope with; a man whom she sensed was beginning to care for her and whose feelings she was in danger of reciprocating.

Marcus felt his throat go dry. He was deeply jealous now. Of a man he'd never met. Of someone who had actually married this amazingly attractive woman.

For the moment, he had heard as much as he could stand about Jack Rutherford. The rest would have to wait.

For a long time.

CHAPTER 3

Cairnmor
Grace

Grace Stewart and her father, Alastair, were out sailing in their two-masted yacht: a ketch called *Spirit II*. It was a beautiful day. The sky was blue, the wind fair and the conditions perfect. Remarkably so for October.

Sailing was Grace's favourite occupation. She loved the freedom and the wide open spaces, and the waters around Cairnmor were part of her soul, having been out and about in boats of all descriptions since the age of two. When the weather was fine, it made for the most exhilarating sailing anywhere.

Both of them were well wrapped up against the autumn chill and Alastair sat in the cockpit, content to let his daughter do most of the hard work, sitting back, admiring her skill and deft movements. When they tacked, he pulled in the genoa or the main, fine tuning the sails to make the most of the wind. He took the helm when she needed to make an adjustment or take in a reef; both of them working as a team without recourse to words or instructions.

This would probably be the last occasion he would come out for this season. At seventy-nine, although physically fit and active for his age, he now preferred the warmer, calmer conditions of the summer months. Well, usually calmer. This was Cairnmor after all…

Katherine, certainly, was happier for him to go out in those circumstances and he liked making her happy. Tomorrow was their sixteenth wedding anniversary, although they had been together for twenty-four years; had known each other for thirty-two years.

Where had the time gone? Surely it was only yesterday when they had first declared their love for each other. Vivid images came flooding back and he smiled to himself.

"Penny for them, Dad," said Grace, who had been watching him for some moments.

"I was thinking about your mother."

Grace laughed. "Of course, I should have known."

She had always thought it wonderful the way her parents cared about each other. She hoped her own marriage one day would be as happy as theirs.

"How are we doing for time?" she asked presently.

"We ought to be heading back very shortly. I think we've had the best of the day."

"Okay."

Grace turned the boat, skilfully going about. They were now almost close hauled; the yacht revelling in the conditions and making excellent headway. Once or twice Grace adjusted course as the boat heeled over too much; the acuteness of the angle uncomfortable even for her. Her father seemed unperturbed by the alarmingly steep deck, merely bracing his feet against the opposite side of the cockpit as she held the tiller firm. Grace knew that he was keeping a careful eye on things and would make suggestions should he became concerned at any time. She always felt very safe when he was on board.

All morning another boat had kept them company, albeit from a distance, appearing from the south as they had sailed out into the Atlantic, then rounding Eilean nan Caorach in their wake and taking the same heading back towards Lochaberdale. Its owner now made great effort to catch up, coming alongside, matching their course and speed.

Grace was impressed with the way the young man handled his yacht. It was very physical; very distinctive. There was a raw energy about him as he stood, legs astride, hauling on the mainsail and genoa as the boat tilted and strained against him, heading almost into the wind as he guided it towards them.

He was tall and broad shouldered, young and vigorous; his broad-brimmed hat adding to his aura of confidence and capability. When he was close enough, he called out to them, cupping his hands to make himself heard, his thigh supporting and taming the tiller.

"Are you headed into the loch?"

"Aye," replied Grace. "Are you?"

"Yes. Is there somewhere I can moor my boat?"

"You can tie her up alongside the quay. There's space for visiting yachts. Otherwise you can anchor out in the bay."

"What's the rise and fall?"

"About six foot at the moment as it's neaps. So there's no problem. The harbour doesn't dry out. You just have to avoid the ferry berth. But it's very obvious once you're there."

They sailed on. Alastair sat still, quietly observing. He could see the impression the young man had made on Grace, who continued to watch him and strayed off course. He tapped her on the arm and pointed to the compass.

"Sorry, Dad."

"It's all right." Alastair smiled and indicated their companion. "He seems like a nice young man."

Grace blushed and laughed because her father could read her so well and that in their closeness, they were able to be very open with each other. Even so, she admonished him good-naturedly by saying, "Da-ad!" They grinned at each other.

Their sailing companion's attention had been drawn to Grace when she laughed and he almost lost control of his boat, experiencing a moment of panic as he came dangerously close to *Spirit II*. Quickly, he moved away to a safer distance. Alastair chuckled. There was something about this young man he liked.

Alastair was very protective of his and Katherine's precious daughter but at twenty-two, she was now grown up and a romance with the right person would do her good. Not that he wished to throw her at the first available young man that she found attractive, including this one, heaven forbid, but she needed to find someone for her own sake. She was far too lovely to stay single or waste herself dreaming about something that could never be.

Grace regarded the young man thoughtfully. There had been no one serious all through university and she had remained aloof from the advances of the boys on her course, where she was one of only two girls. Although she was no recluse,

Grace had preferred to concentrate on her studies. She was popular with her fellow students but there had been no one in particular to whom she had felt attracted. Her girlfriends in her hall of residence always seemed to be falling in and out of love but she had yet to meet someone of her own age who had that effect on her.

Despite her adventurous spirit, Grace knew she was a homebird. She was never happier than when she was on Cairnmor. She had been born on the island, in the little cottage which belonged to her mother, set high up on the hillside overlooking Lochaberdale. Grace stayed there or on Mrs Gilgarry's old croft whenever she wanted to be on her own, making both of them hers, especially the latter, revelling in her solitude and her affinity to the island home she loved so much.

Often she would take her haversack and roam for miles, spending nights out in the open, studying the topography of the land and photographing or sketching the flora and fauna and wildlife that she had always found so fascinating.

It was this hobby, stemming from her early childhood when Jack had first shown her some brightly coloured lichen growing in the secret crevice of a rock, which had inspired her eventually to take a degree in natural sciences and geology at Cambridge University. It combined her love of geography, chemistry and biology and provided her with numerous opportunities to explore the great outdoors on field trips. However, even having experienced all these things and graduated with double honours in June, she had no further desire to venture far afield now that she had completed her course.

Sailing, exploring Cairnmor and being with her beloved parents in the large and spacious farmhouse they shared were the three things that gave the greatest happiness to Grace's life. She didn't ask for or need anything more than this.

Except for Jack, of course. She had always needed Jack.

Once they were inside the harbour, Alastair turned on the engine, bringing the boat head-to-wind where she sat quietly, perfectly balanced, while Grace dropped the mainsail and the genoa, tying them loosely before lowering the mizzen. Then Alastair steered for the jetty, where Grace jumped off and secured the boat as they drew alongside.

Their companion stood offshore and observed them, bringing his yacht alongside once he could see how things were. He threw the bow rope to Grace, who had positioned herself to take it. He admired her lithe movements as she secured his boat behind hers. He smiled and she smiled back. Taking the stern rope in his hand, he climbed onto the jetty and tied it through the metal ring before going over to Grace.

"Hi. I'm Sam MacKenzie."

"I'm Grace Stewart. This is my father, Alastair."

"Hello, sir." Sam stretched out his hand which Alastair took, appraising this young man and liking what he saw.

"Nice to meet you." Alastair stepped off *Spirit II* and stood on the quayside. He would leave these two young people to get to know each other in their own time. He turned to Grace and kissed her on the cheek. "Now, I must go, I'm afraid. Your mother will be wondering where we've got to. You're okay to see to everything?"

"Of course, Dad. I'll be home soon." She gave her father an affectionate hug.

18

He turned to Sam. "Enjoy your stay on Cairnmor. I hope that we shall meet again."

"Thank you. I'll look forward to it, sir."

"Good."

And Alastair walked off along the quayside. After a few moments, he turned back to see that Grace and Sam were already engaged in conversation. He smiled. At last. Someone who would take Jack out of her mind and leave her free to be herself. He wondered how much they would see of Sam MacKenzie. A great deal, he hoped.

Katherine was in the kitchen when he reached the farmhouse about half an hour later. He went up behind her and put his arms round her waist. She turned to him and kissed him. They smiled at each other.

"Hello, you. Good sail?"

Alastair sat down at the kitchen table. "Excellent. The conditions were perfect. We encountered a young man."

"Oh? What do you mean 'encountered a young man'?"

"He sailed up from the direction of Cairnbeg and kept us company. He and Grace have taken quite a shine to each other."

"Really? How old?"

"Mid-twenties, I should say. Perhaps a year or two older than Grace."

"Nice personality?"

"Very nice. Attractive looking too."

Katherine put the kettle on the range. She was curious. "I wonder where he's come from and why he's here. Didn't you ask him?"

"No. I made a tactful early departure. I thought that our daughter needed to get to know him first, without her old dad interfering."

"You never interfere or if you do, it's so subtle that no one ever notices."

Alastair chuckled.

"What's his name?"

"Sam MacKenzie."

"MacKenzie? Be funny if he was related to Robbie."

"It would but I doubt it. There must be thousands of families with the surname of MacKenzie in Scotland."

"How very true."

Alastair was thirsty and tired after his long walk home and the exertions of the day. "I'd love that cup of tea."

"It's almost ready." She took the kettle off the range. "If this Sam MacKenzie does turn out to be someone suitable and Grace really likes him, perhaps she'll be able to let go of Jack at last."

"Let's hope so. It's time."

"High time."

Katherine sat next to her husband and poured out the tea which they drank companionably together.

"I went to visit Robbie while you were out today."

"How is he?"

"Grumpy. Complaining about needing a wheelchair now. But Michael said he's doing fine – especially for his age."

"He's just about the oldest resident on Cairnmor now, isn't he?"

"He's a hundred next month."

"Where does the time go to?"

"I don't know." She experienced a familiar tremor of fear.

Katherine took Alastair's hand and he kissed her palm, both of them aware that he was not getting any younger. They seldom spoke of their desire to hold back time because of their fundamental and overwhelming need for each other. They just spent every minute they could together, savouring each moment; never tiring of each other's company; wasting nothing. In this, they experienced no sense of desperation or restriction but only complete freedom; their individuality enhanced within a relationship that was, and always had been, a very great love story.

"What shall we do for our wedding anniversary tomorrow?" Still holding her hand, Alastair kissed her wedding ring. His wife. This wonderful woman who had shared his life for so long.

"I'd like to spend a couple of days up at the cottage," replied Katherine, without hesitation.

"Then that, my darling, is what we shall do." He smiled at her, his eyes warm. "I love you."

"I love you, too." Inexplicably, her eyes filled with tears. "The years go by so quickly."

Alastair stroked her cheek. "Don't worry. Don't think about it. I'm fitter and more able than a lot of people half my age. So are you. My father lived until he was ninety-six and my mother ninety-five. I have every intention of emulating them and more. You can't be resident here on the island unless you have longevity! Look at Rupert and Mhairi. Your parents take on a new lease of life every time they come here for one of their extended stays."

Katherine smiled, reassured as always. "Shangri-La?"

"No. Just Cairnmor!"

"Perhaps we should market the island as having the elixir of life."

"And forget to tell the tourists about the storms and the wind…"

"And the midges…"

"Especially the midges!"

Laughing, they looked up as the back door opened and Grace came in, her face alight.

"Hi," she said and disappeared up to her room.

Katherine and Alastair exchanged a knowing glance and smiled at each other.

Grace sat on the window seat in her bedroom, smiling; recalling every word of her conversation with Sam. He was doing a Ph.D., he'd told her. His chosen thesis was on a very rare lichen that could only be found on Cairnmor. He'd come to study it for himself and discover the reasons for its scarcity as well as the unusual conditions that encouraged its existence and allowed it to flourish here on the island. There was virtually nothing written about it. He wanted to be the first to investigate it and write a paper that he hoped would be published one day.

His other ambition, he'd said, was to sail round the British Isles, putting off the moment when he had to give up his freedom and begin working for his father in

20

accountancy. The agreement had been that Sam would join the family firm once he had finished his studies. So he kept studying: a B.Sc., a Masters and now a Ph.D. It was no hardship. Botany, the subject that he loved with a passion and wanted to make his career, fascinated and fulfilled him. The longer he could continue to follow his heart, the happier he was.

Sam loved the outdoors as well. This was the direction he wanted his life to take, he told Grace, not to be stuck in some gloomy office in Glasgow with only stuffy old men for company. He loved his father but that was not the place where he wanted to be.

Grace could see he was much too vital for such a restricted life and understood only too well his desire for freedom, for open spaces. She listened quietly, saying very little about herself, other than revealing she had a degree from Cambridge and that she too loved sailing and being outdoors, preferring to allow him to speak; giving herself time to see the person that he was. However, she said just enough; enough to allow Sam to know they had a great deal in common and, on the surface at least, shared the same outlook.

She pictured them sitting on the quayside earlier that afternoon, their legs dangling over the edge of the sea wall, absorbed in conversation; absorbed in each other. He had asked to see her again and she had said "yes" immediately.

There was to be a ceilidh that evening in the Great Hall. Grace suggested that they went to that and Sam had agreed. He'd needed to sort out his boat then and, not wishing to outstay her welcome, she'd said goodbye, happy with the prospect that they would meet again that evening.

Lost in her thoughts, Grace leant her forehead against the glass, looking outwards at the stunning view across the white-gold sands towards the little island of Cairnbeg and the Atlantic beyond.

She wondered how Jack was. It had been an age since he'd written; not since last June, after her graduation, in fact. The longest time ever between letters.

For as long as Grace could remember, Jack had been a part of her life; a part of her family. He had his own room in the farmhouse and spent every leave with Alastair and Katherine. Sometimes, when he was away at sea and her parents were out, as a teenager, she would go into his room and lie down on his bed, burying her nose deep into his pillows, surrounded by his things, wondering what it would be like to be married to him.

He had always been kind to her; right from when she had been very little and Anna had started to be so mean to her. At the time, she had never understood why Anna had suddenly changed and later, when her mother had explained the reasons to her, she still failed to comprehend. As far as she was concerned, nothing had changed. Anna would always be her sister and Alastair and Katherine the kindest, most wonderful parents anyone could wish for. How could Anna reject them? Even Rupert had been appalled by his twin's behaviour. He hadn't changed his demeanour towards Grace. He was still as affectionate as ever; was still her big brother.

Jack had taken Anna out of the house and Grace had felt safe while her sister was away, able to play with her toys unmolested. His kindness had made a deep impression on her, especially when she overheard him tell her parents that he'd keep Anna occupied and out of the way to protect Grace. From that moment on he became her champion, her hero.

She had resented it when Anna and Jack were married, even though she was allowed to be a bridesmaid. If Anna had been nicer to her, then she would have been happier about it all. Anna hadn't wanted her to be a bridesmaid either; that had been Jack's idea. After the wedding, they didn't see very much of Jack for the next year or so as Anna wanted to stay in London.

When Grace was eleven years old, something happened between Anna and Jack. He came to Cairnmor, very upset. *Defeated* was the word that leapt into her mind when he unexpectedly appeared at the farmhouse.

She had never seen him in such low spirits. Like her father, he always had a youthfulness about him, a *joie de vivre* which had now deserted him. That first day, he talked long into the night with Alastair and Katherine. She could hear their muffled voices from the kitchen below as she lay in the darkness of her room. She had crept out onto the galleried landing and peered through the bannisters, trying to hear what they were saying. She could, just about, but at the time, as she didn't understand most of it, she went back to her bedroom and fell asleep.

On her way home from one of her rambles during that week, she had come across Jack sitting half-hidden by the marram grass in the dunes, his head in his hands, tears pouring down his cheeks. She went over to him and put her arms around him, holding him to her while he cried; her comfort given naturally and accepted on his part without embarrassment. She was closer to Jack in many ways than she was to Rupert, of whom she actually saw very little as he was always with Rose and virtually lived with Michael and Mary. In any case, Jack had always been her friend and was, after all, an honorary member of the family.

He wouldn't tell her what had happened. "Perhaps one day, when you're older," he'd said, wiping his eyes, regarding her with tender affection.

Jack was only with them for seven days, going back on the next steamer at the weekend. During that time, she'd kept him company whenever he needed it, staying with him through his strange silences and sadness. Never once did he treat her as some kind of nuisance. Never once did he ask her to go away. She sensed when he wanted to be alone and tried her best not to intrude. He always treated her with courtesy and respect; just as though she was grown up.

Before he left, he gave her a beautifully patterned shell that he had found. He said he would never forget her kindness. Then he hugged Katherine and Alastair and said he would be indebted to them for the rest of his life. Grace cried as the steamer left and that set her mother off as well. Her father had put his arms round them both.

A month later, Ben had come to live with them and her life changed completely, but in a positive way. For Ben was a good baby – most of the time. She'd helped her mother to look after him and Alastair had remarked, with wry humour, that it seemed to be his lot in life to bring up other people's children. Grace had gone over to him then and perched on his lap, telling him that that was because he was such a wonderful father. His eyes had filled with tears and he'd hugged her close to him.

Grace never experienced any jealousy where Ben was concerned because she made herself as much a part of his well-being as her parents. It was the three of them taking responsibility for him; a shared task that brought them even closer.

Whenever Jack came home on leave, he took charge of his son, proving to be a very good father. A deep loving bond developed between the two of them and now, Ben was growing up into a lovely boy, mature beyond his years, with a wicked sense of humour and a very direct expression just like his father.

Grace had always fantasized that one day she would marry Jack and the three of them would all live together as a family in some remote cottage on Cairnmor with their own children. He was much older than her, of course, but age held no significance in her dreams. After all, there was a twenty year age difference between her parents; what did it matter that there was twenty-four years between herself and Jack? He never seemed old. It was why he got on so well with Alastair; both of them young at heart.

Grace heard the sonorous chimes from the clock downstairs, awakening her from her reverie; an unobtrusively gentle reminder of the time. She went along to the bathroom and ran herself a bath, luxuriating in the warmth of the water.

She and Jack had written to each other ever since that time; ever since she was eleven years old. He told her stories of his voyages, sending her pen and ink sketches of his life on board ship; of the places he visited. She wrote about Cairnmor, about school and her friends; about her hopes and ambitions.

She drew pictures of seabirds and mountains; of rocks and plants and he said they were very good. She was proud of that because if the war hadn't intervened, Jack would have become a professional artist. She had asked him once why he didn't take up his scholarship at the Royal College of Art once the war was over.

"Because I needed to support my family," he'd replied simply. "Besides which, a student life didn't really appeal to me by then, especially after my experiences in the war. I was in London, at the Admiralty, part of the Royal Navy, a service I had come to love. There seemed no point," he'd added, as they walked along the spectacular Gleann Cuineas with its views to the mountains beyond.

They'd climbed to the summit of Beinn Rannoch that day and he'd sketched her as she sat quietly contemplating the stunning scenery. He never gave her that one. She often wondered why.

Having dried herself, Grace went back to her room where, holding the towel around her to keep warm, she sat on her bed. Her walls were full of the paintings and drawings that Jack had given to her over the years – oils, water colours, pastels. He had become accomplished in any medium, even without professional training.

Downstairs above the fireplace was a wonderful portrait of Rupert, Anna and herself as children, a present for her parents on their wedding day. She remembered sitting for it: Anna impatient and fretful, Rupert cross with his sister and Grace feeling very calm and, even though she was very little, enjoying the feeling of being sketched, once, that is, she was allowed to see the picture he was creating. All of them were under strict instructions not to tell Alastair and Katherine as Jack had wanted it to be a surprise. Amazingly enough, none of them had said a word.

Above her bed was the watercolour he had painted of her beside the River Cam at the end of her first year at university, hugging her knees, happy and laughing. She had often sat for him; on Cairnmor, in Cambridge.

Amongst these, safely tucked away in her cupboard, was a fine pencil-drawn sketch of the afternoon she had posed for him in London at the family home in Cornwallis Gardens; her nakedness discreetly draped with a strategically placed swathe of material. She had felt embarrassed and shy at first, but had allowed him to arrange the folds of silk according to his artistic needs before giving herself up to the enjoyment she always felt whenever she sat for him.

She had seen desire in his eyes for her then but he didn't touch her. That was a few weeks later when he stayed on after her graduation ceremony; after her parents had gone home; after the Graduation Ball when she had told him she was in love with him. He had kissed her then and held her tightly in his arms, unable to help himself; the memory of her body tantalizing, her lips sweet-tasting. But that was as far as he allowed things to go; as far as they could ever go, he said.

They had walked then beside the River Cam on that beautiful, warm summer's evening, holding hands. She was Alastair and Katherine's daughter, he'd said. He would betray their trust if he took advantage of her. She pointed out that she was an adult now, quite capable of making her own decisions. He said he knew that, but that he wasn't the right man for her.

"Oh, but you are," she'd protested.

He'd shaken his head. "No. You need someone of your own age who will really share your life; your spirit of adventure; your interests."

"But you do."

"Up to a point."

"But I love you."

"I know." He'd stopped walking and pulled her towards him, kissing her lips and her cheeks, running his fingers through her golden hair, absorbing the fragrance of her skin. "And I wish with all my heart that it could be different."

Her eyes filled with tears. "I don't want to lose you, Jack."

"You won't." He'd smiled at her then, taking both of her hands in his. "The ties that bind us are very strong and very deep. I don't want to lose you, either. I couldn't bear to lose you. Ever. Remember that."

And she did. She took on board his reasoning and the world still seemed a happy place, although simultaneously, exquisitely painful. The knowledge that Jack really cared for her sustained her, just as he had known that it would. He put his arm round her shoulders and they walked in silence until the dawn came and they turned for home.

Jack kissed her once more as they said farewell at the door outside her hall of residence and after she had gone inside, he stood on the pavement and waited for her to come to the window, just as she always did whenever he had come to visit her during the past four years. Soon she appeared and waved to him. He blew her a kiss and turned away, only to walk for miles through the deserted streets in order to cool his desire and come to terms with his own feelings for Grace; for things he

24

regretted could never be because he was still, and always would be, in love with Anna.

After this, Jack had gone back to sea and Grace hadn't heard from him since. Any boy she met paled in comparison; their attentions fatuous and immature. She began to think that she would never find anyone who could match his stature. Until today, perhaps, when Sam had sailed into her life.

Quickly, she finished dressing and hurried downstairs, pausing only to kiss her parents goodbye. Carefully, she drove along the winding, single-track road to Lochaberdale and Sam, who would be waiting for her beside his boat.

CHAPTER 4

New York
Family Matters (1)

Marcus and Anna were together now as a couple – a state of affairs that had arisen quite naturally and without fuss. They weren't in love but they found comfort and reassurance in each other and a need to be together. They had been publicly discreet since the incident in the park and few people knew of their association. Most importantly, they had been successful in avoiding speculation in the press.

Marcus never went back to his apartment to live; returning only to pick up his post, collect more clothes and anything else he might need.

He visited his wife occasionally, collected his assignments, went into the office each day and worked on his current novel in the evenings. Sometimes, he went away for a few days to cover a story. He often accompanied Anna to the theatre, sitting in her dressing room while she was on stage, waiting for her; making notes for the next chapter of his book.

Anna surprised herself by allowing things to continue and their relationship to deepen despite her long-held resolve to avoid commitment.

About a month into the play's run, Anna tripped backstage on some rigging that had been carelessly left lying in the wings. She fell heavily, badly spraining her ankle and wrenching her knee. Nothing was broken but the doctor at the hospital said that under no circumstances should she put any weight on the leg otherwise she could do permanent damage.

Anna was prepared to defy the doctor for the good of the play but it proved impossible. She couldn't walk without crutches nor could she negotiate the narrow stairs and corridors backstage with them. She tried using a wheelchair on stage but that upset the whole dramatic emphasis of the story and restricted other cast members' freedom of movement. In the end, Anna had to concede defeat.

She was distraught; the director threw a tantrum; her understudy rubbed her hands in glee and Marcus decided to take Anna away to New England for ten days – the amount of time the doctor had said it would take for the swelling to go down (but only if she was good and didn't try to walk).

His best friend, an attorney called Doug Metcalfe, owned a cottage which he had inherited from his grandmother near Fenton, a small town deep in the heart of Massachusetts. From time to time, he lent it out to trusted friends and on hearing about Anna's predicament was only too willing for Marcus to use it. "Have fun!" he'd said as he handed over the keys.

Before they left, Anna had been fretting so much about relinquishing her part that Marcus went to see the play and was able to say, with total honesty, that her understudy was a poor substitute. Therefore, feeling much relieved, Anna informed the cast and crew she was going to stay with a distant relative who lived Upstate.

No one questioned this; no reporters or photographers seemed interested. It merely mentioned in *Variety* that she had fallen backstage and would not be appearing for ten days and that her role would be taken over by her understudy for the time being. So Marcus and Anna set off for New England, secure in their privacy and anonymity.

The weather was fine and sunny for their journey and Anna lay back in the front seat of the car with her leg supported, feeling safe and relaxed as the powerful car ate up the miles. They listened to the radio and chatted; observing this and that along the way. They stopped at a roadside diner for lunch and Marcus filled up the fuel tank with gasoline. Once they were on the road again, Anna fell asleep and Marcus drove on, content.

She awoke to the sensation of being kissed and after responding, when she opened her eyes, it was as if she had been transported into a world of dazzling flame: deep reds, bright orange and brilliant yellows, all alight and shimmering in the afternoon sun.

"Wow!"

"Aren't the colours spectacular? Have you never seen the Fall in New England before?"

"No, I've only read about it. It's glorious, Marcus."

He helped her up into a sitting position. Before them was a traditional, picture-perfect, white-painted clapboard cottage with a white picket fence.

"Is this it?" she asked. "Is this where we're staying?" Her delight was transparent.

Marcus smiled, taking in everything about her. "Yes."

"It's perfect." She looked up at him, her eyes sparkling. "Quickly then, help me out of the car. I want to see inside."

"Okay."

He got out of the car and went up the front path and opened the front door, revealing a tantalizing glimpse of the interior of the cottage. Then he sat back in his seat, teasing her.

"Not just through the door, dummy. Inside, please!"

"What now? Out here?!" He looked at her and raised an eyebrow. "I don't think those people walking towards us along the lane with their dog would approve."

"I didn't mean that. Even *I* wasn't thinking that at this moment. But now that you've suggested it…" She ran her hand along his thigh.

Laughing, Marcus took her hand in his and kissed it before going round to the passenger side of the car. He bid the couple a courteous good afternoon as they passed by and Anna waved to them. After successfully manoeuvring her out of the passenger seat, he surprised her by lifting her into his arms and carrying her over the threshold of the cottage. He set her down carefully on the large sofa and she watched him as he went back out to the car to collect their luggage. She wondered what it would be like to be with him for always.

Not possible.

She dragged her mind away from the thought. She was not very successful.

This was not good. She would have to rectify the situation when they got back to New York. The thought filled her with anxiety and pain. No, she couldn't give him up just yet; it wasn't necessary to give him up just yet. She'd do that as soon as she was home. Right now, she needed to be with him a little longer.

Not possible.

When he came back into the room, Marcus immediately perceived the change in her mood. Concerned, he knelt down beside her and brushed away the tear that had spilled onto her cheek.

"What is it? What's the matter, honey?" His voice was gentle. "Please tell me."

"I think I'm beginning to care for you." And she promptly burst into tears.

"I care for you, too. Very much."

"Oh."

He kissed her with a new possessiveness. Strangely, she wasn't afraid of it. She had never been afraid of belonging to Jack either. She knew she still loved him; would always love him. She would always belong to him and could never truly belong to anyone else.

Rashly, Marcus said, "I'll leave Virginia and then we can be together for always." She shook her head. "We can't."

"Why not?"

How could she tell him that she had resolved never to be with any man permanently after Jack had left; that, rightly or wrongly, she had resolved to keep herself free of emotional entanglement? On the other hand, Marcus had a wife who was dependent upon him; who was absent for long periods of time. So perhaps it was ideal after all.

No, it wasn't. She resented this other woman who had such a hold over Marcus.

"She needs you."

"And I need her like I need a hole in the head. Quite frankly, I don't care what she does."

"You don't mean that."

He didn't answer.

The sun had gone down and Anna shivered.

"It's getting chilly. Let's see if I can get this fire to light." Marcus busied himself gathering newspaper and sticks.

He sensed they were treading dangerous ground. Anna was not yet ready and he was not yet available for the long-term commitment that ought to follow on from their conversation. But, armed with the knowledge that she was beginning to care for him, the world changed for Marcus and he knew he would do everything in his power to make things as special as he could for Anna; for both of them, within the confines of his availability and her inability to commit.

And where did Jack Rutherford come in all of this? Profoundly, he suspected.

That evening after supper, Marcus sat on the floor with his back to the sofa where Anna lay full length with her leg raised. She stroked his hair absentmindedly as they stared into the glowing flames of the log fire that warmed the room and was the only source of light.

"Where did you study, Marcus?" she asked.

"Harvard. I majored in English Literature and Journalism."

"Clever man." She touched his cheek appreciatively. "Isn't Harvard in Massachusetts?"

He put his hand up to hers and kissed it. "Yeah, in Cambridge, not too far away."

"So you've seen the autumn colours in New England many times?"

28

He smiled. "And I've never tired of it. I think it's one of the most beautiful things on God's earth. Like you." He drew her towards him and kissed her. "Tomorrow, I'll take you out in the car and we'll do a tree-trail."

"Don't you have work to do?"

"Probably. But it'll keep until we get back to New York."

Anna studied the hair at the nape of his neck. She liked the way it curled. At that moment, what they did in the future seemed unimportant. The here and now was what mattered. She would make the most of it before they had to say the inevitable goodbye.

Anxiety touched her heart. Quickly she suppressed it.

"Can we go to Boston as well this week?" she said. "I've never been and Rupert studied there for two years at the Conservatory."

"Your brother? In Boston?"

"Yes." She didn't mind him asking questions now; in fact she liked it.

"Does he look like you?" He'd wondered about this the first time Anna had mentioned him.

"Not really, apart from the usual family resemblance. Although when we were first born my mother always said we were the mirror image of each other. It was only after we were about a year old that the differences began to show themselves more clearly."

"Who does he take after?"

"My mother and her father, both in looks and character, whereas I'm more like my grandmother, who apparently was a great beauty. But not very nice it would seem." She stopped.

"Well, you have her beauty certainly, but not her not very niceness."

Anna was silent. She'd inherited that attribute as well.

Marcus kissed her hand. "I think that the traits we inherit from our families are fascinating. But at the end of the day we are all uniquely ourselves no matter what our heritage is. So, tell me about Rupert."

"I can't tell you about Rupert without telling you about Rose."

"Michael and Mary's daughter?"

"Yes." Anna settled herself more comfortably and Marcus adjusted his position so he was looking at her. "From the moment that Rupert first saw Rose when he was three and she was a baby, he was fascinated by her. Couldn't keep away from her in fact. It was the same story whenever they met. Mary lived with Katherine and Alastair a great deal during the war and of course, Rose was always there. She became as attached to Rupert as he was to her. They were inseparable

"When Rupert was eight years old, he solemnly announced to the family one Sunday tea-time – I remember we were all in London at the time – that they were going to get married and that Rose should have a cello for her fifth birthday, which was the next day. He would play the piano for her and they would make their living giving concerts together."

Marcus smiled. "Early marriages seem to run in your family."

"You'd be surprised."

"Really? You mean there are more?"

"Sort of. Anyway, highly amused by Rupert's pronouncement, Alastair and Michael immediately went out the next day and bought a cello for Rose. She learned the piano as well, although to my mind, she was never very good."

Marcus wondered if Anna had been jealous of Rose in some way but tactfully, he kept that thought to himself.

"One day, much later, after Rose had proved to be quite talented on the cello, I remember Michael saying to the three of us that she must have inherited her ability from Mary whose family all had good singing voices. That it couldn't possibly be from him as he had one tone deaf ear and one that had perfect pitch. He said that whoever was first to guess which one was which would get all the chocolate they could eat and would be able to forget about sweet rationing." Anna laughed, remembering. "As children we used to spend hours trying to work out the right answer."

"I guess that as you have a perfect figure, it wasn't you." Marcus had taken this seriously.

"No, dummy! None of us could. He was teasing us. Gee, kiddo, you Americans don't get verbal teasing do you?!"

Marcus looked confused for a moment and then grimaced with embarrassment. "Apparently some of us don't get irony either. You must explain that to me sometime."

"I'll try. Anyway, Mary replied that it wasn't all her family's doing that Rose was good at the cello because a very eminent French surgeon had once described Michael as having 'sensitive hands'. Whereupon, he tickled her with his 'sensitive hands' until she begged him to stop as she was laughing so much. Then he kissed her. They both enjoyed the whole thing hugely, and at the time I thought that for two adults they were behaving rather childishly."

"But you know better now, of course! When your ankle's recovered, I shall try out *my* sensitive hands on you..."

"You don't have to wait until my ankle's better..." She kissed him before continuing. "Anyway, I don't know how Rupert would have coped if Rose hadn't been musical because he and I absolutely lived and breathed music."

"Did he play any other instrument?"

"We both did. He played the violin and I played the viola. But the piano was always my greatest passion. When Rose was good enough, we formed a piano trio. My grandfather used to coach us whenever he and grandma were over from Canada and we'd give concerts in the Great Hall to anyone who was brave enough to come and listen."

"What's the Great Hall?"

"Village hall on Cairnmor. Named in honour of my mother's first trip to England when all she seemed to see were places that were called 'great hall'. When we were older, we used to give mini recitals at the hotel for the summer visitors and earned a lot of extra pocket money."

"Were you any good?"

"Put it this way, the audiences were always appreciative and usually came back for more."

"Which grandfather coached you? Alastair?"

"No, Katherine's father. A professional musician. He was director of the Music Academy in Halifax, Nova Scotia for many years."

"What about your parents, were they musicians?"

"No. Katherine studied history at Edinburgh University but is a very fine pianist. Alex was a choral scholar at Oxford and an excellent pianist too, but his degree was in law. He became a barrister – a lawyer."

"With a pedigree like that, you ought to have become a musician."

"I didn't though."

"True. Any other musical relatives tucked away?"

"Yes. My Aunt Lily is a professional flautist and used to teach at the Paris Conservatoire. She's married to Phillippe du Laurier."

"The French politician who spent years campaigning for peace?

Anna nodded.

Marcus whistled. "You gotta be kidding me!" He sat up and turned to her, his manner all at once animated. "I've met him. He came to the States some years ago on an official visit to promote his Peace Foundation at the United Nations. He was one of the first people I ever interviewed for the magazine after I got the job. An incredible man."

"I suppose he is. He's always just been 'Uncle Phillippe' to me. He does have a certain presence though."

"You're telling me! Quite formidable. I was completely in awe of him. However, he was very charming and courteous when I interviewed him. But what a personality! And all the things he's achieved. I've still got the article I wrote. I'll dig it out when we get home. He's retired now though, hasn't he?"

"Yes. I haven't seen him in years but my mother tells me in her letters..."

"She writes to you?" Marcus had assumed they had no contact.

"Yes."

"Do you write back?"

"No."

"Why?"

"Too complicated."

Marcus could see that Anna might become upset if he pursued the matter any further, so he asked instead, "So, what does your mother tell you in her letters?"

Relieved, Anna replied, "That he and Lily have five children and two grandchildren with another on the way. He just wants to enjoy family life. Feels he's done his bit for France politically. And the world, I suppose. Aunt Lily has stopped teaching now so she can be with him all the time. He's not always in the best of health these days."

"He was shot during the war by a sniper. I remember him telling me. I guess he was lucky to survive."

"It was Michael who saved his life, together with the French surgeon who said Michael had 'sensitive hands'."

"Michael?"

"Yes."

"So, tell me."

"Michael was a medical officer in the town where Uncle Phillippe was shot. There was a local surgeon but he was too old to carry out the operation himself so he gave instructions to Michael as to how to remove the bullet. Uncle Phillippe often talks about coincidences and forces drawing people together; it's one of his great beliefs. But I always argued with him about this…" Anna never had had much patience with what she called Phillippe's 'fanciful' ideas.

Marcus smiled. "I'd love to hear more about him within the family. But later. We were talking about Rupert and Rose."

"Yes. When he was eighteen, Rupert went to the Royal Scottish Academy of Music in Glasgow and Rose continued at the specialist music school in Edinburgh where we'd all been studying. It was the first time they'd been apart for any length of time.

"Rupert spent his weekends in Edinburgh whenever he could get away and as soon as Rose turned sixteen, they got engaged. They had been childhood sweethearts and nothing has ever changed their love for each other. Anyway, when Rupert was in his final year at Glasgow, a visiting professor from the Boston Conservatory was so impressed that he offered him the chance to study in America on a conducting scholarship. Rupert couldn't afford to turn down an opportunity like that.

"He talked it over with Rose first, who declared he had to do this and that she was going with him and that they'd better get married straight away. He was delighted as this was what he had hoped for. The families agreed. They could see there was no point in them both waiting until they were older or trying to persuade them that America was too far away. Besides, it was seen as the perfect union between two young people who were perfect for each other. It made me want to throw up."

Marcus was shocked. "Why? Weren't you pleased for your brother?"

"Of course I was."

But she'd lost Jack, hadn't she? She couldn't bear to see their happiness; couldn't bear to be on Cairnmor with all the wedding preparations going on. So she'd stayed in the States and didn't come home for the wedding. Said she was sorry that she couldn't get away; that she wouldn't have wanted to miss it for anything. She knew that Rupert and Rose would be disappointed but they had each other, she'd reasoned, and wouldn't have wanted her there with a sour expression on her face that she would have been unable to conceal.

When Anna fell silent, Marcus regarded her carefully: saw the suppressed guilt etched in her face, the sadness in her eyes. He didn't press her further.

"What about Rose and her cello?"

Anna took a deep breath, returning to their present conversation. "Alastair was very concerned about Rose's own career. *Something will come up*, she said. And it did. She auditioned and was accepted for a two year teaching diploma course at the conservatory.

"Before Rupert and Rose returned from their honeymoon, Alastair, Katherine, Michael and Mary flew to Boston and found a wonderful house for the two of them, very close to the conservatory. Rupert and Rose loved Boston and spent two very happy years there."

32

"The Boston Conservatory is hugely expensive."

"Ah. My family is rich." She smiled sardonically. "Very rich."

"How rich?"

"Multi-millionaire type rich."

"Wow! I guess that's another story."

"Of course."

Marcus stood up and stretched. It was time for bed. He damped down the fire and lifted Anna into his arms and took her through to the bedroom.

"What are they doing now?" he asked, as he helped her undress and they got into bed.

"They live in Glasgow where Rupert is associate conductor of the Royal Scottish Philharmonic Orchestra. Rose does some teaching and they do the occasional recital together."

"Are they still happy?"

"Blissfully. It makes me sick." The jealous edge returned to her voice.

"Why?" Marcus questioned her this time.

"Because life isn't like that."

Anna thought of Jack and how blissfully happy they had been; how it had all gone wrong; what a mess she'd made of things.

"It is for them. They're the lucky ones," observed Marcus, defending them.

"Perhaps."

It could be like that for us too, he thought, as he took her into his arms. He sighed. If only. Gently, he made love to her, taking extra care because of her injured leg.

CHAPTER 5

Cairnmor
Family Matters (2)

Rose lay on the hospital trolley outside the X-ray department in the Glasgow Royal Infirmary, waiting to be seen. All was not well. She had just miscarried her baby. The second one. Her body had let Rupert down. Again. Let her family down; let herself down.

She had nearly reached the sixteen weeks which the doctors had said would guarantee a full term. The first miscarriage had been after twelve, almost as soon as she had discovered that she was pregnant. Everyone had been so sympathetic. When she spoke of why she had been unable to teach for a few weeks to the mothers of her pupils, she was amazed to discover how many women shared her experience.

"At least you know you can get pregnant," said one of them.

"And it's a relief to know that your body is working as it should and won't accept anything that's less than perfect," remarked another, who had paid her a special visit at home.

She had drawn strength and reassurance from their words and once she had overcome her immediate sense of loss, felt heartened and although cautious, couldn't wait to try again once the requisite six months were up. She had fallen pregnant almost immediately and had taken extra care of herself, taking plenty of rest, taking things easy. She'd avoided lifting anything heavy, had cosseted herself and then, just when she had almost reached the magic number, she had started to bleed in the night; heavily. Then there was the pain, terrible pain. There was nothing anyone could do. The tiny life growing inside her was lost.

The doctor arranged for her to be taken straight into hospital and here she was now, lying on the trolley waiting for her turn to be X-rayed.

Unchecked, the tears rolled down her cheeks and she let go of all restraint and sobbed her heart out. In distress, Rupert went to find a nurse and she was put onto a ward instead of having an X-ray; the curtains drawn round the bed. He was beside himself with grief for their lost child and concern for his beloved Rose. He held her hand, bravely trying to reassure her.

"It's all right, Rosie. We can always try again."

"No." She snatched her hand from inside his and turned away from him. "No." She was afraid that it might happen again; she couldn't bear it if it happened again. She couldn't put herself through it all again.

"We'll wait a while. It'll be all right. You'll see."

"No." Why didn't he understand how she was feeling? Why couldn't he *see* it?

Rupert was at a loss as to what to do or say. He'd never known his lovely, happy-go-lucky wife to react like this. They had each other, he reasoned. They were both young, there was plenty of time.

"We can wait a bit, Rosie," he said. "Wait until you've recovered completely. There's no hurry."

She didn't answer and closed her eyes, pretending to be asleep.

34

Rupert stroked her hair, playing with the curls, arranging them over his fingers. He knew how much they had both longed for a baby; the miraculous bundle of joy that would be the icing on the cake in their perfect marriage. It had taken them nearly seven years to conceive the first. He smiled to himself. It had been amazing to have been able to enjoy all that freedom beforehand and an incredible feeling when their baby had been conceived at last.

And now this. Again. Poor Rosie. Rupert felt that it would be all right eventually but he realized it was going to be an uphill struggle to persuade his wife that that was so.

He sat beside her bed for a while longer but when she didn't move, he assumed she was asleep. Tenderly, he kissed her forehead and left the hospital. He would come back at visiting time tomorrow after the rehearsal was over. There would be just enough time before the concert.

Once Rupert had gone, Rose opened her eyes. She lay there staring at the ceiling, her mind numb, her body bereft. The house surgeon came by and stood beside her.

"We'll send you down to the theatre tomorrow for a D. and C.," he said. "It's normal procedure. Nothing to worry about. Then in a couple of days' time, you can go home. Take it easy for a fortnight or so. There's absolutely no reason why you shouldn't try for another baby in six months."

Tears spilled onto her cheeks. She turned her head away and closed her eyes. The doctor stood there thoughtfully for a moment or two longer and quietly left. Eventually, Rose slept.

She felt woozy as she came round from the anaesthetic. Unreal; in a sort of dream. Someone said her name and she opened her eyes.

A nurse, her mask pulled down underneath her chin, said, "Good. You're awake, Mrs Stewart." She patted her hand. "I'll just get someone and we'll take you back onto the ward. You've got your own room. Mr Stewart insisted. He felt you would prefer that."

Did she? She had no idea.

"Thank you." Her voice sounded odd; distant. She closed her eyes and when she awoke, her father was sitting beside her. He smiled.

"Hello, Poppet."

Rose smiled and cried at the same time. Michael came to sit on the bed and put his arms round her. She clung to him and sobbed her heart out again. His own eyes filled with tears, sharing with his daughter in her distress. After a while, he helped her find a comfortable position against the pillows and gently stroked her hair, just as he used to do when she was a little girl and she couldn't sleep.

"I've let everyone down."

"No, sweetheart." It was a statement, not a platitude. "No. That's how you feel, but that's not how it is."

All at once, Rose knew what she wanted to do.

"Can I come and stay with you and Mum for a while?"

"Of course. Stay as long as you like," said Michael, his voice reassuringly familiar and kind. "No doubt the doctors here have told you to get plenty of rest, so when we get home to Cairnmor, after we've had you checked out at the cottage hospital, we'll go hiking up all the highest mountains we can find and scrabble down the deepest glens. We'll go shark fishing off Cairnbeg as well. I hear there's a big one lurking there just waiting for you. But you'll have to be quick, the local population on the island is diminishing rapidly..." He smiled. "We'll take the rowing boat out and you can haul it in with Mum's fishing line; you know, the one you used when you were three and caught a piece of driftwood that frightened the life out of you!"

He looked at her and Rose managed a watery smile. This was what she needed. Her father's ridiculous sense of humour. She knew Rupert would fuss her like a mother hen and she didn't want that. Not at the moment.

"How will Rupert feel about it if you do come to stay?" Michael asked presently.

"He's not going to be very happy."

He wasn't. He couldn't understand why Rose didn't want to stay at home with him. The only time they had ever been apart was when he was studying at the Royal Scottish Academy in Glasgow and she was still at St Winifred's in Edinburgh. Even then, he had managed to see her at weekends. What would he do without her? How could she bear it for them to be apart? Minton House would seem cavernous without her.

Privately, Rose thought that she would be glad to get away from its gloominess. Despite their extensive renovations and redecoration over the years, it still managed to retain an air of sadness. She had loved their little house in Boston. It had been so light and airy and such a wrench to leave. Then to come to Minton House...

She had suggested to Rupert many times that they should find somewhere new; perhaps just outside Glasgow, out in the countryside. No, he hadn't wanted to do that, he'd said, as it wasn't very practical. He didn't want a long drive late at night after a concert. Besides, the present house was ideally placed in the centre of town, big enough for her teaching practice and after all, Grandpa had given it to them as a wedding present.

"But he never liked it when he was a child and was forced to go there," she'd protested. "He'd understand if we wanted to sell it." But Rupert had been quietly adamant and she'd let the subject drop.

He came to see her off at Glasgow Central when she and Michael began the journey to Cairnmor a week later after she had come out of hospital.

"I'll wangle some time off and come and stay," he said, as they stood together on the platform.

She could only nod, tearful at their parting; tearful still from her miscarriage.

"It's not right you should go away like this. I haven't done anything wrong, have I Rosie? I haven't done anything to upset you, have I?" he asked anxiously.

"No, darling." She reassured him. "No. It's not you. It's me."

How could she explain that she needed time to herself; time to get over losing a second baby; time to come to terms with the fact that they were never going to have children? She needed time to find the right words to tell her devoted, loving husband that she had decided this was how it was going to be.

Rupert looked puzzled. He didn't understand. But there was no time to say anything else as the guard blew his whistle and Rose climbed aboard. With a low growl, the diesel engine began to pull away from the platform. Rupert walked beside the carriage for as long as he could, holding her hand through the open window.

"I'll come to Cairnmor," he said. "Then we can be together."

"Yes."

"Write to me."

"Oh yes."

The train gathered speed and they had to let go of each other; Rose leaving Rupert behind, a forlorn, lonely figure standing on the station platform.

"How was the ceilidh last night?"

Katherine saw that the door was open to her daughter's room and went in, sitting on the bed watching while Grace packed things into a large haversack: two pairs of trousers, two warm sweaters, socks, thick shirts, clean underwear.

Grace smiled. "Great fun."

And it had been. Sam danced well and Grace had felt comfortable with him. Their individual heights complemented each other and made for an easy partnership. He moved effortlessly and had a good sense of rhythm. He knew all the steps. As did she. All in all, it had been a very good evening.

"Yes, great fun." She looked at her mother and they both grinned at each other. "All right. It was a lovely evening. I really like Sam. He seems like a nice guy."

"I'm glad."

"And yes, you will get to meet him."

Katherine laughed. How well they knew each other. She never ceased to wonder at their closeness.

"In fact, he's coming here this morning before we set off."

"Set off? Where?"

"We're going hiking for a few days."

Katherine couldn't help raising an eyebrow.

"Mu-um!"

"I know you're grown up and everything and that we live in a so-called modern age but…"

"It's nothing like that; nothing like that at all. You should have more faith in me."

"I do. You know I do but even so, you hardly know him."

"I know enough." Grace was firm. "He's doing a Ph.D. in Botany, Mum, so look upon it as a student field trip. That's how I'm viewing it and he is too."

Katherine experienced relief. "What's his thesis on?"

"Lichens that can be found on the Outer Isles but with special reference to a particularly rare one that only grows on Cairnmor. He wants to be the first to write about it."

"Do you know of it?"

"No, but from the way he describes it, I think I know the one and where to find it. It's a three day hike there and back. Out towards Gleann Aiobhneach."

"Well, you're just the person that he needs as a guide." She looked at Grace. "It would seem you both have rather a lot in common."

Grace blushed. "We do."

Katherine was intrigued but said no more about Sam for the moment. Instead, she asked, "What about provisions? Will you take your usual rations?"

"Yes. And I thought Sam could use Jack's tent. It's lightweight and easy to carry."

Grace fell silent for a moment. Disparate images of the trips she and Jack had been on together over the years leapt into her mind: hiking up Beinn Anail; pitching their tents in the pouring rain; of her falling asleep one warm summer's evening while he sat and sketched her in the reflected glow of the camp fire and the setting sun.

Katherine saw her far away expression and guessed where her thoughts lay. So she said, "Doesn't Sam have a tent? I would have thought that would have been a priority if he had come to the island looking for his lichen, especially at this time of year."

Grace returned to the present. "He has but it's rather cumbersome. So Jack's would be better. I'm sure he wouldn't mind."

"No. He won't. At least it's not a solo expedition this time."

Grace stopped what she was doing and regarded her mother thoughtfully. "Do you and Dad worry about me when I go off on my own?"

"Of course we do. You're our daughter; there would be something wrong if we didn't!" Katherine smiled. "But I'm reassured by the fact that you know Cairnmor like the back of your hand. And also, from quite early on, your dad and I made sure the three of you knew how to avoid the obvious dangers and how to survive in an emergency." Katherine paused, then somewhat wistfully, added, "Like you and I, Anna loved to wander around the island on her own. But Rupert didn't, strangely enough."

"I know. It's interesting, isn't it, that it was always us girls that went off by ourselves? Though Rupert only went out anywhere when he was with Rose. How is she, by the way?"

Katherine's mouth took a downward turn. "Not good, according to Mary. She's coming home on the ferry today with Michael to stay for a week or so. There's nothing wrong physically, but she's very down and depressed."

"That's understandable. Rupert won't know want to do with himself on his own. He dotes on her."

"Yes. Perhaps it will do them both good to have some breathing space."

"Rose, maybe, but not Rupert."

"No. He's been attached to her since she was a baby."

"Quite remarkable really."

"Yes." Katherine smiled again, remembering Rupert as a toddler reading his cloth books or playing quietly with his toys while Rose slept peacefully in her cot.

"They're all right though, aren't they? As a couple I mean. There's nothing wrong?" Grace had always regarded her brother and sister-in-law as having a perfect marriage.

"Not as far as I'm aware. I think it's just that Rose has taken the loss of this baby very hard."

"I'm sure she has. I would if I'd been in her position. I'll go and see her when Sam and I get back. Now, Mum, I need to concentrate."

With understanding, Katherine stood up and kissed her daughter. "I'll see you downstairs. What time are we expecting Sam?"

"About ten. And Mum?"

"Yes?"

"Please don't make a big thing about it."

"Oh. And I had the two of you married off already..." she replied, laughing.

"Mu-um! Not even in fun, please."

Katherine smiled. "I know."

After Grace and Sam had left, Katherine said to Alastair, "Well, what do you think?"

"He's perfect for her."

"Isn't he just? But can she let go of Jack?"

"I hope so. Sam is rather a find."

"So it would seem. I wonder what his background is?"

"Well, his father's an accountant. His mother doesn't work but does a lot of charity stuff. Sam is twenty-four, studied biology at Imperial College and then did a master's in botany and now the Ph.D. But you know all this; you were there." Alastair was slightly puzzled by her question.

"I know I was." Katherine was silent for a moment, thinking of Alex and how perfect he had seemed at first. "I'm hoping Sam hasn't got a past."

"Everyone has some sort of past."

"You know what I mean."

"Yes. But I think not."

"I hope you're right."

"Well, I have no doubt Grace will find out. They are bound to swap stories during this camping trip."

"Aren't you afraid for our daughter's virtue?!" Katherine was teasing him, but only slightly, and in doing so, voiced her own concerns.

"Funnily enough, no. And as a father I ought to be suspicious of every young man's motives. No, he seems very trustworthy to me." Alastair took her in his arms and kissed her. "Now, my darling, are we all ready for our joint expedition up into the wilds of South Lochaberdale?"

Katherine laughed. "Yes. The cottage is fully provisioned and our toothbrushes, toothpaste and mountain climbing gear are all in our sponge bags."

"Did you remember to pack the crampons and ice-picks?"

"Of course." They smiled at each other.

"Have you told Ben?" asked Alastair.

"Yes, last night. He's quite happy to spend a couple of days on his own. He's still asleep."

"Twelve going on sixteen!"

"Absolutely!"

"Well, Shona and Angus will look after him. So, Mrs Stewart, let us embark on our trek! I hope the weather's going to stay fine."

"It will."

"How do you know?"

"I asked Robbie yesterday when I went to visit him."

"I should have known! So all of us intrepid adventurers will be all right then?"

"Absolutely."

With that, Alastair took Katherine's hand and, after picking up their one small haversack, they set off for their anniversary weekend.

Grace and Sam took the path that led round the western side of the bay, towards the machair, with the high mountains clearly visible in the distance and with still more peaks off to the east. Gradually, as they covered the miles, the wonders of Cairnmor unfolded around them.

"The topography is amazing!" Sam couldn't get over it. "A complete dune system, peat bogs, fertile plains, moorland... mountains, valleys. Every kind of ecosystem you could wish for. You could spend a lifetime here and never run out of things to study and explore!"

He'd read about it, of course, but no book could have prepared him for the physical impact of the stunning scenery upon his soul. He could barely contain his enthusiasm.

Grace smiled, delighted by his obvious admiration. He had voiced exactly what she had always felt.

"Who owns all of this?" he asked, afraid that it belonged to someone who might not care; some absentee landlord who would allow the land to degenerate.

She hesitated before speaking, not wishing to appear boastful, but very proud of this fact. "My parents. Well, it's my mother actually but she and my father look after the island together as joint trustees."

Sam was silent, staring at her open-mouthed. He couldn't believe it. The kindly, unpretentious people he had just met owned all of this, owned Cairnmor?

From the moment that he had arrived, Sam had taken to his new surroundings. He had walked along the bay out to the eastern headland after Grace had gone home that first day and admired the rugged coastline and the white-gold sands. Afterwards, he had sat on his boat, observing the comings and goings of the unspoilt yet busy harbour at Lochaberdale close up; absorbing the atmosphere, taking everything in.

"Has the island been in your family for a long time?" He assumed their ownership went back generations.

"No. My mother grew up here and Grandpa bought it for her in 1938 but, because of the war, she and Dad didn't come to live here until 1946."

"Is this the grandpa that didn't want to go and work for his father?"

"Yes. Grandpa hated ships. Which was unfortunate as his father founded and owned Mathieson's Shipbuilding and Engineering Company."

"What! Sir Charles Mathieson was his father? Then your grandfather must be Sir Rupert Mathieson!" Sam was stunned. Again.

Grace liked his immediate and wholehearted reaction to things. "It was there that he met my grandmother," she added.

Sam still couldn't get over the fact that it had once been owned by her family. "It was only one of the biggest shipyards on the Clyde! Still is for that matter."

Grace laughed. "Aye. Before the war, Grandpa used to come to Glasgow every so often for board meetings, leaving an excellent managing director to run things. After the war, Grandpa continued to take a deep interest in its development and whenever he and Grandma came over from Canada for their extended stays, he'd spend a great deal of time at the yard. Grandpa sold the shipyard in 1956 to a consortium. He felt he'd done his duty towards his father by then."

"I was twelve at the time and I remember that happening. I'd always been fascinated by this hugely successful shipyard. And Mathieson's is still going strong."

"Aye. Grandpa sold it in a very healthy financial state. Dad thinks it will survive all the latest problems that are hitting the industry."

Sam was thoughtful. "It must be nice to be close to your grandparents."

"It is. Do you not see yours?"

Sam shook his head. "Not very often. My father doesn't like my mother's family and she doesn't like his. They won't have anything to do with either side."

"Goodness." Grace found all that difficult to imagine. She was so close to Grandma and Grandpa Mathieson. After a while she said: "Where does your love of sailing come from?"

"My father. He's a member of the Clyde Cruising Club. *Mallard* is our yacht."

"Does your mother sail?"

Sam laughed. "You must be joking. She hates the water; won't go near it. Didn't want me to come on this jaunt. She made a terrible fuss."

"What happens if you get stuck here? October is rather late to begin a trip like this. The weather can be unpredictable at the best of times but from now onwards, it can get very fierce."

Sam smiled. "Then I shall have to stay."

This had been his intention before setting out. He had needed to be out in the open enjoying one final taste of freedom before committing himself to the future his father had mapped out for him. To be able to combine all this with his Ph.D. was too good an opportunity to miss.

"What about Imperial College?"

"I'm doing field research for my doctorate. As long as I send them written updates of my progress, then they know I'm not idling my time away."

"Don't you have to give any undergraduate lectures?"

"Yes. But not until January when my specialism comes up on the course. So I have three months."

"You could always lay *Mallard* up for the winter in Lochaberdale. *Spirit II* is due to come out of the water later this month. We have a large boat shed where she'll be housed and which my father had built. There's easily room for two yachts."

"Thank you." Sam was surprised by such generosity. "Would that be all right with your parents?"

"Oh yes. Then if necessary you could take the ferry back to the mainland."

Sam didn't reply immediately. For a moment, he had hoped her generosity might extend to inviting him to stay at her house if the weather proved to be inclement. No, that would be presumptuous. "Yes, I could. If necessary," he said, slowly.

Grace was not slow to pick up the reluctance in his voice.

How would she feel if she invited him to stay at the farmhouse? Because that is what she would do if he remained in Lochaberdale. It would only be fair and polite.

How would she feel if Jack came home unexpectedly on leave and Sam was there at the same time? But, came the voice of reason, it would not have to matter because Jack belonged to Anna even though they had separated years ago. Grace knew that; had always known that. She also knew he was still in love with Anna. Anything between herself and Jack was an impossibility, even though he cared for her.

However, Sam would be all hers. But what if he didn't want to go out with her? What if he already had a girlfriend in London or one that lived in Glasgow? She experienced a moment of anxiety and looked at him.

Sam saw the panic in her eyes. The thought struck him that perhaps she didn't want him to stay on the island. That she didn't like him. Or what if she already had a boyfriend? He swallowed hard, his heart beating fast.

They walked on in silence; their easy conversation lost.

CHAPTER 6

Family Matters (3)

Rose sat at the kitchen table, watching her mother as she set about preparing supper. It was very strange to be here in her childhood home without Rupert. He had always been here; had virtually lived with them all the time they were both growing up, except when he went away to boarding school, before she was old enough to go as well. She had missed him then; had felt bereft, as though part of her had been torn away.

When they were very little, they used to share the large single bed in Rose's room and went to sleep holding hands. It never occurred to either of them that they should have a bed each whenever Rupert came to stay. They belonged to each other. Later, she remembered the arguments she had had when her parents insisted they slept in separate rooms, saying that as they were both growing up, it wasn't quite the thing to sleep in the same bed.

Rose was too young to understand but Rupert, being three years older, did. In her innocence, even after this, she would sometimes creep into the spare bedroom at night, climb into bed next to him and put her arms around him just as she had always done, until one day, when she was about eleven and Rupert fourteen, he took her for a walk and explained the facts of life to her. He'd held her hand and said that when they were married, they could sleep with each other every night and that would be all right, but until then, they'd have to wait.

Fortunately, they'd married young, so the waiting was neither too long nor too hard.

Mary looked at her daughter, so pale and serious and wondered what she was thinking. She smiled at her and said, with an intentional brightness in her voice, "What time is your appointment on Monday at the hospital?"

"Dad said he'd arranged it for ten o'clock. Though I don't see any point. It's not going to make a bit of difference."

"Well, it might. Your Dad wanted Mr MacFarland to have a chat with you. He's the new visiting obstetrician. Michael thinks he might be able to shed some light on what's happened."

"I doubt it. If they couldn't find anything wrong at the big hospital in Glasgow, there's no chance that a little cottage hospital will. They just don't have the facilities here."

"Your dad has always said it's the quality of the doctors that's most important and not the equipment. He's always insisted that the best medical people are appointed in the right positions. He's felt like that ever since Alastair asked him to become Chairman of the Cairnmor Hospital Board."

"I know."

"He's done a fantastic job."

"I know that too."

Michael came into the kitchen from his study and sniffed the air appreciatively. "Well, that smells delicious, Mrs Granger," he said, kissing his wife on the cheek.

"I trust that my two favourite ladies have been having a cosy time?" Rose went over to him and he put his arm round her shoulders. "How are you doing, Poppet?"

She sighed, but said nothing. Michael exchanged a raised eyebrow with Mary and asked his daughter what she would like to do that evening.

She shrugged her shoulders. "Nothing particularly. I think I'll go to bed after supper. I'm very tired after the journey."

"Not even a game of cards?"

"No thanks, Dad."

"Monopoly?"

"No."

"Pooh sticks?"

Rose couldn't help laughing at this ridiculous suggestion. "Oh, Dad, honestly!"

"Well, you loved it years ago. I thought a bit of nostalgia and all that, you know…!"

Gratefully, Rose laid her head on her father's shoulder and he smiled at her before turning to Mary, saying, "So, dear wife, is this delicious concoction of yours going to be ready imminently?"

"Even as we speak," replied Mary and with her family's help, she served their supper.

Later that evening, Rose lay in bed listening to the comforting sounds of her parents as they chatted to each other, recounting the day's events in the bedroom next door, just as they had always done at night for as long as she could remember. She gained consolation from its familiarity but nothing could take away the emptiness she felt inside; a sense of utter desolation. Eventually, she fell into a deep, dreamless sleep.

In Minton House, Rupert also lay awake, cold with loneliness, tossing and turning. He got out of bed and paced the floor. Unable to stand it any longer, he decided that next morning, he would call in sick and travel to Oban, catching the ferry to Lochaberdale on Monday. He had to be with Rose; he had to be where she was.

They pitched their tents at the base of Beinn Rannoch beside a fast-flowing stream. The hiatus in their easy conversation proved to be but temporary; they couldn't help themselves. Very soon they were talking non-stop about geology, geography, lichen, university life, plants, birds, the scenery, freedom, field trips. They shared funny stories and spoke of the professors who had inspired them.

They lit a fire with kindling that Grace had brought in her haversack and opened a couple of tins of food and unpacked slabs of cake. They sat together while they ate, watching the flames as they flickered and danced in the gentle breeze. Tired after their long walk, they bid each other a reluctant goodnight.

The next morning was fine but overcast and they climbed the steeply sloping path that led up to the rocky crevices that contained the precious lichen that Sam was seeking. Grace hoped it was the right one, for this was the only place so far where she had discovered any variety that matched his description.

She didn't tell Sam that it was Jack who had first showed it to her, nor did she say that it was this lichen and the many similar rambles she and Jack had taken together that were responsible for her choice of degree. However, the coincidence and significance was not lost on her. She might tell Sam one day. But not yet.

They negotiated the final, awkward rocky outcrop and there, with all its beautiful reddish-gold colours shining out to him within its secret crevice was *lacania decipiens*. Sam couldn't believe it. He'd dreamed of this, ever since he'd heard of its existence. It was the most precious and special moment of his life. Tenderly, he touched its minute surface and at the same time took Grace's hand in his. She was the one who had shown him where it was, his new-found friend.

"Thank you," he said.

Grace nodded, sharing his pleasure. He grinned at her and kissed her on her cheek. She put her hand up to the place, unable to stop herself blushing.

"Now," he said, feeling buoyant and energetic, "We need to take some photographs. You or me?"

They both had their cameras.

"You first," said Grace. "It's your lichen."

"No. It's *our* lichen." He grinned at her again. "But it's my Ph.D. So I'll photograph it first and you sketch it. Then how about we swap?"

"Okay."

His drawing was good, better than hers, in fact. She then sketched him while he was absorbed; a rapid pencil-line sketch. It was a good likeness and he was very complimentary of her skills. So he drew her while she was taking photographs. It was not as accomplished as Jack's and lacked depth but he had a distinctive style, nonetheless.

Sam measured the lichen; took note of its habitat and photographed the surroundings. He measured the air temperature, the humidity, tested the air quality and photographed the terrain: all the details he needed to know on this, his first visit.

As the light began to fade and the temperature dropped, they made their way back to camp and in a rising wind, checked that their tents were securely fastened to the ground.

After supper, they had another early night as Grace felt uneasy and wanted to head off at first light. Her concerns were justified, for the morning dawned with leaden rain-filled skies and ominous dark clouds in the distance. The sea had changed character, no longer the azure blue of the previous day, and was now a muddy grey with white-flecked waves. As experienced sailors they both knew this did not bode well.

They set off at a brisk pace but their progress became slower and slower as they walked into the teeth of the gale. Gusts came whistling down the glens and hit them as they rounded hillsides, almost blowing them off their feet. They were assailed by the rain as it lashed down from the sky, soaking them despite their wet-weather gear. Neither of them were afraid of the physical effort entailed in battling against the elements but they were making little headway, with conditions underfoot rapidly becoming slippery and treacherous.

"I think we'd better take shelter in old Mrs Gilgarry's cottage," shouted Grace above the howling wind. "We'll never get anywhere in this and it's not safe. There's no point in trying."

"Is it far?" called out Sam in return.

"Another fifteen minutes."

They struggled on through the storm, eventually reaching the sanctuary of the cottage. The door flew open as Grace turned the handle and they tumbled in over the doorstep, both of them having to push the door shut against the wind. They were soaking wet, cold and exhilarated. They shrugged off their dripping backpacks and peeled off their sodden outer protective clothing and walking boots.

Without preamble, Sam put his arms round her and kissed her and she kissed him back. He tasted of Cairnmor, of the outdoors and the freshness of the rain. She didn't give Jack a thought.

Breathless, they drew apart and stared at each other;

"Wow!" he said. "I didn't know I was going to do that."

Grace smiled at him. "I'm glad you did."

"So am I. May I kiss you again?"

"Yes, please."

He held her to him and gently explored her lips with his. He was not an expert at this, she could tell, even with her limited experience. And she was glad, oh so glad. She had never subscribed to the so-called sexual revolution and 'free love' and neither, would it seem, had Sam. This was *her* romance; her very own boyfriend. Her first. Possibly so for him as well.

After a moment or two, when they drew apart, he said, "We'd better take off the rest of our wet things. It would be silly to catch a chill."

The interior of the cottage contained only one room and Grace looked at him, her eyes wide with surprise, although she knew he was correct from a practical point of view.

Sam blushed and stammered, "Oh, I didn't mean..." He was embarrassed. "I really wasn't suggesting..."

"I know." Grace smiled, relieved. In any case, she had the solution. "Look, I'll go over there and you stay here. You'll see." She picked up her haversack and walked towards the bed, where she drew two curtains across the width of the room. She poked her head through the middle. "There we are – problem solved!"

And Sam laughed.

When they had both changed into dry clothes, Grace lit the fire in the small lead-blacked range. It took a while for the peat to catch and while they were waiting for it to become hot enough to heat water in the old black kettle and make some tea, they sat together on the wooden chairs either side of the fireplace, one of which was a rocking-chair.

"It's like stepping back into the past, isn't it?" observed Sam, looking round him.

"Yes. This is just the way Mrs Gilgarry kept it when she was alive. She was quite a character. Knew all the herbal remedies to cure all sorts of ailments. She was quite amazing. Before my parents were married, my father went down with pneumonia and it was the potions that Mrs Gilgarry concocted, together with my mother looking after him and giving him the medicines that saved his life. Many years later, when Mrs Gilgarry knew she was growing weaker, she dictated to my mother all her remedies so that they could be kept for posterity. Mum has enough material to make into a book, which she's trying to compile at the moment."

"Will your mother have it published?"

"If she can. We thought we could sell it to tourists as well as the locals who swore by Mrs G.'s ability to cure anything."

Sam smiled at her in such a way that made Grace suddenly feel shy. She blushed. She wanted him to kiss her again, but dare not ask. Little did she know that Sam felt exactly the same.

Instead, he asked, "Who looks after this cottage?"

"I do, along with a few others where the occupants have passed away and there's no family to tend them. I couldn't bear it if they fell to rack and ruin. Someone else might need them one day. While they're empty, I show them to visitors as examples of how crofters once lived in the old days and how many prefer to live today. I've also carved out something of a role for myself as a tourist guide during the summer season, taking guided walks, talking about the history and natural history of Cairnmor. During the winter months at the hotel or in the Great Hall, I do slide shows of my photographs and we show cine film that Dad has shot over the years. He and I are working on a new guide book of the island."

Sam was impressed. Again. She was doing exactly the sort of things he would like to do.

"It strikes me that the area south of Beinn Rannoch would make a wonderful nature reserve," he said. "It has everything – peat bogs, grassland, the loch, heather moorland. Everything."

In his enthusiasm, he leant across and took her hands in his, linking their fingers and studying them as he spoke.

"That's something I've always imagined myself doing. To be some kind of warden, responsible for looking after wildlife and protecting the environment from being built on." He looked at her earnestly. "We're so careless these days with land and buildings. Everything has to be *trendy* or *modern*. Planners and architects say: *Pull all this down; it's old-fashioned. Sweep away the old; forward to the new. We must have progress at all costs. Oh, look – here's a green space; put houses on it. Here's the place for that tower block! Pull down all those terraced houses. It doesn't matter about the communities that live there. It doesn't matter if we create an ugly urban sprawl in the process. We'll call it a 'New Town' or say we've done everyone a favour by clearing out the slums.*" He took a deep breath and contemplated their hands once more, now linked tightly together. "But that's not progress. It's wanton destruction."

Grace was filled with joy. "Oh, Sam. I've always felt exactly the same way. The past is our heritage and the countryside is our present and our future. Both need protecting and preserving not just for the generations to come but for their own sake." Her heart was beating very fast.

He stood up and gently pulled her towards him. "I'm not very experienced at this. At going out with someone, I mean."

"Nor am I."

"I'm glad."

"So am I."

"Let's find out together, shall we?"

"Oh yes, please."

"Gradually, slowly. There's no rush."

They laughed and kissed each other again and added a little more experience to their growing portfolio of life.

High up on the hillside of South Lochaberdale, Alastair and Katherine contemplated the terrible conditions from the warmth and security of their hideaway. The little cottage had seen and survived many such storms but Katherine was worried about Grace and Sam.

"Will they be all right, do you think?" she asked, as she and Alastair stood together, looking out through the kitchen window; the loch and harbour below lost in an obscuring wall of rain, while the wind whipped across the grass and howled round the thatch and under the eaves.

"Of course. Grace will take shelter on Mrs Gilgarry's old croft. It's not too far out of their way. She's very experienced and very sensible."

"Robbie was wrong though about the weather, wasn't he?"

"He was, but he'd be the first to admit he's not infallible!"

"I know, bless him."

Alastair put his arm round his wife's shoulder. She turned to him and they kissed: a gentle, lingering embrace. Time had not dimmed its sweetness, nor had age diminished their desire for each other.

"This place holds so many memories for us, doesn't it?" she said, as they sat down at the table. She poured the tea, which had been stewing silently in the teapot while they had been talking. They took a sip and looked at each other, grimacing.

"Shall I make us a fresh one?" suggested Alastair.

"That sounds like a very good idea."

Katherine watched him as he put the kettle on the range; his movements carefully agile; her contentment deeply felt.

"Was there a particular memory, or just memories in general?"

"In general. My nursing you through pneumonia. Grace being born here. Us standing in the kitchen at the end of the war surveying our 'kingdom' as you called it, discussing the changes we were going to put in place on the island, the improvements we were going to make."

"I remember that well." Alastair smiled. "After that we dug out the survey Ross, John and Michael had done in 1938 and used that as our starting point."

"Do you remember the day when you came up with the idea of the survey?"

"How could I forget? We were going for a walk in the direction of the eastern headlands."

"And we also talked about Michael training as an advocate north of the border. I seem to recall you used the word "*our*" in your phrase "*our* resident advocate.""

"I did, didn't I?"

"And that was even before we were together."

Alastair smiled and raised her hand to his lips. "Perhaps that was because subconsciously we've always been together."

Katherine touched his cheek. "Oh yes. There can be no doubt about that."

Alastair moved his chair next to hers and kissed her properly.

"That survey was quite something," she said after a very long while, resting her head on his shoulder as he stroked her hair.

"And amazingly, most of the things have been put in place – electricity and the telephone reaching most places on the island, a secondary school, the cottage hospital."

"It's a pretty impressive list when you think about it."

"But even so," said Alastair, his mind ever busy and looking ahead, "we can't afford to rest on our laurels. There are still things to be done."

"Oh, I know. But…"

"It's not bad for a life's work, is it?" He held her close to him, his expression full of love. "And the beauty of it, my darling, is that we've been able to do all this together."

"I know." She smiled at him, rejoicing in his embrace.

Eventually, he said, "We couldn't have done it though without your father's financial backing."

"No. But he's only too delighted that his inheritance is being put to good use. Especially the hospital. Selling Mathieson's when he did was a shrewd move and using part of the money to build the hospital and fund it was a brilliant suggestion on your part."

"It seemed obvious to me at the time," he replied self-effacingly.

"I do hope Mr MacFarland will be able to help Rose," remarked Katherine, bringing them back to the present.

"I'm sure he will."

"It must be terribly difficult for her. Mary and Michael are so anxious as well."

"Well, a few days at home will do her good."

Alastair got up from the table and made the tea, bringing it across to his wife. Katherine poured it into cups and they took a sip. "That's better," she said. She regarded her husband with deep affection, knowing the answer to her next question, but asking it all the same. "What would you like to do for your eightieth birthday next year?"

Without hesitating, he replied, "Have a big family get together. Invite everyone."

"Everyone? Even the Australian contingent?"

"Of course. After all, I have a granddaughter whom I've never met."

"That's true."

"Would you mind?"

"Why should I mind? We made our peace with Alex years ago. It wasn't easy for any of us, but I'm very glad we did."

"So am I," said Alastair with feeling, profoundly grateful to have been reconciled with his son before it was too late.

"In which case, dear husband, I shall have to get cracking when we get back to the farmhouse. It will take time for our various far-flung friends and relatives to organize their lives and make their travel arrangements."

"Perhaps no one will want to come." Being a genuinely modest man, Alastair experienced a moment of doubt.

Katherine looked at him, raising an eyebrow. "If pigs could fly…"

He chuckled. "They haven't had much luck yet, so I suppose someone might come."

"Be prepared! Lily and her brood will certainly be here, providing Phillippe is well enough to travel. Although he would want to come anyway, regardless of his state of health."

"In his last letter, he said he was feeling much better now that he can "*laze around*" as he puts it."

"Do you believe him? He's very good at putting on a brave face."

"He's usually honest with me. Perhaps we should pay them a visit. It's been a while."

"Not until I've sent out all these invitations."

"We could take theirs."

Katherine laughed. "All right, we'll go to France but perhaps in the spring when the warmer weather comes. How can I resist it? It's not just Lily and Phillippe being there, it's a special place for us too."

"Yes."

They lapsed into silence, remembering their time serving together in the Royal Navy during the war; remembering their much-missed commanding officer, the very special admiral who lay buried on the hillside at St Germain-en-Laye.

"Perhaps we could make it a nostalgia trip. Visit some of our old wartime haunts," said Alastair. *Before I get too old*, he thought, but didn't say the words. Quickly, he admonished himself. Of course he wasn't old, he just needed to be careful and keep himself fit.

"I'd love to do that."

"Likewise." He smiled. "So, Chief Officer Mathieson, who else shall we invite?"

Katherine chuckled, enjoying the use of her W.R.N.S. name and rank. "Michael and Mary, Rose and Rupert, of course."

"Anna?"

A shadow passed across Katherine's face. Alastair took his wife's hand, gently upholding her.

"We can but try," she said. "I do wish she would answer my letters, even if it's just a line to say she's all right. Her agent is better at keeping us up to date with what she's doing than she is."

"I know. Ten years is a long time without direct communication."

"Oh, Alastair, if only…"

"I know." He touched her cheek.

"Jack will want to be here if he can get leave. He's one of the family in every sense of the word."

"Of course." They exchanged a glance.

"Anna won't come."

"Probably not."

"Do you think that Jack is still in love with her?"

"Yes. And I'd like to think that Anna is still in love with him. Do you think they'll ever get back together?" Even before she spoke the words, Katherine knew it was a forlorn hope.

"No. Too much water under the bridge. On the other hand, stranger things have happened."

"I wish she'd get to know Ben. He's her son for heaven's sake. She's missed out on so much."

"She takes after her father and grandmother – able to sever the link with their children." There was regret but no bitterness in Alastair's voice. "Something that you and I fail to understand."

"Yes."

"Oh, by the way, I meant to tell you, Ben got another commendation for his technical drawing the other day." Alastair was very proud of his great-grandson.

"Really?" Katherine was pleased. "Great-grandpa Rupert thinks Ben should be an architect. So do the school."

"That's another major achievement."

"What is?"

"Cairnmor Senior School, your brainchild."

"Ah, the school."

Katherine was quietly proud of this. The creation of a secondary school on the island was very close to her heart and meant that when they reached the age of fourteen, children from Cairnmor and the surrounding islands no longer had to attend boarding school on the mainland. Therefore, the young people stayed for longer and fewer felt obliged to leave, thus keeping the community vibrant and alive in a rapidly changing world.

For a while, she and Alastair discussed new ways of creating employment for the young people who did not wish to take up crofting or fishing or both. The gradually expanding tourist trade on the island was one such opportunity.

"We need someone who will manage our embryonic industry; someone who truly understands the island."

"Grace?" said Katherine, reading his thoughts.

"Of course, my darling, she's the obvious choice. It's what she's already doing to a certain extent anyway." He stood up and stretched his back. "Now, how about some lunch? All this planning and romancing is making me hungry!"

Katherine laughed and prepared their meal. After they had eaten, they retired to the little sitting room for the afternoon, stoking up the fire with fresh peat. They dozed and read companionably; snug and warm while the storm vented its fury outside.

The inclement weather persisted into Monday, so Michael drove Rose to the hospital even though it was only a mile away. The wind buffeted the car and the narrow road into Lochaberdale was awash with rainwater. The windscreen wipers could scarcely keep up with the deluge and it was with some relief that he parked the car in the space reserved for the chairman. They went inside as quickly as they could.

Opened four years previously, the little hospital had already served the islanders well and their obligatory payment of five pounds per year was but a small, affordable token. It meant that each islander felt they were making a contribution and because of that, the immediately available care they received could be accepted with a clear conscience as it was not as a result of charity. If genuine financial hardship was encountered, payment could be deferred. Moreover, the outstanding amount was never carried over from one year to the next and this generous arrangement ensured that no one went without the treatment they needed.

Alastair, together with Katherine's father, Rupert Sr., had decided from the outset that it was to be a private hospital. In this way, they could run it as they wished without being bound by government bureaucracy. There were stringent rules and regulations to follow, of course, but they had the freedom to develop the care in the way that they wanted and appoint to the staff a small team of visiting consultants and resident doctors and nurses most appropriate to the needs of the islanders. With Michael's legal knowledge, his wartime experiences and continuing interest in all things medical, he had been the obvious choice for its first chairman. He had just been re-elected for a second term of office.

Rose was ushered into Mr MacFarland's pleasant room exactly on time. He asked her several questions regarding her medical history and her pregnancies. Yes, her periods were irregular; yes, it had taken a long time, seven years in fact to conceive the first baby, but no time at all to conceive the second.

Mr MacFarland was silent for a moment. "Did you do any heavy lifting or carrying with either pregnancy?"

"No. I was very careful."

"Did you exercise sensibly and eat fresh food?"

"Yes. All of those things, especially this last time."

"Do you smoke?"

"No."

"Drink a lot of alcohol?"

Rose was shocked. "None."

"You live in Glasgow, I see."

"Yes."

"Well, the area is a leafy suburb, relatively free from pollution."

"Yes."

"Do you like your house?"

Rose thought that seemed like an odd question. She took a deep breath. "No, not particularly. It's very dark and has a rather depressing atmosphere but it was given to us as a wedding present by my husband's grandfather, so Rupert feels that we ought to live there. It's convenient for my husband's work and ideal for my teaching."

"You have a good marriage?"

"Oh, yes." There was no hesitation in Rose's reply. She missed Rupert; wished he were here with her on Cairnmor. She didn't want to go home just yet; she'd rather he was here.

"Do you enjoy your own work?"

"Most of the time. But I'm grateful for the school holidays and I try not to teach too late into the evenings."

"Do you find it stressful?"

"Sometimes. It can be frustrating when talented pupils don't practice as much as they should or if there are parents who insist that their child has lessons when that child really has very little ability. Otherwise, it's wonderful; very rewarding and fulfilling. I have some lovely students at the moment."

The doctor was thoughtful "Is there a history of miscarriages in your family?"

"Not to my knowledge. I am an only child but as far as I'm aware, my mother has never lost a baby. I think that a brother or sister for me just never happened. I know they wanted more children."

The doctor nodded, absorbing the information. "Now, onto your treatment. First of all, I'm going to recommend some multivitamin tablets for you to take. These are quite new onto the market but I think you may find them helpful. It might help to balance your hormone levels."

"Hormone levels?"

"Yes, the menstrual cycle and the female reproductive system are governed by a complex interaction of hormones."

"What are hormones?"

"They are chemical messengers in the body that travel in the bloodstream and influence many of our bodily functions especially, in women, the frequency of periods and successful full-term pregnancy. Stress can affect hormone levels, along with age and general health."

"Are you thinking that my hormone levels could be a factor in why I've had two miscarriages?"

"It's a possibility. However, we first need to rule out any physical reason why you've been unable to carry a baby beyond fourteen weeks. So, Mrs Stewart, if you have no objection, I'd like to give you a preliminary internal examination. It will be brief, given everything that your body has had to contend with just recently. Then, I should like to do a more extensive exam in about six months once everything has healed. "

He pressed a buzzer and a nurse in a starched white apron came in and drew the curtains round the examination couch, handing Rose a gown which she put on, placing her own clothes in the basket provided.

In Oban, Rupert paced the quayside, up and down, up and down, his frustration spilling over.

"Damn this weather," he muttered to himself. "Dammit." He glowered at the sky and pulled his sodden coat closer to him.

The ferry on Monday morning had been cancelled because of the storm and Rupert had spent a frustrating day in the vain hope that conditions would improve. He'd had a dreadful, weather-delayed train journey from Glasgow the previous day and now that he was here, he refused to go home. He had a rehearsal on Wednesday afternoon and a concert in the evening. He'd hoped to go to Cairnmor today and come back tomorrow. Fourteen hours of travel to spend a precious few hours with Rose. But he would have done it, just to see her, to be with her.

The rain poured down and Rupert had never felt so utterly miserable and helpless in the whole of his life.

CHAPTER 7

New York
Virginia

Almost as soon as they returned from Fenton, Marcus received a call at his office from the sanatorium requesting that he come and collect his wife immediately. He debated whether or not to tell Anna straight away. She was about to go on stage for a matinee performance and he knew that to do so before then would be unfair on her. So he sat in the wings and watched her, any number of conflicting emotions going through him.

Afterwards, in her dressing room, while she was sitting at the mirror removing her stage make-up, Marcus drew up a chair and told her.

She turned away from him and resumed her task of applying cold cream; suppressing her inner vulnerability before it took hold.

She saw that this could be the beginning of the end: the opportunity she had been waiting for to finish her relationship with Marcus before it went beyond her control, before she fell in love with him. She must do it now, before her resolve weakened.

"Well, you have a key," she said coldly, acting a part. "Come when you can, although your wife will need all your attention from now on."

Marcus was taken aback. Did she really believe he would walk out on her now, after all they had shared during the previous months? His heart beat faster with anxiety. Quickly, he took hold of himself and made direct eye contact with her via her reflection in the mirror.

"I shall come to you again."

There was firmness in his tone and truth in his words. He wasn't going to be put off that easily by her defensiveness.

Anna paused in her actions and turned to him; the pain of dilemma and truth showing in her eyes. He was too fine a man for such callous treatment from her. He deserved better.

"Thank you," she said more gently. "For everything."

He smiled and touched her cheek, failing to hear the finality in her words.

Anna sat there for a long time after he'd gone, staring at herself in the mirror.

Well, that was that, she thought. Another lover sent on his way. *But this time it hurts like hell and it's hard to let him go.*

She knew it would take her a long time to get over Marcus Kendrick. She had revealed more of herself to him than she should have done and, in responding to her, he had reached deeply into her emotions with his kindness and care. He was in danger of supplanting Jack. She could not allow that to happen under any circumstances; she had to remain inwardly faithful to her husband. It was for the best, therefore, that she and Marcus saw no more of each other.

Anna decided not to go back to her apartment before the evening performance but stayed at the theatre. She wandered into the empty auditorium and sat down on one of the plush red seats in the stalls, staring up at the stage. With Marcus gone, she felt restless; adrift.

On an impulse, she went into one of the rehearsal rooms at the back of the theatre, the one with the grand piano. She sat on the stool for a long time, staring at the instrument. It had been twelve years. Could she still play? Would she remember how?

Tentatively, she lifted the lid, her hands hovering above the keys. Long-suppressed emotions flooded through her and she played a scale – slowly, cautiously. It felt good. She played another, then another; each one faster than the last, her fingers still remarkably supple and responsive. Another scale; some exercises. A study; a prelude; a nocturne until she was completely absorbed in the music.

Afterwards she wept, overwhelmed by the memories and emotions released at her fingertips.

Virginia was quiet in the car all the way home. Uncommunicative. Sullen. It was ever thus when he first brought her back. Always the same pattern: silence, then several days of cajoling, vainly trying to get her interested and involved in things at home; then a week where he would take her for occasional days out in the country or to a museum or an art gallery or the cinema.

Having reached this stage, he knew it would be possible for him to go into the office for a couple of hours each day rather than conduct his business on the telephone. He was able to pay a visit to his agent or his publisher to discuss progress on his latest book or his ideas for the next.

But always, always at the back of his mind there was the fear that he would come home to find empty vodka bottles once more in the wardrobe, the chest of drawers, even the cistern; to find discarded syringes or empty pill bottles on the bathroom floor.

The most dangerous time was when he was sent away on assignment for a few days. It was usually after this that his return would be greeted by a drug-induced high and her breath reeking of alcohol. And the empty bottles. And the overflowing ashtrays and a total mess in the kitchen and bathroom. But, worst of all: Virginia, violent and abusive.

Marcus hated it. He hated the woman sitting next to him. He had absolutely no inclination to try any more with her. He'd had enough of watching her slowly kill herself. It was soul destroying because he was helpless in the face of her self-induced destruction.

When she was released, he became a virtual prisoner in his own home. The only time he was free was when she was in the sanatorium. He had to keep reminding himself that she was suffering from a chemical illness; a disease. She needed compassion not censure.

He needed Anna.

They reached home. He carried her suitcase into their ground-floor apartment and she followed slowly, reluctantly. He made them both a cup of coffee and it was when he took both cups into the sitting room that she turned on him venomously.

"Explain this…!" She hurled a newspaper at him. "And this…!" And another.

One caught him on the side of his head, the other squarely in the chest. This was what he dreaded the most, the violence; the unpredictability of her behaviour towards him.

He picked up the papers from the floor.

There it was. The picture of himself and Anna on the bench in the park. The one that had been taken weeks ago but never printed. It was blurred and difficult to distinguish his identity as he had his back to the camera. Marcus had obviously caught the photographer before he'd had the chance to get a decent shot. Unfortunately, Anna had not been so lucky.

It was part of a new daily competition called, '*Guess the Hidden Celebrity.*' He read the caption. '*Is this Anna Stewart's latest beau? Will he last any longer than the others? Or is he just another dupe waiting to be dumped? Who is he, her mysterious lover in the park? Remember, the $100 prize is up for grabs for anyone who can guess.*' The next day's rag was full of suggestions, none of them hitting the mark.

But Virginia had recognized him. And how had she got hold of the picture? Newspapers were banned from this particular sanatorium. Where had she got it from? Someone had obviously failed in their duty. He would find out.

"Well?" she demanded, her voice shrill; her manner impatient. "I know it's you."

"Really?" replied Marcus, stalling for time while he thought of the best way to deal with this.

"She's nothing but a tart." Virginia was trying to goad him into an admission of guilt. "Everyone knows that. She's renowned for it."

Marcus quelled the urge to defend Anna. He would be wasting his breath and give himself away.

"I might have known you'd go behind my back. Might have known you'd take up with some other woman. That's why you put me in there isn't it? In that place. So you can spread yourself around while I'm out of the way and have your sordid little affairs. How many others are there? How many others have you had? And there's me thinking you were the perfect husband and it was me that was all wrong. That's what I say to everyone: he's the perfect husband." Then she looked at him provocatively. "Even gives me money for my habit."

Marcus was appalled. "I do not. That's a lie. You use your own money, the money that your grandmother left you. The money over which I have no control."

"Only because you give me nothing. You'd keep me in sackcloth and ashes if you had your way. But the public don't know that, do they? The old coot's money is gone now. I'd earn a pretty packet if I went to the newspapers and sold them a sob story of how my famous journalist husband gives me money for drugs and drink so that little wifey can be put safely out of harm's way in a sanatorium while he goes off with his tarts."

"I don't think they'd wear that somehow." Marcus was scathing. And furious. This was unbelievable, a nightmare; like some sort of cheap drama on the television.

"They might when I tell them it's you in the photograph. I could do with the hundred bucks."

"You wouldn't dare."

She laughed in his face. "Believe it, kiddo."

This was not her usual homecoming attitude. Usually she was docile. Ah, but then, she was only about half way through her treatment this time. He'd only seen this side of her when she was hyped up on amphetamines or, after some party, on acid or speed. He looked at her eyes, searching for tell-tale signs of dilation. On the other hand, his picture hadn't been in a newspaper with another woman before.

"I've got a deal for you. You give me a hundred dollars a month to do with as I want and I'll keep quiet. Otherwise, I'll go to the press."

Disgusted, without answering her, Marcus slammed out of the apartment and walked the streets for hours.

As far as he could see, he had three choices.

He could go straight to his attorney and instigate divorce proceedings. Whatever the future might hold for himself and Anna, he wanted to be rid of his wife who was a debilitating millstone round his neck and a drain on his resources. The second choice would be to call her bluff and let her do her damnedest with the papers. With both of these, Anna's name would be brought into it: either through some defence lawyer tearing her reputation to shreds in court or laying her open to further ridicule in the gutter press by dragging them both through the mire. He wasn't prepared to allow Anna to be hurt in that way.

The only other option was to give in to Virginia's demands. There was no guarantee, of course, that she would keep quiet, but at least it would keep her off his back. Perhaps she would find a hippy commune somewhere and live out her remaining days with others of like mind in a drug-filled haze.

It was late when he let himself back in the apartment. Lights were blazing in every room and Virginia appeared out of the bedroom, a vodka bottle in one hand, her eyes wild, her manner aggressive.

Goodness knows what she's on this time, thought Marcus. He didn't even need to look at her eyes.

"Where the hell've you been?" she said, lurching unsteadily towards him. She tripped on the edge of the rug and the bottle slipped out of her hand onto the parquet floor where it smashed, its contents spilling everywhere. "Now look what you've made me do." She stared at him belligerently.

He knew better than to answer her back but he was tired and without thinking he said, "No, it was you who did that with your stupidity."

She started shouting at him, accusing him, hurling abuse. She was in a dangerous, volatile mood. Marcus squatted down to pick up the shards of glass before she could harm herself or him. He had to be careful lest he cut himself and he was so focused on the task, that he forgot to be on his guard.

Deliberately and maliciously, without any provocation or warning, knowing exactly what she was doing, she kicked him in the part of his anatomy which, from the position he was in, was exposed and vulnerable. Caught by surprise, he rolled over onto the floor clasping himself in agony.

"That'll teach you, you unfaithful bastard," she screamed at him.

Thus incapacitated, he knew what was coming next and, strong as he was, for the moment he was powerless to prevent it from happening.

She started kicking him on his chest, on his head and face; her rage and strength drug-induced, her aim surprisingly accurate. It wasn't the first time he'd been used as a punch-bag when caught unawares.

He rolled out of her way, his body on fire as the broken glass cut into him. Painfully, Marcus managed to drag himself to a standing position using the arm of a nearby easy chair but she came at him again, her fists flailing. He managed to shove her back onto the settee, almost losing his own balance in the process. Somehow, she staggered to her feet and lashed out at him again, grabbing whatever was to hand as a weapon. Using all the strength he could muster, he fought her off and pushed her away from him. There was no malice in his action, just self-preservation.

Reeling backwards, Virginia tripped over the edge of the rug and fell heavily, hitting her head on the edge of the glass coffee-table which shattered under the impact. She lay still, blood seeping onto the floor from her temple.

Marcus stumbled over to where she lay and checked her pulse. It was very faint. In agony, his face throbbing and his body burning with pain, he crawled to the telephone by the front door and dialled for the police and an ambulance. He had the presence of mind to put the door on the latch before collapsing onto the floor.

Virginia Kendrick died that night in hospital. The autopsy determined that the immediate cause of death was from injuries sustained to the temple area of her head after it impacted on the coffee table. It also revealed a high level of alcohol and a dangerously high level of amphetamines in her blood stream. She had lacerations on the soles of her feet, indicating that she had stepped on broken glass. Her liver showed the onset of cirrhosis, her spleen was enlarged, her kidneys were in poor condition and there was some degeneration of her nasal passages and lungs. The pathologist estimated that her life expectancy would have been no more than six months had she continued to abuse her body in the way that she had been; if she hadn't managed to overdose before then.

Marcus was arrested on suspicion of murder and kept under police guard in hospital while having treatment for his own injuries. He was tested for alcohol consumption and drug abuse but was found to be clean. He had to undergo two painful operations to remove the glass from his chest and back and for a few days after that, he was unable to lie down. He had stitches on his face and hands as well as his body and although he would bear the physical scars of this episode for the rest of his life, he was fortunate not to be disfigured in any way.

The mental scars were a different thing altogether.

He was questioned by a detective in the presence of his attorney and statements were also taken from the medical team and police officers who responded to his telephone call. The crime scene investigators took photographs and drew diagrams.

There was evidence of a physical struggle having taken place; of the consumption of alcohol; a shattered glass coffee table; a smashed vodka bottle; blood everywhere and empty bottles of amphetamines. The blood was tested and the results showed that most of it, apart from on and around the shattered coffee table and the broken vodka bottle, belonged to Marcus.

His injuries were catalogued and photographed. The apartment searched and documents removed pertaining to Mrs Kendrick's stays at the sanatorium as well as some of her personal effects. His bureau was investigated and various papers, his diaries, letters and some keys were removed.

The neighbours were questioned and statements taken. Had they seen anything, had they heard anything? *Shouting and swearing from Mrs Kendrick but that was nothing new. She was always accusing him of something. This time it was of him being unfaithful to her. Of having an affair. Her poor husband had a great deal to put up with.* Why he didn't just up and leave her, they had no idea. They hadn't heard the sound of anything heavy being thrown against the wall this time.

Virginia's family were notified and her uncle and cousin demanded that Marcus be prosecuted for first-degree murder. After meeting them both, the detective assigned to the case immediately contacted their local sheriff to see if either man had a criminal record. This had already been done with Marcus but with him they could find no trace of any illegality. Not even a speeding fine or a parking ticket. It was very different story with these two, however. When the reply came back, the detective was delighted. He'd hit the jackpot.

The detective also took statements from staff at the sanatorium and discovered Mrs Kendrick's history of violent behaviour when intoxicated or under the influence of drugs and that Mr Kendrick was always caring and considerate towards her. The detective began to think that it would be a waste of time to take this whole thing to court. No jury in their right mind would convict the husband of murder with a wife like that. On the other hand, maybe they would; maybe they'd think he'd had enough and wanted to be rid of her.

Doug Metcalfe advised his client that he should have no contact with Anna. A colleague from the law firm was discreetly despatched to her apartment to explain the situation and collect any personal belongings that Marcus might have left there. Marcus was also advised not to write to Anna or to receive any communication from her. It was best that way and could harm his defence if he did and possibly implicate her if the case went to trial and the prosecution decided to pursue the murder charge once proceedings were underway.

Anna understood. She felt desperately sorry for Marcus. She had been contemplating writing to him to finally end things but in the light of all this, she hesitated. It would not be fair to load that onto him as well. Perhaps the relationship would now come to a natural conclusion if they had no contact with each other. She sent a verbal message of sympathy via the law firm's representative.

A few weeks later, Marcus was well enough to leave hospital. He was brought up before the court for the preliminary hearing where the prosecution presented its case. The Grand Jury decided there was enough evidence for a criminal trial. Marcus was indicted and spent a miserable night in a police cell. Twenty-four hours later at the arraignment, the charges against him were read out. He pleaded not guilty to second-degree murder and was released on five thousand dollars bail, which his attorney paid, and told not to leave the country.

Marcus was shocked and stunned by all of this, as well as deeply upset at not being able to see Anna and talk to her.

He moved out of his old apartment and rented another on the Upper West Side. *Chronicle* magazine suspended him on half-pay pending his trial.

Marcus had no Anna, no job, no inclination or incentive to do anything. His days were empty and, apart from helping his attorney prepare the case ready for his trial, he had nothing to do. He wandered aimlessly through the streets and the parks. He read newspapers and books without taking in a word. He watched television and went to the cinema without enjoyment. He did all these things until he couldn't stand it anymore and hit the bottle.

He drank himself into an oblivion where he could no longer feel guilt, pain, grief, disgrace and the total futility of his life.

CHAPTER 8

Journeys

"I want to move." Rose was adamant. She didn't want to stay in the house a moment longer. She found it depressing and claustrophobic.

"But Grandpa gave it to us."

"Yes, and I had a very long chat with him on the telephone while I was on Cairnmor. He quite sees my point of view and has offered to buy a different house for us."

Rupert scowled. "I don't want him to buy us a new house. I want to stay here."

"You're behaving like a spoilt child," replied Rose.

He had been touchy ever since she had come back. She would have thought he would have recovered by now from the trauma of his abortive journey to come and see her. She had thought it wonderful that he had even tried to come to Cairnmor and had said so, but couldn't help laughing when he described how he had stood on the quayside in Oban for hours in the pouring rain even though he knew all sailings had been cancelled. Why didn't he go into a café and have a hot drink, she asked, instead of standing out in the open like a lemon?

Rupert was upset by her reaction to his efforts and embarrassed that he had failed in his quest. Because of the concert, he had had to give up, admit defeat, and take the train back to Glasgow. All he had to show from that particular escapade was a bad cold. He did the concert feeling very unwell, conducted badly, and the next day, he really did have to call in sick. The remembrance of the whole episode made him tetchy.

"So are you."

"Me?!" Rose was indignant. "Rupert, I've been asking you for ages if we could move. But you don't seem to be hearing me."

"But Minton House is so convenient."

"Yes, but it's ghastly."

"It's just right for a family."

"We're not going to have a family."

"We shall one day. We just have to be patient."

"No. No family. Not ever." Rose had rehearsed so many ways to tell him; had been over and over it in her mind. In the end she blurted it out, the very thing she had wanted to avoid.

"No, no, Rosie. Mr MacFarland said he thought everything would be fine. He said there was nothing wrong, that there was no reason physically why you shouldn't carry a baby to full-term."

"That's not what I meant." Rose spoke quietly.

Rupert took a few moments to comprehend her words. "What!"

"I don't want to try for another baby."

"You can't mean that."

"But I do."

"No, darling. That's just how you feel at the moment. We've always wanted a family."

"Yes, I know we have. But now I don't." Suddenly, she started to cry.

Rupert was beside her in an instant, their argument forgotten, his arms around her, holding her. He couldn't bear to see her so unhappy. She had always been so cheerful and practical. He didn't know what to do; how to react. This was uncharted territory for him.

So Rupert did the only thing he could and listened to his wife, taking on board her fears and longings. After a while, he realized that for Rose to work through her distress and pain, there really would have to be changes. Her anxiety was not going to disappear easily and no amount of love and sympathy or platitudes would provide the answer.

He was not afraid to make changes if it would help her and make her happy. He knew the power of their love was very strong; their closeness inviolate. They would get through this, even though at the moment it was all very painful. And they would have a family one day – he felt certain of it. However, for the moment, Rupert kept that thought to himself and focused on the immediate needs of his beloved Rose.

Their journey to France had been beset by delays and frustrations from the beginning. The crossing from Cairnmor had been choppy and unpleasant; the night sleeper from Glasgow uncomfortable. Their breakfast had taken ages to be served and their taxi from Euston had become embroiled in a traffic jam which seemed to bring out the worst in everyone involved.

Alastair remained sanguine and took it all in his stride, but he sensed Katherine was losing patience when at Victoria, they learned that their scheduled boat-train had 'motor problems' and its departure would be delayed by at least an hour.

"The driver hasn't turned up, more like," remarked one disgruntled passenger, standing next to them, studying the arrivals and departures board as it flapped and clicked its way through its constantly changing cycle.

"You'd think they'd have made such an important train like the 'Golden Arrow' a priority," said another.

"Wouldn't have happened in the old days of steam before the war, before we had nationalization," grumbled an elderly gentleman in a bowler hat, clutching his umbrella and briefcase and heading off in the direction of the station buffet, to consume a dried out ham sandwich, no doubt, thought Katherine.

"We'll miss our connection," she said, turning to Alastair.

"We have time at the moment. Providing the delay isn't too great."

He spotted a British Rail official and went across to speak to him.

"How long is it likely to take?"

"Difficult to say. Depends when they can get another unit. Or if this one can be fixed."

"Is anyone working on it?"

"We're waiting for maintenance to come at the moment."

"We have to catch the boat from Dover at three o'clock. It's the advertised connection. Any chance we'll be there on time?"

"Can't guarantee it, I'm afraid. The unions are on a go-slow as well today. Some dispute about someone being reprimanded for taking too many tea-breaks."

"I see."

Alastair hid his annoyance and went back to join Katherine, who was sitting patiently on a hard wooden bench with their luggage trolley.

"Any luck?"

"None. There's some kind of go-slow, apparently."

"The trains ran better during the war even with all the cuts in services and speed restrictions."

"Lots of things ran better during the war."

"Why can't that sort of mentality be transferred to peacetime?"

"I have no idea. The British seem to have mislaid the conception of pulling together. Now it's every man out for himself."

"And for what he can get. It's pretty depressing really."

They surveyed their surroundings – the dirty station floor, the overflowing litter-bins, the crowded concourse where people jostled each other; their ears assailed by the constant noise of loudspeaker announcements and the slamming of carriage doors.

Katherine sighed. "It's not very salubrious is it?"

"Not really." Then Alastair chuckled. "I'm afraid this is all my fault."

"What, the shortcomings of British Rail?" she said, picking up on and extending the intentional humour.

Alastair kissed her forehead and laughed. "I'd do something about it if it *was* my responsibility."

"I know you would. So, tell me then, efficient husband of mine, how come it's all your fault?"

"I suggested we go to France."

Katherine smiled and tucked her hand through Alastair's arm. "Of course. I therefore hold you personally responsible." After a while, she said, "It's a good job Cairnmor isn't like this."

"Isn't it just?!"

"Mm." She looked at him and said, "Do you know, even with all this chaos, I feel perfectly happy as long as I'm with you."

Alastair tilted her chin up towards him and gently kissed her lips. "Likewise. But I'd still quite like to make that connection."

"So would I."

They both laughed and Katherine laid her head against that of her husband.

Marcus was woken by the shrill, intrusive ringing of the telephone. He yanked the cable out of the wall and sank back onto the floor.

The hammering in his head was very loud and seemed to be coming from the door. It was very insistent. It also had a voice that shouted his name over and over again through the letter box. He ignored it.

There was a crashing sound. Why was the world so noisy? He wanted to sleep. Why was someone shaking him? He wanted them to stop.

"Marcus, Marcus! Wake up! Marcus!"

"Wha...?" He couldn't find any words. He couldn't see straight. He couldn't think. He couldn't feel anything. Bliss.

"C'm on, buddy. Let's get you sober."

Doug Metcalfe looked around the room. It was littered with whisky bottles. Marcus must have been on some bender. What a time to choose. He'd never seen his friend drunk before. Tipsy occasionally, but never anything like this.

With some difficulty, for Marcus was a well-built man, Doug managed to get him to his feet and into the bathroom. He sat him on a chair and supported him while he ran the shower. Then, awkwardly, he removed Marcus's clothes.

With a sigh of resignation, Doug realized he would never stand up by himself so he stripped off and propped up Marcus as the water ran over them both in sharp, reviving rivulets. At least, Doug hoped they'd be reviving.

Sitting him back on the chair, he threw a towel at Marcus but got no response, so he dried him off as best he could and rubbed himself down and put his own clothes back on. He took Marcus through to the bedroom and sat him on the bed where he rolled over onto his side and instantly fell asleep.

Doug found clean clothes, woke him up and with great difficulty, dressed him. If it hadn't been such a crucial day, this whole thing would have been quite comical. He then went into the kitchen to make coffee. Very strong and very black. Marcus could only take a few sips at first, but eventually, he drank a whole cup, then two, then three. He managed to stay awake.

Doug was angry with him but refrained from haranguing him; there was no point. He also had a certain amount of sympathy for him and understood his friend's need for escape. It was a horrendous thing that had happened to him and it was unfortunate that he, Doug, had been called out of town for the past fortnight. He should have kept a better eye on Marcus. He wouldn't let this happen again.

Doug managed to get his friend sober and reasonably awake by the time they were due to leave. They went via a barber's shop, where Marcus was given a shave and a haircut. Doug knew it was vital that he made a good impression in court.

Today was the first day of his trial.

Marcus looked in the mirror at his reflection. He felt terrible but he looked even worse. He turned away, ashamed.

The light cruiser H.M.S. *Leopard* scythed its way through the Atlantic Ocean, en route to the United States for a rendezvous with the American Navy and subsequent participation of its senior officers in joint discussions about policy and manoeuvres for the newly commissioned N.A.T.O. Standing Force Atlantic. A Royal Navy commodore had been appointed as its first overall commander and H.M.S. *Leopard* was transporting both him and members of his staff to New York to lead the talks.

The steward knocked on the door of the captain's cabin.

"Come in."

"Sorry to disturb you, sir. I know how busy you are but I thought you might like a cup of tea and some biscuits. And Lieutenant-Commander Hammond asked me to give you these as well, sir." He placed a letter-package and a bundle of newspapers on the desk.

"Ah, a sure sign that we're nearing land once we receive our mail from the Royal Fleet Auxiliary after refuelling. Thank you, Morgan."

"Yes, sir."

After the steward had left, he glanced at the large, foolscap envelope, recognizing the familiar and welcome handwriting. He decided to save that one until later when his duties were finished for the day and he could enjoy reading it in peace. He glanced at the newspaper headlines and flicked through the inner pages while he sipped his tea. American newspapers were an interesting mixture, he had always thought.

Then an article on page three caught his attention. A murder trial in New York. A well-known Broadway and television actress implicated in the death of her lover's wife. She had been subpoenaed to give evidence.

Anna Stewart.

Shocked, he read on. The detail was well-written and unbiased but he sensed a certain exaggeration in the presentation of the material. He couldn't believe what he was reading.

Anna. Involved in something like this.

His mouth dry and his heart racing, Jack Rutherford paced the floor of his cabin. Suddenly, everything else – his duties, his mission, Grace – paled into insignificance.

PART TWO

APRIL, 1969

CHAPTER 9

The Trial (1)

"Oyez, oyez, oyez. All persons having business before the Supreme Criminal Court of the State of New York are admonished to draw near and give their attention, for the Court is now sitting. God save the United States and this Honourable Court. The Honourable Chief Justice Trelawny presiding."

As the Chief Justice entered, everyone in the wood-panelled courtroom stood. The room was packed with journalists and the public, for the case had generated enormous interest. People were constantly coming in and out of the courtroom and it took a while for the onlookers to settle.

Marcus sat down. He felt nervous and afraid. He knew he would be called to give evidence after the opening statements. He looked at Doug sitting pale and strained beside him. For his part, his attorney felt the total weight of responsibility. Marcus was his best friend and he knew him to be innocent. This should never have become a murder trial but it had happened. An innocent man should never be convicted, but that too had happened.

He thought that Marcus was mad to have allowed District Attorney Mudeford to have his way and put him on the stand as the first witness for the prosecution. It was not usual court procedure. Doug had strongly advised against it but Marcus had reasoned that if he began and ended the trial, then the first and last person the jury saw and heard would be him. It wasn't that he felt overconfident, far from it, but he knew this case hinged on his word and his integrity. It was a calculated risk, but one that he was willing to take. Doug understood his reasoning and went along with it and at the pre-trial hearing, it was agreed that Marcus should be allowed to take the stand, just as the prosecution wanted.

District Attorney Hubert Mudeford went away from that hearing metaphorically rubbing his hands in glee. This case would be over before it began. He'd had many successes using this particular gambit. Poor sucker. What an idiot this defence lawyer was.

Now, as the trial began, the D.A. was invited by the Marshal of the Court to make his opening statement and, once formal introductions were out of the way, proceeded. After giving a rather laboured description of the events as he perceived them, he concluded by outlining his aims:

"It is my intention to show that the accused, Marcus Kendrick, did wantonly and without provocation, murder his wife, Virginia Kendrick, in their apartment. I shall also show that he and his lover, the actress known as Anna Stewart, did plot and conspire to kill Mrs Kendrick in order that they could be together.

"I shall also prove that as an additional motive for murder, Mr Kendrick killed his wife because she threatened to expose his affair with his current mistress and therefore ruin his public reputation. The only way the accused could prevent this and at the same time be rid of his wife was to recourse to murder.

"While it must be noted that Mrs Kendrick had her problems, she was totally dependent upon her husband for financial and physical support. But he consistently refused to help her on either count and she therefore was obliged to use up her inheritance in order to give herself a decent life. She had no immediate family living close enough to be able to assist her.

"For many years, Mrs Kendrick had been through a series of rehabilitation programmes. She was vulnerable and helpless and because he could see no way out of his predicament, I shall prove beyond reasonable doubt that Mr Kendrick murdered his wife as soon as an opportunity arose.

"This was a crime where there is no doubt as to the identity of the murderer. His conduct resulted in the death of another individual – clear *actus reus*. I shall prove beyond reasonable doubt his intent – *mens rea* – to so commit such an act.

"It is disgraceful that Marcus Kendrick, a man in a position of great responsibility to influence public opinion, should commit such a crime. It is my duty to ensure that this crime does not go unpunished and that Mrs Kendrick's family can mourn her loss knowing justice has been done."

At the end of his speech the D.A. sat down and turned to his associate, an expression of self-satisfaction on his face. His associate smiled politely.

His elbows on the table, Marcus hid behind his hands. With the case presented like that, even he would think he was guilty. He regretted agreeing to be questioned first.

Doug was invited to make his opening statement. He took a deep breath and rose to his feet. The door at the back of the courtroom opened and closed. Doug was distracted by this and waited to begin until the distinguished looking man had sat down. Out of the corner of his eye, he also became aware of an unfamiliar woman reporter on the front row taking copious shorthand notes.

Controlling his own nervousness, he started to speak. He outlined the events of the night in question from Marcus's perspective, presenting a very clear and precise picture. He gave no flamboyant denials, no fabrication, just a simple rendition of the facts, leaving an impression of truth and accuracy in his words on the listening public. His conclusion was no less sincere.

"Marcus Kendrick is a well-known and well-respected journalist and novelist with a reputation for fairness and impartiality. He cared for his wife, Virginia Kendrick, for the whole of their very difficult marriage. Unbeknown to him, before they were married, she was already a drug addict with a predilection for alcohol.

"Over time, he came to accept that his marriage was a disaster and, despite his best efforts, it had failed very quickly. Even so, Mr Kendrick steadfastly refused to abandon his wife, knowing that she had no other reliable person to whom she could turn. He cared for her, keeping alcohol out of the house and his wife away from the bars and the drugs, frequently working from home for long periods of time, sacrificing his own freedom and giving up lucrative work so that he might not leave her alone and give her the opportunity to give in to her addictions.

"He tightly controlled her finances as she was liable to use any money she had to purchase illegal substances as soon as he left the house, even to do the shopping. However, he had no control over the way she used the money she had inherited from her paternal grandmother and, if he was required to be absent from home for even a day, would find her missing or high on drugs.

"Mrs Kendrick became unemployable and had been previously arrested for disorderly conduct and possession. She was bound over to keep the peace and put through compulsory rehabilitation programmes. My client paid for each one of these.

"Mrs Kendrick had a history of violent and abusive behaviour towards her husband. I shall prove that he dealt with this in a mature and reasonable manner, especially given the provocation he was forced to endure.

"It is my intention to show that he is a man of good character and that it would be impossible and unthinkable for such a man to commit so heinous a crime as murder, premeditated or otherwise, no matter what strain he was under. I shall also prove beyond reasonable doubt that my client was acting in self-defence on the day of his wife's death and that this unfortunate event was the result of an accident.

"Your Honour, ladies and gentlemen of the jury, there was no malice aforethought, no conspiracy and this also shall be proven beyond reasonable doubt. Thank you."

With a grim expression, Doug took his seat once more and Marcus turned to his friend in gratitude. A murmur of discussion and conversation went round the courtroom but silence fell as the Marshal of the Court called Marcus to the witness box and placed a bible in his hand. Marcus then swore the oath of truth.

The District Attorney rose from his seat and asked Marcus to state his name and occupation. The lawyer then proceeded to question him vigorously, trying to make him falter, to trip him up, to accidentally make an admission of guilt before the court.

"Did you love your wife, Mr Kendrick?"

"At first, yes. I wouldn't have married her otherwise."

"But over time you came to hate her?"

"Given what I endured over the years, it is not surprising."

"A simple yes or no will suffice."

"Yes."

"Did you or did you not want to be rid of her?"

"There were certainly times when I had had enough."

"Please answer the question."

"I wanted to be free of her. As I said, I had had enough."

"Yes or no?"

"Yes."

"So you decided to kill her."

Doug stood up. "Objection, your Honour. The prosecution is making assumptions and putting words into the accused's mouth."

"Sustained."

"Why didn't you just leave her instead of killing her?"

"I did not kill her."

"May I remind you, in case you had forgotten, Mr Kendrick, that you are under oath and your wife is dead."

Marcus blanched and took a deep breath; his heart pounding. "I am very well aware of the former and no one regrets the latter more than I do."

"So you did kill her?"

"No. Her death was accidental. I was defending myself."

"Come now, Mr Kendrick. You are a well-built man. She was a small, incapacitated woman."

"Objection, your Honour. Mrs Kendrick was not a *small, incapacitated woman*."

"Overruled. I shall allow this line of questioning."

Doug sat down, mollified and anxious.

"Thank you, your Honour." The District Attorney gave Doug a condescending glance before moving closer to Marcus. "I find it hard to believe that someone of your height and strength needed to defend himself against someone as frail as your wife."

"Nonetheless, that is what I had to do."

"Your wife was how tall?"

"Five-foot five."

"And you?"

"Five eleven."

"Keep yourself fit, do you?"

"Reasonably."

"Take part in sport?"

"A little."

"Weightlifting?"

"Not since college."

"The truth of the matter is that *you* overpowered *her*, didn't you?"

"Objection, your Honour. The D.A. is leading the accused again."

"Sustained."

"I'll rephrase the question." He turned to Marcus once more. "How could you have possibly needed to defend yourself against a much smaller woman?"

"Objection." Doug was becoming impatient. "We have already been through this."

"Overruled. The accused will answer this particular question."

Marcus turned to the Chief Justice. "Your Honour, at the time of her death, my wife was high on drugs and drink. I knew from bitter experience how this fuelled her strength and made her behaviour volatile and unpredictable. She had dropped a bottle of vodka and it had shattered on the floor. As I squatted down to pick up the glass, certain parts of my anatomy were vulnerable to attack, and attack them she did without any hesitation. Then she started…"

Quickly, the D.A. interrupted as he could see it would not be to his advantage to allow Marcus to continue. "Thank you, Mr Kendrick. Nevertheless, you were still stronger than she was."

Doug was onto him in an instant. "Objection, your Honour. The prosecution has not allowed the witness to finish."

"Sustained. Please continue Mr Kendrick."

"Thank you, sir."

Marcus then outlined what had happened: how she had continued to attack him, how he had tried to avoid her; the injuries he sustained until eventually, how he was forced to push her away from him.

The D.A. pounced on this. "So you used all your strength and pushed her over onto the coffee table, seizing the opportunity to smash her head against it."

"Objection. This is supposition. I can prove that no medical evidence whatsoever exists of such an event."

"Sustained. The last remark shall be stricken from the record. The jury will disregard Counsel's statement. Please continue, Mr Kendrick."

Marcus was vehement in his answer. "Virginia tripped over the edge of the rug which had been disturbed during our... altercation and she landed on the coffee table which shattered under the impact of her body, sending shards of glass into her head as it hit the edge."

Doug's assistant sat making shorthand notes: selecting and sifting the prosecution's line of questioning; making sure no detail of the interrogation was left in mid-air, no stone unturned. Doug thought Marcus was doing well so far. Speaking directly to Chief Justice Trelawny was a moment of instinctive genius.

"Instead of killing her, why didn't you just leave her?" Terrier-like, the D.A. was not about to let go of this line of questioning.

"I didn't kill her. She died as a result of an accident."

"At your deliberate instigation."

"Objection."

"Sustained."

"I didn't leave her because she had no one else to turn to."

"But her uncle will shortly be called to give his testimony."

"I feared for her well-being."

"So killing your wife was caring for her well-being?"

"Objection."

The Chief Justice was stern. "Counsel..."

"I withdraw the question, your Honour." The District Attorney continued. "Are you implying that her own family were not capable of taking care of her?"

"Yes."

"How well do you know them?"

"Well enough."

For the next hour, the D.A. continued with his questions but Marcus did not give way; did not allow himself to be tripped up or trapped. Doug also stood his ground, objecting and supporting his client wherever necessary, keeping the opposing counsel in line. The Chief Justice was good, impartial and fair.

"Do you wish to question the witness, Mr Metcalfe?"

"Not at this time, your Honour."

He and Marcus would stick to their strategy and he felt his friend had held himself together remarkably well. So far, he had given a very favourable impression to the court. However, Doug knew that this was only the beginning. Things would certainly hot up for the afternoon session.

After lunch, the reporter resumed her seat directly behind the accused, waiting patiently in the rapidly filling courtroom for the afternoon session to begin. Marcia Harper read through her notes from the morning's hearing, pleased with the detail she had recorded.

This was her first assignment since her six month's secondment to the *New Yorker* and she wanted to make a good impression. Her Aussie friends back home in Melbourne were all rooting for her while she was here in the States.

Having finished reading her notes, Marcia turned round to look for her mentor, the experienced reporter to whom she'd been assigned, with whom she had sat for the morning session, whom she was unable to find at lunch and who seemed to have disappeared without consulting anyone. It was most irritating and very unprofessional but a regular habit, it would seem.

The article in the newspaper about the upcoming trial had been written by her, under the name of her 'mentor' who had wanted to visit a lady-friend and had told her to get on and write it in his absence. So she had looked at his style, copied it and sent it in as his. Okay, she wouldn't get the credit for it, but it was an unbiased, workman-like report and she was pleased with it.

Marcia had always admired Marcus Kendrick, both as a journalist and author. She loved his work and had always wanted to meet him, ever since she had read his very first article in *Chronicle* magazine when she was sixteen. She had read every book, both fiction and non-fiction, as soon as it was published and had a scrap-book full of articles about him. In fact, it was because of him that she had become a reporter. Even in her wildest dreams, she had never imagined that the first time she saw him, it would be under circumstances such as these, here in New York's Criminal Court building.

Already thus favourably predisposed towards him, Marcia had found herself becoming increasingly drawn towards the real Marcus as the trial progressed. There was no doubt in her mind that he was innocent. Having come to that conclusion, she realized it was going to be difficult to maintain her objectivity as a journalist. But maintain it, she must. This was her first assignment for the *New Yorker* and she had to do it well.

She searched amongst the onlookers and reporters as they arrived, but her mentor had not reappeared. Marcus Kendrick had though, arriving with his lawyer.

Marcia looked up at him as he passed by. She could see he was tired; could see the strain etched on his face. And her heart went out to him.

The afternoon session resumed and Marcus was called to the stand for further interrogation.

Jack Rutherford sat at the back of the courtroom, studying Marcus Kendrick closely as he spoke. He had to admire this man, who looked so terribly haggard and drawn, for withstanding the onslaught of questioning from the prosecution with dignity and steadfastness. He also had some sympathy for Marcus, whom he had come into the courtroom quite prepared to dislike because he was Anna's lover. But for some unknown reason, he couldn't. He actually took to him.

He watched the expressions on the faces of the jurors. Some of them he could read clearly, others were keeping their thoughts very much to themselves. The prosecution's case was building against Marcus, of that there could be no doubt, but the defence lawyer was standing firm, allowing no detail to go unquestioned or unfair accusation unchallenged, successfully deflating the evidence as it was presented.

Jack presumed that circumstantial evidence would play a large part in determining the outcome. Knowing nothing about Federal law, he had no idea if someone could be convicted on this type of evidence alone. There were no witnesses to the actual event and the outcome of the trial would depend on the skill of the defence lawyer and whether the jury believed Marcus's own testimony.

As an experienced captain in the Royal Navy, Jack had been present at standing courts-martial and presided over disciplinary hearings aboard his ship, therefore the due process of law was one with which he was reasonably familiar. As the afternoon session progressed, he became increasingly aware that the murder charge was incorrect. Virginia Kendrick had died, certainly, but accidental death or self-defence were surely more accurate descriptions. As far as he could see, there was nothing deliberate or premeditated about Marcus's actions.

Jack had debated long and hard as to the wisdom of attending the trial but, after his ship had arrived at the U.S. Navy base on the Hudson River and delivered the commodore into the arms of his American opposite number for the first in a series of informal meetings prior to the main event, Jack had seized the opportunity to come ashore – his services would not be required until later when the formal talks began – leaving his very capable executive officer in charge of the *Leopard*.

He reasoned that by coming to the Criminal Court, he would be able to satisfy his need to know and understand the circumstances of the case at first hand. It would give him an idea of the best way to help Anna, should she need his help or indeed, be willing to accept it. However, he now found himself becoming involved in the proceedings for their own sake and was glad that he had come.

"How long did you know Anna Stewart?"

At the mention of her name, Jack's attention was jerked back to the present.

"We were together for about two months."

"And you stayed in her apartment?"

"Yes."

"How many times?"

"We lived together for all of that time."

"What, from the moment you met?" The prosecution attorney pretended incredulity.

"Yes."

"And where was your wife during this time, Mr Kendrick?"

"Undergoing rehabilitation treatment at a Bel Air sanatorium for drug and alcohol addiction."

"So, while the wife's away, the mice do play…" The D.A.'s tone was insinuating.

"Objection. The prosecution's manner is insulting to my client."

"Sustained."

"Was this the first time you had been unfaithful to your wife?"

For some unknown reason, even though it was the truth, Marcus hesitated before speaking. "Yes."

"Really?" The D.A. was disbelieving.

This time his reply was firm and immediate. "Yes."

"Yet you thought nothing of starting an affair with Anna Stewart almost immediately after you met her." When Marcus failed to respond, he added, "Come now, Mr Kendrick, you're a married man. It would therefore seem that faithfulness does not register very highly on your list of priorities."

"Objection," Doug's impatience was beginning to show. "This is irrelevant and once again insulting. My client had no marriage to speak of. He and his wife had not had a normal relationship for many years."

The D.A. was quick to respond. "Your Honour, I'm trying to show the accused's lack of moral character and that he took advantage of his wife's incapacities, using the opportunity for his own... ends, shall we say?"

Chief Justice Trelawny gave the D.A. a quickly concealed look of dislike. "Objection sustained."

Hubert Mudeford glanced briefly at the jury. His words had registered with several of them, so, content with this, he continued to delve.

"Did you ever intentionally supply your wife with drugs so that she could be out of your way in the sanatorium?"

Marcus was so horrified, he almost shouted his denial. "No! Absolutely not! Never!"

"Would you say you were prone to outbursts of anger?"

"Objection."

"Overruled. The witness will answer."

"No. I am generally a calm and patient man."

"Did you or did you not physically assault a photographer in Central Park on 24 October last year?"

"No, I did not."

"I have a statement here from the man concerned – a copy of which is before the court – who says, and I quote, "*I was taking photographs of Marcus Kendrick and Anna Stewart as they kissed and cuddled publicly on a park bench...*'" Hubert Mudeford paused and turned to the jury, a smirk playing around the edges of his blubbery lips, before continuing, "*...when Mr Kendrick spotted me and demanded I hand over my camera. When I refused, he tried to grab the camera, jostling and shoving me in the process. I was obliged to run off for my own protection as I could see he was a very angry man.*'" How do you explain that, Mr Kendrick?"

"Quite easily. Anna and I exchanged one kiss. We heard the camera clicking and I asked the photographer to give me the film, as what he was doing was a gross invasion of our privacy..."

"Come now, Mr Kendrick, you and Miss Stewart are well-known and as such your actions are public property."

"I beg to differ. What we choose to do in public, or otherwise, is our concern and not anyone else's business."

"And I presume that choosing to commit murder comes under the category of 'not anyone else's business'?"

"Objection."

"Sustained. The last question shall be stricken from the record."

"Please tell the court what happened next."

Hubert Mudeford's eyes swivelled across to the jury. Marcus Kendrick could not possibly get out of this one.

"When the man refused to hand over the film, I tried to grab his camera. He sidestepped me rather adeptly and ran off. He was obviously very practised at that particular move."

A murmur of amusement went round the courtroom.

"I did not push or shove him," continued Marcus. "There was no physical contact between us. I did not touch him at all."

"But there is a sworn statement before the court. Therefore, one of you is not telling the truth."

"I am telling the truth."

"And you expect me to believe that?"

Marcus was becoming irritated by this man. His reply was slightly testy. "What you believe is not my concern. What the people in this courtroom believe, is. They deserve nothing less than the truth."

The D.A. snorted his derision. "I'm giving them the truth."

"No, sir. You are not. *I* am speaking the truth."

Jack knew that he was. Marcia knew that he was, but did the jury? The D.A. looked at them again. He couldn't tell. He'd leave that particular thread for now. He'd come back to it when he called the photographer as a witness later on in the trial.

"Would you say that you and Miss Stewart shared a passionate relationship?"

Marcus swallowed hard. This was very near the knuckle. "That is none of your business."

"But it is the court's business. I repeat the question."

"Objection."

"The witness will answer." Chief Justice Trelawny could see the relevance of this particular question. Some members of the jury did not.

"Yes, we shared a passionate relationship."

At these words, Jack felt the first stirrings of jealousy. He knew how passionate Anna could be; knew how passionate they had been together during their short marriage. Surely no one else could have shared that kind of relationship with her? He had always been so certain that what they had had was unique; that neither of them would ever find anyone else who matched what they had known together.

"Would you describe your actions towards your wife on the night of the murder..."

"Objection. Murder has not been proven."

"Sustained."

"Would you describe your actions towards your wife on the night in question as driven by your passion for Anna Stewart?"

"No."

"A crime of passion fuelled by a desperate need to be rid of your wife?"

"No."

"When did you first discuss with Miss Stewart how to get rid of your wife?"

"Objection, your Honour." Doug was once more irritated by his adversary.

"Sustained."

"I shall rephrase." The D.A. smiled ingratiatingly. "Did you and Miss Stewart ever discuss being together for the long-term?"

"Yes, I offered to leave my wife so that we could be together."

"But you said earlier that you could never leave your wife because she was totally dependent upon you. Come now, Mr Kendrick. Be accurate. You can't have it both ways."

"I am being accurate. Both things are true."

"But you wanted to be with Miss Stewart more than with your wife?"

Marcus looked at the D.A. "Wouldn't you?"

A murmur of laughter was clearly audible from the listening public. The prosecution lawyer glared at Marcus before saying, "No, I would regard it as my duty to stay with my wife."

Hypocrite, thought Marcia.

The Chief Justice looked at him but said nothing.

The D.A. cleared his throat and stuck to his task. "So, given the dilemma of wanting to be with your lover but not able to leave your wife, you and Miss Stewart hatched the plan for you to kill off the deceased."

"Objection."

"Sustained. Mr Mudeford, please confine your questions to the facts and not to supposition."

The D.A. took a breath. "In his diary, written several weeks before the…" and he paused deliberately, as though searching for the appropriate word, "…incident…" smirking at Doug, as though to say, 'there you are, try and make an objection to that' "…the accused states that he wanted, and I quote, '*to be rid of this woman who is making my life a misery. I really do not care what happens to her anymore. I've done my best. I can't go on like this. It's a terrible thing to say, but I really don't care whether she lives or dies. All I want is for Anna and I to be together. Perhaps we can find some way of getting Virginia out of our lives permanently.*' The diary is before the court, your Honour, Exhibit A."

The D.A. sat down, an expression of anticipation on his face. The Chief Justice was handed the diary by the Clerk and sat reading for a few minutes, his lips drawn into a tight line.

An excited buzz of conversation went around the courtroom. Marcia sat tense and anxious.

Jack considered the words he had just heard. At best, they were the private outpourings of a desperate man and as such had no substance; at worst, they were a subliminal intention of causing someone harm. Did the final sentence constitute 'malice aforethought', he wondered?

Chief Justice Trelawny banged his gavel and called for order. Once silence had been resumed, the D.A. stood up again and continued, a glint of triumph in his eyes; the smell of victory in his nostrils.

"Here, your Honour, is a clear declaration of intent by Mr Kendrick to kill his wife."

The court went into an uproar.

Doug had to shout to make himself heard above the noise. "Objection, your Honour. It is no such thing. My client was merely at the end of his tether."

The Chief Justice hesitated. Briefly. He looked at the D.A., banged his gavel for silence and said, loudly and deliberately, "Objection sustained."

"*Good*," thought Jack.

Relieved, Marcia sat back in her chair.

Hubert Mudeford was wrong-footed momentarily. Was the Chief Justice biased? Should he call for a mistrial? Unfortunately, there was nothing concrete. He'd watch him closely though from now on. Annoyed, he knew he had no option but to rephrase the question.

Once the room was silent, he said, "Perhaps you could explain to the court exactly what you meant when you wrote, '*Perhaps we can find some way of getting Virginia out of our lives permanently.*'"

Marcus felt sick. He recognized he had to be careful. "I used the term '*we*' and '*our*' because at the time, Anna and I were very much a couple…"

"Even though you still had a wife?"

"Yes."

"And as your wife was in the way of you being with Miss Stewart, together you decided to find some way of getting her out of your lives 'permanently'. Is permanently merely your particular euphemism for murder?"

"Objection."

"Overruled."

"No. Absolutely not." Marcus was vehement in his assertion but there was no anger, no desperation in his manner. His voice was direct and firm because he spoke the truth. "She had become a millstone round *my* neck, in *my* life, and I wanted my freedom. I'd had enough. It never entered my head to kill her. To leave her to her own devices would have amounted to a death sentence and I had no intention of doing that either. My thoughts went no further than to throw her on the tender mercies of her family, such as they are. No, it was not Virginia who was in the way of Anna and I being together."

Jack wondered what that could be. He looked at the Chief Justice's expression and could see the same curiosity there. But the D.A. appeared not to have been listening closely enough and missed the obvious question, carrying on with the previous line of questioning.

"How many times did you discuss with Miss Stewart the possibility of the two of you being together permanently?"

"Once or twice."

"Come now, Mr Kendrick, you can't expect the jury to believe that!"

"It's true. You see, we never got very far in any discussion before the subject of her ex-husband came up."

The D.A. was momentarily taken aback. "Her ex-husband?"

Doug looked at him and smiled. The D.A. had not done his research very well, had he?

"Yes. You see, Miss Stewart is still in love with her ex-husband and because of that cannot commit to any other man. She and I came closer to making a commitment than most, but I remain convinced that she will always love him and because of this, there could never be anything lasting between us even if I had been a single man."

Marcus's words went round the courtroom like wildfire. It was his strongest defence yet but it hit Jack Rutherford like a bolt of lightning. He wanted to leap up and take the stand at the front of the courtroom and declare that he still loved Anna as well; that he was still her husband; that he would always be her husband. That she could never become involved in such a ridiculous conspiracy; that the D.A. was wasting his time. Irrationally, he wanted to rush over to Marcus and shake his hand.

Of course, he did none of those things but, armed with the potentially life-changing knowledge that Anna still loved him, he knew he had to see her again. All thoughts of Grace that he had been trying so hard to put out of his mind these past months, temporarily receded into the background.

Powerful and unbidden, came a vivid picture of Anna running barefoot along the white-gold sands of Cairnmor to greet him, her hair flowing out behind her, her face alight with anticipation. He remembered their kisses as he gathered her to him with absolute joy and his body tingled at the memory and tears pricked his eyes.

CHAPTER 10

Trials and Tribulations (1)

Grace held onto the tiller firmly. The wind had got up suddenly, swirling around all points of the compass; unsettled in any direction. She could see the weather front, a clear delineation between blue sky and a dark grey mass of cloud, catching up with her inexorably,

She knew she had been unwise to come out on this particular afternoon; that had he been at home, her father would have advised against it. But *Spirit II* was ready: newly painted, her hull gleaming blue in the sunlight and Grace had been unable to resist the temptation to take her for a shake-down sail.

She had spent the whole of the previous week fitting out her yacht – putting on the sails, refuelling, filling the water tanks, cleaning the saloon and the cockpit, washing down the white paintwork inside, buffering up the shiny varnished wood (all of which she found great satisfaction in doing herself) and taking back on board everything that had been removed while *Spirit II* had been laid up for the winter – cushions, curtains, sleeping bags, life jackets, oilskins, sea-boots and sou'westers; restocking the food lockers with tins and dried packets for the forthcoming season.

Grace had only intended a short sail in the Loch but the Atlantic had beckoned and here she was, all alone, in the middle of nowhere with no protection from the elements. She turned on the engine, letting it idle, while she hove to. The boat rocked and bucked with the waves as she brought down the mainsail, which in turn banged and flapped dangerously against the mast, the captive main sheet blocks flying noisily backwards and forwards along the metal horse.

With great difficulty, she had just managed to secure the mainsail onto the boom when suddenly, *Spirit II* was caught in a violent gust of wind that sent Grace crashing down onto her knees and causing her to slide off the cabin roof as the boat heeled over, sending her flailing into the safety rail, her lifeline pulling her up short and spinning her round against the metal stanchions.

She lay there, holding on tightly, fighting to regain her breath; her body pinned between the bulwarks and the cabin sides; the boat knocked and battered by the wind and the waves. She had to get to the prow and take the staysail down but she couldn't move. Then the rain started; cold and penetrating. Waves were breaking over the deck and the boat was tossed about every which way. There was a loud graunching and tearing as the staysail ripped with the combined force of wind and water.

In a panic, Grace crawled up to the front of the boat, pulling painfully at the halyards of the shattered sail, her hands numb with cold and fright, working feverishly to gather in the canvas as it flew dangerously out of control. Many times she was enveloped by the remains of the sail; many times she extricated herself and tried to fasten it to the guard rail, only to have it snatched out of her hands by the force of the wind. At last, after a great struggle, she succeeded, tying each part roughly but securely onto the pulpit rail.

Shaking with adrenaline and exertion, Grace crawled back to the cockpit on her hands and knees, holding on to whatever she could find. Once there, she worked frantically to put another reef in the mizzen, needing it as a steadying sail and unwilling for it to suffer the same fate as the staysail.

She knew she had no hope at all of reaching Lochaberdale before darkness fell. She realized she had no option but to head further out into the Atlantic and make for Eilean nan Caorach, the nearest landfall, where the little bay on the eastern side would offer her a sanctuary of sorts from the storm.

But which sail would balance the mizzen best in these conditions? The storm jib was the obvious choice but as Grace looked at the heaving deck, she knew that on her own, it would be reckless and stupid to go back up to the prow of the boat. So, after regaining her bearings and releasing the tiller from its thrall, she turned up the engine revs and headed out into the Atlantic into the teeth of the gale.

"It is so good to see you, *mes amis* !" Phillippe du Laurier was expansive in his welcome. "It has been too long, far too long! I trust you had a good journey?"

"We did, thank you," said Katherine, offering her hand to Phillippe, who, with Gallic charm, took it in his and kissed it. "Eventually, that is, after a somewhat inauspicious start." And she recounted the initial delays followed by what had proved to be a pleasant crossing of the English Channel and uneventful train journey to Paris.

Phillippe smiled. "*Bon* ! Forgive me for not standing, but my back, he plays me up a little today, so I sit. In great frustration on this the very day you arrive!"

"But resting helps?" Alastair was anxious to know.

"*Mais oui, certainement* ! I shall be up and walking more easily tomorrow. And tomorrow, when you have recovered from your journey, we shall visit Eloise and her *deux enfants adorables*. There is another on the way. She is very young for such a large family but she seems to love it; to thrive on it!"

"I'm glad. We know you worried about that when she was first married."

"*Oui*. At sixteen, she was far too young to be married, but right from a little child, all she wanted was family life. She helped her mother with her brothers and sisters and was a natural with them. Armand is a good husband and provider and they share the childcare. Eloise has no ambitions other than family and has always loved the home. Léon, her brother, on the other hand, is full of ambition. He wants to become President of France! I say to him, it is good to aim high but you have to be realistic also. He says that I am only his Papa and that I know nothing. *Moi* ! I tell him to mind his manners and he shrugs and he goes back to his studies and his campaigning." Phillippe smiled at the recollection. "He will make politics his career, there is no doubt. But how far will it take him? Who can tell? But he is twenty and involved with student life at the Sorbonne. He is… a revolutionary!"

"What about François and Frederic?"

"The twins? They do well at the Paris Conservatoire. I cannot believe that they have been there almost a year. They will form a duo when they go out into the world as professional musicians – a violinist and cellist together will be in great demand. But there is the possibility of a trio. They have found an excellent pianist in Gabrielle." Phillippe looked up at his wife, who had just entered the room.

"What's this?" said Lily, hugging her father with great affection, and kissing Katherine on each cheek.

"I was talking about our Trio." They exchanged a glance.

"Ah, yes. Our Trio," Lily smiled, but did not elaborate further.

"And how is Marie?" asked Alastair, wanting to know about his youngest grandchild.

"Marie is so excited to see you. Our little afterthought didn't want to go to school this morning," said her mother.

"She has learnt a new piece on the piano and will play it for you tonight."

Phillippe was proud of his children's accomplishments; proud that he and Lily had such a large family; proud of the fact that despite his infirmities, he was still able to produce such a brood.

"And now, it is time for supper, *n'est-ce pas* ? I think our housekeeper has prepared a special treat for our very special guests."

And with some difficulty, Phillippe raised himself out of his chair and using his sticks, walked to the ornate dining room slowly and carefully.

"I like this one."

Rose felt happy in the light and airy house they had come to see at Strachan of Fairlie, a secluded village fifteen miles into the countryside; fifteen miles away from the grime and clamour of Glasgow.

She loved the sitting room, with its double-aspect picture windows and spectacular views across the glen to the fells beyond; she loved the French doors that led onto the large, well-stocked, sun-filled garden and, once they were open, delighted in smelling the sweet fragrance of the spring flowers that bloomed in the warm April sunshine. She loved the old-fashioned kitchen that had everything they would need and the stable door that also led out into the garden. The house was clean and bright and had been well-cared for.

"Oh, Rupert, this is the one!" She knew they would be happy here; knew it was the right house for them. "The bedrooms are just perfect and I adore the attic rooms. The views are wonderful and there's such a feeling of light and space!"

Rupert hesitated. He knew she was right, it was a lovely house. He could live here quite easily. But it was at least half-an-hour's drive from the centre of the city. He would be reluctant to do that in the snow or the rain. On the other hand, if it made Rose happy…

"It's on the edge of a very small village so there won't be much scope for your teaching," he said, concerned for practicalities; trying to find excuses.

"But Moraytown is only a few miles down the road and I can still use Minton House. I know you don't want to sell it so I'll travel into Glasgow with you on the days that I'm teaching there and you can drop me off. Or I could buy myself a car. It's only a half-hour drive. We're really quite close to Glasgow and yet we have all this scenery."

"Does that mean you won't come to see my concerts anymore?"

Rupert could foresee times when they wouldn't be as intimately involved in each other's activities; times when he would be doing things on his own without Rose by his side. Was it the beginning of the end of their closeness; a closeness he treasured and relied upon, he wondered?

"Of course I'll still come to your concerts! But there may be times when I might want to be at home. Especially if it's this one. I might even give up teaching altogether and just stay here making a home for us both. We could afford that."

Rose went from room to room, planning in her mind how they would decorate; the small changes and improvements they could make; which room could be used for what purpose. She was excited and felt happier than she had for a very long time. Here was their very own house; one that could provide just what she needed; one into which she could grow.

Rupert saw the change in her; saw the sparkle return to her eyes and knew that whatever difficulties this move might throw up for him, he could cope if it made his Rose as happy as this. He had to admit that it did feel like a real family home in a way that Minton House had never done, for all the time they had lived there and for all the redecorating they had carried out.

But he did worry about driving this far out into the countryside when the weather was bad. All those hills... And what would happen if they were snowed in and he couldn't *get* to work?

He looked out of the spacious dining room windows at the view, allowing its sense of freedom to open his mind to possibilities. Perhaps he would buy a land rover and if conditions became impassable, he could always spend a night or two (or even until the weather improved) in Minton House after late rehearsals and concerts. That would save him the anxiety of a potentially dangerous journey. If Rose were willing to keep their present house for her teaching practice, then they would still have it as a base in the centre of town. Whenever she came to his concerts, they would be together whatever the weather because they could stay there afterwards. And in the summer, it would be wonderful to leave the heat and dust of the city behind to drive home to this house and be part of all this lovely scenery.

With his spirits lifting, Rupert began to share Rose's enjoyment of the house tour as the middle-aged vendor showed them round.

The house was large and well thought out, with character and charm, but some of the rooms were slightly shabby and needed redecorating and part of the roof needed urgent attention. Once this had been done, Rupert could quite see that he wouldn't want to leave either, especially if Rose was here all day. Perhaps moving house wasn't such a bad idea after all.

Yes, they would buy this one. But he wanted to pay for it himself, with his own money from the savings he had been careful to make from his generous allowance. They could just about afford it without having to take out a mortgage – and not ask Grandpa for a penny. Then it would be truly theirs.

Rupert took a deep breath and went to find his wife, who was exploring the garden on her own, to share his thoughts with her and to hear anything she wished to share with him.

CHAPTER 11

The Trial (2)

On the morning of the second day, the detective assigned to case was called to the stand by the prosecution as a witness. However, the D.A. failed to extract anything other than a simple description of Mrs Kendrick at the crime scene. The detective seemed unwilling to commit himself to furthering the prosecution's case and the D.A. was obliged to sit down, grim-faced and annoyed. This man was supposed to be *his* witness.

Doug sensed an opening in Marcus's favour and for the first time in the trial, apart from his opening statement, he took to the floor.

"What did you see when you entered the apartment?"

"The obvious signs of a struggle. Blood on the floor. Glass all over the place."

"What was Mr Kendrick's mental state when you arrived?"

"He was unconscious when we first got there but once he'd come round, he was in shock and visibly upset."

"What was his physical state?"

"He was badly injured with blood everywhere on his person. His shirt was torn and there were nasty signs of swelling on his face. He had some difficulty in walking."

"Who had notified the emergency services?"

"Mr Kendrick."

"Before he collapsed." It was a statement, not a question.

"Objection. Counsel is leading the witness."

"Overruled. The witness can continue."

"Thank you, your Honour." Doug repeated his statement.

"Yes, apart from leaving the front door on the latch, using the phone was the last thing Mr Kendrick must have done before he collapsed because he still had the receiver in his hand while he was lying on the floor unconscious."

"Where is the telephone in the apartment?"

"By the front door."

"So my client, in great pain and with great difficulty crawled into the hallway and telephoned for the emergency services. Hardly the actions of a guilty man or someone who had failed to tend to his wife." Doug looked pointedly at his opposite number who the previous day had tried his best to make it seem as though Marcus had compounded his crime by failing to resuscitate his wife. He continued: "Was there anything in his manner that displayed guilt or fear in the presence of so many uniformed police officers, forensic scientists and detectives?"

"No, sir. None whatsoever."

"How would you describe his demeanour?"

"As I said, he was in shock and in a lot of pain. He answered my questions to the best of his ability. His account of what took place has never wavered from that first statement."

"Please would you refresh the court as to what that statement was."

84

"Gladly." And reading from his pocketbook, the detective proceeded to describe the events of that terrible night from Marcus's perspective.

"Do you believe that Mr Kendrick spoke the truth?"

The detective looked him in the eyes and replied, "Yes, sir. I do."

"Thank you. I have no further questions for the witness at this time."

"If the prosecution has nothing to add, then you may step down, Detective Inspector."

The D.A. was a troubled man and remained in his seat looking down at his papers. He had planned to further pursue the idea that Marcus had not gone back to help his wife after phoning the police, but it was too late now. The detective had blown the possibility for that particular line of questioning out of the window.

One by one, the prosecution's witnesses came forward; one by one the cross-examination by the defence found openings which strengthened Marcus's case – the next door neighbours, the pathologist, the autopsy report – with Doug always seeking out details that the D.A. failed to capitalize on or just omitted.

A member of staff at the clinic was next up for cross-examination.

"Please tell the court how long you have been working at the Bel Air Sanatorium." Doug crossed the floor to the stand.

"Two years."

"What is your position there?"

"I am a Senior Carer."

"So you deal with the clients on a day-to-day basis?"

"Yes and keep the records of each one."

"Did you know the deceased?"

"Yes, she was a regular 'customer'."

"What was her attitude when she was in your care?"

"Belligerent and aggressive."

"Was she ever violent?"

"Frequently, especially when she was first admitted. Some of the staff wouldn't go near her."

"So you had to be selective in whom you rostered to help her?"

"Yes."

"What was the reason for her aggressive behaviour?"

"Some people become violent when under the influence of drink and certain drugs. Others are depressive and become morose and lethargic."

"Which category did Mrs Kendrick come into?"

"The violent one, definitely."

Doug paused, allowing the significance of the carer's words to be absorbed by the jury.

"Did anyone visit her, apart from Mr Kendrick?"

"No." The man paused. "But come to think of it, a few days before she died, her uncle paid her a couple of visits, on two consecutive days. He'd never been near the place before, at least not to my knowledge. It was after his second visit that she demanded to be released."

"Is a client allowed to do that, even though they have not finished their treatment?"

"Yes, provided they are not being treated under a court order and have family to go to."

"Did you know why she demanded to be released?"

"No. Well," he thought for a moment, "she did mutter something about an article in a newspaper and that she was going to 'get even with the bastard'."

A murmur went round the courtroom.

"Who was she referring to?"

"I have no idea."

"Could it have been Mr Kendrick?"

"Possibly. I really couldn't say."

"Is it correct that newspapers are banned from the clinic?"

"Yes."

"How did she come by this newspaper or newspapers?"

"I have no idea."

"The only person she had seen was her uncle. Therefore, it seems reasonable to assume that he must be the one who gave it to her."

"Objection. It could have been anyone. Defence Counsel is leading the witness."

"Sustained."

Doug was not worried; he knew the uncle would be called to the stand that afternoon. He'd tease it out of him.

"How would you describe Mr Kendrick's attitude when he came to visit his wife?"

"Caring, but kinda sad."

"How often did he come?"

"Once a week usually, after the initial month when no visitors are allowed. Helps the clients settle in, you see."

"Did you ever see anything aggressive or angry in his manner towards his wife?"

"No. Never. His visits were characterized by a strained silence between them. When his wife came to the end of her treatment, she'd cling onto him and make him promise that he would never leave her, telling him over and over again how much she needed him."

"What was his reaction to this?"

"He'd sigh and promise. But more than once, I saw him leave looking very upset and kinda despairing."

"Thank you." Doug turned to the Chief Justice. "I have no further questions at this time, your Honour."

"This Court is now in recess. We shall resume at two-thirty this afternoon."

Marcus smiled at Doug as he sat down. His friend nodded. "It'll be interesting when the uncle takes the stand."

"Whatever happens, I'll always be grateful to you."

"We'll get there but we're not out of the woods yet."

"I know."

Marcus took a deep breath and stood up. As he turned to pick up his briefcase, the April sun streamed in through the window and highlighted the glossy chestnut-coloured hair of the woman seated on the front row behind them. He regarded her for a moment. There was something familiar about her. Perhaps she had been sitting there yesterday; he had a vague recollection of her while he had been on the stand. Idly, he wondered if she would be there that afternoon.

Marcia had been momentarily blinded by the sun and did not see his brief appraisal of her.

Marcus and Doug left the courtroom for lunch. They circumvented the gaggle of photographers and hacks, many of whom Marcus knew but had no wish to speak to, and found their way to a private anteroom where they could discuss the case and have a respite from the strain of the proceedings.

Jack stayed seated at the back of the court until the crush had eased. Marcus's counsel was doing a brilliant job. He was making the witnesses look as though they had been called by the defence, not the prosecution. By now, Jack was utterly convinced that Marcus was innocent and hoped the jury felt the same.

He was glad he was able to stay for the afternoon session as by now, he had become completely absorbed by the proceedings. However, it was the anticipation of the following day's events that made his heart beat faster and the palms of his hands become damp with anxiety. For it was then that Anna would be taking the stand.

He had decided to surprise her; to hear quietly and anonymously without fuss all that she had to say. Having done his research and found out where her play was being performed, Jack had considered going to the theatre and meeting her there. He had also wondered whether or not to write. In the end, he had decided against all of these things, thinking it unwise to distract her before she gave evidence.

Most importantly, he wanted the first time that he saw her in person to be from a safe distance: keeping his presence concealed amongst the crowd, carefully avoiding any contact with her. Then he'd reveal himself and approach her afterwards at the appropriate time. That would be the best thing. For both of them.

Jack was under no illusion that it would be one of the most difficult things he had ever done. He would have to choose his moment carefully. He wanted her reaction to him to be spontaneous so he could see how she really felt. He also wished to gauge how he felt because, before hearing Marcus declare that Anna still loved him, he had begun to doubt the reality of his feelings for Anna; feelings that he had carried with him ever since the day their marriage ended and which lately had begun to seem unreal and without substance.

The basis for these doubts was Grace. Thoughts of her had occupied his mind since the summer and Jack knew he came alive each time he remembered their kisses and the feel of her in his arms. He was very aware that his feelings towards her were evolving and there was the distinct possibility he might be falling in love with her. Because of the promise he and Anna had made to each other so many years ago, he could not allow that to happen and therefore, had been trying very hard to put Grace out of his mind.

He was not very successful.

Therefore, he needed to see Anna again; to be with her and to be sure that he really did love her still. And, most importantly, that he was, at last, able to forgive her. They had been apart for a very long time. Surely, the wounds would have healed by now? Was it possible for them to be reconciled?

And if that should happen, was it what he really wanted?

The trial resumed after lunch. Marcia took her place and Hubert Mudeford called Virginia's uncle to the stand. He shuffled awkwardly from his seat and, after muttering the oath with only the tip of his forefinger touching the Bible, sat down heavily on the witness chair, his shoulders hunched, turning his cap nervously round and round in his hand. He looked neither at the lawyer nor the jury, but stared fixedly at the floor, his florid complexion shiny with sweat.

"You are Walter Grissom known as 'Wally'?"

"Yeah."

"Please state the nature of your relationship to the deceased."

"I'm her uncle."

"Would you say you were a close family?"

"Yeah."

"Were you close to your niece?"

"Yeah."

"What was she like as a child?"

"Pretty little thing."

"How old was she when her parents died?"

"Twelve or thereabouts."

"Who looked after her?"

"I did. Raised her as my own flesh and blood."

"Did you approve of her marriage to the accused?"

Wally looked up for the first time. He gave a snort of contempt. "No."

"Why not?"

"Too clever fer 'is own good."

"In what way?"

"Tried to tell me how to run my life and how I shoulda looked after Gin, I mean Virginia, better."

"You didn't agree?"

"No." He looked at the floor again.

"Why not?"

"None of his business. At least I give her money which was more'n what he did."

"You mean, he kept her short?"

"Yeah. Tight as a clenched fist he was with his money."

"So without your contribution during her marriage, she would have struggled to keep herself in a civilized manner?"

"Objection. The prosecution is leading the witness."

"Sustained."

"Did your money make a difference?"

"Yeah." He looked at the D.A. "Without my contribution she would have struggled to live in a civilized manner. Especially after she'd nearly used up old grandma's money." His eyes reverted to the floor.

"Grandma's money?"

"Yeah. Her inheritance. The old coot had it hid under the floorboards in her bedroom. Thought it was safe." Wally sniggered. "But Gin found it, didn't she?

88

Went on and on about it and forced the old coot to give it to her. Clever girl, was our Gin. She made…"

Hastily, the D.A. interrupted and brought the Wally Grissom's testimony to a rapid conclusion. "No further questions, your Honour."

When Doug began his cross-examination, he was determined to pursue this matter to its conclusion.

"How did the deceased make her grandmother give her the money?"

"Threw her belongings out of the house one by one and tried to throw her out as well. Quite a battle it was of words and fists. The old woman put up a real fight, I'll say that much fer 'er. Howey and I enjoyed it hugely."

"You didn't try to stop it?"

"Nah. It was their argument, warn't it? Ma deserved it."

A buzz of shocked conversation went round the courtroom. After waiting until this had ceased, Doug continued: "What happened next?"

"The old coot died a few weeks after that. I let Gin hang onto the money. She'd won it fair and square."

The court erupted again. Chief Justice Trelawny was obliged to use his gavel several times before there was silence.

"What did your niece do with the money?" asked Doug, picking up the thread once more.

"How should I know? She was a nearly a grown woman by this time. Her money."

"Didn't you care what she did with the money?"

"Warn't up to me."

"What about when she was growing up? Did you care what she did then?"

Wally shrugged. "It was her life. Warn't up to me to interfere."

"Yet you tried to stop her getting married. Surely that would have been a good thing for her."

"Nah. I warned Gin she'd be marryin' above her station but she took no notice and said it was her ticket out of the hell-hole she was living in with me and Howey. I told 'er, this Marcus Kendrick was a pompous prick and she'd get her comeuppance in the end."

A collective gasp was clearly audible from around the room. The Chief Justice reprimanded Wally Grissom sternly.

"This is a court of law. The witness will temper his language accordingly."

The witness lowered his gaze to the floor.

"Going back to when she was young, did you ever notice anything unusual in her behaviour after she came to live with you?"

No answer.

Doug repeated his question.

No answer.

"If you do not answer the question, Mr Grissom, I shall hold you in contempt," said the Judge.

Wally knew he had no choice. "Yeah. Sometimes."

"In what way."

"She could be a bit wild, like. Difficult." His reply was mumbled, barely audible. Doug asked him to repeat what he had just said, which he did, more clearly, this time.

"Was she ever violent towards you?"

"Objection." D.A. Mudeford rose to his feet.

"Overruled. The witness will answer."

"Yeah. She was headstrong you see. Like a whirling dervish she were sometimes if she didn't get her own way. Especially when she'd had a few..." He stopped suddenly and looked up anxiously at the D.A. who shook his head imperceptibly.

"A few what, Mr Grissom?"

"Nothing."

"The witness will answer the question." Chief Justice Trelawny was not going to let this go.

"Drinks."

"How did that affect her?" Doug continued to probe, allowing nothing to slip by unnoticed.

"She'd be full of moods and used to come at me and Howey."

"Howey?"

"My son."

"What did you mean when you said, '*Come at me and Howey*'?"

Wally was silent again.

"The witness will answer." Chief Justice Trelawny was stern.

"Angry. Out of control. Punching and kicking. Had some strength did our Gin-girl."

"How did you react to this?"

"I'd slap her one and we'd have a rare old shindig. Only in self-defence, mind," he added hastily as another gasp went round the courtroom. The D.A. groaned inwardly.

"How old was she when she started drinking?"

"Fourteen or thereabouts. She might have been a bit older," he added hastily.

"Where did she get the alcohol from?"

Silence. Then very quietly: "It was in the house."

"Do you drink, Mr Grissom?"

"Well, we all like the occasional tipple, don't we?"

"Do we? Do you drink on a regular basis?"

Wally Grissom hung his head. He could not deny this.

Doug took his silence for acquiescence and continued. "What about the drugs?"

The uncle's head came up. "How d'you know about them?" And then stopped, abruptly.

"Please answer the question. Where did she get them from?"

"Some lout on a street corner, I suppose." Wally shifted uncomfortably in his seat.

"Is it true that your son has done time for dealing?"

Wally refused to answer. The D.A. stepped in.

"Objection. His son's previous convictions have no relevance to this trial."

90

"They do, your Honour. I am attempting to prove that Mrs Kendrick was using drugs before her marriage and to discover the source of her addiction."

"You may proceed."

"Thank you, your Honour." Doug turned once again to Wally Grissom.

"Did your son ever supply your niece with drugs?"

"I dunno." He wasn't about to reveal the number of times he'd come into the house to find them both stoned and the atmosphere thick with marijuana. "I wasn't around all that much." He mumbled his answer to the floor.

"Why not?"

"Objection. The question is irrelevant."

"Overruled."

"Where were you?"

In order to protect his son, he'd landed himself in it, hadn't he? Wally knew he had to answer. He didn't want to go to jail for perjury. It would be all too easy for this clever-dick lawyer to find out the truth. "I was in jail."

"Jail?"

"Yeah."

"What for?"

"Objection. Previous convictions are not admissible in court as evidence."

"The witness is not on trial," responded Doug quickly. "Any previous convictions may be relevant to my client's defence."

"Overruled."

"Drunk-driving in a stolen car and resisting arrest."

"How did you resist arrest?"

"I punched the sheriff." Wally couldn't resist a smirk. "Knocked him out cold."

"How long were you inside?"

"Eighteen months."

"So you didn't see anything of your niece during that time?"

"No."

"So, Mrs Kendrick had no one to guide her, to look after her…?"

"She had Howey."

"How old was Howey at the time?"

"Er, eighteen, I reckon. Looked after her while I was away. Gave her stuff."

"Stuff?"

Wally had to make his brain work. He'd nearly given the game away. "Money."

"Which she used for drugs?"

"How should I know? I warn't there."

"Were she and Howey close?"

"Yeah. They was kissin'-cousins, like." He smiled, a horrible grotesque grimace.

"Was she happy about this?"

"Oh yeah. She didn't have much choice, anyway."

Once more, there were shocked murmurs from the courtroom.

"Was she ever violent towards your son?"

"Yeah. He had to watch out and keep 'is guard up. She'd come at him with her fists, throw chairs, bottles, whatever was to hand. Especially when she'd been on them drugs."

"So she did take drugs." Doug knew he'd got him now. "Which ones?"

Wally ignored this. "But Howey's a big strong lad. He soon put her in her place, if you know what I mean. Gin enjoyed that." He smirked again.

"Did she? *Really*? I doubt it."

Doug remained silent for a moment, allowing his words to settle on the jury and around the court. He expected the D.A. to raise an objection as he had just expressed a personal opinion. But none was forthcoming. He glanced at Hubert Mudeford and saw a man who knew the case was running away from him.

"Do you know which drugs your niece took when she was living under your roof, in your care?"

The witness shook his head. "I warn't there. I told you. I were in jail."

"But you know she took them?"

"Yeah."

"How?"

"She told me. They used to do it together, her and Howey. She said it were fun. But he's clean now," added Wally quickly. "He don't do that kinda thing no more."

"I see. Thank you."

Doug gave the impression that he was returning to his seat, but at the last moment, he turned and faced the witness again.

"Oh, one more thing, Mr Grissom. Did you or did you not give your niece the newspapers that contained the articles concerning Mr Kendrick and Miss Stewart?"

Caught off-guard, Wally stammered, "Ye-ah."

"Why?"

In for a cent, in for a dollar. "So that she could get him for it."

"For what?"

"Playing around. It was a way of getting her out of that stupid marriage so she can be where she rightfully belongs."

"And where's that?"

"With me and Howey."

"Did you not consider, Mr Grissom, that it might do more harm than good to your niece's state of mind, given that she was undergoing treatment, to reveal the article to her? Or didn't you care about that? Or was destroying her marriage more important to you? As things turned out, that's just what happened, wouldn't you agree?"

Leaving Wally Grissom squirming in embarrassment, and ending his cross-examination with a suitably dramatic flourish, Doug turned to the Chief Justice. "I have no further questions, your Honour."

He knew there was no need for more. He had exposed the wretched reality of Virginia's young life, demolished the witness's credibility and revealed her violent nature when under the influence of drink and drugs.

"Has the prosecution anything to add?"

The D.A. sighed deeply. "Not at this time, your Honour."

"The witness may step down. The court is now adjourned until ten o'clock tomorrow morning."

Jack shifted uncomfortably in his chair. Wally Grissom was a nasty piece of work, likewise his son. He could see no redeeming features to his character, nor his son's, by the sound of things. And as for Marcus's wife… she sounded as horrible as her relations. She'd had an unfortunate upbringing, there was no doubt about that, and it was obvious there was more to her background than Doug's questions had revealed.

However, Jack respected the lawyer for stopping where he had; it was enough. Virginia obviously saw marriage to Marcus as a means of escape from her tawdry life and that she must have pulled the wool over his eyes very convincingly to persuade Marcus that she was in love with him and for them to get married.

Marcia felt sullied and upset by what she had just heard. She didn't like stuff like this; it was too sordid and not the direction in which she wished to go with her journalism. Poor Marcus. What he'd had to put up with. Virginia was a conniving bitch, there was no other way to express it.

She'd make sure Marcus was well-received by the public when she wrote her report for the paper. She was glad her journalist colleague had disappeared completely from the scene. She could make the article exactly what she wanted it to be – within the bounds of fairness and objectivity, naturally… Marcia smiled to herself as she put away her pad and pencils in her bag.

Walking by, Marcus glanced at her. At least someone had something to smile about, he thought. Which was more than he did. What a fool he'd been to be hoodwinked by Virginia so completely. What a fool he'd been to have married her. She'd used him as a means of escape, that was now blatantly obvious and he berated himself for his utter stupidity.

Jack arrived back at HMS *Leopard* to be greeted with the news that from now on, he would be required to attend the meetings between the Royal Navy and their American counterparts. He knew he had no choice. It meant that he would not see Anna take the stand and, in all probability, the trial would be over before his duties once again permitted him any free time.

Annoyed and frustrated, he snapped at the unfortunate steward who brought him a cup of tea. Because this was an unusual occurrence, the surprised man took it all in his stride and went back to the mess saying that something had obviously happened to upset Captain Rutherford while he was ashore and that they'd all better tread carefully round him for an hour or so and be unobtrusively sympathetic.

CHAPTER 12

Trials and Tribulations (2)

The telephone rang and the housekeeper went to answer it. Sitting in the vast dining room of the château, all lively chatter stopped when the door opened and she spoke discreetly to Phillippe, who blanched at her words.

"*Excusez-moi, ma famille.* I apologise. But I have to go out. There is some urgent business to which I must attend."

Lily looked up in consternation. "What is it, Phillippe?"

Her husband was silent for a moment and looked at his family gathered round the table. There would be no secrets from them.

"Léon has been arrested – again."

"Again?" The word slipped out before Katherine could stop it.

"*Oui.* Again. It happened for the first time last year during the student riots – you have heard of them, I presume?

"We couldn't fail to, even on Cairnmor. The newspapers were full of it," replied Alastair. "If I remember correctly, what began as a student protest escalated into an uprising against the so-called 'establishment' and the 'capitalist society' and led to a general strike here in France."

"*Malheureusement,* Léon was at the forefront of those events." Phillippe's voice was full of regret and disappointment. "*Mon fils,* who should have known better, and who now once again brings dishonour to the family name of du Laurier."

Despite the pressing need to leave, their host seemed reluctant to move from his chair, to leave the sanctuary of his home; reluctant to bail out his errant son yet again.

"Tell us more, Phillippe," said Katherine gently, placing her hand on his arm, sensing his need to talk.

Phillippe sighed. His shame and embarrassment, both familial and political, ran very deep but Katherine and Alastair were two of his dearest friends: a friendship first established almost thirty years ago when they rescued him from Dunkirk. Perhaps it was time for him to talk about his son; time for him to share his thoughts openly and honestly. He would honour that friendship by doing so now.

"It began at the University of Nanterre in Paris in March of last year when certain left-wing groups and students occupied the university council room, meeting to discuss class discrimination in French society and the way political bureaucracy controlled student funding. The authorities did not like this and called the police who surrounded the building. The participants left quietly after their wishes were made public. But then, the students involved were disciplined and threatened with expulsion and this started a series of protests and clashes with the authorities at the university. Things became so bad that the university administration shut it down and in turn, this triggered a wave of protests from their fellow students at the Sorbonne in support. As an official of the national student union, Léon was instrumental in instigating and organizing these demonstrations.

"So, the national student union organized a large, public protest and twenty-thousand students and teachers marched towards the Sorbonne. *C'était incroyable !* However, they were charged by the police wielding batons. There were many injuries and arrests. Both universities were closed and occupied by the police. For the next month or so, there were barricades, petrol bombs and pitched battles between students and the police, who responded with tear gas.

"It triggered a general strike when intellectuals, unions and other political parties became involved and as the violence escalated, there was a great fear of revolution. At one time nearly a million people took to the streets. *Malheureusement,* the whole episode was dealt with very badly and heavy-handedly by President de Gaulle and only served to inflame the situation."

"Didn't he leave the country and go into hiding in Germany?" asked Alastair.

"*Oui.* It caused quite a sensation here in France. Public opinion only turned away from the students when some of them appeared on national television and did nothing to further their cause by behaving like rabble-rousers. De Gaulle was persuaded to return and called a general election, in which his party returned triumphantly to power. The uprising evaporated as quickly as it had begun."

"But it was a terrible, dreadful time." added Lily. "Hundreds of people were injured and arrested."

"Including Léon," added Phillippe, with a sigh. "I had to bail him out and pour oil on troubled waters on his behalf with the university authorities. It is a source of great sadness and shame to me that a son of mine is now regarded as a troublemaker and political agitator. He should put his intellectual abilities to better use. There are other ways of trying to resolve perceived social injustice than violence and public protest." Suddenly, Phillippe banged the table with his fist. "He is an *imbécile ;* an *idiot.* And now I must go again to see what our hot-headed son has been up to this time." He looked at his friends. "We shall talk further in the morning."

Lily took her husband's hand and arm as she helped him to stand up. "I shall come also."

"*Oui, ma chérie.*" Then, to Katherine and Alastair, he said, "I am most upset that our pleasant evening together has been spoiled by this. I am afraid Léon will find his wings severely clipped this time – both by the authorities and most certainly by me."

It was not until very much later that they returned. Katherine and Alastair had gone to bed and in the vastness of the château, it was impossible to hear what transpired, only to know by the headlights of the car and the crunch of wheels on the gravel that Phillippe and Lily had arrived home, presumably with the disgraced Léon in tow.

Grace let go of the anchor, calculating the amount of chain she would need and letting it out accordingly, relief permeating her soul, deeply thankful that she had arrived safely. Her journey to the sheltered waters of Eilean nan Caorach had needed every ounce of courage and strength that she possessed.

She made her way back towards the stern and stood for several moments, bracing her feet against the sides of the cockpit with one arm wrapped around the mizzen mast to maintain her balance in the uncomfortable rolling motion of the boat, taking bearings of the land in relation to her position; checking that the anchor was holding firm. She had tucked *Spirit II* into the shore as closely as possible to give maximum protection and did not wish to add to her difficulties by going aground. After a while, satisfied that all was well, Grace went below and, still shaking from her ordeal, peeled off her sodden oilskins and clothes.

She put them on the hooks in the hanging locker, allowing them to drip steadily into the bilge below. Rubbing herself vigorously with the kitchen hand-towel – for that was all she had – Grace changed into clean dry clothes, thankful that her father had always instilled into her the need for a change of clothes, no matter how short the voyage. "*You never know what may happen*," he'd told her wisely.

She wished he was here now; but perhaps not, for even with his level of fitness, conditions like this were not suitable for someone of his age. Maybe it was better that he wasn't here, then he wouldn't know about her stupidity in sailing out of Lochaberdale in the first place or be anxious when she didn't return home at the appointed time. It was just as well her parents were in Paris. But it was going to be difficult to explain away the torn sail...

Exhausted, she lay down on the saloon berth, pulling a blanket over herself, trying to get warm; trying physically to adjust to the uneven rolling rhythm of the boat, the motion inside the cabin making her feel nauseous and lightheaded.

Everything would have been fine if she and Sam had been out sailing together but he was in London, back at Imperial College, fulfilling his tutorial obligations as part of his Ph.D. and completing his studies before Finals. She missed him and hoped he missed her as well. He had said so in his occasional letters but these were filled mainly with his newfound enthusiasm for lecturing.

Since his arrival the previous October, Grace and Sam had spent two very enjoyable months together. He hadn't returned to the mainland once the weather changed but had come to live at the farmhouse, delighting in his room that overlooked Lochaberdale.

When the weather was good, they had trekked all over Cairnmor, pitching their tents in the lee of a mountain or crag; spending nights in one of the deserted cottages that Grace maintained. He helped her with her work, joined in with island events and spent fruitful hours on his thesis, both of them paying many more visits to the site of his *lacania decipiens*. He was pleased with how his work was going; pleased with his research. He seemed happy and settled and gave Grace every indication that this was where he wanted to make his home.

On Cairnmor. With her. Or so he said.

Sleep proved elusive, as it always did when she thought of Sam or Jack. She got up and put the kettle on the little stove and looked out of the window. The wind continued to howl and the rain lashed down outside. *Spirit II* tugged at her chain but the anchor held firm. Grace pulled on a woolly hat and poked her nose outside into the cockpit to check on her position relative to the land. The boat hadn't moved, apart from swinging and rolling at her anchor.

Grace came back inside, took off her hat, made a pot of tea and sat at the table, her hands round the mug, wrapping herself in the blanket, still trying to keep warm.

They hadn't discussed marriage fully as yet. It seemed that this was a rocky path. There were so many 'ifs' and 'buts' from him and not least from Grace herself. She knew it appeared to be an ideal match but always at the back of her mind, there remained the vivid image of Jack that refused to go away.

It was difficult to let go of someone who had been part of her emotional life for so many years. She knew she was in love with him; had always known it even though she always known that to be with him was hopeless and impossible. Therefore, until she had cured herself of those feelings, she would be dishonest if she married anyone else.

She hadn't said anything to Sam, of course, as that would have wounded him unnecessarily, but her thoughts of Jack were enough to make her doubt whether she was ready for marriage to Sam; whether she actually *loved* him.

Jack's pictures still dominated the walls of her bedroom and although she had replaced a few of them with Sam's sketches and paintings, she couldn't bear to lose any more. Well, she wasn't *losing* them, as they were safely stored in her cupboard, but she liked to see them; they were part of her innermost self. She had never asked Sam how he felt about Jack's pictures filling the walls of her bedroom; he didn't seem to mind, which she thought a little odd. She could detect no trace of jealousy, which she thought would have been natural if he, in turn, really cared for her.

The other obstacle to hers and Sam's future were his parents. She'd met them once and although courteous and polite, she had the distinct impression they did not altogether approve of her. They were dogmatic in their opinions and rather controlling and Sam's father was adamant that his son was going to work for his accountancy firm once he had completed his studies. He made it very plain that he would brook no other option.

Grace knew she could never leave Cairnmor. If they were to be together, Sam would have to live on the island. He knew this and although he said that this was what he wanted to do, he had, so far, prevaricated from raising the issue with his parents.

Before returning to London, Sam had spent many hours talking to Alastair. Her father's advice had been that he should follow his own path; that he *had* to follow his own path, otherwise he would regret it later on and run the danger of becoming bitter, forever dwelling on 'what might have been'. It was inevitable that confrontation with his parents lay ahead and, reluctantly agreeing with her father's tactfully expressed opinion of him, Grace doubted if Sam had the strength of character to follow it through.

Or was it just that he really didn't know what he wanted to do?

She lay down on the saloon berth but, once again, found sleep impossible. The wind kept whistling through the rigging, slapping the sheets against the masts. She couldn't face going up on deck to frap the halyards even though the constant banging kept her awake. With only one change of clothes, she was unwilling to make those wet also by struggling to tie up the offending ropes.

It had been nine months since she had received a letter from Jack; nine months since she had seen him. He had written to Ben, of course, and her heart had skipped a beat whenever she saw his familiar handwriting. He always sent his love to her, which Ben dutifully passed on to her, and that was reassuring, but more than anything, she wanted a letter of her own: a letter of a different kind.

Or did she? Perhaps deep down, she really didn't; perhaps his not writing made it easier for her to get on and live her life without waiting for Jack. However, with absolute certainty, she knew that could never be so. She wondered when his next leave was going to be. Soon. It must be due very soon.

What if he met Sam? How would she feel about seeing them both together at the same time?

The thought filled her with uncertainty but it was Jack who came into her mind and it was his reaction that concerned her most. Incredibly, Sam's features seemed blurred while Jack's were as clear as day. She could feel his arms around her and the depth and strength of his remembered kisses. Sam's perfunctory caresses bore no comparison.

She hugged the thought of Jack to herself, eventually falling asleep while *Spirit II,* rocked and buffeted by the wind and waves, remained secure on her station and protective of her precious cargo.

Rupert had just been to the estate agent. He found the only vacant seat on the underground train on his homeward journey and fidgeted around, impatient and agitated. He was a worried man.

It was not good news. How was he going to break it to Rose that, at the eleventh hour, someone else had put in an offer on the house she had set her heart on; that they had no way of knowing whether this offer was better than theirs until the sealed bids were opened and the decision made?

He'd gone way over the asking price, right up to the limit of what they could afford and their bid had been sent in well before the closing date. Perhaps he should have asked Grandpa for more money and they could have guaranteed the house would be theirs. He would never forgive himself if, for the sake of his pride, they lost this house.

They had been back to Strachan of Fairlie several times and had become friendly with the vendor but the middle-aged lady who was selling the property needed every penny she could get as she intended moving into a large house in Edinburgh as company for her elderly sister. This was an expensive venture as they required a property that was ample enough to accommodate both their needs, and enable them to continue leading independent lives. In the end, no matter how well Rose got on with the current owner, it would ultimately come down to financial considerations.

Little did Rupert know that Rose too had been to the estate agent that afternoon and had received the same information that he had.

Minton House was very quiet when Rupert went inside. He called out Rose's name, but there was no reply. He went from room to room but she was not to be found anywhere. He went outside and opened the garage door. It was empty. The car had gone.

CHAPTER 13

The Trial (3)

"Please state your full name for the court."

"Mhairi Anna Katherine Rutherford."

Marcus looked up in surprise. Anna, still married to Jack? He'd assumed they had divorced a long time ago. It occurred to him that he had never actually asked her and she had never said. He sat back in his chair, all manner of emotions going through him, as the D.A. plied her with questions,

"Are you in love with Marcus Kendrick?"

"No."

Hubert Mudeford was thrown. He had not expected such a definite answer to his question. He tried again. "While you were together, were you in love with him."

"No."

"Come now, Miss Stewart, I mean, Mrs Rutherford, you lived together. Surely you must have had some feelings for him."

"I did. I cared for him very much. We became good friends."

She smiled at Marcus, who smiled back and his heart did a brief somersault. He'd almost forgotten what an amazingly attractive smile she had. No man could possibly be immune from the power of that smile. He wanted her to smile at him like that for always.

"What contact have you had with each other since the night of the murder?"

"Objection!" Doug was very quick to his feet. "It has not yet been proven that murder was committed on the night in question."

"Sustained." Chief Justice Trelawny reiterated Doug's words. "Mr Mudeford, as far as I am aware, the State of New York regards a man to be innocent of the charge until proven guilty. I have not as yet seen any such proof, nor has the jury returned a guilty verdict."

The D.A. took a deep breath and hid his annoyance at the implied reprimand. After a moment's consideration, he continued. "How often have you seen the accused in the past few months?"

"I haven't seen or heard from him since last October when he went to collect Mrs Kendrick from the Sanatorium."

"Surely you must have seen each other, been out together, had some contact at least?"

"No."

"It seems odd that immediately after his wife's death, you and Mr Kendrick stopped seeing each other."

"Nonetheless, it is true."

"Or was it part of the plan?"

"What plan? There was no plan. That's just the way it happened."

"The plan to kill her off so that you could be together." He paused once again to allow his words to have full effect, but the courtroom remained silent and unresponsive. He changed up a gear, becoming more aggressive towards the witness on the stand. "I put it to you, Mrs Rutherford, that you conspired with Mr Kendrick to kill his wife. If you stopped seeing each other beforehand and waited a sufficient length of time before getting back together, then no one would think that there was any kind of collusion and it would put you both above suspicion."

"Objection. The D.A. has been reading too many crime novels or has been watching too many episodes of *Ironside*." Doug felt a sense of satisfaction at the general laughter his remark evoked.

"Sustained." The Chief Justice was sounding weary and gave the prosecution attorney an exasperated look.

The D.A. pressed on regardless. "Do you intend to see each other again?"

"We have no plans at present."

"At present?" The attorney grasped at a straw. "What about in the future?"

"None."

"Do you want to see him again?"

Her reply was unequivocal. "No."

Marcus was shocked out of his physical pleasure at seeing her again. He had been so certain that she had been as upset as he when he had had to collect Virginia from the clinic and it appeared uncertain when they would be able to see each other.

Having been caught out yet again, Hubert Mudeford lost patience and changed tack. "How many men have you been to bed with in the last six months?"

Doug was quick to his feet. "Objection! The question is insulting and irrelevant. The witness is not the person on trial here."

"Sustained."

"I withdraw the question, your Honour." The D.A. paced the floor. "Mrs Rutherford, how long is it since your husband walked out on you?"

"He did not walk out on me."

"Oh? It says here…" and he picked up a magazine and opened it up. "It says here that you were abandoned by him when you were eighteen years old." And he tapped the article for emphasis.

Anna gave him an icy stare. How could she best defend Jack? "I trust that you have sufficient intelligence not to believe everything you read in a magazine."

A murmur of amusement went round the courtroom. Hubert Mudeford went a dull shade of red.

Anna continued. "In my experience, most articles like that are, at worst, pure fabrication and at best, littered with inaccuracies."

"So did your husband walk out on you?"

Anna replied, very quietly. "It was my fault that the marriage ended."

"Oh? Why was that?"

"Objection, your Honour. This line of questioning is not relevant to the case. Also, no new evidence may be introduced to the court without prior agreement."

"Sustained. Mr Mudeford, I am beginning to lose patience with your constant deviation from court procedure. Mr Metcalfe is quite correct. You should know better than that."

The D.A. was suitably chastised. "Of course, your Honour." He paused then said, "How many times did you and Mr Kendrick discuss being together permanently."

"Once or twice."

The D.A. chose to ignore that her answer coincided with Marcus's own. The link was not lost on Chief Justice Trelawny, who referred back to his notes.

"Did you, or did you not conspire with the accused to kill his wife?"

"No, I did not."

The D.A. sat down. He had drawn yet another blank. "No, further questions, your Honour." He had got nowhere.

"Do you wish to cross-examine, Mr Metcalfe?"

"Yes, your Honour, if I may."

Doug approached Anna and very pleasantly, said, "During the time that you lived together, how would you describe Mr Kendrick's character?"

Anna smiled. "Very caring and considerate. He's a very special man."

"Were you sorry when the relationship came to an end?"

"Yes. But that's the way it had to be."

Marcus looked up sharply.

"If Mr Kendrick had not had to collect his wife from the sanatorium, would the relationship have continued?"

"No. I had already decided to end our association. I was just waiting for the right time to break it to him gently."

Marcus was stung. They'd had a wonderful holiday and had come back closer than ever. He'd had absolutely no inkling that she was preparing to drop such a bombshell.

"Why did you want to end the relationship?"

"We were becoming too close."

Marcus felt his chest tighten.

"And you didn't like that?"

"Yes and no. Yes, because I enjoyed his company and he's a very attractive, caring man."

Anna regarded Marcus briefly but Marcus kept his eyes fixed on the table. He couldn't bear to look at her now.

"And no," she continued, feeling guilty, taking her glance away from him, "because I had made a vow to myself after my husband left that I would not allow myself to become emotionally committed to anyone ever again."

"Why?"

"Because I am still in love with my husband and always will be."

"Even though he went out of your life many years ago?"

"Yes."

"Did Mr Kendrick know that you had decided to end the relationship with him?"

Anna looked at Marcus again and he responded to her this time but his eyes reflected the deep hurt that he felt. "No. I never got the chance to tell him."

"Why?"

"Because of what happened to his wife and his subsequent arrest. I thought it prudent to stay away."

"Why?"

"He had enough to deal with. I didn't want to add to his pain. It seemed best that way."

Neither Marcus, Doug nor Anna revealed by the slightest word or gesture that it was Doug who had suggested to Anna initially that she fade out of Marcus's life in order to protect him from any accusation of conspiracy. In doing so, this had played into Anna's hands and Marcus now knew it. The knowledge that Anna had been intending to finish with him anyway, cut him to the quick.

With Virginia gone, Marcus had entertained the secret hope that he and Anna would be able to resume their affair. Although he had always known how remote a possibility it was that they could be together permanently, to have his hopes dashed so completely at this particular time, laid him low. And to discover that she was still married to Jack. That finished him off completely. Alongside the shame and stress of the court case, he now had nothing to look forward to. He sat staring into space, defeated.

"I have to ask you, Mrs Rutherford, is there anyone else in your life at present."

Anna swallowed hard. "No. Nor has there been since Mr Kendrick and I stopped seeing each other."

"Do you miss being with Mr Kendrick?"

"Yes. But I have no wish for us to be together again."

"Thank you, Mrs Rutherford." He turned to the Chief Justice. "I have no further questions, your Honour."

Doug sat down, and placed his hand on his friend's arm. Marcus nodded, accepting the intended comfort. He needed a drink and then oblivion. However, he had promised Doug that he would not touch a drop of alcohol until the court case was over. He would keep his word, then he would go on such a bender… What did it matter now if he killed himself in the process?

He glanced up at Anna as she left. She looked neither right nor left, but walked steadily to the double doors at the back of the courtroom, to be followed immediately by a rush of reporters and photographers, anxious to get her picture and a statement.

Marcia watched Marcus put his head in his hands. He'd obviously cared deeply for Anna. Irrationally, she wanted to take him away from all of this and find some remote, secluded spot where they could be alone. But that was an impossible fantasy. In reality, he was not giving interviews; was not seeing anyone. She had made enquiries along those lines already. All she could do was write about him as favourably as she could for the paper and offer a smile as he left the court room.

She looked at him as he turned to pick up his briefcase and their eyes met but she could not smile; his emotional suffering was palpable and she was caught in its transmission.

Marcus saw the chestnut-haired reporter look at him sympathetically. She had been there every day since the start of the trial and her presence had become familiar to him. Vaguely, he wondered who she was. Not that it mattered. Nothing mattered any more.

He turned and walked out of the courtroom with Doug.

CHAPTER 14

Trials and Tribulations (3)

Phillippe faced his son. He was angry; very angry.

"Tu es très stupide. Tu es un imbécile."

Léon stood his ground, defiant; his mouth set in a determined line. *Just like his mother's*, thought Phillippe. Affection and tolerance usually accompanied any observation of his beloved wife's foibles but this was different and infinitely more serious.

"What on earth were you thinking of?" Phillippe shifted his position uncomfortably, adjusting his walking sticks to give himself a better balance. "You knew your behaviour had to be beyond reproach; you knew you were only allowed back to study at the Sorbonne on a trial basis. What on earth made you decide to lead yet another protest, instigate yet another campaign against the authorities?"

Léon was silent; his expression sullen.

"Answer me, boy."

"Why?"

"Because I am your father and you are not yet of age."

"I shall be in a few months' time. Then you can say nothing."

"Believe me, I shall still have plenty to say."

"Oh, I have no doubt about that."

"Be careful, Léon."

"Why? What will you do? Disinherit me? I don't want any part of your bourgeois life anyway. I don't want to be a landowner, stifling individuality by forcing the proletariat into submission. I want to live life as it should be lived, doing things in the way I want and not kowtowing to authority."

Phillippe laughed harshly. "If only you could listen to yourself and see how immature and ridiculous you sound."

"I'm not being ridiculous." Léon was stung to anger. "It's the establishment that's ridiculous; creating the bureaucracy that kills imagination and creativity with its petty rules and regulations. I can't breathe. I feel enclosed, hemmed in. I need to be free to express myself. To be liberated. And to liberate others."

Phillippe regarded his eldest son carefully before saying: "Well, you will certainly be liberated from the restrictions of your studies." He paused, allowing his next words to have maximum impact. "You have been expelled, Léon. Permanently. They do not want troublemakers like you at the Sorbonne. Your particular way of expressing yourself will not be tolerated any more, particularly after the riots last year."

Despite his bravado, Leon was shocked. "Then I shall gather together my supporters and we shall protest at this unfair act of bureaucratic heavy-handedness." He fell silent for a moment. It suddenly occurred to him that out on his own, he would have no teeth, no political clout. He shrugged. "You'll just have to use your influence then, won't you? You're an important man. They'll listen to you if you tell them to take me back. I'll behave. It worked last time."

"That was last time. And it didn't work. You did not behave. Therefore they sacked you. And I agree with the decision."

"What?!"

"You heard. There are no more chances, Léon. You've blown it. No other university in France will touch you now. You have a reputation as a troublemaker and revolutionary. If you do not like my 'bourgeois life' – and may I remind you that it is just that lifestyle, together with the hard work your mother and I have put into your upbringing, that has given you a decent home and education – then you needn't be a part of any of it. In fact, I am not prepared to support you any more either financially or as a member of this family. You're on your own, Léon. Have a taste of the real world before you start quoting your communist claptrap at me. Then you may come back when you have proved yourself."

And with some difficulty, Phillippe walked out of the room, leaving the door open and Léon standing dumbfounded in the middle of the high-ceilinged *salon*, surrounded by its familiar charm and elegance.

Suddenly, he wanted to smash its wealthy, upper-class smugness and vent his anger on the gracious home his parents had created. Instead, he ran outside through the French windows, leaving them open with the curtains billowing in the early morning breeze; out into the grounds of the château. He sat down on the stone steps leading onto the well-laid out gardens and quickly suppressed a sudden and inexplicable desire to cry.

Grace awoke early the next morning to blue skies and a calm sea. It seemed incredible that the storm had blown itself out so quickly and completely. Because *Spirit II* was close inshore, the little island looked very beautiful in the early morning sunlight, with the grass a brilliant green and the water lapping gently against the white sands of the seashore. The air was fresh and warm. Grace could not believe the contrast with the nightmare that had been the previous day.

She put the kettle on and then took her tea and some biscuits up on deck. The anchor had held firm and she could see they had maintained their position. In the end, she had slept well and, like the new day, was refreshed and ready to embark on the long journey home. With any luck, there might even be time to land on Eilean nan Caorach. Then she realized that she couldn't as the rowing boat was back in Lochaberdale. Another time, perhaps. At least she had food and water and the weather had cleared. Perhaps it was best that she make for home as soon as she was ready.

Despite her longing for Jack, she still wished Sam was with her. She did miss the feel of his arms around her and his gentle caresses, both of them no longer shy with each other. Sometimes though, she wished he would be a bit more passionate. "*One day,*" he'd replied, enigmatically. "*There's no rush.*" So Grace had had to be content with that, telling herself that she should be grateful she wasn't constantly having to keep him under control as some other girls had to with their boyfriends.

Grace had not seen Sam for five months. He had elected to spend Christmas and New Year with his parents without asking her to accompany him, unwilling to go against their wishes. After this, he had returned to London almost immediately to resume his course and fulfil his teaching obligations. His letters resonated with descriptions of his lecturing: how much he enjoyed it; how he saw it as the ideal career path for him to follow. He loved botany and he loved talking about his subject, he wrote.

Grace wondered about all the other enthusiasms he had said he would like to pursue in the future and where his real ambition lay. Perhaps creating a nature reserve and being a warden on Cairnmor was just another of his passing fancies without serious foundation.

She was used to people saying what they really meant and carrying out their intentions. She remembered the Christmas when Jack had declared he wanted Ben to have a decorated tree for his first Christmas and that he was going to go to Oban and buy one, there being no fir trees on Cairnmor. It caused quite a sensation when he walked down the gangplank of the steamer a few days later, carrying the tree on his shoulder like a kit bag, all wrapped up in sacks and tied with string.

They had had great fun decorating it with tinsel and candles and Grace had held Ben on her lap while Jack lit the candles for the first time, all of them reflected in the glow and warmth of the gentle light, with Ben's eyes as big as saucers.

That had been a truly magical Christmas. With Jack at home, the whole occasion seemed more exciting, more sharply focused. The sense of anticipation had been greater; opening the presents after Christmas lunch even more special. On that day Grace had felt truly *alive*.

With a sigh, she washed up her mug and readied *Spirit II* for the long journey back to Lochaberdale. She couldn't remember a time when she hadn't loved Jack. There had never been a 'moment' when she fell in love with him; her feelings for him had always been there, gradually changing and growing with time, just as she had done.

Late into the evening, Rose returned home. As soon as he heard the scrunch of the tyres on the gravel, Rupert was out of the house, down the front steps and opening the car door for his absent wife.

"I've been so worried. Where have you been? Why didn't you leave me a note to tell me where you were going?" There was no hint of reprimand in his voice, just clear anxiety.

Rose sat perfectly still, her hands on the steering wheel. Then she turned to him, her eyes full of tears.

"We've lost the house, Rupert. I went up there, to Strachan, to see Mrs Murdoch as soon as I heard from the estate agent that someone else had put in another bid. I went to see if I could persuade her to let us have the house even if the new offer was higher. She refused to listen, Rupert. She told me to go away and leave her alone. She said categorically that she would accept the highest offer and that there was no more to be said. Just as I was leaving, her phone rang. It was the other people who want the house. They told her what their bid was. That's not right, is it? I thought it was all meant to be done in secret to make it fair."

Rupert was indignant. "No, it most certainly isn't right."

"Anyway, she repeated it – out loud. Rupert, she must have known that I could hear her so she must have been trying to rub it in or boast or something. And it's higher than ours. Much higher. Then she said that she would accept their offer when the sealed bids were opened. She can't do that yet, or can she? I mean there's still another three days before the closing date."

"That's right, there is," Rupert replied thoughtfully. "What did you do then?"

"I left and sat in the car for a bit and then came home."

Rose started to cry, laying her head on her hands against the steering wheel, sobbing her heart out. "I feel so humiliated. And now we've lost the house. And it's all my fault. I wish I'd never gone up there."

Gently, Rupert took her hand, and helped her out of the car. He held her in his arms and wiped away her tears.

"No, my darling. It's not your fault. I think you were very brave to try and persuade her. It's a very special house and I know you've set your heart on it." Swallowing hard, Rupert then asked, "What was the other offer?"

"Much, much more than we could ever afford." She named the figure.

Suddenly, Rupert knew what he had to do. He took Rose into the house and made her a cup of hot milk, which she carried up to their bedroom. He sat with her while she undressed and saw her into bed. When she was comfortable, he went downstairs to his study and picked up the telephone.

He was very aware that this was to be the most crucial phone call he would ever make in his life.

CHAPTER 15

Verdict

The trial was drawing towards its conclusion. Doug had called character witnesses for the defence: influential friends and colleagues. Without exception, they were full of praise for Marcus, commenting on his conscientious nature; how he never allowed the difficulties of his private life to interfere with his work; how he always met his deadlines; how he was honest and reliable.

The prosecution could find no holes in their statements. There was nothing the D.A. could tease out of them that was detrimental in any way towards Marcus; their testimony was solid in his defence.

When Marcus took the stand for the final time, under Doug's skilful guidance, he reaffirmed his earlier statements and once more gave a description of the events exactly as they transpired.

His final words, spoken with such heartfelt simplicity that not one person in the courtroom could possibly doubt his sincerity, were directed at the jury.

"No one regrets more than I do that my wife is not still alive. I shall have to live with that sadness and the memory of the circumstances that led to her death for the rest of my life." He paused before continuing, his expression open; his tone earnest. "I am not guilty of murdering my wife. The mere thought is abhorrent to me. The only guilt I have is that ultimately, I was unable to save Virginia from herself. My only consolation is that I did my level best and that no one could have tried harder than I."

"Thank you, Mr Kendrick." Chief Justice Trelawny regarded Marcus carefully, thoughtfully. "Mr Mudeford, do you wish to cross-examine?"

When the D.A. declined, the Chief Justice said, "You may step down. The witness is excused."

Marcus left the witness stand knowing that he had done everything that could be asked of him. As he had wished, he had begun and ended the trial and, apart from the closing arguments, the first and last person the jury saw and heard was him. The rest was now up to his friend Doug but before that, the District Attorney would present his closing argument: the prosecution's last chance to convince the jury of the defendant's guilt.

Hubert Mudeford was a desperate man. He sensed that the jury were on the side of the defendant and therefore, he knew he faced a Herculean task to convince them that Marcus was guilty. There was a serious danger he was going to lose this case. He'd lost his last two and was under extreme pressure to win this one. Not only was his reputation on the line but possibly his job as well. He decided to go for an all-out attack.

He stood up suddenly, blowing his nose and arranging his few remaining strands of hair into a more comfortable position over the top of his balding head before walking across to the jury box.

"May it please the court," he began, his manner ingratiating; his voice honeyed with deceptive quietude. "This case is a very simple and straightforward one."

Then he let rip, pointing at Marcus, his right arm fully outstretched, his index finger jabbing the air.

"This man, Marcus Kendrick, killed his wife. Make no mistake about it. The evidence is irrefutable. He was a man at the end of his tether and he wanted his wife out of the way so that he could be with his lover, the actress, Anna Stewart. Together they planned and dreamed and he waited like a panther stalking its prey, looking for the opportunity to carry out this heinous crime. Then he pounced, seizing the moment, and smashed this defenceless woman's head against a glass coffee table when she was at her most vulnerable."

The D.A. began to pace the floor in front of the jury. Backwards and forwards he went; his mind-set that of a hunter with the jury as his target. He became an actor taking centre stage, using rhetoric and drama to emphasize the guilt of the defendant; establishing once and for all that this case was *his* and he was going to win it.

"And where is the evidence for this you might ask?" Hubert Mudeford continued expansively, waving his right hand in the air. "Why, it's in Marcus Kendrick's diary! The entries categorically prove, in his own words, written with his own hand, that he planned to get rid of his poor, troubled, vulnerable wife. He didn't care whether she lived or died; he just wanted to be rid of her – this millstone round his neck, this drain on his financial resources. He wanted, and I quote, '*To be rid of this woman who is making my life a misery. All I want is for Anna and I to be together. Perhaps we can find some way of getting Virginia out of our lives permanently.*' The evidence is there. You cannot deny it. A crystal clear example of *mens rea* – the intent to kill. This proves beyond any reasonable doubt that the defendant intended to kill his wife. And this intent, members of the jury, signifies murder."

The D.A., wily old campaigner that he was, looked at his audience. They stared back at him, somewhat shell-shocked by his bombast. He took this to be a good sign. He smiled and for the moment, lowered the volume of his voice.

"As a journalist, Marcus Kendrick occupies a position in which he is able to influence public opinion. His readers, you the general public, listen to what he has to say. I put it to you, members of the jury, a man in such a position of responsibility who has killed his wife should not be allowed to go free but should have the full weight of law brought to bear upon him and be suitably punished for his crime. He should be made an example of and justice must be seen to be done for the sake of Virginia Kendrick's family; for his dead wife's sake."

He moved closer to the jury, leaning over the box; his face inches away from those at the front. A few recoiled from his proximity to them, from his invasion of their personal space.

"Would you want to listen to a man who killed his wife? Would you want him to influence the way you think? Of course not.

"Mr Kendrick has shown himself to be a dishonourable man. While his wife was suffering untold mental agony in a sanatorium, he was out playing around with other women. He is obviously not a man to be trusted.

"Would you want to read the words of a man who cannot be trusted? Of course not! He is an adulterer; an adulterer who killed his defenceless wife. His actions are an abomination and he should not be allowed to operate in the public domain. He is guilty! Guilty I tell you!"

Vehemently, he brought one of his fists down into the other palm, causing the female jury member directly in front of him to jump and go pale with alarm. He looked at her, satisfied that he had made an impact. He made his voice smooth and silky.

"And yet he stands before you as though butter wouldn't melt in his mouth, as though he is the most honest and upright citizen in the State of New York."

He wagged his forefinger again. "I tell you he is not and anyone of you who believes that he is, is grievously mistaken. He committed adultery. He murdered his wife. He seized the opportunity when it presented itself to him and took full advantage of the situation.

"Members of the jury, Mrs Kendrick didn't die because of an accident as Mr Kendrick would have you believe. She was pushed onto that glass coffee table with the full force of a well-built man. We only have *his* word, the word of an *adulterer*, the unreliable word of a *dishonest* man that the events took place in the way that they did.

"Mrs Kendrick cannot tell us exactly what happened that night because she is dead; killed deliberately and maliciously by the man to whom she was married and whom she trusted to care for her.

"I tell you now, the evidence proves beyond all reasonable doubt that Marcus Kendrick murdered his wife. The facts that I have presented to you are sufficient to convict the accused. It is your duty as twelve honest citizens to find him guilty of murder. He is guilty, I tell you. Guilty!

When Hubert Mudeford retook his seat, there were several in the jury who felt assaulted by his verbal diatribe; who found his performance and his attitude offensive. For many members of this particular jury, he had miscalculated badly.

However, his forcefulness and declamatory style had convinced some that Marcus might just be guilty as charged and they began to waver from their previous certainty that the defendant was innocent.

When Doug was called to present his closing argument, he took his time, using the expectant hush that preceded his speech to gain maximum focus from the jury. He waited neither too long, nor rose from his seat too soon. He chose exactly the right moment to approach the jury box and when he did, he had their undivided attention.

"Your Honour, ladies and gentlemen of the jury," he began, his manner calm, his voice measured. "This case is an obvious and straightforward one. There are no complex facts to sort out; no difficult scenarios to unravel. There are no witnesses giving contradictory evidence as to what happened on the night in question.

"To put it simply: the outcome of this case hinges on whether or not you believe the word of my client; whether or not you are convinced he is telling the truth; whether or not you feel that the events as he describes them actually took place in the way that he says.

"You have the testimony of that one man, the defendant, Marcus Kendrick, a highly respected and distinguished journalist and author. There were no other witnesses to his wife's tragic death, no one else can corroborate his statement. So you, each one of you, has to decide within your own heart whether Marcus Kendrick speaks the truth. And let me assure you, ladies and gentlemen, he is speaking the truth.

"I was not there. Nor were you. But the defendant was and you have heard from his esteemed colleagues and friends as to his honest, trustworthy and reliable nature. The prosecution was unable to sway them from their conviction of his good character. That should tell you everything you need to know. These are people who have been his friends for a long time; people who are distinguished in their own right; who have worked alongside him for a number of years. You have no reason to doubt their word. Therefore, you have no reason to doubt Marcus Kendrick's.

"My client once loved his wife. However, the circumstances of their marriage diminished and finally destroyed that love until there was nothing left. Yet he did not abandon Mrs Kendrick or leave her to her own devices. He cared for her, paying for expensive treatment in the vain hope that it would help her. He gave up lucrative work of his own in order to spend as much time as he could at home in order to keep her away from the sources that fuelled her addiction. It upset him greatly that he was constantly fighting a losing battle and that she seemed intent on destroying herself.

"Marcus Kendrick's steadfastness in the face of extreme personal difficulty adds up, ladies and gentlemen, not to a man at the end of his tether who seized an opportune moment to be rid of his wife, but to a fine man; a long-suffering and patient man who endured years of struggle and abuse. Is it any wonder that he sought comfort and consolation in the arms of a beautiful woman about whom he cared deeply?

"His were not the actions of a habitual adulterer, nor were they the actions of a dishonest man. They were the actions of a caring man, who found himself in an intolerable situation. A lesser man would have left his wife, but Marcus Kendrick chose not to do so. He chose to stay and help her because she had no one else to whom she could turn."

Doug paused and allowed the jury to absorb his words. They remained receptive to him, their faces open and alert.

"The prosecution has tried to find evidence of a conspiracy. There is none. The diary entries are merely the private words of a man who knew he had done his best yet realized that this would never be enough; that perhaps it was time to let go of his drunken, drug-addicted wife and let someone else look after her. That, very naturally, he wanted to be with the woman he loved and leave behind a woman who caused him untold misery.

"You have also heard Mrs Rutherford's testimony. That she had already intended ending their affair before the night in question; that she saw no future in their relationship because she was still, and always would be, in love with her estranged husband.

"The words in the diary do not constitute 'malice aforethought' nor do they prove that the defendant and Mrs Rutherford, the actress Anna Stewart, conspired to kill Virginia Kendrick so that they could be together. And, ladies and gentlemen, you have no reason to doubt Mrs Rutherford's testimony, made in this courtroom under

110

oath. It was obvious to me that she was speaking the truth. My client is also speaking the truth."

Doug paced slowly in front of the jury; aware that they were following his every move, his every gesture. They were rapt, attentive.

"Virginia Kendrick was a violent woman. We have heard testimony both from her family and members of staff at the sanatorium to that effect. My client, strong as he is, endured years of physical abuse. On the night in question he did not use his physical strength to kill his wife unlawfully, he used it to defend himself from a vicious and unprovoked attack. Yet, even at the very end, when she lay bleeding on the floor, he tried to save her. In great pain and suffering from the injuries that she had caused and that would hospitalize him and entail two very painful operations, he contacted the emergency services and the police.

"These, ladies and gentlemen, are not the actions of a guilty man. These are the actions of a man who, having been through a harrowing ordeal, unselfishly put aside his own well-being in order to help his wife."

His demeanour calm; his expression one of trust, Doug took a deep breath and half-turned towards his client.

"Marcus Kendrick has never wavered from his testimony of the tragic events when his wife died, not by even the minutest of details; not to the police on the night in question; not to me as his attorney; not before the court during the course of this trial. That is because he is speaking the truth.

Doug paused and looked at each jury member in turn. None averted their eyes, meeting his regard with equal steadiness.

"This man's life is in your hands. If there is the slightest doubt in your own mind that he murdered his wife then you must find him not guilty. If there is the slightest thought that the defendant has been wrongly accused, then you must find him not guilty. If you believe absolutely that Marcus Kendrick is telling the truth, then you must find him not guilty. If there is any hint of uncertainty whatsoever in your own mind, then you must still find him not guilty. There cannot be room for even the slightest doubt or hesitation in what you feel when returning your verdict.

"The prosecution has *not* proven beyond all reasonable doubt that the defendant committed murder or that he was involved in a conspiracy. This court has heard *not one shred of evidence* that supports either of these things absolutely. Therefore, because of that, the defendant is not guilty of the allegations made against him."

Doug turned first to the Chief Justice and then back to the jury. "Your Honour, ladies and gentlemen of the jury, Marcus Kendrick is a good man, an honourable man and he deserves to be a free man. I thank you for your time."

Then he resumed his seat.

Marcia wanted to applaud Doug Metcalfe and sensed that other people around her were suppressing the desire to do the same. But they now had the summing up to come.

Chief Justice Trelawny fixed his eyes onto the jury and spoke slowly and clearly, ensuring they understood the meaning of every single one of his words.

"Members of the jury, it is my task to explain the law to you and to sum up the evidence that you have heard during the course of this trial. You must reach a decision based on the evidence you have heard and decide whether the defendant Marcus Kendrick is guilty or not guilty.

"You should try to reach a unanimous decision. I shall also accept a majority decision. If you are evenly divided, then you must find the defendant not guilty. Remember, it is the job of the prosecution to prove that Marcus Kendrick is guilty, not for him to prove that he is not guilty. You must ask yourself if you believe the prosecution has done this successfully.

"Marcus Kendrick stands accused of the murder of his wife. Not manslaughter, not self-defence, not accidental death but murder. It is your duty in law to find him guilty or not guilty of that one charge. Therefore, nothing else must come into your deliberations.

"There were no witnesses to the events that resulted in the death of Mrs Kendrick. We have only the word of the defendant that they took place in the way that he describes."

Clearly and concisely, the Chief Justice then reviewed the evidence presented by both prosecution and defence, commenting on the testimony of the witnesses and upon the good character of the defendant.

"You must therefore, based upon the evidence you have heard, consider whether Marcus Kendrick intended to kill his wife or whether he did not. You must also decide whether or not he conspired with his lover, Anna Stewart, to murder Virginia Kendrick.

"If you believe that he was waiting for the first opportunity that arose to kill his wife, then you should find him guilty. If you believe he was involved in a conspiracy to kill his wife, then you should find him guilty. If you believe that Marcus Kendrick is telling the truth and that he was defending himself from a vicious and unprovoked attack, then you must find him not guilty. If you believe that he and Mrs Rutherford did not conspire to dispose of his wife so they could be together, then you must find him not guilty.

"Three things must be done while coming to your decision. Firstly, you have to decide if the case against the defendant has been proven beyond all reasonable doubt; that is, you are left with an utter conviction that the evidence presented by the prosecution is accurate and irrefutable.

"Secondly, you must determine whether the defendant's testimony is truthful and that the events occurred in the way that he described.

"Finally, you must 'weigh' the evidence – that is, put it onto the scales of justice. On one side is guilt, on the other reasonable doubt. If there is the tiniest shred of doubt on the scales of justice, the law demands that you must return a verdict of not guilty, no matter how much evidence there might appear to be on the other side.

"Remember, reasonable doubt is what is felt by any fair-minded juror who seeks the truth. I have every confidence that each and every one of you is honestly looking for that truth. It has always seemed to me that it is better to allow oneself to doubt than to have on one's conscience a lifetime of guilt for convicting an innocent man and sending him to a fate that he does not deserve.

"Members of the jury, would you please now retire and consider your verdict."

As the jury filed out of the courtroom, Marcus sat quietly, detached from his surroundings; completely exhausted and drained. All he wanted to do was to hide away. He'd had enough. He could cope with nothing more. The trial had taken its toll on every single one of his resources.

Behind him, Marcia saw his shoulders drop and his head go forward. Seeing he really was near the end of his tether, she once again experienced the desire to take him away somewhere remote to help him recover from his ordeal. Perhaps, she would be able to interview him and afterwards really get to know him; after all, to do that was one of her reasons for coming to America in the first place.

She remained in her seat and smiled up at Marcus as he and his attorney left the courtroom. But he did not see her. It was as much as he could do to make his legs move and put one foot in front of the other.

Skilfully, Doug guided him to an anteroom where Marcus could have some peace and quiet, away from the hordes of reporters and photographers who were poised to engulf him, and await the decision by the twelve men and women of the jury that would determine the course of the rest of his friend's life.

Marcus and Doug barely had any time to sit down when they were called back to the courtroom. They stood as Chief Justice Trelawny entered the room and the foreman of the jury was asked if they had reached a verdict.

"We have your, Honour."

The clerk handed a piece of paper to the Justice, who read it impassively and handed it back to the clerk.

"Please read aloud what it says."

The foreman stood up and cleared his throat.

"We, the jury, in a unanimous decision, find the defendant not guilty of the charge of murder. We, the jury, in a unanimous decision, also find the defendant not guilty of the charge of conspiring to kill his wife." He sat down to lengthy applause from within the courtroom.

"Thank you," said the Chief Justice, once order had been resumed. "I should like to congratulate the jury on an excellent decision. The case is now closed and there are no grounds for an appeal." He looked at Marcus and smiled. "Mr Kendrick, you are free to go."

"Thank you, your Honour." Marcus thought he was going to pass out but he managed to smile and nod at the jury, who were all looking in his direction, and mouth the words, "Thank you."

He sat there for a while before being hustled out of the courtroom by Doug. The onslaught started as soon as he reached the outside steps of the building. He was besieged by cameras and microphones being thrust into his face; of questions being fired at him from all sides.

Marcia couldn't get near him. She tried again and again but was pushed and jostled out of the way and could do nothing to reach the front of the scrum. She could see that Marcus was struggling but she was helpless to offer him support.

"How does it feel to walk free?"

"What will you do now?"

"What are your plans?"

"Over here, Marcus, over here."

"Tell us how you feel?"

"My paper can offer you an exclusive deal for your story."

"Here, here!"

"This way, this way!"

"Where are you going to go after this?"

The questions kept coming and the cameras kept flashing until Marcus could take no more and collapsed onto the steps.

CHAPTER 16

Journeys

Jack Rutherford sat expectantly in the darkened auditorium and looked up at the stage. He had felt thwarted by not being able to carry out his intention of seeing Anna at the trial and, wanting to satisfy his curiosity about her, once he had completed his official duties, he had scanned the listing sections of the newspaper to find out the performance times of her play.

So now he was here, alone, having declined the company of his friend Bob, his executive officer, fidgeting around in his seat, waiting for the curtain to go up, anticipating her arrival on stage.

This was a mistake. He shouldn't have come. He knew he should have been able to resist the temptation. Resolutely, he resolved to watch the play and disappear without Anna ever knowing.

When she made her entrance, his heart lurched and his legs went weak and he saw, not the older but still beautiful actress on the stage, but the young woman he had fallen in love with; the young woman who, when they were first married, had been everything he had ever wanted.

Blindly, Jack knew he had to make himself known to her. It was rash and foolish – he was no longer a carefree young officer but a mature man with all the responsibilities of command. By seeing her again, he risked being hurt again, reopening an emotional wound that had never completely healed.

He wondered who her current boyfriend was; how many there had been since he left her that day so long ago. Too many probably.

She was good in the play, he could see that. She had a charismatic presence and eclipsed the actress in the leading role whenever they were on stage together. Hers was the better part and she was suited to it perfectly, but Jack knew she had been a far better pianist. That was where her outstanding talent lay.

In the interval, he restlessly prowled the bar area: ordering a drink which he didn't touch, lighting a cigarette which he couldn't smoke. The five minute, then the two minute bell sounded. The audience was filing back in for the second half. Jack took his seat and in a surge of recklessness, surrendered himself to the play, to her voice, to her personality.

After it was over, he found his way to the stage door. He asked to speak to Miss Stewart.

"Who shall I say wants to see her?" said the doorman.

"Her husband," said Jack.

After some while, the doorman returned.

"I'm afraid that Miss Stewart is not available. She sends her apologies."

"Is that all?"

"Yes."

"She said nothing else? No message of any kind?" Jack couldn't believe that she would dismiss him so coldly and abruptly.

"No. No message." Having closed the matter, the man returned to the newspaper he had been reading.

Hiding his bitter disappointment, Jack thanked him and left.

Hailing a cab to take him through the rain-wet streets of New York back to the naval dockyard, he once again experienced the overwhelming sense of rejection by the woman whom he had loved and lost so many years previously. Even when his ship began the long voyage home, his renewed pain and disappointment stayed with him.

After a few days, in an effort to lift himself out of his preoccupation, Jack took down from the bookshelf in his cabin a first edition of poems by Siegfried Sassoon that Grace had given him once as a birthday present. This had become his favourite companion on many a journey: his evening solace after exhausting duty. He had read the poems so often, he knew most of them from memory.

He opened the book at random.

In the grey summer dawn I shall find you,
With day-break and the morning hills behind you.
There will be rain-wet roses, stir of wings
And down in the wood a thrush that wakes and sings...

Suddenly, into his mind came a picture of Grace in the secluded rose garden on Cairnmor, one of their favourite places of quietude and rest, sitting for him while he sketched her; her expression one of repose, her body light and still.

He read on:

Not from the past you'll come, but from that deep
Where beauty murmurs to the soul asleep:
And I shall know the sense of life re-born
From dreams into the mystery of noon
Where gloom and brightness meet...

As a sailor and an artist, Jack appreciated the juxtaposition of the disparate words contained in the last phrase where at midday in the summer, how the sun's brightness was so strong that it created an illusion: an aura of indistinguishability, of dimness, in the adjacent land or seascape.

In that moment, in his present state of emotional vulnerability, Jack drew the analogy between Anna (gloom) and Grace (brightness) and he found that the brightness prevailed over the gloom.

Without him even being aware of it happening, his heartache and any residual feelings for Anna dissolved and disappeared for ever.

Carefully, Jack removed from the top drawer of his desk the small rose-garden watercolour sketch of Grace. He studied her image, seeing her character shining out through the simplicity of the pencil lines and muted tints.

Here was faithfulness and steadfastness. Here was a beautiful woman who would never drive him to anger and despair; a woman who was both intrepid and loving. He recalled their last meeting in the summer; how he could do nothing but take her into his arms after she had told him that she loved him.

This time, Jack made no attempt to quell his feelings for Grace but allowed them to surface, savouring them, testing them and seeing where they might lead.

With a sense of urgency, he took out his sketch book, the need to draw her overwhelming.

H.M.S. *Leopard* scythed its way back across the Atlantic and for her captain, the thought of leave and his return home to Cairnmor had all at once taken on a completely different prospect.

After his flight out of the French windows, Léon sat on the steps leading down to the garden for quite some time, trying to work out what he was going to do next. He knew his father well enough to realize that he had meant what he said. Léon really was on his own now.

He wondered what his mother thought about all of this. Had they discussed it? Had she pleaded his case and told the old bastard to get lost and not to be so high-handed and ridiculous? Had she intervened on his behalf in the way that she had often done: standing up for him, making excuses for him when he had been naughty and wayward as a child?

While he was young, Léon knew he only got away with things because his mother would usually take his part, tempering his father's impatience, his strictness; making sure that Papa's constant and nauseating lectures on his son's lack of serious work ethic or unrealistic political ambition didn't last for too long. Phillippe always seemed to be disappointed, never satisfied with whatever Léon achieved. Therefore, he stopped trying and shut his mind to his parent's wishes. It wasn't worth the effort.

In any case, Eloise was his father's especial pride and joy, and the twins, damn them, were always so serious and charming and hard to resist. His little sister Marie had the undivided attention that she craved now that her beloved Papa had retired.

Léon kicked angrily at a large stone under his feet and sent it skittering down the steps. Why had he always been the one left out? Eloise had been married at sixteen but lived close by in the old farmhouse. Marie was too young to be of any use to him. The twins had always had each other and his father had delighted in their musical talents. Especially now they had teamed up with Gabrielle.

Léon could see trouble ahead there, though. Could be interesting if the twins wanted to make the relationship a different one and take her to bed. But Gabrielle was a 'good' girl – he knew that because he'd tried it on with her himself. With anyone that she went out with, it would all have to be very 'proper'. She would make her choice. Perhaps the twins would fight over her. No, he concluded, they were too conventional, too honourable.

Papa had very strict rules about girlfriends for his sons and boyfriends for his daughters. It was just as well he didn't know how many girls Léon had slept with since he'd been at the Sorbonne. Good job *their* parents didn't realize just how many good Catholic girls were willing to relinquish their virginity.

That's what the protests had been about as well – sexual liberation and freedom from the three-headed monster of religion, patriotism and respect for authority. What was needed, thought Léon, was a more liberal moral ideal, not the old conservative one: the one promulgated by his parents and by the establishment to which they belonged. Stuck in the past, that's where they were.

Rebelliously, Léon kicked at another stone.

Fed up and without having come to any conclusion about what he was going to do in order to support himself or even where he was going to live, Léon stood up and took a swipe with his foot at the stone plinth which supported a lichen-covered statue. He cried out with the pain and swore profusely as his foot hit its rock-like rigidity.

"I shouldn't do that again, if I were you," said a quiet voice behind him.

Léon swung round and was surprised to see his grandfather sitting on the ornate metal bench behind him; a picture of studied, watchful calm. He resisted the urge to throw something at the old man.

"It's none of your business what I do. Ever." muttered Léon sullenly. Why didn't they leave him alone? Why couldn't he do what he wanted?

"Is it not? Give me three good reasons why it isn't. Real reasons, mind, and I'll go away and leave you alone. Which is what you really want, isn't it?"

Did he? Léon was suddenly unsure. Three reasons…

"I'm in disgrace."

"True. But not sufficient to deter me."

"Everyone is disappointed in me." There was sarcasm in his voice.

"Also true. But still not enough."

"I've b-----d everything up," he said, trying to shock the older man. "My degree. My career. My life."

"Have you?"

"Everyone thinks so."

"What about you?"

"Me?"

"Yes. You. Do *you* think you've 'b-----d everything up', as you so elegantly phrased it?"

It was all wrong for such language to be coming from his grandfather's lips. Léon shrugged, hiding his embarrassment and shame for making the old man utter a word like that.

"I did what I did."

"And would you do it again?"

Would he? Defensively, he replied that he would.

"Well, at least you have the courage of your convictions and are prepared to stand up for what you believe in, even if that belief is misplaced and you lose everything of true value in the process." Alastair saw his grandson's shoulders drop; the defiance lessen momentarily. "Because you have, you know."

Léon didn't reply. Deep down he knew he had. But he wasn't going to admit it.

"What are you going to do?"

He resisted the temptation to tell Alastair to mind his own business.

"You haven't yet come up with three reasons as to why I should mind my own business."

Was the old man a mind-reader too? Léon shrugged his shoulders. "I have no idea. I could always go and get laid." If he hoped he'd shock his grandfather, he was mistaken.

"Well, that really would solve everything, wouldn't it?" After a moment's silence, Alastair looked at his grandson. "I have a proposition to put to you, Léon."

The young man's head came up. "To me?"

Alastair looked around. "Well, as far as I'm aware, there are only two of us here. Unless you count that statue on which you tried to inflict grievous bodily harm a moment or two ago." He saw Léon's lips twitch in quickly concealed amusement. Alastair smiled and continued. "Yes, a proposition." He paused, regarding his grandson thoughtfully.

Despite himself, Léon found his curiosity aroused. Feigning disinterest, he gave his grandfather a sideways glance. "Which is what exactly?"

"Which is that you come back with Katherine and me to Cairnmor."

Léon was disappointed. "Oh." What a bloody boring thing to do.

"I can see that you're totally enamoured with the suggestion. I can't say I'm particularly excited by it, but I think it will help you."

"I don't need help."

"I beg to differ. I think you need a lot of help."

"How so?"

"Your father means what he says when he is not going to give you a thing. Therefore, you have no money. Your mother will not go behind his back and bail you out this time, as she has so often done in the past."

Léon's face flushed a dull red. How could his grandfather possibly know about his debts and misdemeanours – the former incurred as a result of making overgenerous donations to various political groups and worthy causes; the latter, in other people's eyes at least, seemingly unending?

"Go on."

"You now have no chance of ever being accepted at any university, certainly not in Paris, or probably the whole of France, as the academic world is a small one." Alastair saw his grandson scowl. "Ah, yes, the 'political bureaucrats' you despise so much. It's all their fault, isn't it? And the system, of course. It would have nothing to do with your attitude now, would it?"

Léon started to make a barbed retort but Alastair stopped him. "Therefore, you have no chance of following the career path you set your heart upon."

"So? I'll find a way. If not, I'll do manual work. I'll become one of the proletariat. I'm not proud."

"Good. Because that is exactly what you will be doing. My offer to take you back with us to Cairnmor is not to give you an easy escape route from your transgressions here. Nor am I bailing you out financially. You, Léon, are going to work for yourself. Hard manual labour."

"Doing what?"

"Farming. Farming your own land."

Léon snorted with contempt. "I suppose this is all to teach me a lesson. Well, I'll tell you here and now, it won't work. It won't make me change my attitude or my political beliefs. I think what I think and that's the way it is."

"Good for you. But there are two things you might like to consider. I'm not paying you anything. Nothing. You will be totally self-supporting. Everything you earn will be as a result of your own labours. If you don't work, you won't eat. You can be one of the downtrodden peasants you're so keen on supporting from your lofty intellectual height."

For the first time, Léon's bravado faltered. "I know nothing about farming."

"You'll soon learn. You'll have good help." Alastair's eyes twinkled. "There are plenty of cheerful serfs to instruct you."

Léon had gone very quiet. "Anything else?"

"Possibly. If things go well, I might let you see how we manage our affairs on Cairnmor. See what you think. See if you understand *how* things are done and why: the real process of democratic government. You might be surprised."

"Do I have a choice in all this?"

"No, I'm afraid not. And if you're wise, you'll grasp this opportunity with both hands, especially as you are underage. You are lucky not have been charged with incitement to riot and put in prison."

"Can I leave your wretched island as soon as I'm twenty-one?"

"Only if you have the financial means to do so."

"You mean you won't give me any money?"

"Not a penny."

"That's slavery."

"No, it's not. I'm not the one benefiting from your labours. You are."

"I'll be a virtual prisoner."

"No. You are free to do as you wish. You would end up a real prisoner if you stayed here. But perhaps you'd prefer that, then you could find a new cause and campaign on behalf of the innocent, downtrodden prison population and the injustice of the judicial system." For the first time, an impatient edge crept into Alastair's voice.

"Are you finished?"

"No. I offer you a few words of caution and then I'm done. You are bilingual but Katherine speaks fluent French so you won't be able to mutter insults under your breath and not be understood. Secondly, you'll have to learn Gaelic as that is the language most people speak and understand on the island. Thirdly, the weather on Cairnmor can be atrocious." Alastair smiled. "Now, I suggest you go and get your things together. We leave on the hour."

Following his collapse, Marcus regained consciousness almost immediately and was helped back inside by Doug and one of the doormen. They sat him down on a bench in the entrance hall and while someone brought him a reviving brandy, Doug went back outside where he made a statement to the waiting press:

"My client is delighted with the outcome of the trial and feels thoroughly vindicated by the result. However, he has been under tremendous strain in recent weeks and speaking as his friend and attorney, he now needs to be allowed some time to himself. I'm sure you guys will understand. If you wish to contact Marcus, then please do so through my law firm, where we shall be pleased to take your questions." Finally, he thanked them for their support and interest.

Disappointed but accepting, the reporters and photographers gradually dispersed and Marcia resolved to telephone first thing in the morning to make an appointment. Reluctantly, she returned to the offices of the *New Yorker* to write and submit her report on the trial.

120

Marcia was determined to do an interview with Marcus and hopefully from that get to know him. However, on arriving at work the following morning she discovered to her dismay that she was to be sent out immediately to investigate an urgent story that had its origins in New York but the implications of which spread out as far afield as Detroit and Chicago. She was only left with enough time to pack and leave with her designated photographer at midday. It was an important assignment to cover and she couldn't refuse. Nor did she want to. This could be her big break, her opportunity to make a name for herself here in America and make everyone proud of her back home.

Resignedly, Marcia knew that everything else would have to wait until her return. She hoped that Marcus would be available and all would be well during her absence.

It was not. After his fainting spell, Marcus was examined by his doctor who said there was nothing wrong that an early night and a couple of good stiff drinks wouldn't cure. He slapped him on the back and told him to go back out there and do his stuff.

Marcus did not feel like 'doing his stuff'. What was there to do? He was a free man again but Anna didn't want him and he had not yet been reinstated to his old job at *Chronicle* magazine. He couldn't escape the guilt that Virginia had died after he'd pushed her away from him nor the shame of having to be on trial for murder, even though he had been acquitted.

The nightmares were the worst and he kept having nightmares. She would loom up at him in the darkness shouting and screaming, causing him to wake up, leaving him sweating and shaking. He began to dread going to bed at night and took to staying up, watching the television, prowling the streets or going to late-night movies. Anything to escape his appallingly irrational thoughts.

He didn't tell anyone about all this, not even Doug, but it took its toll on his mental reserves and physical resources that were already stretched to the limit. In desperation, taking the doctor's advice, he took to drinking a bourbon or two in the evening to relax him, in an attempt to anaesthetize his acute feelings of fear and anguish. At first, it seemed to work but then the nightmares returned, and Marcus needed to drink more each day to counteract them: two fingers of whisky then three, then four, then a whole bottle in an attempt to deaden the pain.

Unexpectedly, after a fortnight of silence, *Chronicle* gave him a couple of assignments. With his concentration wrecked by lack of sleep and his mind numbed by alcohol, he failed miserably at both.

A few days later, he was sent on a lowly assignment to the Bronx, 'just to ease him back', but Marcus knew this was the beginning of the end. The Bronx was regarded as the testing ground. If you didn't get this one right, then you were out.

Anxiety caused a return of the nightmares and Marcus sat in his cold and lonely hotel room drinking himself into a comatose state. He was discovered by the maid and thrown out by the management. He missed his deadline and returned to New York to discover he had been sacked for incompetence.

He walked for miles that night not caring where he went; his life in tatters, his reputation in shreds. Drunks accosted him: foul-smelling men with bottles in brown paper bags. He pushed his way past them and stood on the Brooklyn Bridge looking down at the swirling water hundreds of feet below him. He knew he had reached the nadir of his life. There was nothing left to live for.

But in that exact moment, as he prepared to throw himself into the water, words from one of the first conversations he had had with Anna leapt into his mind:

"Where's Cairnmor?" he'd asked.

"Off the west coast of Scotland. It's an island."

"What sort of island is it?"

"Beautiful, spectacular. High mountains and deep valleys. Has the most amazing white-gold sands. Secret coves, magical hidden places. Bogs. Huge storms."

The water beneath him swirled and beckoned, calling out for him to end his agony.

Cairnmor. Beautiful, spectacular.

The water beneath him swirled and beckoned, but its hold on him began to lessen.

Cairnmor. Secret coves, magical hidden places.

The water swirled beneath him but it no longer beckoned and he heard a stronger call.

Cairnmor.

The idea took hold and dominated his thoughts until he could no longer resist its power.

He had to put faces to names; voices to characters; to know, to see, to understand.

He caught a cab back to his apartment and during the course of the next few weeks he phoned Doug, arranged for a visa, cancelled the lease on his apartment, boxed up his possessions ready to be put in storage, packed for his journey and, once everything was in place, set off for the airport.

He had been brought to the abyss but had been pulled back from the brink just in time.

Cairnmor.

That was where he had to go. That was where his salvation lay.

PART THREE

June – August, 1969

CHAPTER 17

Cairnmor
Arrival

When Marcus stepped off the ferry in Lochaberdale, he was overwhelmed by sights and sounds that he had not encountered before, despite the diversity in the vast expanse that was the continent of North America.

He found the scenery of Cairnmor stunning, the atmosphere unique – and the language very strange.

Not everyone was speaking it, of course. There were at least a couple of dozen tourists; some easily distinguishable with their knapsacks and walking shoes, while others were more conventionally equipped with suitcases, sandals and summer clothes.

Listening to their accents, Marcus was relieved to discover he was the only American present. More than anything, he wanted to be anonymous; to be in a place where no one would recognize him, where no one would know of his troubled past.

Marcus had thought long and hard during the course of his lengthy journey, trying to rationalize his abrupt departure and make sense of the inner promptings that had led him to make such a precipitous move.

To come to the place he most associated with one of the people he was trying to forget might seem strange to some but to Marcus, it now made perfect sense. He realized he wanted to come here for two reasons.

Firstly, he was curious. Anna had spoken of Cairnmor with such wistfulness, with such fondness, that from her description, Marcus had formed a picture in his mind: a picture that had grown and expanded until the island took on an identity quite separate from Anna's connection to it. He wanted it to become the place that would envelop him and offer him the solace he was seeking; the place of total escape he so desperately needed. It was to be his starting point in dealing with his past; a past he had to come to terms with if he was to move on and regain his health and his self-esteem.

Secondly, he wanted to see her family. He presumed they knew nothing of his existence, nor did he have any intention of revealing to them his connection to Anna. He wanted to see them for real; to hear them speak and see what they looked like.

This desire had become something he was holding onto: a small positive light in a world which for Marcus had become empty and meaningless, where guilt, remorse and pain still haunted his every waking moment and from which there seemed no respite.

He had no job; no inclination to write; no one to love or who loved him. His visa allowed him to stay in the United Kingdom for six months and he would stay here, on Cairnmor, and absorb himself in the day to day minutiae of the island until everything else was obliterated.

This was where he wanted to be. He had had enough of his homeland and the memories it engendered. Perhaps here, he might find the inspiration to finish his latest novel before his publisher disowned him or, better still, he might begin a new one.

That night, as usual, sleep eluded him, despite the comfort to be found in the faded Victorian elegance of his hotel room. He had eschewed the bar and the general conviviality of the other guests and, tired after his long journey, had gone to bed. He did not wish for company and the proximity of alcohol presented too much of a temptation.

It had offered no solution or cure for his inner despair and his overuse had only presented the double danger of potentially wrecking his health and turning him into a habitual drinker that would have made him no better than Virginia.

He was glad he had heeded the warning bells just in time.

Marcus threw back the covers and walked over to one of the floor to ceiling windows and opened the curtains. He stood looking at the view; the distant headlands silhouetted by a deep red-gold glow from the setting sun, almost invisible below the horizon.

Suddenly, he felt the urge to be outside, out in the fresh air. Quickly, he dressed and made his way down to the lobby of the hotel.

A single oil lamp stood on the large mahogany desk, with its double row of wooden pigeon holes behind, casting gentle shadows on the wall. Marcus tried the main door. It was unlocked. He had been given his own key but the desk clerk had told him, with no little pride, that they never locked the door.

Once outside, he walked down to the quayside and watched a fishing boat come chuntering into the harbour to unload its cargo but Marcus chose not to linger. He took the path that sloped upwards away from the harbour, stumbling sometimes in the shadows; its steepness leaving him breathless and his mind numb with sheer physical effort.

Having reached the summit, the path wound its way downwards to a beach where Marcus stood, gathering his breath, looking outwards – a stationary, solitary figure beside the rolling waves of the Atlantic ocean. It was this same ocean that linked him to his homeland but he felt no special connection, only the loneliness and remoteness of his present existence. He took off his socks and shoes, feeling the cool sand beneath the soles of his feet, walking beside a luminescent sea until he came to a hut, tarred and black, sheltered by the dunes.

The door opened easily and cautiously, Marcus went inside. There was a small wooden bed pushed against one of the walls, its boards bare and hard, together with a couple of oars and some old fishing nets. On a shelf beneath the window stood one or two coloured glass paperweights and some other objects obscured by darkness.

Tired after his walk, Marcus lay down on the cot, using his arm to pillow his head, pulling his coat closer round him and drawing his knees up almost to his chest. Cocooned within the hut's protective walls and lulled by the sound of the waves upon the shore, he fell instantly asleep.

"Hàlo! Cò bheil thu? Dè tha thu 'dol?"

A boy's voice speaking unintelligible words and the early morning sun streaming in through the tiny window caused Marcus to be rudely awakened out of his slumber.

A dog, a golden retriever, came snuffling into the hut, pushing his way through the boy's legs and sniffed energetically at Marcus, who was struggling to regain his bearings after his first deep sleep in months.

"*Cha bhìd e thu.*" He pulled at the dog's collar. "*Come on, Dùghall. Come away, boy!*"

The lad threw a stick in the direction of the sea and Dougal bounded after it before returning and dropping it down at his young master's feet, his tail wagging excitedly, waiting for the same thing to happen again.

Marcus sat up and stretched his cramped back. "I'm afraid I don't understand a word you're saying."

"Oh, I'm sorry." Apologetically, the boy repeated his questions but this time in English: asking who he was, what he was doing here and stating that the dog didn't bite. Then he added, "You're an American?!"

"Yeah."

"So, what *are* you doing in here?"

"I went for a walk late last night and walked too far, I guess. I stumbled across this place and came in here for a rest. I must have fallen asleep. I didn't mean to trespass."

"It's all right. You didn't mean any harm." He regarded Marcus with an open and direct gaze. "You don't look like a tramp."

"I'm not a tramp." He hadn't quite sunk that far.

"But you do need a shave."

His lips twitched at the boy's frankness and Marcus felt the stubble on his chin. "I guess you're right."

"Where are you staying?"

"At the hotel."

"What's your name?"

"Marcus."

"Hi. I'm Ben." The boy studied Marcus once again. "You look tired and rather sad."

"Gee, thanks!" The observation made Marcus smile, although it summed him up very neatly. "Tell me, are all you folks on Cairnmor as forthright as you seem to be?"

Ben looked slightly chagrined. "No. Granddad says I get that trait from my father."

"An honest man, obviously."

"Very. How about you?"

"What about me?"

"Are you honest?"

"Yes." Whatever else he had become, Marcus could say that with absolute confidence. He had to admit it felt good.

Ben looked at him again. "I'm glad. Well, I've got to go." He made a face. "School. And you'd better go back to the hotel for breakfast. They don't like to lose their guests."

Marcus smiled, for the second time. That felt good too. "No, I guess they don't."

"Perhaps we'll meet again."

"Maybe."

"Oh and by the way. It's okay for you to rest up in here. Robbie wouldn't mind as long as you take care of the hut. He doesn't use it now, he's too old and frail, but we all keep an eye on it and make sure it stays in good repair. It's a sort of special place on the island because Robbie is a special person and our oldest resident." Ben picked up the stick once more and threw it for Dougal, who scurried away across the sand to retrieve it. "Bye. See you."

"Bye."

Marcus stood in the entrance to the hut and watched the boy and the dog make their way along the sand, wondering about his encounter. Once they were out of sight, he left the hut, closing the door carefully behind him.

Outside, the air was warm and he stood by the shoreline again, just as he had done during the night, but this time shielding his eyes from the dazzling sunlight reflected off the water. For a brief wonderful moment, he was unaware of his inner disquiet but as it crept back into his consciousness, he turned and began the long walk back to the hotel.

When he arrived, the lobby was busy with many guests setting off for their day's activities. Fishing tackle, nets, and baskets littered one corner of the room, and a couple of older men, complete with deerstalker hats and binoculars slung round their necks over tweed jackets, were seated on the sofa, deep in conversation.

A young man with sandy-coloured hair went over to them and introduced himself and the three of them went outside together. Marcus couldn't catch his name but the young woman who had come in with him, spoke to the man at the desk nearby.

"Those two tweedy-types will be disappointed!" she said, nodding towards the departing figures. "I think they were expecting to go shooting but Dad and I are discouraging that. Also, now that we've sold so many deer onto the mainland, it's quite difficult to find them on the hillsides, thank goodness. People can still go deer-stalking, but it's with a photograph as the end result rather than a dead animal. I used to hate it when visitors came to Cairnmor specially to 'bag a trophy'. It's better this way – though you might lose a few guests because of it, David."

The manager smiled. "I never liked the sort of people it brought in anyway. When my grandparents ran the hotel and I used to come and visit over from the mainland, Grandma used to say that she was glad when the season stopped."

"But your granddad was far more philosophical about it."

"True."

"Are you coping all right with John and Marion popping in all the time? I think they find it difficult to keep away from the hotel even though they've retired now!"

"Och, I don't mind. They're a real help and they're delighted I've taken it on. I couldn't abide the city life anymore and I'm grateful to Katherine for giving me this chance. And it's a far better place to bring up the kids. Speaking of which, how is your mum?"

Marcus's thoughts raced ahead… *Katherine? Her mother? Then this young woman must be…*

"Struggling with Mrs Gilgarry's herbal remedy book! Says she can organize all the herbal remedies into lists and categories, but thinks it'll end up being very boring in its present format. She says she needs to find an interesting way to dress it up, but it's beyond her at the moment."

"Well, the islanders will buy it, however it's presented."

"Perhaps, but we want it to sell to the tourists as well." The young woman picked up a clip board from the desk and scanned it briefly. "Now, how many have we got for the guided walk tomorrow?"

"Nine, so far, Grace."

So it is her. Grace. Anna's half-sister; the little girl that Anna was so mean to. All grown up. She's really lovely… Marcus pretended to look at the newspaper at the far end of the desk, all the while listening in on the conversation and surreptitiously observing Grace.

"That's great. Have they all got suitable walking shoes and wet-weather clothes in case it rains?"

"I hope so. They've been given the leaflets you had printed and Brenda's doing a packed lunch for all of them. Her usual ridiculous amounts of food!"

"They'll need it with all that fresh air." Grace looked at her watch. "Goodness, I must go. Dad and I ordered a new sail for *Spirit* and it's arriving this morning on the ferry. I said I'd meet him down by the quayside."

Marcus's heart beat a little faster. *Her father. Alastair?*

She turned to go. "Oh, I meant to ask you the other day but I completely forgot. How's the Gaelic coming on?"

David grimaced. "Still can't make head nor tail of it."

Grace laughed. Marcus, absorbed and therefore vulnerable, found her captivating.

"Never mind. It is difficult at first."

"Will it matter if I never get the hang of it?"

"Ooh yes, terribly," she said, teasing him. "Honestly, don't worry. It's not for everyone and as most of the people you deal with can only speak English anyway, it really isn't going to matter too much."

"I'm glad. But I'll keep trying."

"You do that. Now – *mar sin leat. Bidh mi gad fhaicinn.*"

"Huh?"

"I said, 'I must go' and 'I'll be seeing you'," she replied good-naturedly.

"Oh." David smiled but shook his head. He knew he'd never get the hang of this. "*A-màireach.* Tomorrow. *Aig leth-uair an dèidh ochd!* At half past eight!"

Ignoring the hint, he didn't respond in Gaelic or copy her words. Instead, he settled for a cheery, "See you, Grace!"

With curiosity getting the better of him, Marcus discreetly followed her out of the hotel and, keeping an unobtrusive distance, looked on as Grace and Alastair greeted each other affectionately. They were immediately engaged in conversation and to Marcus it was obvious that they were very close.

He envied that. It was something that he had never really known. With his parents both in the diplomatic service, he had seen very little of them while he was growing up, having spent most of his early life at an exclusive boarding school in Connecticut, then later, of course, at Harvard. His parents had chosen not to take him with them on their various postings around the world, being convinced that it was better for him to have a stable education in one place than be dragged from pillar to post every few years. In that sense, Marcus felt they were right, but he had missed out on family life as a result and the chance to see the world.

He sat on the harbour wall at a safe distance and observed Grace and Alastair as they boarded the ferry to collect the sail and once they were out of sight, he decided it was time to make his way back to the hotel for a bath, shave and some breakfast. He was glad he'd seen them though. Alastair seemed a kindly man and Marcus wondered if they would ever meet. And Katherine, for that matter.

And Grace.

As he ascended the sloping path from the harbour, it suddenly occurred to Marcus that if he wanted to meet Grace, he should go on this guided walk the next day. He wondered how far it was. He was not very fit and hadn't got any walking shoes, his only footwear being that of a city-dweller.

Tough. He would just have to manage.

Spurred on by the thought of joining the walk, Marcus went up to the desk and asked the clerk – David, the manager, seemed to have disappeared – for a leaflet. He read it quickly.

The tour was about four hours long, covering as much distance as the party felt able to walk, taking in the bay, something called the machair and the spectacular *Gleann Aiobhneach* (what was that?) with its stunning views to the mountains beyond. They would stop for a picnic lunch and the post-bus would collect them and bring them back to the hotel in time for afternoon tea. Maximum number of persons to be accommodated was ten. Equipment needed: rainproof coat, suitable walking shoes and a knapsack for the picnic lunch.

Quickly, Marcus asked to have his name added to the list. He hoped that Grace had never heard of him.

"That's fine, Mr Kendrick. All done. Now is there anything else I can help you with?"

"Is there some place on the island where I can buy a pair of walking shoes?"

"Yes, sir. If you go along to Ron's Stores, he'll fix you up with whatever you need."

"Ron's Stores?"

"Just along the main road. Old Ron's just about retired now but his son runs the shop and sees to the business side of things, but the old man himself is still in there every day serving the customers and coming up with new ideas. He's quite a character and likes to chat with whoever comes in. Rescued from Dunkirk by Mr and Mrs Stewart, who own the island."

"Thanks." Marcus smiled. It was turning out to be an eventful and interesting day. And this was only his second on Cairnmor.

Feeling a little more energized, he went up to his room for a quick shave and a bath. He managed to slip into the dining room just before they stopped serving and chose a 'Full English Breakfast' from the menu, which to him as an American, seemed slightly incongruous on a remote Scottish island.

Having satisfied his hunger, Marcus walked towards the main street, which was little more than a row of single-storey cottages, some of which had been converted into shops. He saw no sign of Grace and her father as he passed the quayside and assumed they had collected the sail and gone about their business.

The main street was quaint and totally in keeping with the general ambience of the island, with a post office-cum-village store, a bakery, a butcher's shop, a greengrocer and the smallest bank that Marcus had ever seen. There was also what looked like a chandler's shop with a large sign over the door, indicating that this was 'Ron's Stores'.

Intrigued, he opened the door and was greeted by fishing nets festooned across the ceiling and the smell of tar. There were oars, fishing rods, tackle, tents, thick clothing, lifejackets, small farming equipment and other myriad objects for both sea and land. Towards the back of the shop, which had clearly been extended from the original cottage, were large drum-like containers marked with 'Grass Seed', 'Barley' and 'Oats' in capital letters. It was a veritable Aladdin's cave.

For a moment, Marcus was overwhelmed, his mind trying to assimilate the sheer complexity and variety of the contents. He jumped when a voice behind him said, "Can I 'elp you?"

Marcus turned and stammered, "Gee, I'm er, I'm er, looking for a pair of walking shoes."

The man, whom Marcus assumed to be Ron, chuckled at his discomfiture. "Visitor to Cairnmor?"

"Yeah."

"Been here long?"

"No, I only arrived yesterday. I'm staying at the hotel."

"Well, there's very few other places to stay. What size?"

"Sorry?"

"Walking shoes. What size?"

"Oh, er, well, I'm size twelve back home in the States, but I've no idea what that would be over here."

"I dunno either. We'll try twelve to start with."

"Okay."

"Brown or black?"

"Brown. I think."

"Just as well as that's the only colour we sell." Ron chuckled. "But I'm thinking of stocking black as well if enough people ask for it."

The man carefully manoeuvred himself from his stool and from the lumbering way he walked, Marcus could see that one of his legs was false. It didn't seem to deter him as he climbed a stepladder to bring down one of the boxes from the rows that filled the shelves.

"Here, try this on for size." Ron extracted one of the shoes and gave it to Marcus.

"Best have the other one as well. Sometimes people's feet is different, see. One of 'em might be bigger than the other."

130

Obediently, Marcus tried both shoes on. They were too big. "I guess I need the next size down."

These were a better fit but tight.

"That's the newness, see. They're the right size…" and Ron pressed the ends of the shoes to see how much room there was "…they just need to be broken in a bit. Wear them around indoors off and on for a few hours before you go out in them, otherwise you'll end up with feet full of blisters."

"Thanks."

"Anything else?"

"Yeah. Do you have a waterproof jacket of some kind and a knapsack?"

"Ah, going on one of Grace's guided walks are you?!"

Marcus nodded.

"Well, you're very wise to follow her suggestions. She knows what's doing, does our Gracie."

"Do you know her well?"

"Oh, yeah. Her parents rescued Angus and me from Dunkirk and after the war was over, I brought my family here and we made the island our home. I've known her since she was a nipper."

"A nipper?"

"Child. Lovely girl she is. Always has been."

It was good to have his first impressions confirmed. He wondered about Ron. He seemed willing to talk and Marcus always used to enjoy hearing other people's stories before… Quickly, he changed the direction of his thoughts.

"Who's Angus?"

"My best mate. He moved here too after the war and became the farm manager of Alastair and Katherine's farm. His wife Shona is housekeeper there. His missus and mine get on like a house on fire."

More nuggets of information to store away about Gra… Anna's family, thought Marcus. He had almost thought 'Grace's family'. She seemed to be taking precedence here. "What did you do before the war?"

"Regular in the army. Went across with the B.E.F. when the balloon went up…"

"Balloon went up…?"

Ron looked at him quizzically. "Ask a lot of questions, don't you?"

"One of my worst traits, so I've been told!" Marcus smiled. It felt good to be asking questions again, to have his curiosity aroused.

"Well, I suppose, being an American, it's only natural you don't understand some of our Limey phrases." Ron scratched his cheek. "Well, to answer your question, I suppose 'the balloon went up' means the war was declared. When the thing we'd been afraid might happen actually did happen. The emergency situation, so to speak."

"Right." Marcus waited for Ron to continue.

"Anyway, when the Germans invaded France, we was forced back to the coast in a fighting retreat. Angus and I was badly injured at Dunkirk and I eventually lost one of me legs, but Angus was okay, just lost a bit of his heel. Katherine and Alastair brought us back to Blighty and saved me life. Can't praise 'em high enough.

Anyway, Angus went back on active service when he had recovered and I got invalided out of the army."

"That must have been hard."

"It wasn't easy. The wife was glad, though. Devastated about the leg but she took the attitude that she had me home for the duration. And she was 'appy to look after me until I could get about a bit. Treated me right royally she did." Ron chuckled at the memory.

"What did you do then?"

"Well, after the war was over and I was well again, I set about thinking about what I could do. But first, Angus and me came here with our families as guests of Katherine and Alastair. Anyway, seeing 'ow we all liked it 'ere so much, they invited us to stay. Which we did." Ron moved back to his stool and sat down before continuing. "As soon as I saw this place, I knew what it needed. There was no shops anywhere, apart from the post office. I'd always wanted to run a shop of some kind, you see, so Alastair helped set me up. He and Katherine have always been good to me an' the missus and the little 'uns.

"Little 'uns?"

"Children," replied Ron, with obvious pride.

"How many do you have?"

"Four. And every one a blessing, I always say. They're all grown up now and have families of their own. Live on the island too, so I see 'em most days. And when the eldest said he wanted to work in the shop and run it one day, I couldn't have been more delighted. And the others are doing well and thriving on their crofts."

"Crofts?"

"Their own little farms, you might say."

"Ah." Marcus surveyed his surroundings. "Was the shop like this from the beginning?"

"You mean as stuffed as this?" Ron smiled at his customer. "Nah. I started off by making a little hardware store and that seemed to go down well. Then the locals kept coming up with suggestions and ideas of things that they needed or which would be useful to stock on the island rather than having to order and then wait for them to be delivered from the mainland on the steamer. So I listened to 'em and, Bob's yer uncle, now look at it! In the last few years, I've begun to cater for the tourists as well – hence all the hiking gear. My eldest is talking about extending the shop still further, but I says to him he should wait and see."

Marcus couldn't help but be impressed. He looked around him appreciatively. "It's great!" He didn't ask who Bob was, but assumed that it was another one of Ron's colloquial phrases.

"Are you a Scot?"

"Nah. London born and bred I am. Near Clapham Junction is where I grew up. But I wouldn't go back there for all the tea in China. Love it here. It gets to you, this place does. Here, in the heart," he tapped his chest with his thumb, "So be warned!"

Marcus chuckled and promised to be careful.

"Now, you needed those waterproofs and a knapsack… I've got a nice line in windcheaters," and Ron stomped over to where the required items were kept and Marcus made his choices.

He paid for his purchases and as he was leaving, he said, "I guess you must be Ron?"

"That's me. And if you're staying a while…?" Ron looked enquiringly at Marcus, who nodded, "Then you'd better tell me your name. We always like to know who's who and what's what." He smiled.

For some reason, it gave Marcus a feeling of immense pleasure to be able to say: "I am staying a while and I'm Marcus."

The two men shook hands.

"Nice to meet you, Marcus. Well, don't forget to wear those shoes and break 'em in gently. And remember, Cairnmor will weave a magic spell on you as well if you're here for any length of time. You'll be hooked. There's no escape and don't say I didn't warn you!"

"I'll remember and thanks for the advice."

As he walked out of the shop and back towards the hotel, Marcus considered Ron's last words. He sat on the harbour wall to rest, suddenly feeling tired again after his exertions, looking out over the bay towards the headlands and the distant mountains.

Immersed in the beauty of his surroundings and the all-absorbing atmosphere, he realized that Ron's warning had come too late. He had, without noticing, already succumbed to its enchantment.

Cairnmor had gone right into his soul and it felt *good*.

However, Marcus recognized that the old doubts and demons were very powerful and still within him. He consoled himself with the thought that perhaps it would be all right; perhaps here, he needn't be afraid. Perhaps here, he could find the strength to banish them forever and be able to put the recent events of his life into some kind of perspective.

Marcus sighed. That was the hope, anyway. He was not there yet and that state of mind was a long way off. But inexplicably, he experienced a momentary surge of optimism and, dragging his tired legs up the slope, went back to the hotel to break in his new walking shoes.

CHAPTER 18

The Walk

Despite his optimism and enjoyment of the previous day, Marcus slept badly, as had become his wont, and woke up feeling lightheaded and disorientated. He needed to spend the day in bed until the dizziness had passed but that was impossible, for today he was going on a four hour hike. Reluctantly, he got out of bed and went along to the bathroom where he washed and shaved with difficulty, his hands trembling uncontrollably. He nicked himself three times with the razor. Annoyed, he dabbed at the cuts with his flannel and the towel.

The sight of blood brought back the nightmare and he had to fight with every breath to control his panic and fear.

Quickly, he returned to his room and finished dressing, making his way down to the dining room which he found was busy even at this early hour. Marcus forced himself to eat something, opting for fruit juice and scrambled eggs on toast followed by three cups of strong, black, bitter-tasting coffee. He concluded that the British had no idea how to make good coffee and that perhaps he should learn to like tea.

He ascended the stairs to his bedroom, holding onto the bannister for support. He guessed that in his present state, all the travelling and physical exercise of the previous couple of days were beginning to catch up with him.

Was he really that unfit? Well, today would sort him out, then he could rest up for a week if necessary.

He put on his walking shoes which were much more comfortable after the hours spent pacing his room, collected his knapsack and windcheater and made his way back down to the lobby. David's wife was handing out the packed lunches and he put two rounds of sandwiches, a huge slab of cake, an apple, a bottle of water and a small packet of biscuits into his knapsack. It felt very heavy. He decided to sit down while he was waiting and his heart beat faster in anticipation of Grace's arrival.

She came through the door almost as soon as he had sat down, accompanied by the young man he had seen the previous day.

"Hello, everyone," she said. "I'm Grace and this is Sam and we're going to be your guides for today. Can I just check that you all have your lunch?" She looked round the assembled party who all nodded in affirmation. "Good. And a waterproof coat? Excellent. We've got a good day for our walk as the weather is forecast to stay fine until later this afternoon, but we'll have you all safely back here before then." She smiled. "Now, as we go on, if anyone has any questions, please don't hesitate to ask. I hope that we'll have a chance to chat to you individually as the day progresses. If you'd care to follow us, we'll get started, shall we?" And Grace led the way out of the door.

They walked down to the harbour where they stopped to look at the ferry which had just docked and was unloading cargo and disembarking passengers.

"Everything we need to live on the island has to come by sea," began Grace. "There is no airport and in rough weather sailings are often cancelled. The car ferry comes every other day under normal conditions. Until ten years ago, the Royal Mail Steamer only came once a week and when the winter storms set in, the islanders could be without contact with the outside world for weeks or even months at a time. It meant they had to be self-sufficient and self-reliant, building up stocks of food during the summer for the long winter days ahead. Many of the older generation still continue with this tradition and very wise they are too!

"The harbour here is very much as it has been for generations. There is little room to extend or expand. This was tried at the end of the last century, but the alterations only succeeded in silting up the entrance so had to be taken away again. Lochaberdale is the only suitable place on the whole of Cairnmor in which larger ships can dock and therefore, it's vital that the harbour is kept clear and to a good depth. As you can see, it is a busy, thriving working environment with fishing boats and pleasure craft as well. There's actually plenty of room for everyone."

They ascended the path that Marcus had taken two nights previously, keeping the harbour in view. His legs felt weak and he struggled to keep up with the group, pausing to rest every so often. Leaving Sam to continue with the commentary, Grace came back down the hill towards Marcus, who had stopped yet again to regain his breath.

"Are you all right?" she asked, her voice and manner full of concern.

"I'm just not very fit, I guess." He looked at her and tried to smile. "I'll be okay in a moment or two."

"Are you sure you don't want to go back to the hotel?" Grace felt anxious as they had only just begun the walk.

"I'll be fine. I don't want to miss out on anything."

She smiled reassuringly. "Don't worry. There'll be another one of these tours at the weekend."

"I'm all right now."

Together, they walked slowly upwards and rejoined the group. Once Marcus was safely back in the fold, Grace went on ahead to Sam.

"Is he okay?" he asked.

"He says he is. But he looks very tired."

"Ashen would be a better description."

"From his accent, he sounds like an American. Do you think he's the man that Ben encountered asleep in Robbie's hut?"

"He could be."

Grace chuckled. "I suppose I could always say to him: 'Are you Ben's sad American?'" When Sam didn't respond to her humour, she added, "So, do you think you'd still like to do this for a living even though looking after tired, sad people comes with the territory?"

"Of course I would, and especially if you come with the territory."

"I'm a permanent fixture."

Sam sighed. It was all so difficult. He looked across to the horizon. "I think I'll broach the subject with my father after my graduation ceremony next week."

"Really?"

Since Sam had returned to Cairnmor at the end of his course, Grace had begun to wonder whether he was serious about moving to the island. Each time he had said he was going to 'broach the subject', nothing had happened – either it wasn't 'the right time' or his father was 'too busy'. She had become sceptical, beginning to believe that he would never do so.

"He'll cut me off without a penny probably, or never speak to me again," said Sam morosely.

"Well, the money doesn't matter, my family's rich enough to keep us going for ever..."

"I keep forgetting that..."

"Good. Because I would want us to be self-supporting. Anyway, my dad has immense powers of persuasion and diplomacy. I'm sure he'll be able to bring your father round."

"I doubt it."

"Well, we'll have to see. In the meantime, we'd better give these folks their money's worth."

So they continued, down the hill, onto the beach.

"This particular stretch of sand extends for six unbroken miles and there are further examples all over the island. Its white-gold colour and texture are unique to Cairnmor and the surrounding islands and cannot be found anywhere else in Great Britain. The sands are pristine, washed clean by the Atlantic Ocean, the body of water you see before you. There is nothing between us and the continent of North America," said Grace, allowing the party to take in the view.

"During the winter months, storms uproot vast quantities of seaweed which the crofters have always used as a fertiliser but we'll talk more about that once we come onto the machair. About a hundred years ago, the seaweed was harvested to make potash which was used on the mainland to make glass. However, cheaper imports from abroad meant that potash from seaweed was no longer considered viable. This was probably just as well from an environmental perspective, as the whole conversion process was very polluting, but the loss of the industry was disastrous for the people who made their living from it. These days," added Grace, "there is still an industry here using seaweed but one that is kinder to the environment. It is collected from the beach and taken to a special factory in the north of the island where it is dried and ground into a powder. Then it is sent to the mainland to be processed into a thickening or gelling agent for foodstuffs. This growing industry," she continued, "provides a vital source of employment for many islanders."

The walkers then moved along the sands, towards a rocky outcrop that protruded onto the beach.

"We come now to an old tarred hut, built over eighty years ago, and very typical of the island." The group gathered round Grace while they contemplated the hut. "It was constructed by Robbie MacKenzie, a local fisherman and widely regarded as one of the greatest characters to live here. When he wasn't at sea, he could always be found seated outside the hut mending his nets, dispensing advice on the weather or discussing the latest goings-on with whoever happened to be passing or had come to see him. He celebrated his hundredth birthday a few months ago and is

Cairnmor's oldest resident. He has a rich fund of stories to tell, which he's willing to share with anyone who cares to listen…"

Marcus looked with longing at the hut where he had spent his first night. His dizziness had returned and distracted himself by asking, "Did he use it as some sort of base? Because there's a bed inside."

Grace and Sam exchanged a brief glance. So the tired man *is* Ben's 'sad American'.

"Yes," she replied. "He often used to spend the night here. Said he always slept better in his hut than in his bed at home."

Marcus managed a smile. He could believe that.

After stopping for tea and biscuits beside the hut, they left the sands via the rocky outcrop and climbed up the path through the dunes.

"This dune system, like the sand, continues in an unbroken stretch for six miles," said Sam, "and is one of the finest examples anywhere in the British Isles. The tough, spiky marram grass keeps it secure and whereas coastal erosion seems to be affecting similar places on the mainland, here on Cairnmor, the dunes just keep growing larger. It's a rare phenomenon which has scientists puzzled and the residents delighted, so I'm reliably informed." He smiled at Grace, who took up the thread once more as they left the dunes behind.

"We've now come to the machair which, as you can see, is a large fertile plain, mainly composed of sand and light soil. The island is divided between a few large farms and hundreds of crofts, which are like smallholdings. Everyone has the right to use the machair to grow crops and the right to graze their animals within the enclosures.

"The seaweed that I told you about earlier is not only used as a fertilizer but also binds the loose sandy soil together giving it a weight and depth it would not have otherwise. The principal crops grown on the machair are barley and oats, the varieties of which are native to the island. They grow very low to the ground as this gives them some protection from the wind which is a force to be reckoned with here!

"Potatoes are also a staple crop and the potatoes on Cairnmor are the best tasting anywhere in the world," added Grace, with a smile. "Also, as you can see, the meadows look and smell particularly lovely at this time of year, with their profusion of summer flowers. Again, there is a greater concentration and variety of flowering plants than can be found…"

Suddenly, the world started to spin for Marcus. There was nothing for him to hold onto and as his legs buckled under him, he collapsed onto the soft cushioning grass of the machair.

Grace was beside him in an instant. She checked his pulse and his breathing. Both were fine but there was nothing she could do to bring him round.

Sam looked at Grace in a panic. "What shall we do? What shall we do? We're in the middle of nowhere. We can't just go and call an ambulance!"

Calmly and clearly, as though talking to a child, Grace said, "Run and fetch Angus and get him to bring the land rover. We'll take him home first of all as that's nearest and then you'll have to go for the doctor. After that, we can take him to hospital if necessary."

Sam ran off while Grace removed her jumper and made a pillow for Marcus's head. The other guests sat down on the machair to wait, most of them full of sympathy for the "poor man, who had looked so pale right from when we left the hotel."

However, one of the group was not and made his feelings clearly felt. "We've paid for this tour, young lady," he said, his voice full of irritation. "I hope we're not going to have to sit around and wait for too long."

"Don't you worry, dearie," said his wife, addressing Grace and giving her husband a despairing look. "We can carry on with our walk once the poor man's been sorted."

Grace smiled distractedly in acknowledgement while at the same time scanning the tour list. What did Ben say his sad American was called? Marcus. There was only one Marcus written down but she couldn't read the surname. Kranrick or something. David really was going to have to take the desk clerk in hand and ask him to improve his hand writing.

Within fifteen minutes, Sam had returned with Angus and two of the farmhands. They lifted Marcus carefully into the back of the vehicle onto some clean sacking and set off cautiously across the machair. Sam went with them and an anxious Grace continued the guided tour, her mind very naturally elsewhere.

When she got home later that afternoon, Katherine, Alastair and Sam were seated around the table drinking tea.

"How is he?" she asked.

"Tucked up in bed upstairs, fast asleep, wearing a pair of Sam's pyjamas," replied her mother.

"Has he come round yet?"

"Yes, just before we brought him indoors."

"That's a relief. Did he say anything?"

"He kept apologizing for being a nuisance and insisting he was fine."

Alastair chuckled. "I said if he was fine, then I was a monkey's uncle. He went very pale again at that point."

"I'm not surprised." Grace smiled at her father. "Has the doctor been?"

"Yes, he came straight away," replied Katherine.

"What did he say?"

"That he couldn't find anything wrong with him. He's not ill, apparently. But Doc thinks he's suffering from complete exhaustion. He wonders if he's been through some kind of trauma recently. Thinks this could be a physical reaction to it," said Alastair.

"Goodness!" Grace was shocked. "Will he have to go into hospital?"

"Not at the moment. Martin thinks that total bed rest for at least a week is what he needs most right now. However, he did say that when Marcus is feeling a little stronger, he should come to the hospital for a physical examination, just in case there's some other underlying reason why he is so exhausted. He said that what would be most beneficial for him is to be looked after properly in comfortable, friendly surroundings."

"Could they look after him at the hotel?" Grace was doubtful even as she asked the question.

"Not really. They just don't have the resources at the moment with the tourist season at its height." Katherine smiled at her daughter, yet there was a hint of resignation in her voice. "So I said he could stay here."

"Oh, Mum, thank you!" Grace hugged her mother. "I know he's a stranger and all that, but I sort of feel a measure of responsibility for him. I don't mean that I feel it was my fault that he fainted, it's just that it seems right he should be here with us. I can't say why exactly; it's just a feeling. Especially with Ben having discovered him in Robbie's hut yesterday."

"Well, it just seemed the natural thing to do. He needs proper rest and care and he can't get that at the hotel. I couldn't very well leave him to fend for himself."

"Ben will be delighted when he gets home from school. He was very taken by his encounter yesterday. I must admit, it fuelled my curiosity as well," said Alastair. "However, on a more practical level, our guest will need his clothes and things from the hotel if he's to be with us for any length of time."

"I hope he's trustworthy." Grace experienced a sudden moment of anxiety. "Because we know nothing about him."

"The same thought did flit through my mind," responded Katherine, "but I overrode it."

"Well, Angus'll sort him out if he turns out to be an axe murderer!"

"Oh don't say things like that, Dad, please!" but Grace couldn't help smiling. "Somehow, I don't think that description fits him."

"Who's an axe murderer?" said Ben enthusiastically, as he came into the kitchen, dumping his satchel and games kit on the floor and helping himself to a handful of biscuits from the tin on the table.

"Bloodthirsty boy!" exclaimed his great-grandfather equably. "We're thinking about starting a new line in gruesome guests." He chuckled at Ben's wide-eyed expression. "We were just speculating because your 'sad American' is upstairs fast asleep in the blue guest room."

"What?!" Ben spluttered crumbs over the table and everyone laughed, but not unkindly, at his reaction. "How come?"

Grace explained the circumstances and Ben's response was a heartfelt: "Wow!" and "Can I go up and see him?"

"Not yet, impatient idiot. He's fast asleep," said Sam. "Give the poor man a chance. He needs peace and quiet, not clodhopping boys like you tramping into his room."

Ben responded by putting his tongue out at Sam, who air-punched him – an action which Ben neatly sidestepped. He bent to pick up his satchel. "Well, I've got homework to do. Let me know when it's dinnertime or when Marcus wakes up; whichever's first. I'm starving."

"Yes, your lordship," mocked Sam, as Ben went out of the kitchen.

"I wonder how long our unexpected guest intends to stay on the island?" asked Alastair, all the while regarding Sam carefully, deciding that he would speak to him later about the number of times he derided Ben, who was beginning to dislike it.

"Sam and I could go down to Lochaberdale now, if you like, in the car and find out, as well as collecting his stuff from the hotel. Couldn't we?" suggested Grace.

"I want to check the moorings on our boats anyway, and make sure they're secure, especially if the weather forecast is correct."

"Don't be tempted to go out anywhere, though," said Alastair good-naturedly to his daughter. "It doesn't look too good for later… lots of wind…"

"Da-ad," chided Grace. "You're not going to let me forget my little escapade in a hurry are you?!"

Alastair chuckled. "No. And it was no 'little escapade' either. But you coped incredibly well by the sound of things and brought yourself and *Spirit* home safely. And that was the most important thing. However, if I'd known… I would have been beside myself with anxiety."

Grace kissed her father on his cheek. "Well, I'm glad you didn't know and it's taught me a useful lesson. But I wouldn't have gone out had you been at home."

"True. In that case, perhaps I shouldn't go anywhere…"

"Don't be daft!" and father and daughter smiled at each other with deep affection and mutual understanding.

Marcus awoke in a totally strange place but wherever it was, it was very comfortable. He tried to get up, but the effort was too much. He was too tired and his head was swimming. He flopped down into the soft pillow, pulling the sheet, blankets, eiderdown and bedspread further up to his neck.

Feeling safe and warm, he promptly fell asleep once again.

The news of Marcus's fainting spell had travelled like wildfire and when Grace and Sam reached the hotel, they were beset by questions from every side. Parrying the enquiries as best they could, they made their way to the front desk. Even before they had a chance to say anything, David, the manager, said, "I expect you'll be wanting our American guest's things. I'll take you up and away from this mayhem. He's in room eight."

"How long is he booked in for?" asked Grace, as they ascended the stairs.

"Three weeks but he did mention to me that he intended staying on Cairnmor for six months."

"Six months?!" Grace was surprised. "I wonder if he'd thought ahead as to where he would stay later on?"

David shrugged. "I've no idea. Because we're fully booked from now until October so it couldn't have been here."

He left them at the door and Grace and Sam went into Marcus's room. They found two large suitcases under the bed and his clothes put away neatly in the chest of drawers. They packed these as well as his hair brush, his shaving things, soap and flannel and his pyjamas and dressing-gown. In his bedside cabinet was a leather pouch which obviously contained some personal documents, and resisting the temptation to look inside, Grace put those in the case as well. In the wardrobe were his coat, shoes, some winter clothing as well as a small, locked valise.

Having emptied the room of all his belongings, Grace and Sam shut the door, locked it and went back downstairs.

"Got everything?" asked David.

"Yes, thanks."

"What shall I do about his room?"

"Keep it for the moment until we know what he's doing."

"Righty-ho, Grace," he said, putting the key on one of the hooks on the wall behind the desk.

"See you, David." And they left, having completely forgotten to ask what Marcus's surname was.

A week later, Marcus was sitting in the kitchen eating breakfast with Katherine and Alastair, Grace and Sam having left for London two days previously to attend the ceremony at which Sam's doctorate was to be conferred.

It was Marcus's first morning to be up and dressed and although he felt a trifle unsteady on his feet, he had insisted that it was time, even if it was only for an hour or so. Katherine had relented and now, here he was at the table. They had not conversed a great deal during the previous week, as he had spent most of the time asleep, apart from waking up for meals. They had left him to rest and not disturbed him with too many extraneous questions, reasoning that there would be plenty of time to get to know him once he was up and about.

Katherine had begun to feel very protective towards their unexpected guest and his presence in the house had not been a disturbing one, nor had the task of looking after him been an onerous or difficult one. They were curious about him though, particularly Ben, who had been allowed to take the occasional meal up to his 'sad American' on condition that he didn't ask too many questions and came downstairs more or less straight away. Being the good boy that he was, Ben did as he was told and while he was delivering the tray, talked about Robbie or Cairnmor or school, snippets of information that he thought might interest his newfound discovery. Alastair supplied Marcus with a few books and magazines to look at – nothing too demanding that might require effort on the part of their guest – and Katherine had kept the room fragrant with flowers.

For his part, Marcus was filled with gratitude for their kindness towards him, a mere stranger, and for the first time in months, he found he could put his immediate past out of his mind and give himself up to the blissful release and restorative powers of sleep and safety.

That first morning, just as Katherine was pouring them a second cup of tea, the back door flew open with a flourish made all the more dramatic by the strong wind that had been blowing since first light. They all looked up in surprise as a very good-looking man in the unmistakable uniform of a Royal Navy captain stood before them in the doorway.

He smiled broadly and was about to greet the assembled group when he was stopped in his tracks by the sight of their guest.

"Good God!" he exclaimed, his expression one of complete astonishment. "Marcus Kendrick! What on earth are you doing on Cairnmor… and of all places, in Katherine and Alastair's kitchen?"

CHAPTER 19

Discovery

"Marcus Kendrick?!" exclaimed Katherine. "The journalist and author?"

All eyes turned on Marcus and he wished that he could pass out again and escape the recognition and explanations that now inevitably would follow. Perhaps he should leave before they discovered his past. Perhaps they knew about it already now that they had discovered his identity.

However, the week's sleep had taken him past the fainting stage and all he could do was stare at Jack Rutherford. It had to be him. A Royal Navy officer.

"Do you two know each other?" asked Alastair incredulously.

"Not exactly," replied Jack carefully, all the while regarding Marcus whose face had gone very pale. "But I would hazard a guess and say that we know of each other."

"Yes," said Marcus quietly. "But I don't understand how you know me... unless..." His thoughts were racing: were Jack and Anna back together? If they were, would Anna have talked to Jack about him? Surely not.

"I was there at your..." but something in Marcus's expression: a warning, a look of fear and panic made Jack stop in mid-sentence.

This exchange was not lost on Katherine and Alastair, who diffused the moment by standing up to greet the new arrival with affectionate hugs before Katherine said, "Why didn't you let us know you were coming?"

"I didn't know myself until two days ago. You see, I've had a bit of a promotion. They want to make me a commodore."

"Congratulations! That's wonderful news!" and Alastair shook Jack's hand with his firm grasp.

"Well, yes and no."

"What do you mean?"

Jack hesitated. "I haven't yet decided whether or not I shall accept."

"Why?"

"Oh, a number of reasons." He smiled at Alastair. "I'm not sure I understand all of them myself at the moment. But we'll talk when I do."

Discreetly, Marcus observed the newcomer and found something about him that he liked. Very much. It wasn't logical. This man was the reason he couldn't be with Anna, therefore, he ought to resent him, to be profoundly jealous of him but, to his surprise, Marcus found that he wasn't.

Not at all.

"How long can you stay?" asked Katherine.

"I've six weeks before I'm supposed to take up my new job."

"Six weeks! That's wonderful."

"It means I'll be here for your birthday jamboree."

Alastair's eyes became suspiciously moist. "I'm so pleased. It wouldn't have been the same without you. So what's the new post going to be?"

"I've been offered Naval Assistant to the First Sea Lord."

"At the Admiralty?"

"Oh yes."

"Well done, Jack. I'm proud of you."

"Thank you but I haven't accepted yet."

"Ah, but they offered it to you and that's the main thing."

Jack smiled again and, as casually as he could, asked, "Anyway, where's Grace?"

"Gone to London with Sam," replied Katherine.

"Sam? Who's Sam?" Jack was shocked.

Alastair and Katherine exchanged a brief glance before the latter said, "Her boyfriend."

"Boyfriend?" He was worried now. "She never told me. But then we haven't written to each other in ages and that's my fault." His buoyancy diminished, his mouth dry, Jack asked, "How long have they known each other?"

"About eight months, although she hasn't seen a great deal of him since January because he's been in London finishing his doctorate at Imperial College. He's back there to have it conferred."

"A clever chap then." Could he be glad for her? She needed an intelligent man. But Grace – in a relationship. Jack wondered if they'd slept together and had to work hard to conceal an immediate surge of jealousy. "What's his specialism?"

"Botany."

"Is the relationship serious?"

"Yes, and he's absolutely right for her. Sam says he wants to live here on Cairnmor, but he's going to have a bit of a fight on his hands as his father wants him to take up accountancy in the family firm in Glasgow once he's finished his studies."

"Have they made any plans to get married?"

Again, Katherine and Alastair exchanged a glance.

"Not exactly," she replied carefully. "They can't really until things have been sorted out with Sam's family and also, Grace keeps wavering."

"She does?" A nugget of hope began to replace his resentment. "Has she said as much to Sam?"

"Not as far as we're aware. It's how she feels in her own mind."

"And you two being the mind readers that you both are…" Jack smiled at them, allowing himself to experience a small feeling of relief.

However, before they could say anything further on the subject, from overhead they heard thumps and bumps and footsteps clomping down the stairs.

"Now where's that young scallywag of mine?" called out Jack.

"Dad!" and Ben came running through the open doorway and straight into his father's arms.

Marcus wished he could faint again.

Seeing him blanch, Jack looked sympathetically at Marcus. "You didn't know?"

He shook his head. "She never told me."

His words were almost inaudible but Katherine heard them as well as Jack, who nodded.

"Are you home for a long time?" asked Ben, claiming his father's attention.

"A very long time. Six weeks. Most of your summer holidays. So, young man, now that I'm here, what shall we do today?"

"I don't mind, as long as we're together. I'd like to go fishing."

"It's a bit windy for that today," observed Alastair. "You'll not catch much."

"Your great-granddad is a very wise man." Jack put his hand on Alastair's shoulder and then said to Ben, "How about you come upstairs with me while I get changed and you can see all the presents I've bought you. Then we'll go and kick a ball around on the beach until lunch. We can go fishing tomorrow if the wind's died down a bit."

"And go rock-pooling?"

"Of course."

"Goody-goody. In that case, today can be a catch-up day and I can tell you all about my science lessons at school and what the teacher said about my artwork… And then we can go for a walk this afternoon. There's heaps to tell you!"

Ben grabbed Jack's hand and pulled him in the direction of the stairs.

"Hang on a minute, Samson, my arm'll be out of its socket at this rate. Now, let me collect my suitcase and we'll go and stow all this kit in my cabin." As they moved off, Jack looked at Marcus and said, "Perhaps we can talk later?"

Marcus nodded, but said nothing. So Jack smiled and Marcus, reassured, smiled back. Perhaps it would be all right after all.

There was silence in the kitchen after Jack and Ben had gone upstairs. Then Katherine said to Marcus, "Don't go away. I'll be back in a moment."

Alastair stirred his tea, thoughtfully. "We thought your surname was Kranrick."

"What?"

"Apparently on Grace's list from the hotel the desk clerk's handwriting was so appalling, that your surname was virtually indecipherable. Hence we didn't know who you really are. I do apologise!" Seeing an expression of anxiety in Marcus's eyes, he added, ever perceptive: "Would you rather we didn't know who you are?"

"Yes."

"Is there a reason?"

How could he tell these kind and good people that he had killed his wife, drunk himself senseless and been sacked from his job for incompetence? They'd ask him to leave straight away and Marcus didn't want that; oh how he didn't want that.

Sensing his reluctance to reply and mindful of the doctor's words that he'd been through some kind of trauma, Alastair said, "Well, my friend, there's no hurry. You can talk when you feel able. We'll not press you."

"I can't thank you enough for all your hospitality. You've been so kind."

"Don't mention it. And stay as long as you would like to."

"Thanks. I appreciate that." Would they let him stay after they knew…?

"Here, it is," said Katherine, coming into the kitchen once more, "I thought I could lay my hands on it quickly."

She placed a carefully preserved copy of *Chronicle* magazine on the table, together with a book.

"There!" she said. "The article you wrote on Phillippe du Laurier. We kept it, of course, as it was about a family member, and also because we're all so proud of him and his achievements in striving for world peace. We thought it was wonderful that someone from America wanted to write an article on him. And to think that you're here now, with us, and we didn't even know who you were!"

"It was my first interview for *Chronicle*."

"Yes, I remember Phillippe telling us. He was terribly impressed by your professionalism and thought your questions were most intelligent and not the usual run-of-the-mill, superficial stuff he had encountered before."

She smiled at Marcus, who blushed and somewhat sheepishly turned to the page and scanned the article.

"And then, a couple of years after that came out," continued Katherine after allowing Marcus time to look properly at his article, "I was browsing through Foyle's Bookshop while we were staying in London and found this…" and, with another smile, she handed the book over to Marcus, who opened the front cover.

"My first novel." He swallowed hard, suspiciously near to tears.

"Yes."

Alastair, who had been quietly observing Marcus, said, "We seem to have in our possession two of your firsts."

"Yes."

Suddenly, for Marcus, the room began to swim and, seeing him go very pale, Alastair and Katherine immediately went to his aid and carefully helped him up to his room where they settled him onto the bed.

"I'm so sorry to be a nuisance."

"You're not. You just need to get yourself well again."

Emotionally exhausted, Marcus was asleep even before Katherine had finished her sentence.

"Poor chap. Something very unpleasant has happened to him, I think," remarked Alastair once they were back in the kitchen.

"I know. I wonder what it is?"

"So do I. No doubt he'll tell us in his own good time."

"And he knows Anna."

"*Knew* her is the more likely scenario." Alastair kissed his wife's forehead. "And you'll be wanting to hear all about her."

"Of course. But I shan't probe, although I want to so much." Katherine's eyes filled with tears. "I want to know all about her, how she is, what she's been doing. Marcus has suddenly become a tangible link, our only one, apart from her agent, who has had very little to say recently."

"We're going to have to be very patient."

"A hard thing to do."

"Yes." Alastair held her close and suddenly, he looked at her. "An idea has just struck me. Why don't you involve Marcus in your book about Mrs Gilgarry's remedies? It would be therapeutic for him, excuse the unintentional pun, but you know what I mean. It will certainly be helpful for you. I know you're stuck for ideas at the moment. After all, he's a published author and we both enjoyed his first novel. He has a very readable style and his storytelling is vivid. There's integrity too in his writing. It'll be a little light relief after the serious stuff he must be doing for *Chronicle* magazine. Provided he's willing, of course. We wouldn't want to force him into it."

Katherine brightened immediately. "You are a brilliant man! He might even have some ideas for your guidebook as well."

"Give the poor chap a chance! We don't want to swamp him with work. He needs his rest too, remember?"

"I haven't forgotten. Oh, Alastair, what a good idea! He'll feel better if he's helping us in some way, because I'll hazard a guess and say that he feels guilty about having to be looked after like this."

"Then he doesn't know *us* very well, does he?"

"Not yet. But he will."

"Of that I have no doubt!"

Katherine looked at the clock. "Goodness, is that the time? I must go into Lochaberdale."

"Another secret errand to do with my birthday bash?" Alastair's eyes twinkled mischievously.

"How do you *know* these things?!"

"Aha! I have vays and means of finding you out," he said.

"Vell, it iz a gut job I am a good vife."

"Ya, but it vud never occur to me to tink othervise! Don't be long, darling."

"Of course not."

And they smiled at each other.

That evening, after supper, Jack went up to Marcus's room to collect his tray.

"Feel up to talking for a little while?"

Marcus sighed. "Yeah, I guess so. At least if I feel faint, I can pass out in comfort." He managed a smile, which Jack returned and made himself comfortable in the easy chair. Then, without preamble, he said, "I was at your trial."

"I guessed as much."

"Don't worry – I was impressed."

"You were?" Marcus was surprised.

"I thought you parried that obnoxious district attorney's questions with great dignity."

"You did?"

"Yes."

"He was rather unpleasant, wasn't he?"

"Pompous ass more like."

The unexpected observation so surprised Marcus that it made him laugh. "Yeah!"

"You'll have to tell me what happened in the end, though, as I was called back to my ship and couldn't stay."

"Did you hear Anna's testimony?"

Jack shook his head. "I wanted to. She was the reason I'd come in the first place. But I never got that far."

"Where did you get to?"

"The uncle's testimony. He really was a nasty piece of work."

"Yeah."

"And his son. So what happened in the end?"

"The jury found me not guilty."

146

"Obviously, otherwise you wouldn't be here now," observed Jack. "Unless you'd managed a spectacular jailbreak!" he added. "I should have sued them for a miscarriage of justice if you hadn't been acquitted! It was obvious to everyone in the courtroom that you weren't guilty. I'm pleased for you. How long were the jury out?"

"Five minutes." Marcus couldn't help smiling.

"Ha! That lawyer of yours was first-rate."

Marcus smiled again. "Yeah! He was fantastic. Doug's my best friend."

"From before or after the trial?"

Marcus laughed. "Before."

"I expect he felt quite a weight of responsibility then?"

"You're telling me! He took a week off afterwards to recover."

"And what happened to you?"

He hesitated. "I hit rock bottom."

"Hardly surprising."

Marcus wasn't expecting understanding. He'd spent so long beating himself up for sinking into the abyss that he'd ceased to realize that his stupidity could engender a sympathetic response like Jack's.

The two men sat in silence for several moments before Jack said, "Well, you can tell me about it sometime, if you want. It might be good to get it off your chest."

"Maybe. But not yet."

"No, give it time." Then, unexpectedly, Jack asked, "Would you like me tell Katherine and Alastair?"

"What about?"

"The trial and the events that led up to it? Might be easier for you."

"They'll ask me to leave."

"No, they won't."

"You're sure?"

Jack smiled. "I know them very well."

"I guess." Marcus considered Jack's offer. Instinctively, he knew he could trust him. "Yeah, okay. I'd appreciate it. But why would you do this for me? You never know, I might still be a rival for Anna's affections."

Momentarily disconcerted, Jack retorted with no little irony, "Not a chance. You said it yourself at the trial. She's still in love with me." *For all the good it does me*, he thought.

"Ouch!" said Marcus.

"Well, Anna is another conversation," replied Jack, smoothing out the moment of mutual discomfort. "If we can bear it."

"Too true."

"Perhaps we should cover that thorny subject when we know each other better."

Marcus nodded, suddenly feeling weary again. Seeing this, Jack stood up. It was time to go downstairs and let him rest.

"You know, I really admired you for the way you handled yourself in the trial, whatever happened afterwards."

"Thanks. I appreciate that." He reached for his book and as Jack picked up the tray and turned to go, Marcus said, "I'm glad we've met. When Anna and I were together, she told me a great deal about you – all of it good – and I'm glad you've turned out to be the decent sort of guy I always thought you were."

Jack nodded and gave Marcus a half-salute in acknowledgement as he went out of the room.

Later that evening, he went for a walk with Katherine and Alastair and told them of the trial and what had befallen Marcus and why he, Jack, had gone in the first place.

"So, the doctor was right when he said he'd been through a traumatic time," said Katherine, once Jack had finished. "Poor Marcus. It's an awful story. It's impossible to imagine what it must have been like for him."

"I wonder what happened to him after the trial?" asked Alastair.

"We may never know. It depends on whether he's able to talk about it."

"He must have been laid pretty low."

"Yes."

"Well," said Alastair, "if he's going to talk to anyone about that episode in his life, I'm thinking it will be to you. I can quite see the possibility of a friendship developing between the two of you."

"I know. Ironic, isn't it?" observed Jack. "Given that he loved Anna and lived with her for a while."

"You don't feel any resentment or jealousy?" asked Katherine.

"Oddly enough, no. Well, some. I wouldn't be human if I didn't." Jack sighed, then said quietly, "I tried to see her before I left New York. I had one day left after we'd finished the meetings, so I went to the theatre to see her play. Afterwards, I sent a message backstage asking if she would like to see me but she was apparently not available."

"Well, at least you tried," said Alastair, sensing more but not enquiring.

They walked on in silence for a while and sat down in the shelter of the dunes not far from Robbie's hut.

"What was she like in the play?" asked Katherine, wanting to hear any news of her daughter, no matter how small.

"Very good. She has a real stage presence. However, overall I think she's a better pianist; that's where her true talent lies. She's still very beautiful," he added quietly.

"What will you do now, Jack?" asked Alastair.

"If she's not willing to see me, there's not much I can do, is there? I'm not going to go on bended knees and beg her to see me if she doesn't want to."

"Perhaps it's for the best."

"No, it's not!" Katherine suddenly expressed some of her pent-up frustration over Anna. "The two of you should be together. Why is she so foolish? And how can she bear not to have anything to do with Ben. He's her son for goodness' sake! She's missed out on so much. Just like her own father."

Alastair reached out for her hand, calming her agitation.

"You know," he remarked philosophically, "there is a trait in our family that seems to have been handed down through the generations. I can't say it's one I'm particularly proud of, but it's there nonetheless. There's physical beauty in the

148

women and good looks in the men but with that comes a high sex drive and the ability to walk away from marriage and children without a backwards glance."

"Roberta, Alex and Anna," said Katherine. "All very alike."

"Yes."

"My parents walked away from me."

"True, but the circumstances were different. It was done through the best of motives rather than purely selfish ones."

"The end result was similar, though."

"Not quite. You thought the people who brought you up were your real parents…"

"Anna grew up believing you were her father."

Alastair sighed. "That's true. And because we never told her when she was younger, it was our fault that she took it so badly when she did find out. And by accident, which made things even worse."

"I've always reckoned that she's never come to terms with that discovery," said Jack. "When she does, maybe she'll stop running away."

"Perhaps. But when she won't have anything to do with us, or you, or Ben, it's difficult to try and effect any kind of reconciliation," said Alastair.

"Were we wrong in waiting to tell her?" asked Katherine.

Jack smiled. "No. We all of us do what we think is best at the time. And then just have to muddle through and deal with the consequences afterwards."

"Dear Jack," said Katherine. "It's so good to see you."

He took her hand and kissed her cheek and put his other hand on Alastair's shoulder, his eyes full of warmth.

"It's good to see both of you, too."

However, Jack knew it was much, much more than that. Katherine and Alastair meant more to him than anyone else; more, that is, except Ben. And Grace.

Especially Grace.

With that thought, he helped them both to their feet and they walked home together in reflective silence.

CHAPTER 20

New York
Decisions

Marcia was late for work. Her cab was stuck in a traffic jam and she was thoroughly fed up. She had begun to hate New York. There seemed to be no escape from the constant noise, fumes, crowds of people on the sidewalks but above all, the loud brashness of it all.

She missed Australia. There was no doubt about it. She missed her friends; she missed the genteel surroundings of Melbourne. She was not like her mother who loved her work and the outback and could spend any amount of time in either place. No, Marcia liked her home town and her home comforts. She was very much like her father in that respect; not her stepfather, whose surname she had taken, but her real father who, before he died when she was twelve, had spent most of his time at home. True, he had had bouts of frustration when his ill-health stopped him from working and supporting the family, but her mother had told him not to be silly and that she was earning enough for all of them to live comfortably and that she would rather have him safe and well at home than risk his being ill yet again. He would acquiesce, but always rebelliously, and she remembered her mother laughing and them both kissing each other.

Marcia had loved her father. Whenever he was well enough, he had put what energy he had into her upbringing and her education: taking her to the theatre or the cinema or the public library and, when she was eleven, to the law courts to watch the trials. You were supposed to be fourteen to watch the trials, but Pa had always said to anyone who questioned it that she was the correct age and because he said it with such conviction, no one argued with him. Being tall had helped. She didn't understand most of what was going on in the courtroom, but he explained it to her clearly and with real understanding. She'd always felt proud that he knew so much.

However, one thing always puzzled her. He would never talk about his past and always avoided giving her a direct answer when she'd asked (as young children always do): "What did you do when you were little?" She'd then asked her mother why he would never tell her anything. She always replied that when Pa was ready, he'd talk about it, but if not, then it was best to leave well alone.

Marcia still missed her father. She and her mother had been devastated when he had died; things had been emotionally very difficult for a long time. Then, a couple of years later, her mother had met an old friend, someone she had gone out with before she'd known Pa and eventually, they got married.

She liked her stepfather. He was a kind man and made her mother happy, but Ma was never quite the same person after Pa died. A light had gone out of her life and she never completely regained her drive and energy. Marcia always reckoned that Pa was the love of her mother's life.

The cab driver woke Marcia out of her reverie.

"I'd walk if I was youse, sweetheart," he said. "We's not goin' nowhere."

Marcia sighed. "Okay." She paid him off and got out into the sweltering heat of a New York summer's day, eventually arriving at the offices of the *New Yorker* hot, harassed and extremely late.

Her day did not go well. She was harangued by the editor for her tardiness and then required to run tedious errands which the office boy should have done. Finally, when she collected her assignment, she found she'd been given, yet again, a murder case to cover. So back out onto the burning-hot pavements she went and hailed another cab to take her downtown. When she arrived, the crime scene was crowded with uniformed police, plain clothes detectives, forensic specialists and gawping members of the public.

She showed her journalist's pass and was allowed under the police tape. She managed a brief interview with the overworked and irritable detective assigned to the case and another with one of the ambulance crew who asked if she wanted to see the body. She declined.

Feeling sick with the heat and the gruesome details of the murder, Marcia wanted to escape. She'd had enough of this. Enough of America; enough of the unpleasant assignments that were being thrust upon her. When she'd brought the subject up with her immediate superior a while back, he'd told her to get on with the job and that if she wanted to be a reporter, then she had to take what she was given. Recently appointed, this editor wasn't in the business of pandering to her sensitivities, he'd said. She should either shut up or get out; he'd never wanted to take on some Aussie greenhorn in the first place.

After that, things had become considerably worse and Marcia found herself covering every obnoxious crime the editor could find in the city of New York. She felt sullied by her work; demeaned by her treatment. It had not turned out to be the aspirational, trailblazing job she had hoped.

Marcia had taken to wondering whether she could stick it out; whether she could complete her six-month secondment. If she didn't, then no newspaper would look at her; if she did, what damage might be done to her emotional wellbeing? Either way, her self-esteem would be in tatters. Perhaps she just wasn't cut out to be a journalist.

Resignedly, Marcia took another cab back to the office. That was something else that got her down about much of New York. No one walked anywhere. Well, you could walk in Manhattan, on Long Island, on the Upper East Side, in the wealthy business, shopping and residential areas. However, just turning a corner a few blocks down the street could take you into some sleazy, gang-infested area where every honest citizen went in fear of their life. This rapid change presented an uncertain environment in which to live and work and made her feel very insecure. She hated her noisy apartment block situated in a neighbourhood that she found threatening.

Upstairs at her desk in the drab, crowded, smoke-filled room that passed for the main office, she began to write up her report. But the words wouldn't come. She had no desire and no inclination to complete her assignment. Instead, she tore out the pages from her typewriter, screwed them up and threw them onto the floor in disgust.

Her sojourn in the States had been three months of progressive disillusionment. She had learned nothing of value; had been subjected to the most unpleasant of situations and all she wanted was to go home.

On the spur of the moment, Marcia put a fresh piece of paper into her typewriter and typed her resignation, requesting that she be released from the remaining three months of her secondment. In doing so, she knew she was saying goodbye to any hope she might have of pursuing a career in journalism; most certainly in America and most likely for the newspaper back home who had sponsored this trip with such naïve hope and enthusiasm.

Had they known each other, she wondered what Marcus Kendrick would have thought about her actions. Would he have said she ought to have more courage and stick it out, or would he have understood and said she was doing the right thing?

She wondered where he was at that moment. Despite her best efforts to track him down after returning from Chicago, he seemed to have disappeared off the face of the earth. His attorney was the only person who knew where he was and when Marcia had gone to his office and said she wanted to contact Marcus Kendrick, she had been given short shrift when she had revealed that she was a reporter and, after intimating that she was a friend, had been told that if Marcus had wanted her to know, then he would have told her. She had come away from this abortive attempt to find her idol with the feeling that altogether her trip to America had been a total waste of time.

Having tendered her resignation, Marcia realized she would now be able to go to Scotland after all. Once the inevitable fireworks had died down and she had served whatever notice she was required to do, she would make the travel arrangements and attend the birthday celebrations of a grandfather she had never met.

Back in her apartment that evening, Marcia reread the invitation she had brought from home. Perhaps this grandfather would be able shed light on Pa's mysterious past. Perhaps she would at last be able to understand why he would never talk about it.

She took out a pad of paper and wrote her acceptance.

Anna stood backstage in front of the noticeboard, unable to believe her eyes. The closure notice had just been posted for the play. Her play; her very successful play. True, audience numbers had dwindled in direct proportion to the soaring summer temperatures outside, but she could not believe what she was seeing. Usually in the searing heat at this time of year, Broadway theatres closed down for several weeks before the new season began and the plays, old and new, went out on tour into the provinces.

But not hers it would seem. Anna telephoned her agent and told him the news.

"Yeah, yeah, I know. It's a bummer," his laconic drawl offering her cold comfort. "Still, you've had a good run for your money. But try not to fret, honey. Something'll come up. Actress like you – a successful Broadway play under your belt, several TV shows to your credit. You'll be in great demand. I'll put out a few feelers, set up some auditions. It'll be all right, just you see."

But it wasn't all right. Even when the closure was made public, nothing came up and Anna knew she would be obliged to spend the remaining time in a sort of limbo; knowing the play would be ending, but not having any useful employment to look forward to.

She had been invited to a party that night and went along: the first since she and Marcus separated. She hadn't wanted to start a relationship with anyone else after she stopped seeing him or resume her casual affairs. He'd changed everything for her. It wasn't that no one could measure up to Marcus or that she had fallen in love with him. She hadn't, but her carefully buried emotions had been reawakened and all she could think about these days was Jack. She dreamed about him at night and thoughts of him filled her waking moments. Even when she was on stage or when she was practising the piano.

Ever since the day when Marcus had gone to collect his wife, Anna had been doing a great deal of practice and had applied, and been accepted, for lessons as an external student at the prestigious Gilliard Conservatory of Music. Her professor had been very impressed and his keen interest and praise for her playing had restored her confidence and her own enthusiasm. With all the work she was doing, even after a twelve year layoff, her facility had gradually returned to its former power and experience of life had given an added emotional depth to her playing.

She had been very happy these past months, dovetailing the play and the piano. It had worked well.

Her music was home; this was what she knew best. She couldn't wait to wake up in the morning and open the piano lid. She loved being on stage; she loved the feeling it gave but the deeper satisfaction came from her music. As time progressed, it began to take over her life and to exert a more compelling hold on her than the theatre.

After a series of lessons, her professor asked if she would be willing to perform in a benefit concert that he was organizing at the Carnegie Hall the following July. This was the second such benefit to be held and the previous year's event had proved to be a popular and prestigious occasion, he said, raising thousands of dollars for underprivileged children, giving them the opportunity to experience how music could transform their lives

He also told her that one or two famous soloists would be performing individual items or a movement from a concerto, giving their services for free, alongside specially selected students from the conservatoire. As a famous actress, she would be a considerable draw. The Gilliard Symphony Orchestra would be there to accompany the whole event, this in turn giving the students invaluable experience in performing with outstanding musicians at the top of their profession.

With fear and trepidation, Anna accepted. She wondered how she would feel performing among such illustrious company; she who had not played in public for so long and had abandoned her professional training after only three years. Perhaps, if by some remote possibility, it went well and no acting jobs came up, she might return to her original ambition and become a concert pianist. She knew she had been good enough at one time.

Jack had wanted her to be a concert pianist; Jack who had always supported her, who had loved her and who loved to hear her play, who had encouraged her when she'd found the pressures of performance too demanding, who had given her confidence when self-doubt in her abilities crept in.

They had spent hours together – she practising, he sketching and painting in the same room; neither distracting the other; happy and content in each other's company; happy in each other's talents.

What an idiot she'd been. To mess things up in the first place and then to refuse to see him when he'd come to the theatre a few weeks back. What a fool she was. Perhaps she should contact him.

Immediately, anxiety assailed her. No. She wasn't ready to do that. She was scared they'd never get beyond the inevitable impasse they had reached all those years ago.

But could they now? Had she left it too late? And what if, having been refused, Jack never came to her again; never wanted anything to do with her?

Wanting to escape, she opened the piano lid and, after warming up, played through the first movement of the Rachmaninov Second Piano Concerto. It was this movement she was to play at the benefit concert; the movement her professor had said would be ideal because it had been used with great success for the film *Brief Encounter* and would be perfect for her, as a famous actress, to perform.

What he didn't know, and what Anna didn't tell him, was that the whole concerto, which she'd first learned as a sixteen-year old, had always been hers and Jack's favourite and the film, about the sacrifice of romantic love, always made her cry, no matter how many times she saw it.

So, Anna went to the party that evening after the play and was introduced to a pleasant man with whom she spent an innocuous few hours. But she came home early and went to bed alone. The only person she wanted now was Jack.

Perhaps he would be at Alastair's eightieth birthday celebrations. Having decided not to bother, she thought that perhaps she would go after all; providing nothing came up, of course, on the acting front in the meantime.

A few days later, the innocuous man from the party called her and they went out for a meal. He was very attractive and very good company. Eventually, Anna succumbed and went to bed with him.

For the time being, all thoughts of Jack and the birthday party went out of her mind until one morning a few weeks later, after the benefit concert was over (to great critical acclaim for her performance) and the play had closed and nothing had come up, her new lover said he had to go to London on business and asked if she would go with him.

Without hesitating, Anna said yes. She didn't want him to go without her; she didn't want to be too far away from him. Perhaps she would go to the birthday jamboree; if she did, she needn't be absent from London for long, she told him.

It was time she faced up to her family. And Jack. And met her son. Or would that take more courage and more nerve than she possessed?

CHAPTER 21

Cairnmor
The Book

It had been a month since his collapse and Marcus was beginning to feel a great deal better. After an initial assessment by the doctor a fortnight after his collapse to confirm there was nothing seriously wrong, he had just spent two days in the cottage hospital undergoing a thorough physical examination and having various tests.

The doctor was very pleased with the results. His blood count was within normal parameters; his liver showed no abnormalities and his kidneys were functioning perfectly. His heartbeat was strong and even and his chest clear.

"Well, Mr Kendrick," he said, "I'm pleased to say that you are in perfect physical shape. Your collapse was no doubt due to the exceptional stress you've been under these last months, the lack of sleep and the unaccustomed consumption of alcohol. How do you feel now?"

"Fine, thanks, Doc. I couldn't be in better hands."

The doctor smiled. "I would imagine that is the case."

"But I still feel exhausted much of the time."

"That's only to be expected, given what you've told me. You've had a major trauma to deal with, as well as years of strain and abuse. It's bound to take its toll. A lesser man would have thrown in the towel a long time before you did." He looked at Marcus and smiled again, "But you can leave all that behind now, fortunately. Make a new start; a clean bill of health, so to speak," and he chuckled at his own witticism.

Marcus was pleased. To hear someone voice the very thing he had hoped for by coming to Cairnmor raised his spirits. To know that he had done himself no permanent damage by his stupidity engendered such relief that he felt his fear lift away.

The doctor consulted his notes. "What you do need, though, is to recover your physical strength and fitness. Good food, lots of rest in friendly surroundings and gentle exercise for the next month or so should do the trick. Mentally, you're recovering, but complete restoration will take time. Remember, be patient; don't rush things."

"Sure."

"How long are you able to stay on the island?"

"I have six months on my visa; well, five now."

"Good. This is the best place you could possibly be. Not having to rush around from pillar to post will be just the thing. Take it very easy."

"Gee, that means I'll have to cancel the day trip I was planning to make to Australia!"

The doctor laughed. "Yes, sorry about that." He stood up and offered his hand, which Marcus took. "Well, Mr Kendrick, it's nice to meet you and if you could make an appointment at the desk on your way out, I'd like to see you again in a month's time."

"Okay Doc, and thanks."

"You're welcome."

Having done as he had been asked, Marcus walked along to the hotel and paid his bill, cancelling his reservation. Alastair had said he would come and collect him in the land rover when he came out of hospital but the lobby was bustling with people and, as there was a long queue to use the telephone, Marcus didn't wait around.

It was a lovely day and feeling energized, he decided to walk. With only pyjamas, robe and shaving things to carry, he hoisted the knapsack that contained them onto his shoulder and set off. Even though he took his time, he was obliged to take frequent rests. By doing so, he had plenty of time to admire the view – and what a view it was. Stunning was the only way to describe it and he could not help but be drawn in by its beauty.

Ron was absolutely correct. This place does get to you. If I carry on like this, I shall never want to leave. Marcus felt his throat constrict at the thought of going away. Could he stay? Could he make a life for himself here?

After a couple of hours, he reached a sort of crossroads in the track and had to admit he was lost. He chose a path off to the left that meandered its way round the hillside and suddenly, he came upon a sunny spot sheltered from the breeze by a small wood where, tending a fragrant and colourful rose garden, he found Katherine.

"Hi!" he said.

She turned round in surprise and stopped what she was doing; secateurs poised in her gloved hands. "Marcus!" she exclaimed. "Goodness, did you walk?"

"Yeah. And maybe I shouldn't have. I'm exhausted."

"I'm not surprised. Here, come and sit down and have a drink of lemonade."

She retrieved a large bottle from the stream and poured some into a plastic tumbler. Marcus drank the cool, refreshing liquid gratefully.

"That's wonderful. Thanks."

Katherine came to sit beside him on the grassy bank. "So, what did they say at the hospital?"

"The doctor gave me a clean bill of health, but said I should take it easy for the next month or two."

"Anything else?"

"Good food, lots of rest and gentle exercise."

"So you decided to walk the two miles home... That's definitely taking it easy!" Katherine grinned at him.

"Yeah. Well..." he said sheepishly. "I guess I thought that as it was a lovely day..."

"Well, you seem to have survived, so that's something."

"I'm all right. Don't worry, Katherine, I'll be careful."

"You'd better," she said sternly, but with a smile, "I don't want my handiwork being undone."

"No, ma'am!" replied Marcus. "But I don't want to be a nuisance."

156

"You're not. Stay with us as long as you need to," she added, with genuine warmth.

He looked at her gratefully. "Thanks, I'd love that. But I'd hate to be a burden."

"You're no burden."

"I'm glad. Perhaps in a while, when I'm better and feel I can cope, there might be a cottage I could rent? I'd like to get back to my writing sometime. I have a novel half-finished and a publisher who very soon is going to start breathing down my neck."

Katherine laughed. "I know of just the place. It's one of the untenanted cottages that Grace looks after. But not quite yet." She knew he wasn't ready. However, she decided to seize the moment and put forward Alastair's idea. "In the meantime, Alastair and I have a suggestion to make that might just ease you gently into the world of work once again."

Marcus was immediately interested. "Yes?"

"I hope you won't consider it to be an imposition… it would be a tremendous help to me…"

"Anything. If I can repay your hospitality in any way, please tell me."

"It wouldn't be too arduous a task…"

"Katherine, just say it…!" and Marcus smiled at her.

Now that he has some colour back, he has a very attractive smile, she thought. *There's a great deal of character there, too. I'm not surprised that Anna got involved with him. Well, she has good taste in men, at least, with Jack and Marcus.* Katherine wondered how many other relationships Anna had had in between and sadly came to the conclusion that there would probably have been too many.

"Well, there used to be a resident of Cairnmor, a Mrs Gilgarry, who was an expert in herbal remedies. She knew her cures worked and had spent a lifetime experimenting and perfecting them. So, having lived to a ripe old age, when she realized she was growing frail, she asked me to write them all down for posterity. I did so and after she died, I thought they would make a very good book. So I started to compile all the information. Well, that was fine in itself and I've made good progress, but I wanted something more for the book; something more than a list of herbs and methodology for the cures."

"A peg to hang the coat on…"

"Exactly."

Marcus was silent for a moment. Then he asked, "What sort of person was she?"

"A real character. Feisty, independent and very decided in her opinions. She had an unending fund of stories to tell and was highly regarded by most people on the island who would walk miles to see her and be given a cure for their ailments. She gave short shrift to timewasters and malingerers but would do anything for someone whose need was very great. She came herself to treat Alastair when he went down with pneumonia in 1937."

For a few minutes, Marcus sat very still, then he smiled. "It seems to me that what you need to do is to incorporate Mrs Gilgarry herself into the book. Her life story, her character, some of the stories she told, the things she did. Are there other people, as well as yourself, who would remember her?"

"Plenty. Cairnmor seems to encourage longevity."

"Then I shall have to stay here, obviously."

Katherine smiled at him. "That's a wonderfully positive thing to say, Marcus. And we'd all be glad if you did. But wait and see how you feel a few months down the road; it would be a tremendous decision."

"Huge. But I've no desire to go back to the States, at least not at the moment." He went to help himself to another tumbler of lemonade. "May I?"

"Of course, go ahead. What you're suggesting for the book is just the sort of thing I had in mind, although I hadn't quite put it into coherent thought. In any case, I don't have the skills or the time to do it." She looked at him.

"But I do."

Katherine smiled. "Exactly. I'll help you all I can, but the creative side of it would have to be completely yours."

Marcus felt the glimmer of enthusiasm. "Okay, I'll take it on. Is there a deadline?"

"No, take your time."

"Will folks on the island mind if I ask them all kinds of questions?"

"No, not if you say that you're writing a book about Mrs Gilgarry. You'll get some interesting reactions but everyone who knew her will want to talk about her. I'll point you towards the right people and tell them what we're doing. I'll come with you if it's necessary to do any interpreting." She hesitated. "It'll be a lot of work for you."

"That's okay. If there's no deadline, then I can take my time and enjoy it."

"Thank you so much, Marcus. Now, what about money? Because writing is your profession."

"Money?" Marcus was caught by surprise. "I couldn't take a cent!"

Katherine regarded him, thoughtfully. "But you do have to have the means to live."

"I have enough. If I never worked again and my books continue to sell, I could make quite a respectable living from the royalties. Besides which, would you take any money from me for my board and lodging?"

"Of course not."

Marcus smiled. "Well, there we are, then."

"All right, I'll give in gracefully."

"Look on it as a favour and the perfect way to repay your kindness."

"Thank you, Marcus. Now, I must finish these roses and I suggest you find a comfortable spot and have a sleep. If you give me that tumbler, I'll have some lemonade."

"I'm so sorry Katherine, I didn't realize that was the only one."

"I wasn't expecting a friend, you see," and she smiled. "Besides which, you've just been given a clean bill of health from the hospital, so I think I'm safe from germs as we're having to share!"

Contentedly, Marcus lay back onto the soft mossy grass and was asleep within moments.

On the table after supper, Katherine spread out all the material she had collected on Mrs Gilgarry's remedies. Most of it was in shorthand but Marcus couldn't understand a word of it. "I'm not familiar with this system," he said puzzled. "As a reporter, I have to know and use shorthand, but I don't understand any of this."

Alastair, comfortably ensconced in his easy chair beside the range, said, "That's because it's in Gaelic."

"Gaelic?"

"The language that all the natives speak on Cairnmor," said Jack, who together with Ben, was laying out fishing flies at the other end of the table. "And some of us incomers as well."

"You speak Gaelic?"

"A little. Though as my sojourns here tend to be irregular, I don't have time to hone my very limited skills."

"Take no notice," remarked Alastair. "He speaks it fluently."

Marcus laughed. "I've always used Pitman's."

"What, to speak Gaelic?" asked Ben innocently.

"No, shorthand, dummy," and Jack gave Ben a friendly nudge with his elbow.

"I know. I was just teasing."

"That's what I use," said Katherine, "And this *is* Pitman's, but in Gaelic."

"That neat!"

"Do you remember," said Alastair to Katherine, "when you first decided to teach yourself shorthand while you were waiting for the twins to be born? We couldn't make head nor tail of it at first and we joked about Gaelic in shorthand being even worse than English."

Katherine laughed. "Yes, I do remember. I never thought I'd actually need to do that one day."

"What speeds can you do?" asked Marcus.

"Could – it's been a while. At one time I could do a hundred and twelve words per minute and sixty-five typing. In English, that is."

"Wow! I can do hundred words per minute and I thought that was pretty fast. My typing is about fifty."

"Katherine had the fastest speeds of any Wren we came across during the war," observed Alastair proudly. Katherine blew him a kiss.

Marcus smiled. "You don't use it now?"

"Occasionally at Island Council Meetings."

"Island Council Meetings?"

"The governing body of Cairnmor," said Alastair. "We meet once a month to discuss all sorts of things."

"Who's on it?"

"It's open to any resident on the island. They have to be elected, obviously, and then serve for two years after which, they must put their name forward for re-election should they wish to do so. Katherine and I, as joint trustees of Cairnmor, Cairnbeg and all the outlying islands, are ex-officio and permanent members of the council."

"Can anyone come and listen?"

"Yes. Why do you ask?"

"I'd like to do that, someday."

"You'd be more than welcome. Young Léon is coming to the next one. You can keep him in order."

"Who's Léon?"

"The family rebel!" said Jack. "Brought here in disgrace, I'm afraid, after getting thrown out of the Sorbonne for challenging the authorities once too often. He's been assigned to look after an untenanted farm to give him a dose of surviving in the real world. He's Phillippe du Laurier's eldest son," he added.

"Phillippe du Laurier's son?"

"Yes, the black sheep of the family and a right know-it-all!" said Ben. "Argues about everything. Thinks I should rebel against the system. When I said I was quite happy with the way things are and there was no point, he said I'd been 'cowed into submission by the wealthy ruling classes.'"

"What did you say to that?" asked Jack.

"I laughed at him and told him he was talking utter rot."

"Good for you."

"He wasn't very happy."

"I'm not surprised."

"Angus isn't very happy with Léon, either," continued Ben.

"Oh?" Alastair was immediately alert. "He hasn't said anything to me."

"I overheard him say to Shona that if he caught Léon playing fast and loose with Fiona again, he'd take a shotgun to him even if he was Phillippe du Laurier's son. What's 'fast and loose' mean?" he asked feigning ignorance.

"Ben!" exclaimed Katherine and much to her grandson's amused embarrassment, the assembled company laughed.

"It would seem that our latest family arrival still has a lot to learn," observed Jack, coming to the aid of his son. "He's been here how long – three or four months?"

"Yes. And he's been doing extremely well," added Alastair. "However, it sounds like I need to pay him an additional visit and have a chat with Angus about Fiona and Léon."

"Who's Fiona?" asked Marcus.

"Angus and Shona's eldest daughter," replied Katherine. "Angus is our farm manager and you may also be very interested to know that just by using his fist, Angus felled the sniper who shot Phillippe."

"Wow! It's a pity I didn't know all this when I interviewed Phillippe du Laurier. And the fact that you rescued him from Dunkirk!" said Marcus, thoroughly enjoying this conversation.

"Ah, you've been talking to Ron," said Alastair.

"I bought some stuff from him. He's quite a character."

"Aye, that he is."

Marcus continued to sift through the papers, reading the remedies that Katherine had already transcribed from shorthand.

"You know, it strikes me that what this book needs are illustrations for some of the herbs. You could use photos, but it would make it different and special if they were drawn or painted." He looked at Jack. "You're an artist. Could you do something?"

"Possibly." He stood up and came over to where Marcus and Katherine were seated and studied the documents. "Watercolour would be the most appropriate, I should think."

"But where would we get hold of examples?" asked Marcus.

"How about Mrs Gilgarry's cottage?" suggested Alastair, with a twinkle in his eyes. "It's the obvious place."

"Her cottage?"

"Yes, left exactly as it was the day she died. Grace has been looking after it."

"But that's great! Living history!" Marcus felt his spirits lift again.

Seeing this, Jack turned to his son. "When did you say you were going to spend a few days with your school-friend on Cairnbeg?" he asked.

"From Saturday. Is that okay?"

"Absolutely fine. In which case, Marcus and I will take a gentle hike over to Mrs G's and spend a few days soaking up the atmosphere. I can do preliminary sketches and take some photographs. How does that sound?"

"Sounds great," replied Marcus. "I'll bring my camera too. Is it far?" he added, looking at Katherine.

She smiled. "You'll manage."

"Okay, then. You're on." He turned to Jack. "I'd like to see some of your artwork, if I may."

"To make sure I'm good enough, huh?" teased Jack.

"No... no... I didn't mean that at all!" Marcus was embarrassed.

Jack put his hand on the American's shoulder, "It's okay, my friend, just weird British humour."

Marcus relaxed and shook his head. "I've never understood verbal teasing."

Jack chuckled. "We'll have to initiate you in that case. You mentioned seeing my handiwork? Come on then, now's as good a time as any," and he led the way into the sitting room.

"I saw this the first time I surfaced from my room," said Marcus, admiring the portrait of Anna, Rupert and Grace that hung over the fireplace. "It's an amazing painting. It's so vivid, the three of them seem as though they're here, in the room."

"Thanks." Jack smiled as he recalled: "Anna hated posing for it. She complained and squirmed and squiggled the whole way through. Grace, on the other hand, was as good as gold even though she was so much younger. She's always been willing to sit for me, even when she was little. She's an artist's dream. Her beauty may not be as obviously striking as Anna's but," and he considered for a moment, "it's softer and more classical in origin. She has a wonderful bone structure and an inner loveliness that shines out and makes her personality captivating and irresistible. In repose, her facial expression is gentle and kinder than her sister's. I could paint and draw her forever."

The wistfulness and longing in his voice caught Marcus's attention and he studied his companion with renewed interest.

"Anyway," continued Jack, taking a deep breath, "upstairs, I can show you some more examples of my stuff."

He took Marcus to Grace's room where they stood in the doorway. Marcus was astonished to see the walls covered with pictures.

He turned to Jack in surprise. "Are these all yours?"

"Yes."

"Their range and depth are tremendous."

However, it struck him forcibly that here before them, was the undeniable evidence of Grace's feelings for Jack.

"She's in love with you isn't she?" observed Marcus.

Jack nodded. But, when he spoke, his voice held uncertainty. "Or was. I'm not sure which now."

Marcus took this in, but chose not to remark upon it at that moment. Instead, full of admiration for Jack's ability, he said, "Some of these are fantastic." And he moved around the room looking carefully at each sketch, painting or drawing. "You're a talented guy. You should give an exhibition of your work."

"I'd love to do that one day," said Jack.

For Marcus, it was also obvious that surrounding them was the undeniable evidence of Jack's feelings for Grace.

"Grace is your muse," he said unexpectedly.

His words caught Jack by surprise. His heart beat faster and a frisson of pleasure went down his spine. "I'd never thought of her that way before."

It was odd, he considered, given the amount of time he had spent in her room over the years, that he had never before appreciated how much artwork he had done specifically for Grace. They were all here: his portraits of her, views of Cairnmor, its flora and fauna, life on board the Royal Navy ships that he had served in, as well as the ships themselves; all carefully mounted and displayed.

"Seems obvious to me." Marcus regarded him again. "And I'd hazard a guess that you care for Grace," he added.

"Oh yes, very much so," Jack replied quietly, his thoughts racing. "However, I'm so much older than she is."

Marcus shrugged. "Alastair is much older than Katherine. They've never let it worry them. Yet you say you're still in love with Anna?"

"I thought I was," responded Jack honestly. He took a deep breath and changed the subject, moving across the room to inspect a few drawings in a completely different style that were tucked away in a corner of the room. "I don't recognize these. They must be some of Sam's."

Marcus joined him. "His style's not bad but he's nowhere near the same league as you. You oughta quit the day job and take up painting fulltime."

Jack chuckled. "That was my original ambition. I'd been offered a scholarship to study at the Royal College of Art when the war broke out and then afterwards, I decided to stay on in the Royal Navy as I needed to support my family. I'd come to love the service and I'd seen too much action to want to go back to college, anyway."

"Do you regret that decision?"

"Not for a moment."

"Well, if you ever decided to quit the navy, you could make a very decent living as an artist."

"Perhaps, but art rarely sells."

"Illustrations do, though!"

Jack laughed. "I'll consider it. When we've finished this book, do you think it would be the sort of thing that a publisher would be interested in? Because I'd love to see that happen for Katherine's sake. Mrs Gilgarry would have been tickled pink as well, if she'd still been alive."

"You knew her?"

Jack nodded. "Yes."

"I'll pick your brains when we're at her cottage. To answer your question, if the book turns out well, I'll certainly send it to my publisher."

"Thank you. However, we'll keep that between ourselves for the moment. I would rather like it to be a surprise if we're successful." He smiled. "Well, my friend, you're looking tired. I suggest you go and get your beauty sleep. You're going to need all the energy you can muster in a couple of days' time."

Gratefully, Marcus said, "Night, Jack, and thanks."

"You're welcome. Goodnight."

Once in his room, Jack stayed up late looking through his portfolios. There were pictures of Anna but there were many, many more of Grace and his heart stirred at the sight of them. When they'd been together, Anna hadn't always wanted to pose for him and she'd often made it difficult for him to work on his other paintings by constantly demanding his attention.

However, she'd always wanted Jack to sit with her and do his art work while she was practising the piano and to please her, he had done so without complaint but, if he were honest, he never managed to achieve a great deal because he had to be as silent as possible so as not to disturb her concentration. Because he'd loved her and admired her talent, he'd coped and when he could, completed the pictures later while she was attending her classes at college. Jack had always been careful never to let her see his reluctance.

Grace, on the other hand, had always been willing to sit for him. His thoughts strayed to the day in London just after she had finished her degree when she had, in all innocence, offered to pose for him because he was bemoaning the shortage of good life-models. He had hesitated at first because she was Katherine's and Alastair's daughter but in the end he had agreed, salving his conscience by covering her nakedness with discreet swathes of blue material that perfectly matched the colour of her eyes.

Seeing her in this way had affected him profoundly. For the first time he had wanted to make love to her; for the first time he had thought of her as someone other than just the girl who had always held a very special place in his heart. For the first time he saw her as the woman she had become. The memory of their subsequent kiss after the graduation ball and of holding her in his arms came back vividly to him and he realized it was quite possible that he really was, after all, in love with Grace.

But what of Anna, the woman he had cherished in his mind for so many years? Perhaps she was just a dream; an illusion of remembered love that had no basis in the reality of his present life. Perhaps, he reasoned, instead of trying to leave Grace behind emotionally and cling onto the memory of Anna, he should dismiss from his mind once and for all the woman he had married and once loved so passionately.

He sighed. If only it could be as simple as that.

Jack stared into the middle distance for a very long time debating within himself; worrying about Grace and Sam; dwelling on the irony that the understanding of his feelings for Grace may have come too late for him to have any hope of realizing them.

Eventually, he put his artwork away, climbed into bed and slept.

CHAPTER 22

Realization

London was busy. The traffic and hot, crowded pavements were making Grace feel hemmed in. At Cambridge she had coped with being away from Cairnmor because her surroundings were aesthetically pleasing and the open spaces of the Fens not too far away. And she had loved the Backs and the gentle River Cam.

Grace understood how difficult it must have been for her mother to have made the adjustment when she first came to live in London. Her mum always said that she wouldn't have coped at all if it hadn't been for her friendship with Grace's dad.

She was alone in the house; her solitude welcome. Sam was at Imperial College for the day, rehearsing for the ceremony and seeing friends. Grace had chosen to stay in Cornwallis Gardens where it was cool and peaceful. This was the only place she liked when in London. And Horse Guards Parade, strangely enough, with the wonderful Admiralty Building. The parks were all too small and the traffic fumes all-pervasive.

Grace went into the sitting room and put her feet up on the sofa, staring into the empty fireplace. She thought of Jack and the day he had painted her, here, in this room, and how, watching him as he worked, she had seen such an intense expression of desire for her in his eyes that, as the minutes ticked by and she had felt less embarrassed by her semi-nakedness, she had wanted to brazenly cast aside the swathes of material and reveal everything to him.

Grace blushed at the memory. She had, course, been too shy and innocent to do anything as reckless as that.

She had never seen the same desire for her in Sam's eyes. Nor did she have any inclination to throw herself at him in quite the same, shameless way she had resisted with Jack. For all his physical prowess when they were out sailing together, her boyfriend was not a passionate man and Grace needed someone who was passionate. She and Sam had not slept together; neither of them having suggested nor pressed the point, despite moments of intimate exploration. If they should get married, as they had often discussed, might she feel differently when they actually went to bed with each other? Would Sam be right for her physically?

Did she even want to get married to Sam? She wasn't sure. Did she want to marry Jack? Of course she did, but that was the impossible dream; had always been the impossible dream. Perhaps she should forget the dream and settle for a less than perfect reality. After all, she did care about Sam and find him attractive. They were good friends and had everything in common.

However, the prospect of marriage to Sam didn't exactly fill her with joyous anticipation. A tiny niggle at the back of her mind set her wondering if the relationship itself had run its course. Latterly, they had not talked with the same ease and spontaneity as they had done in the past; indeed, since coming to London, they had hardly talked at all.

Grace lay down on the sofa and slept, experiencing an unusual, overwhelming sense of *ennui*.

The day after Sam's doctorate had been conferred, the congratulations and celebrations completed and recovered from, Grace, Sam and his parents went to the Savoy Grill for a celebratory meal. Grace was very quiet throughout, waiting for Sam to raise the subject of his living on Cairnmor. He didn't, so, at the end of the meal, Grace did, jumping in with both feet.

"When Sam and I are married," she announced, "we're going to live on Cairnmor."

"No, no, my dear," said Sam's father soothingly. "Sam is going to be working in the family firm in Glasgow, aren't you, my boy?"

"Er…" Sam's face was as white as a sheet.

She waited for him to speak but he said nothing. *Well, if he can't talk, then I shall do the talking for him*, thought Grace, frustrated by his lack of gumption.

"He loves the island and wants to make his home there. His ambition is to become warden of the nature reserve he's going to help my father and me create," she said, going right to the heart of the matter, cutting Sam no slack whatsoever. There had to be a definite decision. It was make or break time.

"What?" Sam's mother was horrified. "A *wildlife* warden?" She couldn't believe what she was hearing.

"Your son loves the outdoors. He loves fresh air and wide open spaces, or hadn't you realized that? His doctorate is in Botany. He doesn't want to be stuck in some stuffy office in the centre of a city."

"Grace! That's enough!" Sam looked at her aghast and then at his parents, his expression full of fear and anxiety.

"It's always been understood that when Sam finished his education, he would come to work with me." His father was stern.

It's now or never, thought Grace. "Perhaps he doesn't want to."

"Doesn't want to?" spluttered Sam's father. "This is the first I've heard of it. Is this true, my boy?"

"Well, er…" Sam looked at Grace in a panic. *What on earth was she doing?*

"We've discussed it so many times. He's talked about it at length with both my parents."

Some impish, mischievous side of her character made her persist with landing Sam in a place where he obviously did not want to be; where he, for whatever reason, had misled her into thinking that he wanted to stay on Cairnmor – with her.

Sam's father thumped the table with his fist. "Be quiet, girl, and let the boy speak."

"He's not a boy, he's a man of twenty-four and you're not allowing him to make up his own mind." Grace was not going to be deflected.

Sam's father ignored her and addressed his son who had covered his face with his hands. "Well, do you?"

"I don't know; I don't know," he muttered.

"This is ridiculous," said Grace, losing patience. "If you meant what you've always said to me ever since I've known you, then stand up for what you really want. Fight for it. But make a decision. I need to know one way or the other."

Sam looked at her, distraught. "How can I?" he said.

166

"Just do it," she replied.

Sam's father wagged his finger at his son. "If you do this thing and go to live on Cairnmor, then you will have broken every promise you ever made to your mother and I. Let me warn you now, if you go and live on this... this island and pursue this ridiculous idea, you will no longer be welcome in our home as our son."

"It's all right Father," said Sam, taking a deep, shuddering breath. He turned to Grace and took her hand in his. "Being on Cairnmor was like being on a wonderful holiday in a very special place that I came to love but now, the holiday's over. I really do have to work for my family."

"And what about you and I?" she asked, her eyes filling with tears, all impatience gone. "Were we just part of your 'wonderful holiday' as you so aptly phrased it?"

"No, of course not! Surely, we don't have to live on Cairnmor to be together?"

"Oh, but we do," she said, removing her hand from his. "You know we do," she added sadly.

Grace wiped away the tears that were spilling down her cheeks. How little he understood her; how little he loved her; how little she really loved him.

Quietly, Grace got up from the table, carefully replacing her chair under the table.

"Goodbye, Sam," she said and turning, walked out of the restaurant.

She took a taxi to Cornwallis Gardens, packed her things and caught the first train she could from Euston Station back to Scotland and *home*.

Imperceptibly, the days on Cairnmor were beginning to shorten. Twilight didn't seem to go on forever; darkness came early again to the northern hemisphere.

Léon stood outside his cottage, surveying his croft; waiting for Fiona to come to him as she had promised. He had been on the island for nearly four months now; four months of hard, back-breaking labour and the greatest inner satisfaction he had ever experienced. He had gained weight and strength and revelled in being physically fit, able to join with the other crofters on equal terms. He still had much to learn, but the greatest joy to him had been Fiona, who had taught him so much and worked alongside him on the croft and on the machair.

He remembered the first day he had been taken to the cottage where he was to live and make his living; how he had been appalled by its rundown state, its lack of facilities and home comforts. He recalled how he had rebelled, refusing to do anything.

On the defensive and feeling very afraid, he had flown into a rage, berating his father and his grandfather in an abusive torrent of French, completely forgetting the latter's warning that Katherine, standing by Alastair's side, spoke the language fluently. Upset at the way Léon had insulted her husband, she had replied in kind, pointing out the errors of his ways in no uncertain terms, sparing him nothing.

He hadn't expected such a vitriolic reply and Léon now remembered with embarrassment how he had sat on the floor after everyone had gone and wept like a small child; how Fiona, on her way back from school had come into the cottage, curious to see the new arrival, and found him; how her soft voice and gentle manner had soothed him. He had listened to her after that while she told him exactly what he needed to do now that he was a crofter.

However, her parting words were very firm. She told him he should pull himself together, stop behaving like a spoilt brat and just get on with things; that she would come again the next day, as it was a Saturday, and help him clean the range so that at least he could be warm and cook himself some food.

"But I don't know how to cook," he'd protested.

Fiona was kind, but uncompromising. "Then ye'll just have to learn, won't ye?" she'd replied. "I'll teach ye."

So she did. After overcoming his initial reluctance, Léon learned quickly and over time after enduring many disasters, came to be proud of his culinary skills.

Together, on that first day, they swept and cleaned the little cottage and made it habitable. During that first week, after Fiona had finished school each day, they went out searching for furniture, enquiring about any castoffs that other crofters might have. Through this, Léon acquired a small table and a couple of easy chairs, a saucepan or two, some cutlery and plates and, most importantly, he gradually became acquainted with the generous folk whose fate he now shared.

When Angus and Alastair brought him his first animals, Léon was once again at a loss.

"Ye'll figure it out, lad," said the big man. "Look after them kindly, keep 'em fed and watered and they'll repay ye a hundred-fold," he'd added. "There's enough feed in yere little barn to keep ye going until ye earn some money from yere own labours. The pasture on this croft is first-rate. Let the cows graze. The grass is good at this time of year. Don't worry, we'll not let the animals starve."

"What about me?" he'd muttered, still surly.

"Ye've chickens and the cows. They'll provide yere immediate needs. And as for yere flock of sheep, when it's shearing time, ye can make a pretty penny from a good fleece at the mainland markets."

They'd gone away then and when Fiona came after school, she'd shown him how to milk the cows and they shared part of his first bucketful. The milk tasted creamy and was full of flavour, far better than any Léon had had back in France. He drank greedily, for he was hungry, and after she had shown him how to fry some eggs, with good food inside him, Léon began to feel more able to cope.

The next morning, after he'd collected the eggs from the hens and finished his breakfast, Angus appeared and took him in the land rover to the machair, showing him the strips of land and the enclosures that were to be his.

"Somewhere under these weeds, lad, ye'll find a crop of potatoes. The previous tenant planted them before he died and they've been sadly neglected these past weeks. They need hoeing and the beds raised up afterwards."

"Why?"

"Stops the sun getting to 'em and making 'em green. They're poisonous when they get like that."

Léon had never realized that potatoes could be poisonous. They'd always come exquisitely prepared at home and heaped on his plate at the Sorbonne. The Sorbonne. His other life seemed a world away.

"Now there's oats over here. Again, ye'll have to clear the weeds."

"Oats?"

"Cereal crop."

"Qu'est-ce que ? What?"

"Cereal crop. You can use it to make bread and porridge."

"I cannot make bread."

"I expect Fiona will teach you. She's been spending enough time at yere cottage." His expression darkened.

"Fiona has been very helpful."

"Yes, she's a good girl." Angus had looked at him then. "Be careful, lad. Remember yere manners when yere around her."

Although Léon didn't quite understand all the words, he understood the inference.

He shrugged. "Of course."

Angus looked at him again and his final words as he drove away, were, "Ye'll be able to make some money from the potatoes and the oats. The bakery needs a regular supply and the grocer sells vegetables and eggs. Keep enough for yere own needs and sell the surplus to the shops."

Léon watched the land rover disappear and then looked across the machair to the mountains beyond. It was a beautiful landscape but for the present, he had no time to enjoy it. With a sigh, he began the back-breaking task of clearing the weeds on his allotted land.

He began by using just his hands but other crofters labouring nearby took pity on him and lent him tools to make his work easier. They worked alongside him to get him started, showing him how the potatoes would be harvested in the time-honoured way once they were ready and explaining why the oats grew so close to the ground.

"Aye, it's the wind, ye see. If the poor little stalks were any higher, there'd be nothing left of the crop once the wind's whistled its way across the island. Have ye got any peat yet?"

"Peat?"

"For the fire."

"Oh, that. There's a stack of it next to the house."

"Aye, but ye'll need more. Ye'll use that up, soon enough. Tomorrow we'll show ye where the peat is for your croft. We'll help ye to cut it when the time comes."

Léon had felt overwhelmed by their generosity.

Soon after that, he'd experienced his first storm. Fiona arrived unexpectedly on his doorstep, the wind howling through the eaves.

"We must go and bring the cows into the barn and shut up the chickens. The sheep will have to take their chances. It's too late to bring them in from the machair. Did ye not look up at the sky and see the storm brewing?"

"The sky?"

"Yes, the sky," she repeated impatiently. "Let's just hope they'll be all right. Well, don't just stand there. We must get to work!"

So they did. The rain lashed down and when they had finished, they ran into the croft, pushing the door shut behind them.

Léon had found the whole experience exhilarating and Fiona smiled at him as she rubbed her hair with a towel. She put the kettle onto the range to make them a cup of tea and told Léon to put more peat on the fire. They needed to keep warm; they didn't want to catch a chill, she'd said.

She'd asked him about France, then, and university. For the first time in weeks, he was able to talk about politics and what he believed.

"Has being here changed your views?" she'd asked him.

He hesitated before replying, but when he did, it was reflectively. "The people here on Cairnmor are not downtrodden slaves to the wealthy ruling classes," he finally admitted.

Fiona smiled. "Aye, I agree with ye there and I'm very glad to hear ye say it. We live the life we do because it's what we want to do. We have the freedom to choose exactly how we want to live."

"But you do not own the land."

"Aye, that's true. Mostly everyone is a tenant farmer, but they regard their crofts as their own to do with as they wish and I know that Alastair and Katherine are trying to find ways of enabling the crofters to purchase their land if they should wish."

"And what about you, Fiona, what do you want to do?" He'd been curious.

"Have my own croft one day, though Pa is dead set against it. He says I'm the clever one in the family and that I should go to the university. But I think not."

"Why?"

"I like it here. I leave school next month and they've told me that if my Higher results are good enough, I can apply for a correspondence course and get my degree that way."

"Which subject will you choose?"

Fiona had laughed. "Believe it or not, social and political history!"

He'd kissed her then and she hadn't resisted his embrace.

So, tonight, she had agreed to share his bed for the first time. The anticipation was almost too much for him to bear. They had come very close many times but she had always drawn back; wanting to be certain of his feelings for her; unwilling to take the risk of committing herself to him until she was. Léon understood and had been patient but knew that the time had now come for them to belong completely to each other.

He spotted her as soon as she appeared at the base of the hill and impatiently he waited for her to reach him. When she did so, they stood for a moment looking at each other before he took her hand and led her inside.

"Any problems?"

"No. No one knows. Yet."

Much later, as the remaining hours of darkness crept towards morning, inside the little cottage – with its check curtains and matching cushion covers that Fiona had made, and the quiet orderliness and cosiness that she had created – the lovers slept peacefully in each other's arms.

However, there was no peace in Angus MacKellar's household when Fiona's younger sister discovered that she was not in her room and that her bed had not been slept in. She immediately went to tell her father.

170

What happened next became legendary across the island – how Léon, the reprobate son of a French aristocrat used his considerable Gallic charm to seduce Fiona, the lovely, innocent peasant's daughter, and have his wicked way with her; how Angus, her outraged father, thrust a loaded shotgun at Léon's throat and was about to pull the trigger when Alastair came charging up the hill in the Morris Traveller and bravely disarmed him before anyone was hurt.

The truth was far more prosaic, yet no less dramatic because of it, and went like this:

Alastair and Katherine were seated at the breakfast table having an early morning cup of tea – Marcus, Jack and Ben had not yet surfaced – when Shona, Angus's wife, burst into the kitchen utterly distraught.

"He's going to kill Léon. He is! He is! He's taken the shotgun and a whole box of cartridges and gone in the land rover over to Léon's croft."

"Whatever for?" exclaimed Katherine, taken aback by her housekeeper's unexpected entrance.

Shona burst into tears. "Fiona's spent the night with him. He's a wicked boy and has deflowered my daughter"

"Ah." Katherine put her hand over her mouth to hide her amusement; trying to stop her shoulders shaking with suppressed laughter. She shouldn't really find it funny. Perhaps it was the phrase, 'deflowered my daughter', that set her off.

Alastair looked at her sternly. It really was no laughing matter.

"You don't know that for certain," he said, in a vain attempt to calm things down.

"Oh yes, I do. Many times Fiona has arrived home with her hair dishevelled and her clothes all untucked in a most unbecoming way. Angus has even caught them together kissing and canoodling…" her bottom lip trembled in indignation, "…on Léon's bed. My husband warned him; said he'd take a shotgun to him if he didn't stop playing fast and loose with his daughter."

"Where is Fiona now?"

"At Léon's. She must be. Her bed hasn't been slept in all night. She's only seventeen. She's much too young."

Alastair sighed. "I'll go up there," he said. "I'll take Morris as Angus has got the land rover. I hope it can manage the slope."

"Shall I come with you?" asked Katherine.

"No, my love, stay here with Shona."

He regarded the weeping woman with impatience. Thank goodness *his* wife was more level-headed than this.

Alastair set off and drove the car up the hill as far as it would go, then quickly walked the rest of the way. He arrived to hear shouting and sobbing coming from inside the cottage.

Angus was bawling at Léon, "I warned you. I told ye to stay away from my daughter but ye wouldna listen. Yeve been nothing but trouble since ye arrived. I wish ye'd never come here. Yere nothing but a disgrace to your father who is a very great man and whom I am proud to know. But ye…" and Angus spat on the floor, "…are nothing but a no-good waster and an insult to the name of du Laurier."

Léon couldn't utter a word with the shotgun against his throat, nor could he risk it going off accidentally by trying to fight his way out, but he was not going to be cowed. Oh no, he was not. Defiantly, Léon stood his ground, matching Angus's stare, not giving way by so much as a flicker of an eyelid.

When Alastair entered the cottage, the scene was thus: there, pinned up against the wall was Léon, while Fiona was sobbing into her apron at the kitchen table.

"Angus, put the gun down," he said quietly, but with unmistakable authority. "It's not worth wrecking your life by killing someone."

"He's wrecked my daughter's life."

"We don't know that."

"Oh yes, we do. When I arrived, they were in bed together fast asleep and as naked as the day they were born." He gave the gun another thrust into Léon's throat. "How dare ye force yereself on my daughter."

"He didn't, Pa. It was both of us."

"What do ye mean? Both of ye? Ye mean ye let him?"

"Yes." Fiona could be defiant too.

"Then yere no better than a common hussy and no daughter of mine."

Fiona began to cry again. "I love him."

"Yere too young to know what ye want."

"Angus, this is not helping anything."

Alastair looked round the kitchen as he spoke and saw the bright domestic changes everywhere. Within its friendly comfort, he realized that these two had been quietly building a home together over the past few months. He looked at Léon and winked at him.

Léon saw this and his eyes lit up. His grandfather knew, he understood.

"Put the gun down, Angus, and let's talk about this in a calm and reasonable manner."

Knowing that Alastair was his friend as well as his employer and that he had outranked him during the war, reluctantly and carefully, Angus lowered the gun and put it on the table. Immediately, Fiona rushed over to Léon, her eyes full of love for the young man standing beside her. He put his arms around her, wiping away her tears.

After a moment or two, Alastair broke the ensuing silence by saying to Fiona, "I think, my dear, a cup of tea would be most welcome then perhaps we can all sit down and talk together like civilized human beings."

Alastair watched Léon carefully as Fiona went across to the sink and filled the kettle with water, placing it on the range. The young man's eyes never left her and from his expression, his grandfather knew with absolute certainty that Léon was truly in love.

He picked up the shotgun and opened the barrel. It was empty. He looked up in surprise at his farm manager.

"Och, Alastair, ye don't think I'd be so daft as to stick a loaded shotgun at someone's throat, do ye?"

Alastair didn't know whether to laugh or punch him on the jaw. He exchanged a glance with Léon and saw the same expression mirrored in his face.

With the tea poured and on the table, Léon was the first to speak, addressing Angus. "Before you threaten me or demand anything, I want to say something to you. What happened last night was not some random event. I love your daughter and she loves me. We want to get married."

"Never. I'll never give my consent."

"Then we'll run away," said Fiona. "I'm eighteen next month and anyway, across on the mainland, I can get married legally without your say-so."

"Yeve corrupted my daughter, ye no-good…"

"He's done no such thing, Angus." Alastair could see the irate parent's expression darkening, so he added quickly, "Well, in a manner of speaking, perhaps…" Having pacified him by this small act of diplomacy, Alastair continued: "But that's not what's important now. What's done is done and cannot be undone. So, we must look to the future. These two young people are in love. It's very obvious to me. And look around you. The evidence of their desire to be together is here in the cottage, on the machair, in the animal enclosures. We've been so pleased, you and I, with the practical progress that's been made on this croft that we've forgotten to look at the most important thing: they've been working together, Angus, and falling in love in the process." Here, Alastair paused and smiled disarmingly. "And I would have said that for them to get married was rather essential, wouldn't you, given the circumstances of your discovery this morning?"

Clever Grandpapa, thought Léon. He picked up Fiona's hand, choosing that moment to show off the ring with its tiny diamond that sparkled on her third finger.

"This has taken every penny I've managed to earn," he said proudly, recalling all the original and enterprising things he had done to supplement the income from his croft.

Alastair chuckled. "Well, you won't be going anywhere for a while then."

"Non. C'est vrai. I am staying here. *Ici.* This is where I now belong and shall make my home." Nothing was going to make him change his mind.

"What about your inheritance?" asked Alastair, proud of the way his grandson had turned out and in such a short space of time as well.

"Your inheritance?!" exclaimed Fiona, her eyes wide with surprise.

"I am the eldest son of a French aristocrat, *ma chérie.* I stand to inherit a fortune one day."

"But…"

"Do not worry. To have so much money would not sit well with my conscience. Besides, I have two brothers and two sisters who are far better suited to looking after the family pile than I am. I shall forever be the wayward son…"

"…who redeemed himself by hard work," interrupted Alastair, "and found his true identity and his true love on a remote Scottish island."

Léon looked at him gratefully. *"C'est vrai. Merci, Grand-papa."*

"'s ur beatha." And they both laughed.

Alastair persuaded Angus to let Fiona stay with Léon. There was work to do on the croft and it needed both of them to complete it. The wedding date was set for the beginning of September and once they were outside, Alastair said to Angus, "Look upon it this way, my friend. Whatever you may think of Léon at the moment, I don't think it would be too fanciful to suggest that Phillippe would say it was one of those occasions when forces beyond our control bring people together. I think it's rather special that your daughter and Phillippe du Laurier's son are to be married."

"As long as he does marry her," said her father, who, after Alastair's clear appraisal of the situation, was exhibiting a complete reversal of his previous attitude. Outwardly, Angus remained dour but somewhere inside him was an appreciative spark for Alastair's words.

"Oh, he will. He'll have me to answer to if he doesn't! No, my friend, it will work out fine. And they'll be happy too. Your daughter is a clever girl and all your grandchildren will be trilingual."

Angus looked puzzled. "What do you mean?"

"Léon has been teaching her French and Fiona's been teaching him Gaelic. They both speak English, so there's your third language. Katherine's been having great fun with them when they've come to visit us. Shona will tell you." Alastair put his hand on Angus's shoulder. "Don't think too badly of them. There's a lot of his father in Léon that has yet to manifest itself and a lot of you in Fiona's character. They'll be fine together." He opened the door of Morris. "See you back at the farm. There's a few things we need to talk about regarding those new enclosures."

"Aye, that there is."

After Angus had gone, Alastair sat in the car for several minutes and closed his eyes. He felt very tired. Perhaps it was time he eased off a bit and handed the reins over to someone else. But who? Grace already had her contribution to the running of the island mapped out and it would be too much for Katherine to manage on her own. Sam, should he figure in Grace's future (and Alastair doubted that he would), just didn't have the strength of character and Rupert wasn't interested.

There was only one person whom Alastair wanted to work alongside him and then ultimately take over from him and that was Jack. He sighed. He knew it was impossible given Jack's commitment to the Royal Navy and unfair even to suggest it to him.

Alastair started the car and carefully drove home. He'd have to manage for a few more years yet, it would seem, until a suitable candidate could be found. At least it kept him active and he did know how to pace himself. And he and Katherine did share the load. And more than anything, he loved working with Katherine. Except for just being with her, of course.

CHAPTER 23

Remedies

Jack and Marcus set off for Mrs Gilgarry's cottage in good spirits. They travelled as far as the track in the post bus and once it had driven away, surveyed the belongings strewn at their feet. They had a great deal of luggage: sleeping bags, rucksacks, provisions, an easel, cameras. Jack looked with some concern at Marcus.

"How much of this stuff can you manage? It might be better for me to make a second journey."

"I'll be fine. I don't need a nursemaid."

"I know that," replied Jack, wondering at his friend's tetchiness. "Actually," he added tactfully, "It's not you I'm thinking of. It's me. Or rather, Katherine's reaction to me when I get you home bent double and bandy-legged with all the weight I've insisted you carry!"

"Sorry. For some reason I suddenly feel irritable."

Jack smiled at him. "I hadn't noticed."

"Sure you had. You're just too polite to say. Very English."

"Ah, but you should hear me on the occasions when I do let rip."

"I'm not sure I want to!"

"Very wise." And the two men smiled. "Now let's apportion out this lot. You take all of it and I'll just stroll nonchalantly beside you and make sure you don't topple over."

Marcus looked at him aghast.

"Verbal teasing, my friend."

"I guess I'll never get the hang of that, ever."

"In that case, I'll do my best to spare you."

Between them the two men sorted out the luggage and set off along the narrow grass track. It was a lovely morning, warm and sunny. Marcus remarked on the scenery of Cairnmor.

"It's beautiful, isn't it?" replied Jack. "In all my travels, I've never come across anywhere quite like it. Now, if you think Lochaberdale is stunning, wait until you see Gleann Aiobhneach. It's just the most spectacular place I've ever been to."

"You love this island, don't you?"

"With all my heart. It's been my home for a very long time now. I can't imagine living anywhere else, nor would I want to. When I eventually leave the navy, this is where I want to be, even when Ben has grown up and possibly moved away."

"What about Anna?"

"Anna?" The question caught Jack by surprise. He hadn't given Anna a thought in his deliberations as to where he would live. He had always known it would be Cairnmor and she had not figured in his plans, despite his remembered feelings for her; despite being unable to let go of her emotionally over the years. "I have no idea. When we were first married, she couldn't wait to leave. However, when she was young, she'd always enjoyed rambling and exploring but never with the same passion that Grace has for the island."

"Anna is definitely a city girl." Marcus stared ahead and fell silent.

"It's odd, isn't it," remarked Jack, "us meeting like this, forming a friendship?"

"Yeah."

"Anna meant a great deal to you, didn't she?"

"Yeah."

"But she threw you over without so much as a 'by your leave'."

"Yeah."

"If it's any consolation, in effect, she did the same to me."

"Yeah?"

"I don't suppose she ever told you why we split up?"

"No, she didn't but I've always been curious. For two people who supposedly loved each other as much as you and Anna, it must have been something major."

"It was. Look, why don't we take a breather? We've been walking for a while and I could do with a drink and something to eat."

They shrugged off their backpacks and dumped their other bags on the ground, finding the sandwiches, cake and lemonade which Katherine had thoughtfully provided. Marcus sprawled on the grass, while Jack chose to sit on a rocky outcrop, looking across to the ocean where sunlight sparkled and danced on the water. He took a deep breath.

"This is not going to be an easy conversation. For either of us."

"Well, I'm over her now, I guess. That's the hope. In any case, I'm a good listener and I want to put the final piece into the puzzle."

Jack nodded. "It also makes it easier that you already know something of our history. When Anna and I first moved to London, we were blissfully happy. There is no other way to describe it. Anna was revelling in her freedom and independence and making excellent progress at the Guildhall while I loved being at the Admiralty. Those first two years were the happiest I had ever known. However, at the beginning of her third year, things began to change.

"She became friendly with some students at one of the London drama schools and began spending more and more time with them and less time with me. She also neglected her music studies to such an extent that she had to attend an interview with the principal of Guildhall.

"Naturally very concerned, as soon as I found out about this from one of her friends on the music course, I lectured her on her responsibilities, how she was being unprofessional and wasting her talent. She said she didn't care about music anymore, that all she wanted was to be an actress. I said that that was impossible; she declared it wasn't and we had the most almighty row.

"With her being so young, I felt it was my responsibility and duty in the absence of her parents to keep her on an even keel. At my insistence, she gave up her drama ambition and newfound friends and focused on the piano once more.

"For a few months things seemed to be going smoothly again for us until she fell pregnant. I was over the moon with joy but she was distraught and threw a huge tantrum. Even though I pointed out that the baby would be born after she had completed her three years at the Guildhall, Anna was still hysterical. She didn't want a baby, she said. She didn't want to be saddled with a child and have it wreck her career. She said she hated me for getting her pregnant and restricting her freedom. She also said I was a stuffy, boring old man whom she didn't dare tell her friends about and she was embarrassed by being married to me."

"My God," said Marcus. "That must have hurt."

"It did."

"But she was so in love with you."

"I know or at least I thought she was. But I've often wondered since then if before we were married, I perhaps represented some imaginary sophisticated outside world and that was the basis for her feelings rather than real love."

"I think she saw you as a mature, very handsome, sexy man."

Jack laughed. "I'm hardly that. However, I felt I was her protector as well as her lover. She needed that otherwise…"

"…knowing Anna as we both do…"

"…her libido would have got the better of her." Jack grimaced, knowing what was to come.

"Yeah. So, what happened next?"

"You can imagine how I felt at that point. Upset and shocked doesn't even begin to describe it. But then she absolutely floored me by declaring she was going to have an abortion. That she didn't want the child. That she'd already made enquiries and found a safe, clean and reliable place that had a good reputation where she could go. That she had already made the appointment. That as she was only three months gone, it wouldn't be a problem." Jack took a deep breath, the memory still painful. "Of course, I forbade it, cancelled the appointment and employed a private detective to make sure that she didn't go anywhere near this… this… clinic or any other."

"A private detective?"

"I couldn't be sure, could I, that she wouldn't have the abortion behind my back. She'd tried to already by making the appointment."

Marcus exhaled and shook his head.

"Anyway, Ben was born the following September and Anna refused to have anything to do with him. She didn't want to know. She pretended he didn't exist. I cared for him as best I could and employed a nanny to look after him as of course, I had to work."

"What was Anna doing all this time?"

Jack sighed deeply. "Way before the private detective came on the scene and around the time she must have fallen pregnant, she had auditioned for and been accepted at the drama school where her erstwhile friends were, even though she'd already been offered a fourth year at Guildhall. I had absolutely no idea about either of these things until the drama course was presented to me as a *fait accompli*. I could do nothing to change the situation, so I just had to accept it and live with it as well as pay for it. And that's where she went and spent most of her time."

Marcus shook his head in disbelief.

"Well, I was furious with her – both for her deception and for throwing away a potentially brilliant career, for she is an outstanding pianist, Marcus, whatever her personal problems. She might be all right as an actress, but she's a much better musician."

177

"I never heard her play the piano. She said she never touched the instrument again after you left."

Jack was surprised. "I wonder why?"

"I always assumed it was because she was upset after you went away."

"Perhaps. But I doubt it." Jack was thoughtful. Could that be the reason? However, he felt certain that it was not. "So, for about two months, I supported my family as best I could. Anna went to her drama school and I looked after Ben. But it was very hard. Then, she began staying out all night. When I questioned her, she said that rehearsals had finished late and she was with her friends. Against my better judgement, I believed her but something was making me uneasy and uncomfortable when I was around her. Then one day, while Ben and the nanny were staying at her parent's house for the weekend, I came home early from the Admiralty feeling very unwell with a heavy cold, to find her with some man in *our* home, in *our* bed. It was the classic scenario."

"What did you do?"

"I dragged him out of the bed and punched him on the nose then together with his clothes, bundled him down the stairs and out into the street."

"He was still naked?"

"Starkers."

"Ha! Good for you. But oh, Jack, I'm so sorry."

"Oh, it gets worse."

"Worse?!"

"Anna pleaded with me to forgive her. She said it would never happen again. She begged me not to leave. So I didn't. But I couldn't bear to touch her after that. Our marriage ended for me on that day. For the next few weeks or so, we lived a total nightmare and when I found out she had started sleeping with someone else, my whole world collapsed. Angry and defeated, I walked out on her, taking Ben with me."

"I'm not surprised."

"Soon after that, the nanny gave in her notice but, before she left, I travelled here to Cairnmor and poured out the whole sorry tale to Katherine and Alastair. Ben needed a loving and stable environment in which to be raised so I asked them if they would be willing to take on that responsibility. Without hesitating, they both agreed and a month later, I brought my son to his new home. I was still legally committed to the Royal Navy, so I couldn't care for him myself full time."

"But you're a great dad, anyone can see that."

"Thanks. I try."

"And Ben has never had any contact with his mother?"

"No, none."

"How does he feel about it?"

"Philosophical. He says that he's luckier than most children because he has two mums…"

Marcus was puzzled. "Two mothers? You mean Katherine and Anna?"

"No – Katherine and Grace. You see, when he first arrived, even though she was quite young at the time, Grace took it upon herself to help care for him and a grand job she's made of her share, too. Ben also regards himself as having two dads – myself and Alastair. He says that's plenty; why would he need another mother?"

"Ben's a very special boy."

"Yes."

"After all that she did to you, how can you possibly imagine that you're still in love with her?"

"That's a very good question. I'm not sure that I am any more but Anna is not a woman easily forgotten."

"No," replied Marcus. "She's not."

Jack stood up. He had said enough. It was time to resume their journey. They helped each other on with their respective burdens and continued along the narrow, winding, achingly beautiful path to Mrs Gilgarry's cottage.

Completely lost in his own inner sound world studying scores for the concert he was to conduct that Saturday, Rupert nearly jumped out of his skin when the telephone rang: a harsh intrusive sound that was completely at odds with the mellifluous sounds in his mind.

He waited for Rose to answer it but when it continued to ring with shrill insistence, he reluctantly put aside his score and went out into the hall. Rose had obviously not yet returned from the shops, where she had gone to buy some material for a dress she wanted to make. They had then planned to go to the cinema after lunch to the matinee performance of *Ring of Bright Water*.

After her precipitous and unsuccessful flight up to Strachan of Fairlie, Rose had thrown herself into her work, taking on more teaching and accepting additional playing engagements. When she wasn't out and about, she was to be found sitting at home, staring into space, an open book lying unread on her lap or her knitting put down mid-row beside her on the settee.

So Rupert had helped her with the housework and devised activities that they could both do together; anything that would serve as a distraction and help his beloved Rose overcome the continuing pain of their lost child and her disappointment at not getting the house upon which she had set her heart.

They went cycling in the countryside, putting their bikes in the back of the land rover that Rupert had purchased, or walking up into the hills when the weather was fine or going to the theatre or the cinema whenever they were free in the afternoons or evenings.

Gradually, Rose became more cheerful again, more like her old self. They began to laugh and have fun together again and to share the closeness and intimacy that had always come so naturally and spontaneously to them.

They had a thousand memories upon which to build and a lifetime of friendship and love to sustain them.

"Mr Stewart?" enquired the voice at the other end of the telephone.

"Speaking."

And the conversation that followed meant that afterwards, Rupert went out for a short while before coming home and pacing the floor in the hallway, impatient for Rose to arrive home. When she did, he put his arms around her and kissed her, his face alight with love and joy. He followed her into the kitchen and stayed with her while she put away the shopping.

"I thought we could have ham and cheese for lunch and I bought some wonderful bread that the baker had just made," she said, chattering away happily. "I met Mrs McTavish, you know from number forty-two and she was telling me all about her grandson. It's why I'm so late. I couldn't get away!"

Rupert smiled. "I have a suggestion to make, darling. It's a lovely day so, instead of going to the cinema, why don't we put together a picnic and head out into the hills. The things you bought sound perfect for that."

"Why not? We can always save the film up for a rainy day."

Together, they concocted the meal and set off in the land rover. Rupert took a very circuitous route, one that Rose would never have driven so that she would have no idea where they were going. When they reached a place he had previously and secretly pinpointed on the map, he told her to close her eyes and to keep them shut.

Obediently, she did so and when he stopped the land rover, Rupert told her not to peek under any circumstances. Carefully, he helped her out of the vehicle and they walked a short distance before he brought them to a halt.

Then he told her to open her eyes and watched his beloved wife's reaction as she stood before the Old Rectory in Strachan of Fairlie. He saw the transformation in her expression as realization began to dawn upon her.

Rose's heart beat quickly. It couldn't be, surely?

Rupert led her along the path to the front door. There he put a key into her hand and watched her again in anticipation while she, in utter amazement, turned it in the lock and opened the door. Without hesitating, he picked her up in his arms and carried her over the threshold into their very own house – the house of their dreams.

Speechless at first, she walked from empty room to empty room.

"Is it ours?" she asked eventually, over and over again. "Really ours?"

"Yes," he reassured her each time.

Finally, when she had convinced herself that this really was not a dream, she asked him how it was possible.

He smiled. "Well," he said and took her by the hand, opening the French doors, where they sat on the carpeted floor inside the sitting room, with their legs and feet resting on the flagstones outside – warmed by the early afternoon sun, enclosed within their large and completely private garden.

"Well," he repeated, "you see, my love, this all came about because of the day you came here to speak to Mrs Skinflint."

It was not her real name, of course, but they had decided it suited her and the name stuck.

"Really?"

"Yes. You see, in being deliberately nasty to you, she actually did us a favour and gave the game away when you overheard her say the amount that the other prospective buyers had made in their sealed bid. So, that night after you were asleep, I rang Grandpa and Grandma Mathieson at their house on Cairnmor, having first found out from Mum that, as luck would have it, they'd arrived early for the birthday jamboree. After I told him what had happened, Grandpa immediately instructed his solicitors to put in a rival bid, telling them that it had to be submitted on the closing day."

"What about the note of interest?"

"I'd asked him to put that in ages ago."

Rose was slightly huffy. "How come? I thought we were going to buy the house without asking him for any money?"

"We were." Then Rupert smiled, looking pleased with himself. "You see, I asked him to put in a note of interest as a sort of insurance policy, yet all the while hoping we wouldn't have to call upon his services."

"Oh, I see! You clever man. And you never said a thing to me!"

"No. I was hoping we'd never have to ask Grandpa."

Her spirits restored, Rose asked, "So what happened next?"

"Naturally, Grandpa's bid beat the other one hands down and *he*, which of course meant *we*, got the house."

"Isn't that a bit dishonest?"

"Why? Grandpa is perfectly entitled to bid for any house he likes. The fact that he's going to sell it onto us a few months down the line – at a loss, I might add – is completely up to him!"

"We must pay him back."

"Of course. I've already said that, because we want this house to be really ours, don't we?"

Rose nodded, her eyes filling with tears.

"But I did say that we would always be grateful to him."

"Oh, so grateful."

Tenderly, Rupert wiped her tears away with his fingertips.

"I'll write and thank him as soon as we get back to Minton House," continued Rose. "Though it'll be hard to put into words everything that I feel."

"Everything that *we* feel." He touched her cheek and kissed her lips.

"Oh yes," she murmured, closing her eyes in utter bliss as he took her into his arms and began to undress her. "Everything that *we* feel."

Afterwards, warm and replete, they sat together and ate their picnic lunch – another first in their very own home.

CHAPTER 24

Surprises

Grace stepped off the ferry with a profound sense of relief. She was home. She didn't want to go back to the farmhouse just yet. She needed a few days to herself; a few days in which to come to terms with her breakup with Sam. She had not indicated when she would be returning from London to her parents but as soon as she was seen in Lochaberdale, they would know and wonder why she hadn't come home.

So Grace went into the post office and quickly scribbled a postcard to Alastair and Katherine to say that she was spending a few days on her own at Mrs Gilgarry's cottage and would see them soon, knowing they would understand. She caught the new, young postman just as he was starting out on his rounds and, as he'd always had a soft spot for her and had other post to deliver to the farmhouse, he readily agreed to take her card. She then purchased some bread and other provisions, and went up to the hotel, using the Ladies cloakroom to change into something more appropriate for a hike. She left her suitcase with David and set off for Mrs Gilgarry's croft, her knapsack containing a change of clothes, food and water.

The day was sunny and fine. Cairnmor was enjoying a settled period of warm weather and soon, Grace discarded her sweater and tied it round her waist. She was grateful to be wearing just a sleeveless t-shirt and shorts and as she strode along, revelling in the fresh, clean air, she gave herself up to the freedom of the wide open spaces where she could be completely herself.

She needed solitude above all else; a place where she could retreat and lick her wounds in private without having to talk to anyone. For she was wounded – by Sam's enthusiasms that proved to be ephemeral; by the intentions he had not followed through but, most of all, by the loss of him as a friend as well as a boyfriend. That was the hardest thing perhaps, for they had shared a great deal during the time they had known each other.

The thought occurred to her that maybe, despite this, they had never truly known each other at all.

When Grace arrived at the croft, she didn't go into the cottage immediately but made her way down to the beach, where she sat hidden in the dunes listening to the sound of the waves.

Eventually, she gave into her feelings and wept.

Jack and Marcus spent their first afternoon studying the herb garden, deciding upon the most likely illustrative candidates for the book. Jack knew most of the names, although not what they were used for, and had come armed with a list of suggestions that Katherine had given to him before they left home. His idea was to sketch the interior and exterior of the cottage as well as the herbs as this would add to the atmosphere of the book and the verbal portrait of Mrs Gilgarry that Marcus might be hoping to create. Enthused by this, Marcus readily agreed and they spent time discussing various artistic and literary possibilities.

Once they had completed everything they needed for the moment, Jack left Marcus to his own creative devices and decided to take a stroll down to the beach before returning to cook supper. His own concept was taking shape in his mind but, not in the mood to start that afternoon, he decided to begin sketching and painting the next day.

The narrow, rocky path led steeply down to yet another broad expanse of sand dunes and Jack took his time, enjoying his surroundings. It was so different to South Lochaberdale; the dunes here were on a smaller scale, the sand a golden fringe to the towering mountains nearby. He and Grace had often camped here; it had become a favourite haunt for them over the years. It seemed an age since he had been here last; it seemed an age since he had last seen her...

He stopped.

Grace.

She was there, seated, half-hidden by the marram grass; her head buried in her hands, her body racked by silent sobs. Without hesitating, he went over to her and sat down beside her and when she had seen it was him, he took her into his arms and comforted her.

"Jack, oh, Jack!" she said, burying her face in his shoulder.

"Is it Sam?" he asked gently

"Yes."

"A row?" He knew it was more than that.

"No."

"Is it over?"

"Yes."

Jack experienced an overwhelming sense of relief. "Do you want to talk about it?"

She shook her head. "Not yet."

"Too soon?"

"Yes."

"I understand."

"I know."

She looked up at him then and Jack had to use every ounce of his self-control not to kiss her. However, it was not the right moment; Grace was too vulnerable, too hurt.

But oh, how he wanted her.

Instead, he lifted clear of her cheek a strand of hair that had become mixed up with her tears and gently pushed it back from her face.

A shiver of pleasure travelled down Grace's spine and she wanted him to kiss her. However, she recognized that it was too soon; her breakup with Sam was too close, too real.

But oh, how she wanted him.

Instead, she laid her head on his shoulder again until her tears gradually subsided.

"Do you remember when you came across me sitting in the dunes all those years ago?" he said.

How could she forget? "Of course." She managed a watery smile. "Except it's you comforting me, this time."

She wished they could always be together to comfort each other.

How he wished he could always be there when she needed him; when they needed each other.

"Why haven't you written to me, Jack?"

He hesitated. "Because there was a danger that... that I was beginning to care for you too much."

"Too much? What do you mean?" She turned to him, hope flooding her heart, despite her grief.

He knew he had to be honest. "Because there was a danger that I was falling in love with you. Had fallen in love with you."

She hardly dared to believe what she was hearing. "And is that such a bad thing?"

Jack touched her cheek and smiled. "No."

"And what about Anna?"

"Anna?" Until that moment, Anna hadn't entered his head. But at the sound of her name, she was there, his constant emotional companion. So he obviously wasn't over her – yet. "Ah, the perennial unanswered question."

"Yes."

He stared into the middle distance. He couldn't give her a definitive answer at that moment so he said: "And what about Sam?"

"In the end, he wasn't the one for me. I cared for him, certainly, but I could never love him properly because I'm so in love with you."

Jack gathered her to him then and kissed her without any hesitation and Grace put her arms round his neck as he laid her back against the sand, responding to him, matching the intensity of his embrace. After a while, they let each other go and sat together, side by side holding hands.

Grace was the first to speak. "Oh, Jack, it's so silly for both of us to keep trying to overcome our feelings for each other. Why do we need to? It's ridiculous."

He laughed. "I know and I agree with you. Therefore, after this, we should stop trying. But, my dearest, sweetest Grace, you have to get over the pain of losing Sam before we can be truly together. There is always danger in starting a new relationship on the rebound, no matter how well we might know each other or how much we feel for each other."

"I know. And by the same token, you have to leave Anna behind. Completely. I want you to come to me free and clear, Jack. I don't want even the tiniest part of you still belonging to her."

He was silent for a moment. Then he nodded. "Yes. I understand." He smiled suddenly. "It would seem we both have some emotional unpacking to do."

Grace returned his smile. "And when it's done, I'll be here. Waiting."

"And when it's done, I promise I shall come to you."

Jack stood up and offered his hand to Grace who took it in hers. He picked up her haversack and together, they walked back up to the cottage.

After supper, Grace banked up the fire, for the evening at this higher altitude had turned chilly and the three of them sat in the glow of the flames and talked of Mrs Gilgarry.

Marcus could not help but notice how close Jack and Grace were; how easily they laughed together; how they finished each other's sentences; how they sparked off each other; how well they knew and understood each other; how comfortable they were together.

Anna was a fool to have let Jack go but ultimately, she had done him a favour as Grace was by far the kinder, more sweet-natured sister and Jack deserved someone as lovely as her. Marcus knew that Grace would never be unfaithful and the age difference was of no consequence. Jack was, as Anna had told him, just like Alastair: young at heart and most certainly youthful in appearance. Yet he had the gravitas of someone used to being in command and was a man with strength and depth to his personality. Marcus felt proud to know him and be able to call him a friend.

Marcus began to take notes as they talked about Mrs Gilgarry; notes establishing the personality of the old lady in whose cottage the three of them temporarily resided; recording events in her life; learning about the clearances and her lost relatives; about some of the people she had cured and her attachment to the island she had never left.

He began to understand what it was like to live here; the hardships that had had to be endured; the isolation as well as the sense of community forged across generations and which still held sway even in the rapidly changing modern age.

And through his notes, Marcus began to find his way back into writing.

Eventually, they lapsed into silence. Jack took out his sketchpad and with quick, confident strokes, drew Grace as she sat on the floor in front of the open hearth, bathed in the glowing firelight. She sat very still, conscious of what he was doing, lost in its execution; finding consolation in familiar actions of which she had always loved being a part.

Marcus was absolutely correct when he had described her as Jack's muse. All afternoon, Jack had not drawn a thing, yet now, with Grace's unexpected appearance, his hands were busy crafting a picture that perfectly captured her poise and beauty.

That night, Grace insisted that Marcus slept behind the curtain in the double bed as he could not afford to have a disturbed night's sleep, while Grace and Jack camped out in front of the fire; she in his sleeping bag and he lying on the cushions taken from all the chairs and covered by a spare blanket or two for warmth. Innocently, they lay close together and fell asleep holding hands.

So the days passed, filled with creative endeavour. Jack completed his artwork, leaving the finishing touches to be done at home, while Marcus began expanding his notes, his inspiration taking him deeper into his writing. Grace took photographs with Jack's camera and went for long walks, finding the solitude she needed but not wishing to stray too far or be away too long from the companionship of Jack and Marcus.

Especially Jack.

In the evenings, they talked of life's experiences, of love, philosophy and friendship and when their brief sojourn came to a close, they reluctantly packed up to leave, bidding a silent farewell to the cottage that enshrined the spirit of Mrs Gilgarry and that had helped each of them on the pathway to healing.

They caught the post-bus at the end of the track and arrived back at the farmhouse laughing and talking. Jack teased Grace about her first attempts at painting and as they entered the kitchen, they looked at each other with such open affection that it was obvious to everyone that they were in love.

And there, seated at the table was Anna.

It was hard to know who experienced the most shock – Anna, Jack, Grace or Marcus and for a moment they none of them moved or said a word but just stared at each other.

Alastair and Katherine immediately took in the situation and knew that, despite their delight and surprise at seeing their errant daughter-granddaughter again, the fireworks from the past were only just beginning.

It was a potent mix. Jack and Anna; Marcus and Anna; and now, judging by the expression on their daughter's face and his reaction to her, Grace and Jack.

Grace and Jack.

Katherine looked at Alastair with her mouth open. He smiled and shook his head. In that instant, every assumption and preconception they had ever held had been turned upside down. How could they have been so spectacularly wrong?

They saw the icy glare that Anna gave to her sister; they saw Marcus go pale at the sight of Anna and as for Jack, well, he just stood there holding onto the back of a chair, apparently calm and detached, his command experience enabling him, for the moment at least, to reveal little of what he might be feeling.

Anna was the first to recover and break the shocked silence.

"Hello, Jack," she said, flashing him her smile; a smile that was both seductive and vibrant.

All at once anger, remembered love and desire flooded though him and Jack knew he was now having difficulty concealing his emotions.

"Hello, Anna."

He looked at Grace, who was watching him in consternation; whose beautiful eyes had filled with tears; who knew he was struggling but who could do nothing to help him. His lovely Grace who could only trust that he would keep faith with all that he had said to her.

Anna took in their expressions; her envy of the little sister who had everything as strong as the day she discovered that Alastair was not her real father. But Grace and Jack? Oh no, she was not going to have that.

"Hi, sis," she said.

Grace could only stare at her.

And Marcus? thought Anna. *Here on Cairnmor? How? Why? Looking so thin and pale...* "Hello, Marcus," she said. "This is a surprise."

He blanched even more and could not move.

Eventually, he nodded at her. "I guess it is."

Marcus found her as beautiful as ever but now he saw the hard lines around her mouth; the emptiness in her eyes – something of which he had not been aware when they had been together. It alienated him and served to alleviate his memory of their relationship and the later humiliation and pain of being cast aside so easily and without explanation.

"Well," said Anna to the assembled company, "this *is* interesting."

Grace shrugged off her knapsack and went into the cloakroom where she took off her walking boots, quietly padding upstairs in socked feet to the sanctuary of her bedroom.

Katherine followed her immediately and found her standing by the window, looking out over the sands to the ocean beyond. There was so much to say but her mother knew exactly where she had to begin.

"You really are in love with Jack, aren't you?"

"Yes."

"And all the while your dad and I thought it was just a girlish fancy."

"It was never that."

"I can see that now. And funnily enough, in accepting the two of you being together, everything's fallen into its rightful place. I'm so sorry that we were so mistaken."

Grace smiled. "It's okay. I knew what I felt, despite what everyone thought and tried to tell me what was possible and not possible; real and unreal."

"And what about Jack? What are his feelings for you?"

"Can't you tell?"

It was Katherine's turn to smile. "Yes. And I think it's wonderful. He's a wonderful man and your dad and I both care for him deeply. But he's so much older than you…" Katherine faltered and then laughed at Grace's disparaging look. "Oh, all right. I know, I'm a fine one to talk. I should have known better than to say anything!"

Grace gave her mother a hug. "You know that age makes no difference for you and me where love is concerned. And he's so like Dad in that he's one of these people who seems ageless."

"Yes, he is." Katherine was thoughtful. "But Anna coming home unannounced has made things rather complicated."

"That's an understatement."

"It will certainly test whether or not Jack is over her. We've always believed that he still carried a torch for her, despite what happened. We also thought that Anna might still be in love with him. However, we could be wrong."

Katherine smiled ruefully: she and Alastair weren't infallible in their judgement.

"Jack and I talked about all this, Mum, when we were at Mrs Gilgarry's and it is partially true, at least on Jack's part. I said he had to come to me free and clear and that I wouldn't have any part of him if he still wanted Anna."

Katherine looked at her daughter with admiration. "That was a very brave thing to say."

"But is it too much to expect of any man? It seemed the right thing to do with Anna just a distant reality, but now that she's actually here… Is Jack strong enough to finally let her go?" Grace hardly dared ask the question.

"I believe he is and you were right to ask it of him but Anna's untimely arrival will certainly be the acid test. In the meantime, you'll probably have to go through all sorts of agony."

Katherine kissed her daughter's forehead, wishing she could protect her child from the emotional pain that was to come.

Grace took a deep breath. "Yes, I know."

"But your dad and I are here, supporting you, you know that. Jack is, when you think about it, ideal for you. Even more so than Sam."

"But you thought Sam was ideal." Grace couldn't resist chiding her mother a little.

Katherine took it in good part. "We did and he proved in the end to be a disappointment. But you weren't ever sure about him, were you?"

"Not completely, no."

"So what happened in London?"

"We split up."

"I had assumed as much when you didn't come straight home from the ferry. Can I ask what happened? Do you feel able to talk about it?"

"Yes."

So Grace outlined what had happened and also added that she too needed to be over Sam before she and Jack could be together.

"But that will take less time, I imagine, than for Jack to leave Anna behind?"

"Perhaps." How wise her mother was. "And what about Ben?"

Katherine raised her eyebrows. "I shouldn't say this but I'm so glad he's not here at the moment. I don't want his equilibrium upset by the sudden reappearance of a mother he doesn't know and who rejected him even before he was born."

"He's a very sensible, mature boy. I'm sure he'll deal with it." However, Grace sounded more certain than she felt.

"Perhaps so, but this is going to be an unprecedented situation for him. It's not going to be easy at all."

"Well, he knows we all love him. Has Anna mentioned Ben?"

"Not so far."

"She's probably still pretending he doesn't exist."

Katherine looked at Grace and laughed. "Ooh!"

"Sorry about that."

"Don't be. It's probably true."

"How long is Anna staying?"

"I don't know. Certainly until after your dad's birthday party."

"Are you glad she came back?"

"Of course, I am. She's my daughter and your sister and we've all been apart for so long. But..." and Katherine hesitated.

"There are so many issues to be resolved, aren't there?"

Her mother sighed. "And I'm not convinced that Anna is capable of resolving them even now. But it is still good to see her. I think."

Grace regarded her mother thoughtfully for a moment before saying, "You may be forced into making some kind of choice."

"What do you mean?"

"Between giving support to me or Anna."

"Then there's no contest. My greater loyalty is with you. Anna made the decision to leave us behind many years ago and she can't expect to waltz in here and claim automatic rights."

"So you don't see her as the prodigal daughter then?" Grace smiled.

"Certainly not. So far, there has been no emotional reaching out on her part. Her arrival was more along the lines of, 'Here I am. I've come to see you. Aren't I gracious to do that?' and I think she expected us to fawn over her with unbridled joy."

Grace chuckled but she could sense the underlying pain and bitterness in her mother's words. "But you didn't?"

"No. We're all keeping our feelings well-hidden and under control otherwise all the hurt and anger and recriminations might just come pouring out."

"I wish she'd never come home."

"You may be right. But there might ultimately be some kind of resolution because of it."

"Perhaps."

The two women sat together in silence and wondered exactly what was going to happen: Grace full of ambivalence about her sister and Katherine with a premonition that there would be stormy times ahead for all of them.

Meanwhile, downstairs in the kitchen, with Alastair having taken a shaky Marcus into the study for his own sake as well as to alleviate the tension in the room, Anna suggested to Jack that he should take her out for a meal at the hotel where, she said, they could "talk things over."

He accepted, knowing that this would be the ultimate and final test of his feelings for Anna.

CHAPTER 25

Decisions

The hotel dining room in Lochaberdale was busy and the staff were run off their feet trying to keep up with the rush. Jack and Anna had to wait for a table as residents were always given priority, even though the hotel was also open to the general public.

Jack bought them both drinks at the bar and they sat in the lounge waiting for their turn. Anna smiled at him; nervously, he thought.

"Thank you for agreeing to come out with me this evening," she said.

Jack nodded in reply.

She raised her glass. "Here's to us."

Jack kept his glass in his hand. For himself, he had to be cautious and deliberate, testing each reaction; for Anna, he had to be careful not to give her the slightest indication that he was interested in her.

It seemed very strange to be with her after all this time. Strange and yes, unnatural. Yet he had to do this; he had to prove both to himself and to Grace that he was no longer in love with Anna; that he could spend an evening in her company and not want to take her to bed with him afterwards.

"Cheers." He lifted his glass to his lips.

He regarded her carefully, taking in her exquisite beauty and air of sophistication, which had turned heads as soon as they walked into the hotel, but which seemed out of place in the homely comfort of their surroundings.

"You're staring at me, Jack," she said encouragingly.

"Am I? I do apologize." His reply was matter of fact, given without embarrassment. "If you'll excuse me, I'll go and see when our table will be ready."

Anna took a deep breath. This was all turning out to be much more difficult than even she had anticipated. Jack seemed distant, unwilling to communicate and, if she had hoped for a rapturous reception when she had arrived at the farmhouse earlier that day – a warm welcome back into the bosom of her family – then she was sadly mistaken. It had been strangely muted; stilted even. Perhaps this was all a terrible miscalculation on her part; perhaps she shouldn't have come at all. Perhaps, just as she had always feared, she'd been away too long.

When Jack returned, he said that their table was ready and he allowed her to go first into the dining room.

For Anna, childhood memories came flooding back; of the recitals that she and Rupert had given in here; of the impromptu concerts with Rose that became regular events. Yet, as she looked around at its old-fashioned elegance, it felt strange after her life in New York; so dull and staid, so utterly *parochial*.

They studied their individual menus and Jack watched her again while she made her choices. Almost thirteen years had passed since he had last seen her; nearly fifteen since they were married. Had he forgiven her? Yes, but he had not forgotten.

"So, what have you been doing with yourself?" she asked, opening the conversation as casually as she could.

"The navy keeps me occupied."

"You were in the States a while back?"

"Yes. I saw your play. You were very good."

She accepted the compliment graciously. "Thank you."

They sat in silence.

When Jack failed to ask why she had not been willing to see him, as she had expected him to, Anna said, "I'm sorry I wasn't able to see you. Things were pretty hectic back then, you know."

How could she tell him she had been afraid?

"I'm sure they were." He was giving nothing away.

She decided to bite the bullet. "How's Ben?" she asked.

The question caught Jack by surprise. "Forgive me, but after rejecting him at birth and years of ignoring his existence, why should you take a sudden interest now?"

"I just wondered."

"He's fine. Thriving. Doing well at school."

"He must be at boarding school now on the mainland."

"No, there's a secondary school here on Cairnmor, and very fine it is too. Things have changed a great deal since you've been away."

"If you remember, Jack, we left together."

"True. But I returned. Frequently."

He gave her one of his direct looks and she averted her eyes, unable to meet his gaze.

"How often do you see him?"

"Every leave. Our home is here on Cairnmor with Alastair and Katherine."

"Do you tell him about me?" Her voice wavered.

"Of course."

"Does he ask after me?"

Jack had to be honest. "No, not very often. He's happy and settled just as he is."

"I'm glad."

Did he detect a note of longing in her voice? "The decision was yours, Anna."

"Yes." Unexpectedly, tears pricked at her eyes.

As gently as he could, he asked, "And has it been worth the sacrifice?"

She was silent. There was no easy answer. She shrugged her shoulders. *Of course it had.* "Maybe. But I think I'd like to get to know him now."

"Really?" He didn't believe her. "Why?"

"Because… because I should."

Anna was faltering now. Her desire to know Ben was just an excuse: a lead into what she had intended to say – that she still loved Jack, that they should forget the past, that she wanted them to try and repair their broken marriage, that she was sorry she had made such a mess of things.

At the last minute her courage failed her. For some reason she couldn't bring herself to say the words she thought she wanted to say.

"Why?" Jack repeated his question.

"Every child needs their mother."

"Ben has Katherine and Grace."

"Grace?!"

"Yes. From the moment Ben arrived on the island, she took it upon herself to help care for him."

Anna felt a surge of jealousy and resentment. Her little sister looking after *her* son. It should have been her. Guilt and anxiety surfaced once again.

The starter arrived and they ate in silence.

Anna felt she was getting nowhere. This distant and guarded man was not the same person that she remembered. Jack had always been so communicative and caring; so friendly, so *amiable*. The old-fashioned word fitted him perfectly. They had been blissfully happy once. And like a fool, she'd wrecked their life together.

Suddenly, a picture of Greg, the innocuous man from the party, leapt into her mind; the man whose apartment she now shared; the man who even now was waiting for her at the hotel in Oban.

For the first time, Anna began to question whether or not she still loved Jack – this man who had loved her so much and for whom she had carried so many years of regret for the way she had treated him and caused him to leave. For the first time, she questioned whether she really needed him after all.

But was she ready to let go?

The waiter cleared away their plates. The main course arrived. Jack felt he ought to say something; Anna did too. They both started to speak at the same time.

"I'd like…" he said.

"I'm still…"

"You first."

Anna took a deep breath. She had to give it one last try before she finally laid the ghost of her failed marriage to rest.

"I'm still in love with you, Jack."

Until the journey home from New York after she had rejected him again, until his recent passionate embrace on the beach with Grace, his immediate reaction would have been to declare that he was still in love with her, that he would always be in love with her, that he felt so intensely about her that he had never truly loved anyone since.

Now, as he studied this flawed, desirable woman sitting opposite him, he saw no warmth of love in her eyes and he shook his head. "No."

"What do you mean, 'no'?"

"You're not."

"How do you know?"

"I just do. You only think you are."

"And what gives you the right to tell me what I think?"

"I have no right," Jack replied equably. "None at all. Why have you come back, Anna?"

"To make amends?"

"It's too late."

"No. It can't be."

"It is with me."

"I thought you still loved me. I thought we had something really special that would last forever whatever happened."

192

"So did I."

He wouldn't accuse her; they had hurled enough recriminations at each other before he walked away from her. He wouldn't talk about his love for Grace either, which was becoming more real to him with every passing moment.

"I messed everything up. I regret that now," said Anna.

Jack nodded. Thirteen years too late, but at least it was a start.

"And what about the family? Katherine and Alastair? Can you let go of that hurt too?"

"You don't mince words, do you?"

It was all too much too soon for her. His honesty disturbed her carefully cultivated equilibrium.

"It's not all that hard," he said.

"It is for me."

"Why?"

"They betrayed me."

"Not intentionally."

"But it still hurts to discover that the man you thought of as your father is in fact your grandfather and that they'd omitted to tell you that your real father was living somewhere else. And then to find out that this real father didn't give a damn about you." There was deep bitterness in her voice.

"Rupert coped."

"He had Rose."

"You had me."

"Yes, I did and you were very good to me. But Rupert didn't have the shock of reading that letter."

"The one Alex wrote to Katherine, you mean? Where he apologized for not being a proper father to you and Rupert and for being such a rotten husband; how he had found real happiness in his new life but would always regret what he left behind?"

"You've read the letter?" Anna was surprised.

"Yes. Katherine showed it to me so that I could better understand what had upset you so much."

"And did you?"

"Of course, but I've never understood why you held it against them for so many years. Why didn't you get in touch with Alex when Katherine suggested it? When she offered to write to him and suggest that the two of you got to know each other? And why were you going through your mother's personal correspondence in the first place?"

"Her bureau was open and it was raining and I was bored."

"That's no excuse."

"No, it was just teenage Anna being nosey and behaving badly, *again*."

Her sudden sarcasm cut through Jack like a knife; this hereditary trait that was a direct throwback to Roberta, Alastair's first wife: the mother of Alex and Lily and Edward, whom Jack had served with during the war and who was not Alastair's child and a thoroughly nasty piece of work. At least Anna had enough of Katherine in her to act as some kind of saving grace.

Grace. Suddenly, he was impatient to go home and be with Grace. He'd had enough of this futile conversation.

Their sweet course arrived. Jack decided that the time had come for general conversation to end and for him finally to declare his hand.

"There's no easy way to say this, Anna..." he looked at her. "But I'd like a divorce."

She appeared to be shocked. "A divorce? Why, Jack? I thought we agreed we'd never get a divorce; that we'd always stay married."

"I know we did. But surely you can see that it isn't right to hang onto something that ended years ago?" He smiled at her gently. "It would seem we've both of us been clinging onto a vague notion that one day we'd get back together because our love for each other was so strong that it would survive adultery, separation and subsequent relationships. But life isn't like that, Anna. We have to move on to what's real and not live in the past or dwell on the illusion of lost love."

And Anna knew that Jack spoke the truth.

"Yes," she said, accepting his words simply and quietly.

"However, having said all that, there's no reason why you shouldn't get to know Ben," he added, waiting to see her reaction.

Anna was silent. Did she really want to get to know a teenage son?

"We'll see." Hardly drawing breath, she then said, "I'll have my lawyer contact yours and we'll hammer out some kind of agreement. It shouldn't be too complicated and we can go for one of these new no-fault divorces. We could be free of each other in about twelve weeks."

Jack had the strong impression that she'd already been considering this.

"You'll naturally have full custody of Ben and I don't want any kind of settlement," said Anna, her facial expression and voice matter-of-fact. "I'm probably wealthier than you anyway."

Jack smiled. "Perhaps I should ask you for alimony in that case!"

Anna failed to see the humour. "I suppose you only want a divorce because you've met someone else."

He wasn't quick enough to hide the way his face lit up and Anna was about to ask who it was when she recalled Grace and Jack as they had entered the kitchen that afternoon.

Grace. It was Grace. Why, that conniving little...! How could he possibly be thinking of marrying her little sister; the little sister who had everything Anna had ever wanted? And now she would even have Jack.

Anna felt sick with jealousy. *She* couldn't have Jack, nor did she really want him if she was honest, but she'd make damn sure that Grace didn't have him either.

They ate their ice-cream, didn't stay for coffee and drove home in strained silence.

Socially, the evening had not been a conspicuous success but it had taught Jack one very precious and valuable lesson: that he was no longer in love with Anna, nor would he ever think of her again in that way. It had been much easier than he had anticipated and he knew he would be able to keep his promise to Grace. The thought filled him with delight.

As soon as they reached home, Jack decided to speak to Alastair first before going upstairs to find Grace. The two men went into the study and sat down in the two easy chairs either side of the fireplace.

"So, how was your evening?"

"Difficult."

"I imagined it would be."

Jack smiled. Without preamble, he said, "If I said to you I was thinking of leaving the Royal Navy, what would your reaction be?"

"I'd naturally ask why, but I would also know that you wouldn't consider such a thing without good reason." Alastair regarded him carefully.

"You wouldn't think I was throwing away what promised to be a spectacular career?"

"Not necessarily. You've had a pretty good run for your money already! Reaching the rank of captain with the offer of commodore is no mean achievement."

"You wouldn't be disappointed?"

"Of course not. It's your life, Jack. You're a mature and responsible man, I hardly think you would take any decision lightly."

"You really are a master of diplomacy!"

"It's my middle name. Come on, Jack, out with it!"

"I haven't asked her yet, but I know she'll say 'yes'." Jack paused. "How would you like it if I became your son-in-law – *again*?"

A momentary frown flitted across Alastair's face. Surely not Anna? Not after all this time; not after the way she had treated him?

Jack read his thoughts. "Not Anna. Grace. I'm in love with *Grace*, Alastair, and have been for some time. Do you mind?"

"Why should I mind? Well, she's always been in love with you and we'd always put it down to some kind of girlish fancy."

"I don't think it was ever that."

"So it would seem! And it appears we were very much mistaken." Alastair smiled. "You know Katherine and I would be absolutely delighted without you even having to ask. For the second time, I shall say to you that I couldn't ask for a better son-in-law. Although this time around with Grace it feels completely *right* whereas before with Anna it didn't. For me, technically, you were only a grandson-in-law then!" He chuckled. "And I'm hardly in a position to mention the age gap!"

Jack laughed. "No. As you and Katherine are very aware, it makes no difference."

"So, how does leaving the Royal Navy come into all this?"

"Grace won't live anywhere but on Cairnmor, you and I both know that, no matter how much in love she might be."

"That is very true, I'm afraid." Alastair paused, "And you would consider giving up your career for her in order to live here permanently? That's very noble of you, Jack."

"I wish I could say it was. But it's only part of the story. Ben is also here and it means I can be with him long term. Also, the service is changing, Alastair. It's not the navy that we came to know and love during the war. There's the same pride among the officers and men in the Royal Navy's history, in its traditions, customs and achievements; the same discipline and excellent training. But there are big changes coming. The politicians hold the purse strings and no matter how much we senior officers may argue for a strong navy right across the board, the government is cutting back. The Cold War is the name of the game at the moment and most of the available resources are being put into antisubmarine warfare."

"That's not altogether a bad thing."

"No, but you have to have a balance. We need a strong surface fleet as well. You see, if I were to accept the post they're offering me, then I would have to play a big part in implementing those changes. I'm reluctant to see the service I love very deeply hacked about by politicians who have no idea of the ramifications those changes will bring. It's already happening and I can do nothing to prevent it. The navy will adapt and survive as it has always done but I'd rather leave with my memories intact."

Alastair understood only too well. "However, it's still going to be very hard for you nonetheless as I know from experience. Well, my friend, we shall just have to spend the long, dark winter evenings reminiscing together about the good old days. You know that I'll talk for any length of time about the Royal Navy." Alastair rubbed his hands with satisfaction. "And I shall look forward to doing that very much."

Jack laughed. "So shall I."

"Have you considered what you'd like to do?"

It was a natural question but for Alastair, it contained so much hope. He was not going to ask Jack directly to take over his responsibilities for Cairnmor – the suggestion had to come from Jack himself. He had to *want* to do it.

"I've given it a great deal of thought, particularly since I've been here on leave these last couple of weeks. Firstly, I'd like to fulfil my artistic calling and see if I really do have enough talent to make a go of it professionally. Marcus has been encouraging me to do this and says I should go for it. Secondly," and Jack deliberately paused knowing the effect his next words would have on his friend, "and most importantly – and this is something I've always wanted to do but have never spoken about it – I was wondering if, when you retire, you would like me to..."

Alastair's face lit up with joy.

"Yes, please!" he said without hesitation. "It would be perfect."

"Mind reader!"

"It's beyond my wildest dreams." Fired up with enthusiasm, Alastair spoke quickly. "Initially, we could work together and when the day comes that Katherine and I finally decide to step down, then you and Grace can take over the administration of the island as joint trustees. I can't think of anyone better qualified or better suited to the job. You love the island and have all the necessary administrative experience into the bargain. And you'll be married to our precious Grace, who will inherit Cairnmor one day. I can't tell you how delighted I am." Alastair's eyes filled up with tears. "By handing over the reins to you and Grace together, my dear friend, I know that the future of the island couldn't be in better hands. I can't wait to tell Katherine. I've been worrying about what would happen."

"I know. It means I can also repay you in some way for the time and effort you've spent in raising my son."

196

"That isn't necessary, but I understand what you're saying. Now, when is all this likely to happen?"

"At the end of January."

"The powers that be will be disappointed."

"Perhaps. However, I've given the Royal Navy twenty-four satisfying years of my life and it's time I moved on in a different direction."

"Shall we go and tell the girls?" said Alastair, getting out of his chair.

"Or in my case, ask the girl!"

Alastair chuckled. "I don't think you'll have any problem there!"

"Nor do I!"

However, as they left the study and mounted the stairs, they heard the back door slam and came upon a furious row on the landing between Anna and Marcus, with Katherine looking on, her face white with suppressed anger.

CHAPTER 26

Searching

"You are nothing but a cold-hearted bitch. You can't stop bullying her even now, can you? What you've just done is despicable beyond words. If you weren't a woman, I'd punch you on the jaw."

"What, like you did to Virginia?"

"How dare you!"

Marcus went to move forward but Jack grabbed him from behind.

"It's not worth it, Marcus. Whatever has happened just now is not worth it." He felt Marcus relax and let him go. "But would someone like to tell me what the hell is going on here?"

Marcus and Anna glared at each other. Then she dropped her gaze, fear replacing blind anger. She knew she'd just made yet another stupid mistake. She began to plead with Marcus.

"Don't. Please don't. Remember the good times we shared."

He scowled at her. "Why should I? Did they stop you from unceremoniously dumping me when it suited you?"

"I gave evidence at your trial."

"You were subpoenaed. You had no choice."

"I was on your side and said good things about you."

"And I was grateful back then. But this is now. Grace has never done you any harm, Anna, and yet you still treat her like a piece of…"

And Marcus stopped, not wishing to offend Katherine. In that moment, he became aware that his friendship with Jack and Grace had become greater than any previous loyalty he might have felt towards Anna.

Very slowly and deliberately, never taking his eyes away from her, he explained what happened.

"I came up the stairs to see Anna loitering in the corridor, in this get-up," he indicated her negligée, "and as soon as she saw Grace come out of her room, she opened the door to your bedroom, Jack, and called out, 'I'm here, darling. I hope you're ready for me!' Of course, the room was in darkness and Grace had no reason not to believe you weren't in there waiting for Anna."

Jack stared at Anna in shock. "Why? Why would you do that?"

Marcus didn't give her a chance to reply. "She's always been envious of Grace and because she couldn't have you, Jack, she wasn't about to let her little sister have you either." Marcus was sparing Anna nothing. "Grace burst into tears and disappeared down the stairs, having made the assumption that you and Anna had returned from your meal at the hotel having got back together. I opened the door to your room completely and put the light on to check for myself. Of course, as Anna well knew and I had surmised, it was empty."

Without saying a word, Jack ran down the stairs and out of the house after the woman he truly loved.

For the first time, Katherine spoke and there was no mistaking the resolve in her voice. "There is a ferry to the mainland tomorrow. I would like you to be on it, Anna."

She had made her choice.

Anna burst into tears and disappeared into her bedroom. Marcus leant back against the wall and slid down to the floor, exhausted.

"She's not all bad, you know," he said, looking up at Katherine and Alastair.

"No, but the good parts are often hard to find," said Alastair.

"I'm so sorry," said Marcus.

"Why should you be sorry?"

"Because I was brutally frank. She's still your daughter and granddaughter and I am a guest in your house. I should have been more tactful."

Alastair shook his head. "Desperate actions call for desperate words sometimes." He offered his hand to Marcus who took it and stood up. "I think we could all do with a cup of tea. Late as the hour is, we none of us would be able to sleep if we went to bed now. And not at all until we know where Grace has gone and is safe."

Gratefully, Marcus accepted his offer and Alastair put his arms around Katherine and held her close to him, comforting and supporting her. Together, the three of them went downstairs into the kitchen.

Grace slung her knapsack onto the back seat of Morris and tied up the laces on her shoes which she had grabbed on her way out. She started the engine and drove down the hill quickly, blinded by tears. She had no idea where she was going; she just needed to get away, away from Anna.

And Jack.

She couldn't believe he would do that to her and yet she had no reason to suppose he was not in his room waiting for Anna. Grace knew she should have checked further but she hadn't wanted to just in case he was there. In bed. Waiting. She felt sick at the merest thought of Jack and Anna together…

The car bumped along the narrow track. She was driving much too fast and she knew it, but did nothing to slow her pace. She wanted to get as far away as quickly as she could.

Perhaps she'd take a job on the mainland. She couldn't bear to be in the same house as them now.

She'd trusted him. Jack. He was the last person she would have thought would have let her down. Surely he would have taken her to one side and explained gently and clearly that he couldn't be with her because he really couldn't let go of Anna? She would have been devastated, certainly, but that would have been the honourable thing to do and she had always taken Jack to be an honourable man.

But this? The car lurched suddenly and she had to wrench the steering wheel over to stop it careering off the track into the bogs that lined either side of this particular stretch of road. She only needed to get away, not kill herself.

Perhaps all men were unreliable. No, she knew that wasn't true. Her father was as solid as they come; so were Michael and Angus. And Rupert. Even Léon had turned out to be a good man. Fiona was over the moon that he had asked her to marry him; she had never doubted his love for her and that one day they would be together, she said.

Why couldn't she find someone like that? Sam had been special but in the end, he'd proved to be unreliable. And now Jack, the same. But surely he couldn't be? Not Jack. The more she thought about it, the more unlikely it seemed. And yet she had no reason to suppose that Anna wasn't telling the truth.

Grace slowed down as she reached Lochaberdale but once she was beyond the school on the outskirts of the little township, she put her foot down hard on the accelerator and the car careered along the narrow track once again.

Where could she go? Somewhere she could not easily be found. On the spur of the moment, she veered left up the slope that took her out towards the eastern headlands.

About fifteen minutes later, the track ran out and she stopped the car. It was pitch black and even with her torch it was difficult to see where she was going. She wondered whether she should spend the night in the car. She knew only too well how treacherous her beloved Cairnmor could be in the dark; how treacherous her beloved Jack was being at that moment.

She burst into tears again and sat down on a rocky ledge until her sobs had subsided. Then, pulling herself together, she put on her jacket, picked up her knapsack and began walking to her chosen refuge: the place that she had heard about as a child but where she had never been.

She hoped the tide was out.

Jack ran down to the beach calling Grace's name, but received no answer. He searched among the dunes as far as Robbie's hut, but she was nowhere to be found. He called out again and again but to no avail. He ran up the steep slope to Katherine's old cottage, one of Grace's favourite hideaways, but it was dark and empty.

Winded and anxious, Jack bent over with his hands on his thighs trying to get some air into his lungs. It was dark and he was seriously worried. Surely she would have returned home by now? After recovering his breath, he made his way down the hill and back to the farmhouse.

As he entered the kitchen, he found Alastair, Katherine and Marcus seated at the table.

"Any sign?" asked Alastair anxiously.

It had now been two hours since Grace had run out of the house. Her father knew she was sensible and knew she was used to being on her own, but this time it felt different; this time they had to search for her.

Jack shook his head. "No. I'm going to try the path down to Lochaberdale next, but I came back for a torch."

"I wonder if she took her car?" said Katherine suddenly. "We've all been assuming she went on foot. If I was that upset, I'd want to get far away as quickly as I could. I don't know why I didn't think of that before."

Jack was out of the door even before she'd finished speaking. He was back again in a moment. "You're right. Morris has gone."

Alastair got to his feet. "I'll go and fetch Angus and the land rover. Jack, you get together whatever you think we may need. We'll catch up with her, I'm sure."

He was out of the door and back within ten minutes.

"Och, Alastair, this is a sorry business," remarked Angus as the three men made their way down to Lochaberdale in the land rover. "Would ye be agreeable to us picking up young Léon on the way? Ye never know, but an extra pair of hands might be useful and he's a strong lad now. It's best to keep it in the family, if you get my drift."

"Of course," said Alastair feeling pleased, despite his present disquiet, that relations were now good between Angus and his future son-in-law and grateful for his farm manager's discretion.

They made a brief diversion to pick up Léon and retraced their path back onto the main track. Jack then suggested that he search Katherine's rose garden, another favourite place of refuge for Grace, but found it to be deserted. Disappointed, he climbed back into the land rover.

There was no sign of Morris as they travelled slowly down the hill, nor was Grace to be found anywhere in Lochaberdale. *Spirit II* was swinging gently on her mooring as the tide turned, so they knew Grace had not gone out to sea.

"She could be anywhere, *Grandpapa*," remarked Léon.

"I know, my boy, and she's probably perfectly safe and will come home in the morning. But my instinct tells me something's not right and that we need to find her.

"Aye, but it'll be like looking for a needle in a haystack in the dark," observed Angus.

"Yes, but that's what we've got to do." Alastair then hesitated for a moment before saying: "I think we should collect Michael. Just in case, you know." He said no more, but he needed his friend to be there.

Michael was out of the house almost immediately and Mary drove up to the farmhouse to be with Katherine, who had elected to stay at home with Marcus in case Grace returned.

He slung his medical kit into the back of the vehicle amongst the jumble of ropes, climbing gear, blankets, torches and Tilley lamps that Jack had brought. They would probably not need any of it, but it was better to be prepared.

With agonizing slowness, they travelled over the bumpy terrain. They went as far as they could beyond Michael's croft and Angus brought the land rover to a stop at the edge of the loch and let the engine idle.

"Well, that's as far as we can go this way," said Michael.

"Yep." Jack sighed.

He got out of the vehicle and walked along the shore for a little way. This had never been one of Grace's haunts. She hadn't come here – he could feel it. But where on earth could she have gone? Mrs Gilgarry's cottage? Unlikely. They had just spent three very happy days together and, in her present frame of mind, thinking that he had acted dishonourably towards her, it would be too painful for her to stay there. But where was she?

Then some memory stirred at the back of Jack's mind. *Of course!* Quickly, he ran back to the land rover.

"I think I know where she is!" he exclaimed. "Turn round, Angus and drive back the way we came. Go slow, mind. We need to look out for some kind of turning up onto the eastern headlands. It'll be on our right."

Michael was aghast. "It's very tricky underfoot in the daylight, let alone in the dark."

"What makes you think she went up there, Jack?" asked Alastair, his heart pounding. Surely Grace was too level-headed to take any stupid risks?

"It's just some random memory that popped into my head. On one of our more recent camping trips, she told me a story that Mrs Gilgarry had told her about several families who sought refuge in some caves along the eastern seaboard after their village had been burned during the clearances. Grace said that these caves could only be reached from a very small beach at low tide. The rest of the time they were completely cut off because once the tide came in, a treacherous undertow made access too dangerous."

"And you're sure she's gone there?" Michael was seriously worried.

"It's a bit of a long shot, but it's possible."

They drove on in silence.

Grace slithered and slipped over the uneven surface as she ascended the path towards the headland. Mrs Gilgarry had spoken of a steep-sided gully that was the only means of access down to the little beach from where it was possible to climb into the caves. If she did find them, no one would think of looking for her there. Grace had no reason to suppose anyone would be worried. She was used to wandering the island on her own; they'd know she would keep herself safe and come back eventually.

She could hear the waves pounding against the rocks over a hundred feet below her. Suddenly, the moon emerged from behind the clouds: lighting her way, aiding her progress. She walked nearer to the cliff edge and there, just in front of her, the grass seemed to disappear.

She shone her torch down the precipitous incline. This must be it: the gully. Her heart beat faster with adrenaline and anticipation; all thoughts of Anna and Jack taken out of her mind.

Grace knew she had to concentrate; to focus. She couldn't afford to slip. Perhaps she should wait until morning before attempting this.

No.

She was too close to her objective; the challenge of it too great a temptation to resist. She would have to manage without the torch, though. It would be impossible to make the descent and hold a torch at the same time so she tucked it safely into her haversack. She might need it later.

Slowly, she began on the downward path, using tufts of coarse grass or rocks protruding from the gully sides as hand-holds. She felt her way cautiously with one foot at a time, wedging her walking boots against the rocks to give her better purchase. After a while, with moonlight to help her, she found that her eyes were adjusting to the darkness and she could see quite well. While still being careful, she began to move with greater confidence.

Some fifteen minutes later, they found Morris. It didn't look as though the car had been abandoned with desperation because the driver's door was shut with the key still in the ignition. It was parked at the end of the track and they knew they would not be able to take the land rover beyond this point either.

They apportioned the equipment between them all, apart, that is, from Alastair whom Jack would not allow to carry anything.

"You might be physically fit," he said, when Alastair protested, "But you're still nearly eighty and this is going to be a tough enough hike as it is without any extra burden."

Alastair acquiesced without protest. "I take your point. Thank you, Jack."

They set off in single file, Jack in the lead with Angus bringing up the rear and Alastair, Michael and Léon in the middle. The pre-dawn light was beginning to emerge on the horizon and soon they could see their way without the aid of torches and lamps. They decided to keep two of the torches but set the others down along with the lamps. They could collect them on the way back; there was no point in carrying unnecessary weight. The equipment would be quite safe.

As the grey of pre-dawn began to lighten the sky above her, Grace peered back through the gloom to view her progress. It was quite spectacular and yet she had a long way to go before she reached the beach at the bottom of the gully. Her view below was obscured by some kind of overhanging rocky ledge, so she had no idea as to the state of the tide.

She lay down and peered gingerly over the edge. It appeared to be no more than a very thin layer of shale. This was going to be very awkward. She wriggled forward as far as she dared, looking for hand and footholds, for some way to lift herself over safely.

Suddenly, the ledge gave way and she was propelled downwards, tumbling and rolling, her body thrown against rocks that protruded beside and beneath her. Helplessly, she went down and down. She told herself to relax; she must relax. She had read somewhere that if your body was relaxed when you fell, you could avoid serious injury.

So, Grace closed her eyes and gave herself up to the forward motion she could do nothing to prevent, keeping her body as light as possible, and prayed that she would be all right.

When they reached the start of the gully, there was no sign of Grace.

"This must be the right place. It has to be," declared Jack.

He called out her name but there was no reply. He called again and again, but all they could hear was the pounding of the waves below.

"Now, we need to decide what to do." He looked over the edge. "It's horrendously steep but I can get down there all right."

"I'm going with you."

"Och no, Alastair," protested Angus, holding onto his friend's arm.

"She's my daughter. I must." Fear made him insistent and he pulled away from his friend's grip and prepared to lower himself over the edge.

"Don't be daft, man. Look, if it makes ye feel any better, I cannae go either. With my limp, I'd only be a liability. I'll wait up here with ye. It'll need two of us to be here in case..."

"Absolutely," interrupted Michael, looking at Angus gratefully, knowing the farm manager could manage perfectly well. "You really can't go, Alastair. I would never forgive myself if anything happened to you. Think of Katherine. Would she want you to go?"

"No." Alastair had to give in. Again. *Damn it*, he thought, frustrated by the aging process that negated every youthful inclination. Well, nearly all... at least he still had that.

Jack was becoming impatient. "Look, whoever's coming with me, we must get a move on."

He and Léon took the ropes and blankets, tying them securely onto their backs, leaving their hands free, while Michael slung his medical kit across his shoulders. At sixty, he knew he would find it tough going but years of living and working on Cairnmor had kept him fit and reasonably agile.

Léon was apprehensive. He'd never attempted anything like this before but he relished the challenge. *Perhaps when he hears of this*, he thought, *Papa will be proud of me at last*. The thought spurred him on and he followed his companions into the gully.

Carefully, they made their way downwards with Jack in the lead, showing them the best places to hold onto; how to wedge their feet against the sides to give them better purchase, how to keep the weight evenly distributed and their bodies balanced.

Slowly, cautiously, they descended until they came to a place where there had been a recent landslide. Jack's heart began to pound and for the first time he felt real fear.

"You two stay here," he commanded.

He undid his homemade backpack and took it off, moving forward cautiously. Small rocks, stones and shale skittered downwards under his feet and he almost lost his balance. Just in time, Léon grabbed him before he went careering head first down the slope.

"Thanks," said Jack. "I'll have to try it a different way."

He manoeuvred himself in a sitting position from which he could move with more control by keeping his hands on the ground. Even so, he slipped and slithered to the bottom of the incline.

And there, lying unconscious at his feet, he found Grace.

CHAPTER 27

Echoes

"No, oh, no!"

Jack threw himself onto his knees by her side. He felt her pulse and checked her breathing. Both were strong and even. Relieved, he said her name but she gave no response.

He called up to Léon and Michael and they came, carefully and slowly down onto the beach in the same way that Jack had done, bringing the blankets, rope and the medical kit with them.

"She's breathing comfortably and her pulse is strong. I've checked both," said Jack.

"Good."

Michael knelt down beside the still, prone figure of Grace and examined her carefully. He looked up in amazement.

"As far as I can tell, there's nothing broken. You have a look."

Gently, Jack began to feel along the length of one of her legs, moving upwards from her ankle as far as her thigh. His breath caught in his chest and he stopped.

"I'll take your word for it," he said, clearing his throat.

Michael smiled at him. "Er… yes… absolutely. I take your point."

"What about her back and neck?"

"That's the hardest part to tell."

Very carefully, Michael felt up and down her spine.

"One or two vertebrae slightly out of place but that's all, I think." He looked at Jack. "She's covered in cuts and the bruises are beginning to show but all in all, she seems to have been incredibly lucky. However, we need to get her to hospital as soon as possible. I'd like her to have some X-rays, especially here…" and very gingerly, he touched the back of her head. "She has a bump the size of a duck-egg but there doesn't appear to be any compression. However, only an X-ray will tell for certain. I'd like to know how long she's been unconscious."

"It's going to be impossible to get her out of here without a boat. There is no way that we can get her back up that gully."

"*Mon Dieu !* Jack, Michael! *Regardez la mer !* Look at the sea! It's coming in very fast," shouted Léon, making the two men jump.

Without warning, the water was surging round the promontory, hissing and foaming into the tiny cove, rapidly flooding the beach.

"Bloody hell!" said Jack. "Where are those caves?"

They scanned the rock face and then Léon shouted out, "Look! *Regardez à droite !* Look to the right! A path going upwards and they are there!"

"We shouldn't move her, let alone carry her up that slope," declared Michael.

"We have to. There's no choice." Jack stood up. "Between the three of us, we should manage it."

They lifted her up carefully, Jack cradling her head and shoulders with Léon holding her legs and feet while Michael supported her waist and back.

Slowly, they carried her. The water gushed round them, covering their feet, their knees, their thighs and by the time they reached the path, it was almost up to their waists. With a profound sense of relief, they climbed upwards into the safety of the caves.

Gently, they laid Grace down on the floor onto one of the blankets.

Jack stood at the entrance, surveying their situation. He knew what had to be done next.

"I'm going to swim over to the ledge and climb back up the gully to tell Alastair and Angus we need a boat," he said.

"No! I'll do it!" Léon wanted to make a real contribution to this adventure. He was young; he was strong; he was his father's son. "I'll go!"

"Can you swim?" Jack was dubious about allowing Léon to tackle such a dangerous assignment.

"Mais oui ! My father insisted that all his sons learned to swim. It was the one thing he could do with us boys physically. He could not play football or tennis, you see."

"Okay." Jack put his hand on the young man's shoulder. "There's a dangerous undertow if Mrs Gilgarry's story is to be believed, so what we'll do is to tie all of these ropes together and if they're long enough, you should be able to swim to the ledge…" and Jack pointed.

"Mon Dieu ! But that is the one we waited at. It is almost at water level!"

"I know. Help me with these ropes."

The two men laid them out on the floor of the cave. Jack tied each of them with a water bowline and secured the last one tightly round Léon's waist using the same knot. Suddenly, Jack began to have second thoughts.

"Look, it's too great a risk for you to do this, Léon. It has to be me."

"Non !" Léon was emphatic. *"Non !* You are stronger than I am, *certainement.* But I shall need your strength to hold onto the rope and pull me back if the current takes me away. I could not do that for you. Even though I now have much muscle." He flexed his arm, making Jack smile. "Besides which, if that was Fiona lying there, I should want to be by her side. You stay. I shall be all right."

Jack took a deep breath and gave in. *"Merci, Léon. Tu es très brave."* He then tugged at each section of rope before saying, "Well, they all seem to be secure."

They walked to the entrance of the cave and Jack placed the final section of rope around his shoulder, holding on to it tightly, the rest poised and ready in his other hand. At the last moment, he removed the signet ring he always wore on his little finger lest it should become lost or damaged as he took the strain on the rope. Carefully, he placed it deep into his trouser pocket.

"When I say 'now', off you go."

"Good luck!" said Michael, standing behind Jack, ready to tail the rope if extra strength was required.

"Merci. I may need it."

Léon looked at the swirling water below his feet. Despite his brave words, his legs felt like jelly.

"Ready?"

"Oui."

206

"Now."

Léon lowered himself into water that was so cold, it took his breath away. As he left the sanctuary of the cave, he felt the current take him. There was no predictability to its direction and he had to use all his strength just to keep afloat. His goal seemed an impossibility.

He struck outwards with a strong crawl, feeling the rope pull tight around his waist as Jack helped keep him on course; then feeling it slacken as it was paid it out little by little, fine judgement being used by Jack, allowing him to make progress and be secure but without being hindered.

The tide was still coming in and the undertow began to make itself felt as Léon left the protection of the promontory. Jack had to use all his strength to hold on as the sea asserted its power.

Léon had almost reached the ledge when suddenly, the rope snagged. Jack stood helpless and horrified as Léon disappeared beneath the surface of the water.

Quickly, he paid out more rope.

Anna sat on the sands of South Lochaberdale and lit a cigarette, watching the gulls as they wheeled and circled in the air. She had no desire to prolong her stay in the farmhouse. She just wanted to go home and leave the scene of her absolute stupidity. But she couldn't. This was Cairnmor. There wasn't a ferry until that afternoon.

Her mood was a mixture of defiance and embarrassment. Whatever had possessed her to act in the way she had last night? And as for Marcus... By exposing her in that way, he'd caused her to lose every last shred of any dignity and credibility she might have had left. She should have landed him in it when she was giving evidence at his trial. No, that would have been unfair and unjust. He had always been kind to her when they were together and very good in bed.

She thought of Greg. He was kind and also very good in bed. And he suited her better, even more so than Jack. She wished she could be with Greg. He always managed to sooth away her fears and troubles and make things right again. He would restore her equilibrium after this foolishness on her part, as he had done so often since she had known him.

He'd fallen in love with her almost immediately and what was more, Anna didn't mind. She really didn't. He understood her moods, her needs. He supported her acting and he positively encouraged her musical ambitions. But he could be quite censorious if he felt she was overstepping the mark with him. She liked that in a man. Control with intelligence; strength with gentleness.

Just like Jack.

She really had to stop this now; this habit of comparing every man to Jack. She had done it for so many years, it had become an ingrained part of her psyche. She wasn't in love with him anymore – the reality of seeing him again had proved that beyond any doubt.

However, it seemed odd to be able to say with absolute certainty that she was *not* in love with him when for so long he had been the dream in her head. It was hard to believe that the illusion could have been swept away so quickly and easily.

Perhaps she was in love with Greg. The thought struck her like a bolt from the blue and her heart pounded. If that was the case, she must finish with him before it impinged on her feelings for Jack; before she was unfaithful to her husband yet again by loving someone else.

Anna experienced confusion. She had to stop doing that as well. If she was in love with Greg, there was nothing to feel guilty about. She and Jack were going to get divorced. He no longer wanted her nor did she want him. Therefore, he wouldn't have the right to be angry with her any more if she loved someone else. She could do exactly as she wished.

It took her several moments before she could assimilate the significance of the thought. She could love Greg with a clear conscience and she could allow herself to stay in love with him.

But what if he wanted children?

She didn't want another baby. She was not cut out to be a mother: that much she knew for certain. Anna felt anxious and confused again. Perhaps she should finish with Greg after all, then she wouldn't have to worry about having children nor would he be forever disappointed with her when she refused to have any. Besides which, he already had a family to whom he was devoted. His divorce had been an amicable one and, for the sake of his two grown-up daughters and son, he had remained on good terms with his ex-wife.

He was divorced and had children already. The thought struck her forcibly. Might it be that he wasn't worried about having any more? If that was so, then she could go to him and stay with him.

For the first time in her adult life, Anna felt emotionally free from the guilt that had kept her tied to Jack. She began to wonder about the other events in her life which had distressed her and from which she had run away, suppressing guilt for the pain she had caused others.

Up on the cliff top, Angus was becoming increasingly anxious. As soon as the three men had begun their descent down the gully, he had, with great difficulty, persuaded Alastair to walk back to the parked vehicles and take a proper rest. There was nothing they could do for the time being, he said. It was better to be alert and able to deal with any eventuality.

They talked for a while, sitting in Grace's Morris and very soon, completely exhausted after the exertions of the night, Alastair had fallen asleep. Angus sat for a while and made sure that he was warm enough by covering him with the last remaining blanket before trudging back along the track to keep a solitary vigil waiting for the reappearance of their companions.

They had been gone a very long time. Angus felt doubly frustrated that, in order to dissuade Alastair from going with them, he had not been able to go down the gully and use his great strength to help and also, that he could not see what was going on at the base of the cliff.

Eventually, his curiosity got the better of him. Very carefully, he began to make his way downwards. He had to know exactly what was going on.

Restless and anxious, unable to stay in the farmhouse, Katherine had gone for a walk along the beach. Grace had not returned and they had heard nothing from Alastair or Jack and the others. She felt helpless and useless.

It had been comforting to see Mary though and, after they had talked, she had left her and Marcus distracting themselves by looking through Mrs Gilgarry's remedies, putting them into some sort of order and talking about the old lady. She had stayed for a while but, unable to concentrate, Katherine had decided to come out for a walk.

She smelt the cigarette smoke a long time before she saw Anna. The rising wind had blown it in her direction and its pungent aroma caught in her throat and made her cough. When she came upon her daughter, perched in the shelter of the sand dunes, she stopped and the two women stared at each other.

"I suppose you're going to make some derogatory remark about my being addicted to the pernicious weed," began Anna defensively, stubbing out her cigarette in the sand.

"No, but you know how I feel about you smoking."

"Yes. You made that very plain when I was fourteen."

Katherine sat down a little way away from her errant daughter.

After a while, Anna said, "I'm sorry about last night."

"So am I."

Anna forestalled her mother before she could say any more. "Please don't lecture me. I'm a grown woman."

"Then act like one."

"Grace will be all right."

"Let's hope so."

"I'll never forgive myself if anything's happened to her." Yet even as she spoke the words, she knew her mother would sense the ambivalence in the sentiment.

Katherine looked at her sharply, but said nothing.

"I've been playing the piano again," began Anna, after a lengthy, uncomfortable silence, her voice hesitant and uncertain.

"Oh? I didn't know you'd stopped."

"After Jack left, I wanted to cut the ties to my old life completely."

"And did you achieve your goal?" Katherine was unable to keep the bitterness out of her voice. All that talent, all those years of hard work wasted.

"Perhaps. It's also why I didn't write."

Katherine was stung. Anna had been loved and cared for. Was that such a terrible thing that she had felt the need to turn her back on them all so completely?

"Twelve years without any kind of communication is a very long time."

"But you must have known I was all right"

How unfeeling and unimaginative her daughter could be sometimes. "Your agent has become something of a distant friend."

"Yes." She hesitated. More guilt to overcome. "I'm sorry I haven't kept in touch."

"So am I." The words were the same, though the response was slightly softer.

"Thank you for your letters."

"I'm glad you read them and didn't just toss them into the bin."

Anna blushed. She had done that with the first ones.

"It's always good to hear from you."

"Really?" Katherine found it hard to tell whether Anna was being sincere or offering mere platitudes. "And what about Ben? He comes home tomorrow from staying at his friend's house on Cairnbeg. Will you stay to see him? You could delay your departure by a couple of days."

Anna wondered whether her mother was beginning to regret ordering her to leave so peremptorily. "I don't know. It's probably better that I don't. For your sake."

"I'm not that hard-hearted. It's more important that you see your son."

"No. I can't."

"Why?"

"My life is in the States. It wouldn't be fair on him if his mother suddenly breezed into his life and then breezed out again. Therefore it's better that we have no contact at all." More long-buried guilt pricked her conscience.

"Better for whom? You or him?"

"I've no idea. Me probably. I never was cut out to be a mother."

"How do you know? Have you ever tried?"

"No."

"It's not too late to get to know him. You're missing out on something very special, Anna. He's a lovely boy."

"And I'm grateful to you for raising him."

Katherine regarded her daughter carefully before saying, "What if he resents you for ignoring him?" She refrained from saying, *Like you did with Alex.*

"He won't."

"How do you know?"

"Because all of you give him so much love that he won't even notice."

"You can't be certain of that. Alastair and I loved and cared for you."

"I know and I threw it back in your faces. I'm such a *wicked* girl."

Katherine sighed. Nothing seemed to have changed since she was fourteen. When would Anna learn?

"I'm sorry, Mum. That was unfair."

She moved closer to her mother and said, so quietly that Katherine thought she'd misheard, "I've been an absolute fool all these years."

Warmed by her daughter's unexpected use of the word 'Mum', not unkindly Katherine replied, "You have rather, I'm afraid."

The two women sat in silence; a silence that edged them a little closer to some sort of reconciliation.

Jack felt the line slacken again and saw Léon surface, gasping and coughing for air before resuming his epic swim. The water was surging in eddies and whirlpools and Jack held on grimly, gasping with pain as the rope bit into his hands and wrists. Michael came to help him, the two men holding on with difficulty, struggling to keep the rope under their control.

They both knew that this was the only thing keeping Léon safe but they had now reached the end of the rope. There was no more left to pay out. Jack was also at the limit of his physical endurance. He could only imagine what Léon must be feeling.

Léon surfaced again tantalizingly close to the ledge, coughing and spluttering. The rocks were slippery but he wasn't quite near enough to get a grip. Time and again he tried, only to be swept back by the water. In vain he tried to loosen the knot round his waist; in vain he struggled to reach the safety of the ledge. The rope was too tight: there wasn't enough left to allow him to haul himself out of the water. He'd come all this way and made all that effort for nothing.

The thought of Grace lying there unconscious on the floor of the cave spurred him into making one last monumental attempt.

"Tell me about my father. Tell me about Alex."

Anna's words caught Katherine by surprise.

"I don't want to know the bad bits: how he was unfaithful to you, how he ran off and made a new life for himself in Australia and never contacted us again for years and years. I want to know what he was really like as a person: his character."

"Well, he was funny and kind, charming and very handsome."

"As handsome as Jack?" She was off again but Jack was her emotional yardstick against which all things were measured. She would use it this one last time and then let it go forever.

"Oh, yes, perhaps even more so. He was highly intelligent; a barrister at the top of his profession. He loved the drama of the courtroom."

Anna took this in. "Perhaps that's where I've inherited my acting ability from."

"Perhaps."

"Was he a good pianist?"

"Very."

"As good as me?" This was a simple acknowledgement and understanding of her ability, not boastfulness.

"No. You were exceptional."

"Did you love him?"

"Very much."

"It must have been difficult when you thought he'd been killed during the war."

"It was."

When Anna asked her next question, Katherine realized just how far along this particular road her daughter was now travelling.

"How did you and Alastair fall in love?"

"We just did. After we were told that Alex had been killed, we turned to each other for comfort. Gradually, over time, we came to realize that we felt a great deal more for each other than the affectionate friendship and companionship we had always shared."

"Alex's reappearance must have made things very, very awkward."

"That's an understatement."

"And then when you found out he'd been unfaithful while he was in Singapore…"

"I knew the marriage was finally over and that Alastair and I could be together for the rest of our lives as Alex could say nothing."

"Alastair was always a wonderful father to Rupert and me, wasn't he?"

Katherine's eyes filled with tears. "The very best. He loved you and cared for you as though you were his own children."

"He was always there for us, wasn't he?"

"Oh yes, even when Alex was alive, before the war." She had to be honest.

"Do you mind my asking all these questions?"

"No. You need to know and I'm glad you have found the courage to ask them at last."

"Am I really like Alex, I mean my father?"

"Oh yes. Incredibly."

"I wish I could remember him but I was too young. And now it's too late because he's dead."

"Yes."

Anna was silent for a moment. Then she asked, "What was I like as a child?"

"Strong-willed and naughty sometimes but surprisingly sensitive to other people's emotions. Although you often used that awareness to get your own way."

"Manipulative, you mean?"

"Yes. Sometimes. But you had this great passion for music. It was your life, your *raison d'être*. I'm very glad that you've found your way back to the piano again."

Anna moved closer to her mother. "Tell me how you and Alex met."

"He arrived one day on the steamer and asked me the way to the Lochaberdale Hotel…"

"Was it romantic?"

"Very. Like a novel."

And Katherine told her daughter about her father and the first wonderfully happy weeks that she and Alex had spent together on Cairnmor at the start of their relationship. She told Anna about her first visit to London and how he had proposed to her; of the Christmas spent at Mistley House when Roberta walked out on the family. She recounted how she and Alex worked together in the search for her real parents, Anna's grandparents, Mhairi and Rupert Senior. And finally, she told Anna about the Appeal at the House of Lords where Alex had spoken so eloquently in defence of the islanders, winning what became the most important and prestigious case of his career.

"Was he happy when Rupert and I were born?"

"He was delighted and very proud."

"But he didn't get involved with us did he?"

"No."

"Why?"

"He was married more to his work than he was either to me or his family."

"And that's why Alastair became like a father to us."

"Yes. You see we all of us lived in the same house and your granddad adored you both, just as you and Rupert both adored him."

And Anna nodded, understanding at last.

"Here, lad, give me your hand."

Léon reached up and Angus leaned outwards as far as he could, grabbing hold of Léon's hand and arm. He felt the line go slack and he pulled Léon towards him until he could grab the rope round his waist, lifting him bodily onto the ledge, where the young man lay panting with exhaustion and shivering with cold.

"That's it, lad. Just lie there and get ye breath back. Yere a brave one and no mistake. I'll just gather all this lot in."

Angus pulled hard on the rope which Jack had released as soon as he saw that Angus had hold of Léon. When he had collected it all in, he threw it onto the ledge and waved at Jack, who responded in kind.

"Now, we'll just get this knot undone."

However, as hard as he tried, he couldn't. Jack had done his work too thoroughly in providing a knot that strengthened as it became wet. There was absolutely no prospect of undoing it, so Angus produced his trusty Swiss army knife from his jacket.

"Hold still now," and he sliced the rope round Léon's waist in one quick thrust. *"Merci."*

The young man sat up and lifted his shirt, viewing with some dismay the red weals that were already visible on his skin.

"We'll get those looked at when we're back in civilization again. Now, what news of Grace?"

Léon explained what had happened and what was needed. Angus looked at the gully towering above them and said, "Well, if yere up to moving straight away, we'd better get going. There's no time to lose. The climb will warm ye up."

As soon as Jack saw them begin the ascent, he went into the cave and knelt beside Grace who looked up at him.

"When?" he asked Michael, his face suffused with joy.

"Just now, just after we released the rope."

"Thank God."

"Is she all right?"

"Yes."

He took her hand, gently brushing her hair away from her face, and kissed her forehead.

Discreetly, Michael moved out of earshot and went to sit at the mouth of the cave, leaning against the wall, looking outwards as the retreating water still swirled around the cove. He could just make out the tiny figures of Angus and Léon making steady progress up the narrow gully.

"Hold me, Jack."

Carefully, he took her into his arms, grimacing at the pain in his hands but not allowing her see.

"Of all the stupid things to do."

"Ssh. Don't talk, my darling, just rest."

"I fell. The outer part of the ledge collapsed. I wasn't trying to be reckless."

"I know," he said soothingly, while at the same time thinking that attempting a perilous descent on her own wasn't exactly sensible.

Slightly incoherently, her words tumbled out. "It doesn't matter about Anna. I don't care what went on. I love you too much, Jack. Everything else doesn't matter."

He held her close to his heart. "I wasn't with Anna yesterday evening."

"You weren't?" At the back of her mind, she'd always known that but even so, relief flooded through her.

"I was in the study with Alastair, discussing our future."

"You were?"

"Yes. I love *you*, Grace. And *only* you."

"You do?"

"Yes."

"And Anna?"

"She can go to hell for all I care, especially after that stunt she pulled on you."

"You don't mean that."

He looked at her.

She smiled then said, "I just panicked. I didn't really believe that you were waiting for her in your room but I could never be completely sure about anything where Anna is concerned. And I was afraid to look in case you were."

"I understand. But please believe me when I say you have absolutely no reason to doubt me, and neither shall I ever give you cause. I love you with all my heart and soul."

"Oh, my darling. I love you so much."

"I know."

For a while they sat together in silence. Then Jack said, "There's a poem called *Idyll* by Siegfried Sassoon in the book you sent me for my birthday. It's always been my favourite. I've read it so many times."

She thought for a moment. "*In the grey summer garden I shall find you, with day-break and the morning hills behind you…*"

"That's the one."

"It's my favourite as well."

"There are two lines that capture perfectly what I've finally come to understand; about finding you, I mean…"

Gently, Jack kissed her and Grace leaned back against him, listening to him, safe at last in the arms of the man she had always loved.

"Please tell me what they are."

He smiled at her, his eyes alive.

"*Not from the past you'll come, but from that deep where beauty murmurs to the soul asleep.*" He caressed her gently. "You see, darling, my true love lay not in the past with Anna, but with you, my dear sweet, beautiful Grace; you, who speaks to the very essence of me. I didn't realize. I'm sorry it's taken me so long to wake up to that."

Tears filled her eyes and she pulled him towards her and kissed him.

"We're together now and that's all that matters. At last we've found each other." Grace smiled, content. After a while, she could feel her eyes closing. "I'm so tired, I can't keep awake."

Jack kissed her again and covered her with the blankets. Almost instantly, she fell into a deep healing sleep.

He went to find Michael.

"Will she be all right? Does it matter that she's fallen asleep?"

Michael smiled. "Not at all. The best thing for her. Now, let me take a look at those hands."

And Jack winced as Michael put on ointment and bandaged them up.

214

The terns cried out above them, circling and wheeling.

"I wish I'd asked you all this sooner."

"So do I." Katherine didn't say that she had tried many times to tell her, but each time had been met with tears and tantrums. "It would have made things much easier for you."

"Yes. I realize that now."

"And for all of us. But maybe you had to be ready within yourself…"

Katherine stopped speaking, losing the thread of what she was saying; losing any sense of what she was doing at that moment.

She had to go to Lochaberdale. Now. She was *compelled* to go to Lochaberdale.

"I'm so sorry, Anna. I have to go."

"Why?"

"I don't know. I just do. Please don't be offended." She stood up and touched Anna's shoulder briefly and gently. "I'm glad we've talked like this but I really do have to go."

Disconcerted by her mother's abrupt departure, Anna watched as she disappeared through the sand dunes, walking quickly, taking the shortest route down to the main township on the island.

CHAPTER 28

Spirit of Adventure

As soon as Angus and Léon reached Alastair in the land rover, they told him that a boat needed to be despatched with some urgency. Angus drove them as fast as he dared down into Lochaberdale and straight away took Léon into Ron's shop where he could be looked after.

Meanwhile, Alastair went to the lifeboat station but as luck would have it, the lifeboat had been called out on a difficult rescue involving two fishing boats and was likely to be away for some time, they told him. The rest of the fishing fleet were also out.

Instantly, Alastair knew exactly what he had to do. Moreover, he would allow no one to dissuade him from this particular course of action. With decisive strides, he went to his motor boat, *Spirit of Adventure*, tied up alongside the harbour wall.

At exactly the same time Katherine arrived and Alastair immediately held out his arms to her. For a brief moment they kissed and held each other close.

"I needed you," he said.

"I know. That's why I came."

Katherine was anxious; wanting to know about Grace.

"Did you find her?"

"Oh yes."

"Is she all right?"

"Unconscious but safe."

"Oh, Alastair. What happened?"

"We don't quite know what the full story is, as yet. Jack and Michael are with her."

"Where?"

"Some caves along the eastern seaboard that Mrs Gilgarry must have told her about."

"How did you know where to look?"

"Jack remembered a conversation he'd had with Grace on one of their more recent camping trips."

"He's a remarkable man."

"He is and very much in love with her. But I'll tell you more as we go."

"Go where?"

"To rescue our daughter, of course."

"What?"

"Apparently, these caves are only accessible at high tide by boat or by climbing down an impossibly steep gully to a tiny stretch of sand when the tide's out. However, it may be possible to be picked up from the little beach. We won't know until we get there. Did Mrs G. never tell you about them?"

"No! Goodness, what a discovery to make after all these years! I presume you're intending to take *Spirit of Adventure*. In which case, I'm coming with you."

"I'm counting on it." He smiled and kissed her again.

"Now, now you two. What's goin' on 'ere?" and Ron stumped over to greet them. "Léon's nice and snug now. Hot drink and a couple of blankets and some dry clothes. He'll be all right. Brave lad 'e is by all accounts."

He watched as Alastair and Katherine removed the cockpit cover.

"Angus and I ought to be goin' wiv you both. Just for old times' sake, you know," he said, hiding his inner anxiety for their wellbeing under a nostalgic exterior.

Alastair chuckled. "Nice as that would be, we'll go faster with fewer people. As it is, on the return journey there'll be five of us." He began making preparations to start the engine. "Now, I need cans of fuel. Lots of them. It'll take us several hours at least to reach the caves. There's enough in the tanks but it would be disastrous if we ran out."

"Okay, guv," and Ron ambled off as fast as he could to the fuel store, where he enlisted the help of his two sons.

Within an hour, *Spirit of Adventure* was pulling away from the jetty. Ron had supplied them with fuel, blankets, flasks full of hot tea and food. He and Angus stood on the quayside watching the boat as Alastair opened up both engines, and they remained to see it recede rapidly into the distance.

"Will they be all right, do ye think?" asked Angus. "He's no' gettin' any younger. Nor is Katherine."

"Nah. They'll be fine. They've travelled far and wide over the years and *Spirit*'s a good sturdy motor boat. Besides which, they'll take it in turns. Katherine's still a dab hand at the wheel which means Alastair won't have to do all the driving."

"Aye, tha's true. And they brought us back from Dunkirk just fine, didn't they? But," he added, "they were much younger then."

"We was all much younger then," remarked Ron. "They'll bring our Gracie back all right and at least they won't have no enemy to contend with like we all did at Dunkirk!"

"Aye, there is that indeed," and the two men smiled at each other before returning to Ron's shop to await the intrepid little ship's return.

Anna remained seated for a while, deep in thought, after her mother had left. Then she returned to the farmhouse. She went straight up to her room without speaking to anyone and penned two letters: one for Jack and the other for her mother and grandfather. After this, she packed her suitcase and caught the afternoon ferry, which departed just after *Spirit of Adventure* had disappeared out of sight beyond the headlands.

With only a small amount of regret, Anna bade a silent farewell to her family and the island that had once been her home.

She knew she would never return.

Fighting against an increasingly hostile sea, they approached the little cove a couple of hours before the next high tide.

"Well, we seem to have timed it just right," remarked Katherine.

"Yes, but it's more by luck than judgement," replied Alastair. "Can you take the wheel for a moment? I just want to check the chart again."

Adjusting rudder and engines, Katherine kept the boat at station-keeping but it was not easy.

"The currents are very unpredictable here. It's quite difficult to keep the boat steady."

"I know and that worries me."

Having studied the chart once more, Alastair decided that it would be risky but possible to enter the cove, despite the footnote warning of eddies and whirlpools that appeared under certain tidal conditions. He hoped those conditions would not be present that day.

"I'll take her," he said and skilfully, he brought *Spirit of Adventure* around the promontory, holding her steady opposite the little beach.

As soon as Jack and Michael heard the sound of the engine, they walked down to the water's edge. Alastair motored slowly towards them, constantly checking the depth gauge.

"How's Grace?" called out Katherine, cupping her hands round her mouth so she could be heard.

"She's regained consciousness and apart from some concussion, seems to be fine. She's asleep at the moment, but I want to get her to the hospital as soon as we can," replied Michael, doing the same.

"Thank goodness she seems to be all right." Katherine's legs suddenly went weak and she had to sit down.

"What's the water like out there?" asked Jack.

"Volatile," replied Alastair, sharing Katherine's relief but fighting to keep *Spirit of Adventure* under control. "I don't want to hang around here for too long. Can Grace walk to the boat? I'd rather be away before the tide comes in too much further."

"That's wise. The sea absolutely surges round that headland and the cove fills up with water very quickly. There really is a nasty undertow once that happens. It would be impossible to control the boat, especially with this onshore wind."

Jack and Michael made their way quickly back to the cave. It took a few moments for Grace to wake up and several minutes before she was ready to walk. Supported by Jack and Michael on either side of her, she made slow but steady progress towards *Spirit of Adventure*.

Alastair brought the boat as close to the strip of beach as he dared while Grace waded out and climbed up the ladder, which Katherine had attached to the port side, to be followed by Michael, both of them aided by Jack, who was now shoulder deep in water.

Katherine kissed and hugged her daughter and although Alastair wanted to do the same, he knew he had to use every ounce of concentration to keep them in the same place. It was impossible to anchor.

Absorbed in watching them, as he prepared to mount the ladder, Jack looked up too late as, without any warning, the tidal surge rushed towards them. The power of the water slewed the motor boat round, wrenching his fingers from the rope ladder and winding him as the hull slammed into his chest. The wave dragged him away from the boat, the undertow sucking him beneath the water.

Spirit of Adventure yawed and bucked and Alastair fought frantically to regain control, terrified that Jack might have been swept under the propellers, using all his strength and skill as the gallant little ship was forced nearer and nearer towards the rocks, tossed about like a child's toy in the foaming water.

Grace was screaming, her voice barely audible above the hissing maelstrom, frantically looking out for Jack. Katherine and Michael held onto her, both of them clinging grimly onto the safety rail; desperately trying to stop themselves from being thrown overboard.

There was no chance to look for Jack; no chance to see where he was. Alastair was fighting for all their lives and his passengers could only hang on with all their might for theirs.

After the initial surge had passed, his heart pounding and his legs weak and shaking, Alastair brought the boat under his control, steering it away from the cove, standing off in relatively calmer water.

"We've got to look for Jack! We have to!" Grace was hysterical.

Katherine and Michael, pale with shock, looked at the empty water and knew there was nothing that anyone could do.

Grace tore herself away from the arms that restrained her and went to her father and, ignoring her dizziness, ignoring the fact that her legs were buckling under her, pleaded with him.

"You have to save him, Dad, you must!"

Alastair, white as a sheet, shook his head.

"It's far too dangerous. All I can do is to stand off for a bit and see if he surfaces."

"You have to do more than that. We can't just leave him."

"If he hasn't appeared in the next few minutes..."

"Don't say it. Please don't say it. He has to be here somewhere. He must be here somewhere. He can't have drowned. He can't... not now, not ever."

Alastair looked at his daughter and ignoring his own exhaustion and the expanding pain in his chest, he opened up the engines again and they motored to the next cove and the one after that and the one after that, returning to their original place one last time. But there was no sign of him anywhere.

Jack had gone.

With profound sadness and great reluctance in an increasingly rough sea, they turned for home. Michael took over the wheel, while Alastair and Katherine comforted their shocked daughter downstairs in the saloon; the three of them holding each other close, trying to come to terms with the tragedy that had just taken place.

Angus met them at the quayside just as darkness was falling. He knew something was very wrong as soon as they stepped off *Spirit of Adventure*. Ron made the boat secure, while Angus took them straight to the hospital, where a trance-like Grace was examined, her head X-rayed and she was pronounced fit and well apart from concussion.

While Katherine was with Grace, Alastair had a quiet word with the doctor on duty, who listened carefully to his chest, checking his heart rate, breathing and blood pressure.

"Och, you're fine, my friend. You'll outlive us all! A bit of tension caused those chest pains, which given what's just happened is hardly surprising. Go home and get some rest, if you can. There's nothing anyone can do until morning when the lifeboat and the fishing fleet return."

Alastair nodded and thanked him, before going to find Grace and Katherine. The doctor wanted to keep her in overnight for observation but Grace insisted that she wanted to go home. Under no circumstances did she want to stay in the hospital.

Angus drove the sad and silent party slowly back to the farmhouse where they sat around the kitchen table in stunned silence before Katherine helped an exhausted Alastair up to bed and Angus returned home to give the sad tidings to his family.

They decided to wait until Ben returned from his friend's house on Cairnbeg before giving him the devastating news about his father.

CHAPTER 29

Idyll

That night, unable to sleep, eschewing the proffered comfort and consolation of her mother, her head throbbing from grief and concussion, Grace sat on the window seat in her bedroom, her burning forehead resting on the cool glass, staring out into the darkness.

In the grey summer garden I shall find you
With day-break and the morning hills behind you…

The words of the poem that Jack had shared with her in the cave were going round and round in her mind. She remembered that birthday, celebrated on Cairnmor, when, as a present, she'd given him a first edition of Siegfried Sassoon's Collected Poems which she'd found in an antiquarian bookshop in Cambridge.

She remembered how delighted he'd been; how he'd hugged her joyously for a long time; how that afternoon, they'd gone for a long walk, ending up in the rose garden where he'd sketched her and asked her to read aloud from the book.

It was one of the most special afternoons that she had ever spent. Even now, she could see the loving expression in his eyes as he paused to observe her and listen while she spoke – a testament to his feelings for her. Yet, until the moment when she had told him that she loved him after the graduation ball, he hadn't made any move to kiss her because, she supposed, he was still under the influence of his feelings for Anna.

Oh, the irony of it, the cruel and bitter irony, thought Grace, that at the moment they had declared their unfettered capacity to love each other, Jack was lost.

It was too harsh; too unkind.

Unable to stay in her room any longer, Grace went across the hall to Jack's bedroom, quietly closing the door behind her; every action slow and deliberate; every action calculated to try and prevent her eyes filling with yet more tears; to stop the dizziness from completely taking over.

His curtains were open and in the moonlit room, she could see his personal things – his hairbrush, his comb, his wallet, his cufflinks box with its distinctive Royal Navy insignia – all laid out exactly in the way that he always left them: objects with which she was so familiar.

Glancing down at the floor, she saw one of his portfolios. Carefully, she reached up to the bedside lamp and switched it on before kneeling down and opening it, sifting through the bundle of sketches and paintings.

They were all of her.

Her hands trembling; her vision blurred by the tears that filled her eyes and spilled down her cheeks; her actions full of exhaustion and dizziness that she could no longer contain, Grace looked at each one until she could bear it no more.

Leaving the drawings and paintings strewn on the floor, she climbed into his bed, pulling his covers over her; burying her face in his pillows and breathing deeply, falling asleep with his scent in her nostrils.

Disturbed by some extraneous noise from outside, she awoke a few hours later from a deep, dreamless sleep.

Grace lay still for a long time, staring at the ceiling, cocooned for the briefest of moments by the drowsiness of sleep and the comfort of Jack's bed, before the pain and grief of shattering reality once more overtook her.

She needed to escape; to be out in the fresh air, away from the confines of the house. Grace pushed back the covers and, as though in a dream, returned to her own room and dressed.

Without thinking, she let herself quietly out of the house and in the first grey light of dawn, slowly walked the short distance to her mother's secluded rose garden. Surely here, in one of her favourite places of quietude and solace, she could lessen the heartache and despair of loss?

In the grey summer garden I shall find you
With day-break and the morning hills behind you...

She spoke the words aloud, uncontrollable tears pouring down her cheeks. It was all too much. She knew she could never find the comfort and consolation she sought.

Grace lay her aching body on the soft dampness of the mossy bank, her grief mingling with its wetness; its coolness a balm for her burning forehead.

She didn't know it was possible to feel such agony; didn't know how the human heart could survive such onslaught. She would never find him again, never share another day-break with him; never be with him again, out in their beloved hills.

"Oh Jack, I need you so much."

She rested her head on her arm and wept again until there were no more tears.

There will be rain-wet roses; stir of wings;
And down the wood a thrush that wakes and sings...

Mantra-like, she whispered the words over and over again as if by doing so she could bring him back; could bring him to her once again. He had so nearly been hers; they had come so close to sharing the life of which she had always dreamed. It was too cruel. How could life be so cruel?

Not from the past you'll come, but from that deep
Where beauty murmurs to the soul asleep...

He had told her that his greatest love came not from the past, but was all for her, Grace, who spoke to the deepest part of him, in the same way that he spoke to her.

In the state beyond exhaustion, her eyes closed and she drifted towards sleep. She heard his voice in her dreams...

And I shall know the sense of life re-born
From dreams into the mystery of noon
Where gloom and brightness meet.

His voice was so soft, so gentle, so close...

And standing there
Till that calm song is done, at last we'll share
The league-spread, quiring symphonies that are
Joy in the world, and peace, and dawn's one star.

He said her name.

"Grace."

He touched her cheek.

"Darling Grace, wake up."

He kissed her lips.

Drowsily, she put out her arms for him and he came to her and she held him close to her.

It was a wonderful dream; a cruel dream.

He was not here with her. He couldn't possibly be here with her.

He kissed her again and stroked her hair.

Suddenly, she was awake.

"Jack, oh, Jack!"

And all at once, they were both crying and laughing and hugging each other.

"You're here! But how? We thought…"

"I know." He buried his face in her shoulder, hiding from her the excruciating pain in his ribs. "I thought so too."

She took his head between her hands, searching his face, making sure he was real.

"I never want to be apart from you again," she said urgently, desperately. "Ever. I don't care what it takes. I have to be with you all the time. I don't ever want to lose you again. I couldn't bear to lose you again."

Jack kissed her then, urgently, passionately, his stubble rough on her cheeks. But she didn't care. He was safe. He was alive.

Eventually, they drew apart but Grace kept as close to him as she could.

"Tell me…"

Adjusting his position so that he didn't gasp out in pain, he recounted what had happened in the intervening hours since they had last been together:

"The undertow dragged me beneath the water and the tidal surge swept me round the headland and into the next cove. Somehow, I managed to surface and found myself in some sort of rock gully. There was no way that I could make myself visible to you, I was completely hidden from view. It was as much as I could do to cling onto the rocks with the water swirling all around me. I was trapped, I couldn't move.

"Eventually, the incoming tide carried me up higher and I was able to climb onto a small grass-covered ledge where, too exhausted to do anything else, I managed to wedge myself in safely and then lay down and slept. You must have gone by that time."

"We looked for you in all the nearby coves, but we couldn't see you. It was awful. Eventually, the surf became too strong and Dad was finding it impossible to control *Spirit*. We had to go otherwise the boat would have been smashed against the rocks. Oh Jack, I can't tell you how terrible it was when you disappeared and we were powerless to do anything to save you and then we couldn't find you and had to leave."

"I felt the same when I couldn't let you know I was safe."

"What did you do then?"

"When I woke up a few hours later, the tide had gone out and I could better assess my predicament and how to get out of it. The rocks below were no help and the cliff above me was sheer, but with no other options, I had to climb it. There was no other way out."

"Oh Jack, I'm so sorry. This is all my fault."

He kissed her forehead. "No one could have foreseen the repercussions of your understandable need for solitude." He smiled, and grimaced as he moved his hands. He would not let Grace see the state they were in.

"What happened next?"

"I reached the top of the cliff eventually. It was the most difficult climb you or I have ever attempted but, despite shaking with exhaustion when I reached the top, I did feel an enormous sense of achievement." He smiled at her and Grace nodded with understanding. "So, spurred on by this, I began to walk in the direction of home. I knew it would take me a long time and I was anxious to get back to you and let everyone know that I was safe. I can't tell you how glad I was when I passed the gully and even more delighted when I saw Morris still sitting there – and with the key in his ignition!"

Grace laughed. "I'm glad I did leave the key. I nearly took it with me but decided not to as I couldn't risk dropping it. I knew the car would be safe. No one ever goes up there and also no one ever steals anything on the island."

"Fortunately! Anyway, feeling immensely relieved, I drove down into Lochaberdale and sent word to all and sundry that I was all right. Everyone was immensely kind and, even though it's still so early, messages were despatched in all directions. I then went to the hospital but they said that you were fine and had gone home. I was on my way up to the farmhouse, when Morris ran out of petrol."

"Where?"

"Here."

"Here?"

"Yes. And I found you."

"Good old Morris!"

Jack laughed and kissed her again. Inadvertently, he put his hand up to her face and she saw the shredded bandages and the raw state of the skin underneath. She lifted up the other one and held them both. She looked at him in consternation.

"What happened to your hands?" she whispered, disparate images of him not being able to paint again filling her with sudden fear.

"Oh, nothing."

Grace looked at him. Jack smiled back at her ruefully.

"Oh, all right, then. They got rubbed raw when I was holding the rope for Léon and then bruised when I was trying to hold onto *Spirit*. The climb didn't do them any favours, either."

"Oh, my darling. Will they be all right?"

This had been worrying Jack as well, but he didn't say anything. "I expect so."

"You've got to have them looked at straight away. We've got to go to the hospital."

"Now?"

"Yes, now. Immediately."

"Yes, ma'am." He saluted and winced. "But are you up to the walk?"

"I'm fine," she said firmly. She could do anything now Jack was with her. "They said at the hospital there was nothing wrong; that there was no compression and that the sleep I had in the cave meant that my concussion is less than it would have been. I've got to take it easy for a week or so but I can manage to walk down into Lochaberdale."

"And then home," he said. "I could stay in bed for a week after all this!"

Grace gave him an impish smile.

He returned her look with wonder and said, "We ought to wait until we're married," but his words belied his desire; his pressing need of her.

"Why? I know we'll be together for always and remember, I said I wasn't letting you out of my sight ever again."

He laughed. "I know. But we should still wait."

"Why? I'm over twenty-one and anyway, I've already waited for you for such a long time," the tone of her voice betraying *her* need of him.

He touched her cheek thoughtfully and said very quietly, "Yes, you have." He hesitated and then added, "But what happens if you should become pregnant? Even in this day and age, it still carries a certain stigma."

"I won't. Besides which, I hardly need remind you that I was six years old when my parents got married. I was at their wedding. So were you. No one on the island worried about that."

Jack chuckled. "I know but even so, I don't want that for us."

"I won't get pregnant. Not yet anyway."

"How can you be so certain?"

She hesitated, still unsure whether what she had done was the right thing. "I'm on the contraceptive pill."

Jack was horrified. "Why? You and Sam didn't...?"

"No! Of course not, but when we first started going out with each other, I thought it would be wise, you know, just in case..."

"My ever practical Grace," he said relieved. "However, I can't tell you how glad I am that you didn't sleep with him. But you must stop taking it as soon as we're married."

"I intend to. I want us to have lots of children. And straight away. But you haven't asked me yet."

"Asked you what?" He was teasing her.

"If I'll marry you. I might not accept." She was teasing him back.

He smiled and took her hand, which he kissed tenderly. Then, ignoring the agony in his chest, he went down on one knee.

"Will you marry me?"

"Oh yes, a thousand times, yes."

Gently, he brought her to her feet and pulled her close to him and kissed her. He then took his signet ring from his pocket and put it on the third finger of her left hand.

Jack looked at her with his wonderful open and direct expression and said, his eyes full of love for her, "With this ring, I thee wed. With my body I thee honour. With all my worldly goods with thee I share."

And Grace repeated the age-old words, tears of joy filling her eyes.

He picked one of the roses then and after shaking the raindrops from the petals, placed it in her hair.

As they walked out of the hidden glade to begin their new life together, Jack didn't even give it a thought that the rose garden was where he had also proposed to Anna.

It was as though the memory of her had been erased from his mind.

CHAPTER 30

Celebrations

It was the morning of the birthday dinner-dance in the Great Hall in Lochaberdale. At the farmhouse, Katherine was fully occupied with last minute preparations, Alastair had been despatched to his study for a game of chess with Ben (along with strict instructions not to come out until he was called), Jack and Grace were supervising the arrangements in the Great Hall while Michael and Mary, together with Rupert and Rose, were organizing the group of volunteers who had offered their services for the catering.

Léon and Fiona had gone to meet with Phillippe and Lily at the hotel: Fiona nervous at the prospect of meeting her future father-in-law whom she had grown up regarding as some kind of god from the way her father had always spoken of him, while Léon was nervous because he wanted his father to have a good opinion of him at last.

Marcus was helping Katherine in the kitchen when she suddenly said, "Goodness me! The Australian contingent is arriving on the ferry today and I haven't organized anyone to meet her."

"Who's the 'Australian contingent'?" asked Marcus.

"Alastair's unknown Australian granddaughter."

"You mean Alex and Rachel's daughter?"

"That's the one." Katherine looked at Marcus imploringly. "Would you be a dear and meet her?"

"Of course. You know I'm glad to do anything to help. What time's the ferry?"

"Midday."

"Have Grace and Jack got Morris?"

"Yes and Angus is off with the land rover on an urgent mission of his own. Something to do with escaping sheep. So you'll have to walk, I'm afraid."

"In that case, I'd better leave very soon. It's a lovely day and I could do with some exercise. When I've met her shall I bring her back here?"

"Not immediately. She's staying at the hotel so give her a chance to settle in first. She can come and have tea with us later this afternoon if she'd like to. I thought it best that she gets to know us gradually and have some space of her own to start with rather than suddenly be faced with thousands of strange relatives, even though the du Laurier clan and some of our friends have taken over most of the hotel for this week."

"Really?"

"It's true. I booked the rooms last October as soon as I knew what we would be doing."

Marcus laughed. "Very wise. Where are the tourists staying?"

"With local people on their crofts."

"Could give a whole new dimension to the tourist industry on the island."

"That's exactly what Grace and Jack said."

"Do you have any idea what she looks like?"

"Our family guest? None. We should have arranged for her to have a rose in her teeth and carrying a book!" Katherine smiled.

"I'll find her. What's her name?"

Before Katherine could answer, Ben burst into the kitchen.

"Grandma, I'm starving."

"We only finished breakfast an hour ago," observed Marcus.

"I know but I'm still hungry."

"You'd better look in the fridge and see what you can find," said Katherine.

"Ah, 'the locust phase of adolescence'," quoted Marcus good-naturedly. "I remember it well!"

Ben laughed. "I like that. Where's it from?"

"I've no idea. But it's rather appropriate. Well, I'd better get going. See you later, guys. Enjoy your grazing, Ben!"

Marcus took his time walking down to the harbour and timed his arrival to perfection. He sat on the harbour wall and waited while the ferry berthed and discharged its cargo of a couple of cars and a crowd of foot passengers, looking out for anyone who might qualify as the 'Aussie contingent'. He realized he'd forgotten to ask for her name again before he'd left the farmhouse.

Suddenly, coming towards him, a familiar face and a head of thick chestnut hair, glossy in the sunlight, caught his eye. He knew this lady, but from where?

Realization dawned.

At the same moment, she looked up and stopped dead in her tracks in front of him, her mouth open in amazement.

"Marcus Kendrick?"

"Yes."

"I was at your trial," she said, the words tumbling out of her mouth before she could stop them.

"I know. Every day. You sat behind me. I used to look out for you." Marcus's response to her was instant.

"You did? I tried to find you afterwards but you'd gone."

"I came here. To recover."

They looked at each other in wonder.

"Please tell me your name."

"I'm Marcia Harper."

It was impossible to miss her accent. "From Australia?"

"Too right."

"Then you must be Alastair's mysterious granddaughter?"

"Alastair Stewart? Yes, I am. You know him?"

"I do. I'm actually living with your family."

"How come?"

"This is a small island and it's a long story!"

They looked at each other again.

"Do you have time to tell me?"

"All the time in the world."

The words slipped out before Marcus knew he was saying them. He couldn't stop looking at her. Marcia couldn't stop looking at him.

"I'm supposed to be staying at the hotel."

"I know." Marcus picked up her suitcases and smiled. "Shall we?"

"Yes."

They continued to regard each other with astonishment as they walked up the slope to the hotel. When they reached the door, they stopped and Marcia put her hand on Marcus's arm.

"I'd like to know about my Scottish family before I meet them," she asked him quietly. "Please will you tell me? I know nothing, you see."

"I'd be happy to."

"My father wouldn't tell me anything when he was alive."

"Alex."

"Yes. You know about him?"

"Oh, yes."

Marcia looked at him again.

"Look, why don't we get you booked into the hotel first and settled in your room, then we can talk as much as you like," said Marcus.

"Really?"

She smiled for the first time and Marcus was struck by its similarity to Anna's. But Marcia's smile was natural and spontaneous, revealing character and an inner vulnerability, whereas Anna's did not.

He wanted Marcia to smile at him again and again.

As soon as they entered her room, she immediately went over to the window and admired the view.

"Stunning, isn't it?" said Marcus, coming to stand beside her. "I slept in this very room when I first arrived."

"You did?"

"Yeah."

"I can't believe this."

"What?"

"Me standing here next to you like this." Then she blushed.

Marcus was curious. "What do you mean?"

"I've admired you ever since I was sixteen," she blurted out. "I've always wanted to meet you. I love all your books and I've read all your articles. And I absolutely knew at your trial that you were innocent." She blushed an even deeper shade of red. "And I shouldn't have said all that."

He smiled and touched her hand. "Of course you should. It's wonderful."

Marcus felt his spirits soar. Here was someone to whom he wouldn't have to explain about Virginia and risk losing as a prospective girlfriend before he'd even got to know her. He'd been so afraid of this – that it would be difficult for him to establish any relationship in the future; certain that his past would act as a barrier that could never be overcome.

But, Marcia knew all about him. She'd been to his trial and he wouldn't have to explain about Anna and go through the difficult process of trying to prove his innocence. He grinned happily at her.

"Now, what if I leave you to unpack before we talk?" he suggested. "After that, I know a lovely place where we can go."

Marcia shook her head. "Please stay. I'd rather you did."

Marcus didn't need much persuasion. "Okay. I'd be glad to."

While she put away her things, Marcia told him of her life in Australia; of her father and her mother; of her desire to become a journalist; how Marcus had inspired her. He listened and occasionally asked questions to which she responded naturally and openly.

By the time Marcia had finished unpacking, they both knew that something very special was happening between them.

As they left the hotel, Marcus took her hand in his and while they walked, he told her about Cairnmor: why he had come here; how he had come to love the island; about the book he was writing with Katherine; about Jack's illustrations and his great talent as an artist.

By the time they had reached the white-gold sands of South Lochaberdale, they both knew they were falling in love.

Sitting hidden from view amongst the dunes, with the gentle summer's breeze blowing round them and the sound of the waves lapping against the shore, Marcus told her about her family: of Katherine and Alex; of Katherine and Alastair; of Grace and Jack; of Rupert and Rose; of Anna.

"So Anna Stewart is my half-sister?!"

"Yes."

Marcia was stunned. "I had no idea! I saw her when she gave evidence but I never realized. I never made the connection with the surname!"

"And why should you? There must be thousands of families with the surname of 'Stewart'. How come yours is Harper?"

"My stepfather adopted me when he married my mother. So I took his name."

Warmed by the sun and their conversation, together they watched the red-legged oyster catchers and brown speckled dunlin as they fed at the water's edge.

They talked of New York, of her secondment, of her resignation.

"Did I do the right thing?"

"Absolutely."

"Have I wrecked any chance I might have had of journalism?"

"Not necessarily." Marcus was thoughtful. "Working on a good quality magazine might suit you better, though."

"I hadn't thought of that." She smiled at him again and Marcus wanted to kiss her.

"What will *you* do?" she asked him a moment or two later.

"Well, I had planned to stay on Cairnmor until my visa runs out."

"When's that?"

"December. What about you?"

"I have no plans. I don't have to be back in Aus for a while. I could always stay here..." she said cautiously.

They looked at each other again.

"I'd like that," he said, touching her cheek.

"You would?" she said in wonder.

"Yeah."

"And then what?"

"I could always come to Australia. I've no particular desire to go back to the States."

"You haven't?"

"No."

"Marcus?"

"Yes?"

"This is all happening to us very suddenly, isn't it?"

"Yes. Do you mind?"

"No. Do you?"

"No. I think it's wonderful."

"Please will you kiss me? I don't think I can wait a moment longer."

"Nor me."

And Marcus took her into his arms and kissed her. For a very long time.

Later, together, they stood up, brushed the sand off their clothes and he led her by the hand to the farmhouse where he introduced Marcia to her extended family and to Alastair, the grandfather whom she had never met.

It was early morning. The sun was already warming the land, dispelling the shadows cast by distant mountains. The lovers stirred and smiled at each other, greeting the new day, happy and content in their thatched-roof cottage perched high upon the hillside.

He put his arm out for her and she came to him, resting her head on his shoulder.

"Alastair?" murmured Katherine, still sleepy.

"Yes, my darling?"

"Happy birthday."

"Thank you." He kissed her forehead.

"Was it a good party last night?"

"It was a wonderful party."

"Did you like the theme?" She knew he had but she just wanted to hear him say it again.

"I *loved* the theme. To have a nineteen-forties occasion was an inspiration on your part. Very nostalgic."

Katherine smiled. "Everyone looked so elegant. And handsome. Especially you in your Royal Navy mess uniform."

"Jack and I did cut a particular style, I thought." He chuckled. "Not that I should say anything, of course."

"Of course you should! It's your birthday, you're allowed to say anything you like! I thought everyone really got into the spirit of the occasion."

"They did. The swing band were excellent and the dancing afterwards was a delight. Very romantic." He stroked her cheek. "You looked particularly beautiful. I've always loved that dress."

"I know. That's why I wore it."

Alastair kissed her lips and Katherine responded to him, his caresses still as blissful for her as they always had been.

After several moments, he said, "Jack and Grace looked stunning together."

"Didn't they just? I'm really looking forward to their wedding, whenever that might be."

"So is Ben. He said he couldn't be happier that Grace and his Dad were going to be married. And, what's more, Jack thinks his divorce will be finalized by the end of October, so he and Grace plan to get married then. He's heard from Anna's lawyer already."

"Goodness, that was quick!"

"It's a very straightforward thing, apparently, as there's no complicated settlement to draw up or difficult circumstances to overcome."

"Unlike mine."

"I know, but we got there. In the end."

"Oh, yes."

Alastair propped himself up on one elbow. "Do you mind that they're already living together before getting married?"

"Not in the slightest! They truly love each other and Grace was determined she wasn't going to let Jack out of her sight ever again."

"I can't say I blame her after what happened."

"Nor me. How about you, do you mind?"

"No. After all, we didn't want to wait, did we?"

"Of course not."

"There's a lot of us in Jack and Grace."

"Oh yes."

They lay together in companionable silence before Alastair said, seeing that Katherine was now fully awake, "Breakfast and a cup of tea would be nice."

"Your wish is my command, O husband!"

They dressed and went into the kitchen where Katherine prepared bacon and eggs for them both.

"I'm so glad that Phillippe is proud of Léon," remarked Alastair, after Katherine had finished cooking their breakfast and was seated beside him at the table. "Léon deserves it thoroughly and was delighted by his father's praise. He's longed for that moment, I think. They talked about politics too, both of them surprised to find a great deal of common ground, which pleased Phillippe especially. I think that Léon might make an excellent member of the Cairnmor Council one day. He's learned so much so quickly."

"And Phillippe and Lily both really like Fiona. She's such a moderating influence on Léon."

Alastair chuckled. "Angus strutted around like a peacock after they had spoken to him! Ron told him not to be such a daft beggar but I could see he was pleased for him."

"They're such characters. It was a fortunate day when we found them at Dunkirk. I'm so glad they came to live on Cairnmor."

"So am I. It's one of those unexpected yet welcome bonuses in life."

"And what about Marcus and Marcia? Now there's a lovely bonus! Do you think they'll stay together and maybe even settle here?"

232

Katherine had been surprised and pleased by this unanticipated romance. They had been inseparable since Marcia's arrival and Marcus deserved some luck after all he had been through. She thought Marcia to be a lovely young woman and was amazed to discover that she was the same age as Grace. Katherine smiled to herself. Rachel must have been pregnant when Katherine met her at the hospital in London after Alex had suffered yet another bout of malaria. She wondered if Rachel had known then. Perhaps she might be able to ask her one day.

"I have a feeling that they will stay together," observed Alastair, "but I don't think they'll settle here. I reckon Marcus will move to Australia and they'll make their home there."

"I hope they will come back to see us, though."

"I'm sure they will. Hopefully for extended visits, just like your parents still do from Canada."

"I wonder if Mhairi and Rupert will *ever* settle on Cairnmor? The journey is becoming more and more difficult as they get older."

Alastair didn't make the observation that he was a year older than Rupert but took his wife's hand, reassuring her; knowing that she had always felt the pain of separation keenly from those whom she loved. She lifted his hand to her lips, grateful for his unspoken understanding.

"Maybe not after all this time. Despite their original intention many years ago, I think that Canada is their permanent home. But we've had some wonderful holidays over the years when they've come here or we've visited them."

"Yes, that's true."

"And we have seen an awful lot of them considering they live so far away."

Katherine smiled. "Yes, and I'm so glad."

"And what about Rupert and Rose?" observed Alastair, moving the conversation on.

"I thought she looked radiant."

"Your parents are delighted that they're so happy in their new home."

"Which of course, Rupert has already been able to buy back from his grandfather."

"And hopefully, he and Rose will be able to have children one day."

"Michael and Mary feel certain of it," said Katherine. "Especially now that Rose is taking that herbal remedy Mary and Marcus discovered while sorting through my notes, that is supposed to balance the hormones."

"Good old Mrs Gilgarry! Her legacy reaches far and wide!"

"She would have enjoyed all this hugely, especially if she'd stayed at the hotel."

Alastair chuckled. "It was always her favourite building on the island." He finished his last mouthful of breakfast before saying, "Were you sorry that Anna wasn't there?"

"No. I think it was right that she left when she did. However, if the letter she wrote is anything to go by, she finally seems to be facing up to her past and is also beginning to accept and forgive us at last. Hopefully, she'll keep in touch with us now."

"I think she may, but we'll have to wait and see."

"If we had told her sooner, would she have turned out differently?" asked Katherine.

Alastair took a deep breath. He too had asked himself this question. He shook his head. "No, I don't think so. She's very like Roberta. If it hadn't been that, it would have been something else."

"She was such a loving child."

"Most of the time. It's all too easy now to forget that despite her apparent sweetness, she was often wilful and deceitful. Especially as she grew older. Even before she read that letter."

"Yes, that's very true."

Lightening the mood once more, Alastair said, "Well, with everything that's been going on, I forgot to tell you that Jack's heard from the medical board. Because his hands and ribs will take a several months to heal and because of his long service, the navy's going to put him on the retired list. It means he won't have to go back and serve out his remaining time. Nor will he have to resign. And he can remain part of the Royal Navy."

Katherine smiled, cheerful once more. "That's marvellous news. Grace will be pleased, although she did say that she would go with him wherever he was posted."

"I know. I find that quite remarkable."

"Me too."

They took their tea outside, putting their cups down on the little table where they had sat so often over the years, drawn to the magnificent view across the bay to Lochaberdale.

"The future looks full of promise, doesn't it?" said Alastair, suddenly feeling energized by all the possibilities. "And what's more, our beloved Cairnmor will be in very safe hands."

He smiled tenderly at Katherine, his wife, his companion, the mother of his favourite child. He put his arms round her and held her close to his heart.

"I love you," he said.

"I love you too," she replied simply.

There was so much to look forward to; so much to look back upon. Best of all, they would continue to share everything, just as they had always done for so many wonderful years. Filled with profound joy, they saw Grace and Jack walking up the hill to meet them, a picture of complete happiness.

Katherine and Alastair smiled at each other knowing that here was the future – as certain and everlasting as the beauty of Cairnmor.

OTHER PUBLICATIONS FROM ŌZARU BOOKS

The Call of Cairnmor
Sally Aviss

Book One of the Cairnmor Trilogy

The Scottish Isle of Cairnmor is a place of great beauty and undisturbed wilderness, a haven for wildlife, a land of white sandy beaches and inland fertile plains, a land where awe-inspiring mountains connect precipitously with the sea.

To this remote island comes a stranger, Alexander Stewart, on a quest to solve the mysterious disappearance of two people and their unborn child; a missing family who are now heirs to a vast fortune. He enlists the help of local schoolteacher, Katherine MacDonald, and together they seek the answers to this enigma: a deeply personal journey that takes them from Cairnmor to the historic splendour of London and the industrial heartland of Glasgow.

Covering the years 1936-1937 and infused with period colour and detail, The Call of Cairnmor is about unexpected discovery and profound attachment which, from its gentle opening, gradually gathers momentum and complexity until all the strands come together to give life-changing revelations.

"really enjoyed reading this – loved the plot... Read it in just two sittings as I couldn't stop reading." (P. Green – amazon.co.uk)

"exciting plot, not a book you want to put down, although I tried not to rush it so as to fully enjoy escaping to the world skilfully created by the author. A most enjoyable read." (Liz Green – amazon.co.uk)

"an excellent read. I cannot wait for the next part of the trilogy from this talented author. You will not want to put it down" (B. Burchell – amazon.co.uk)

ISBN: 978-0-9559219-9-5

Changing Tides, Changing Times
Sally Aviss

Book Two of the Cairnmor Trilogy

In the dense jungle of Malaya in 1942, Doctor Rachel Curtis stumbles across a mysterious, unidentifiable stranger, badly injured and close to death.

Four years earlier in 1938 in London, Katherine Stewart and her husband Alex come into conflict with their differing needs while Alex's father, Alastair, knows he must keep his deeper feelings hidden from the woman he loves; a woman to whom he must never reveal the full extent of that love.

Covering a broad canvas and meticulously researched, Changing Times, Changing Tides follows the interwoven journey of well-loved characters from The Call of Cairnmor, as well as introducing new personalities, in a unique combination of novel and history that tells a story of love, loss, friendship and heroism; absorbing the reader in the characters' lives as they are shaped and changed by the ebb and flow of events before, during and after the Second World War.

"I enjoyed the twists and turns of this book ... particularly liked the gutsy Dr Rachel who is a reminder to the reader that these are dark days for the world. Love triumphs but not in the way we thought it would and our heroine, Katherine, learns that the path to true love is certainly not a smooth one." (MDW – amazon.co.uk)

"Even better than the first book! A moving and touching story well told." (P. Green – amazon.co.uk)

"One of the best reads this year ... can't wait for the next one." (Mr. C. Brownett – amazon.co.uk

ISBN: 978-0-9931587-0-4

Reflections in an Oval Mirror
Memories of East Prussia, 1923-45
Anneli Jones

8 May 1945 – VE Day – was Anneliese Wiemer's twenty-second birthday. Although she did not know it then, it marked the end of her flight to the West, and the start of a new life in England.

These illustrated memoirs, based on a diary kept during the Third Reich and letters rediscovered many decades later, depict the momentous changes occurring in Europe against a backcloth of everyday farm life in East Prussia (now the north-western corner of Russia, sandwiched between Lithuania and Poland).

The political developments of the 1930s (including the Hitler Youth, 'Kristallnacht', political education, labour service, war service, and interrogation) are all the more poignant for being told from the viewpoint of a romantic young girl. In lighter moments she also describes student life in Vienna and Prague, and her friendship with Belgian and Soviet prisoners of war. Finally, however, the approach of the Red Army forces her to abandon her home and flee across the frozen countryside, encountering en route a cross-section of society ranging from a 'lady of the manor', worried about her family silver, to some concentration camp inmates

"couldn't put it down... delightful... very detailed descriptions of the farm and the arrival of war... interesting history and personal account" ('Rosie', amazon.com)

ISBN: 978-0-9559219-0-2

Carpe Diem
Moving on from East Prussia
Anneli Jones

This sequel to "Reflections in an Oval Mirror" details Anneli's post-war life. The scene changes from life in Northern 'West Germany' as a refugee, reporter and military interpreter, to parties with the Russian Authorities in Berlin, boating in the Lake District with the original 'Swallows and Amazons', weekends with the Astors at Cliveden, then the beginnings of a new family in the small Kentish village of St Nicholas-at-Wade. Finally, after the fall of the Iron Curtain, Anneli is able to revisit her first home once more.

ISBN: 978-0-9931587-3-5

Skating at the Edge of the Wood
Memories of East Prussia, 1931-1945… 1993
Marlene Yeo

In 1944, the thirteen-year old East Prussian girl Marlene Wiemer embarked on a horrific trek to the West, to escape the advancing Red Army. Her cousin Jutta was left behind the Iron Curtain, which severed the family bonds that had made the two so close.

This book contains dramatic depictions of Marlene's flight, recreated from her letters to Jutta during the last year of the war, and contrasted with joyful memories of the innocence that preceded them.

Nearly fifty years later, the advent of perestroika meant that Marlene and Jutta were finally able to revisit their childhood home, after a lifetime of growing up under diametrically opposed societies, and the book closes with a final chapter revealing what they find.

Despite depicting the same time and circumstances as "Reflections in an Oval Mirror", an account written by Marlene's elder sister, Anneli, and its sequel "Carpe Diem", this work stands in stark contrast partly owing to the age gap between the two girls, but above all because of their dramatically different characters.

ISBN: 978-0-9931587-2-8

Travels in Taiwan
Exploring Ilha Formosa
Gary Heath

For many Westerners, Taiwan is either a source of cheap electronics or an ongoing political problem. It is seldom highlighted as a tourist destination, and even those that do visit rarely venture far beyond the well-trod paths of the major cities and resorts.

Yet true to its 16th century Portuguese name, the 'beautiful island' has some of the highest mountains in East Asia, many unique species of flora and fauna, and several distinct indigenous peoples (fourteen at the last count).

On six separate and arduous trips, Gary Heath deliberately headed for the areas neglected by other travel journalists, armed with several notebooks... and a copy of War and Peace for the days when typhoons confined him to his tent. The fascinating land he discovered is revealed here.

"offers a great deal of insight into Taiwanese society, history, culture, as well as its island's scenic geography... disturbing and revealing... a true, peripatetic, descriptive Odyssey undertaken by an adventurous and inquisitive Westerner on a very Oriental and remote island" (Charles Phillips, goodreads.com)

ISBN: 978-0-9559219-1-9 (Royal Octavo)

ISBN: 978-0-9559219-8-8 (Half Letter)

West of Arabia
A Journey Home
Gary Heath

Faced with the need to travel from Saudi Arabia to the UK, Gary Heath made the unusual decision to take the overland route. His three principles were to stay on the ground, avoid back-tracking, and do minimal sightseeing.

The ever-changing situation in the Middle East meant that the rules had to be bent on occasion, yet as he travelled across Eritrea, Sudan, Egypt, Libya, Tunisia and Morocco, he succeeded in beating his own path around the tourist traps, gaining unique insights into Arabic culture as he went.

Written just a few months before the Arab Spring of 2011, this book reveals many of the underlying tensions that were to explode onto the world stage just shortly afterwards, and has been updated to reflect the recent changes.

"just the right blend of historical background [and] personal experiences... this book is a must read" ('Denise', goodreads.com)

ISBN: 978-0-9559219-6-4

Ichigensan
– The Newcomer –
David Zoppetti

Translated from the Japanese by Takuma Sminkey

Ichigensan is a novel which can be enjoyed on many levels – as a delicate, sensual love story, as a depiction of the refined society in Japan's cultural capital Kyoto, and as an exploration of the themes of alienation and prejudice common to many environments, regardless of the boundaries of time and place.

Unusually, it shows Japan from the eyes of both an outsider and an 'internal' outcast, and even more unusually, it originally achieved this through sensuous prose carefully crafted by a non-native speaker of Japanese. The fact that this best-selling novella then won the Subaru Prize, one of Japan's top literary awards, and was also nominated for the Akutagawa Prize is a testament to its unique narrative power.

The story is by no means chained to Japan, however, and this new translation by Takuma Sminkey will allow readers world-wide to enjoy the multitude of sensations engendered by life and love in an alien culture.

"A beautiful love story" (Japan Times)

"Sophisticated... subtle... sensuous... delicate... memorable... vivid depictions" (Asahi Evening News)

"Striking... fascinating..." (Japan PEN Club)

"Refined and sensual" (Kyoto Shimbun)

"quiet, yet very compelling... subtle mixture of humour and sensuality...the insights that the novel gives about Japanese society are both intriguing and exotic" (Nicholas Greenman, amazon.com)

ISBN: 978-0-9559219-4-0

Sunflowers
– Le Soleil –
Shimako Murai

A play in one act
Translated from the Japanese by Ben Jones

Hiroshima is synonymous with the first hostile use of an atomic bomb. Many people think of this occurrence as one terrible event in the past, which is studied from history books.

Shimako Murai and other 'Women of Hiroshima' believe otherwise: for them, the bomb had after-effects which affected countless people for decades, effects that were all the more menacing for their unpredictability – and often, invisibility.

This is a tale of two such people: on the surface successful modern women, yet each bearing underneath hidden scars as horrific as the keloids that disfigured Hibakusha on the days following the bomb.

"a great story and a glimpse into the lives of the people who lived during the time of the war and how the bomb affected their lives, even after all these years" (Wendy Pierce, goodreads.com)

ISBN: 978-0-9559219-3-3

Turner's Margate Through Contemporary Eyes
The Viney Letters
Stephen Channing

Margate in the early 19th Century was an exciting town, where smugglers and 'preventive men' fought to outwit each other, while artists such as JMW Turner came to paint the glorious sunsets over the sea. One of the young men growing up in this environment decided to set out for Australia to make his fortune in the Bendigo gold rush.

Half a century later, having become a pillar of the community, he began writing a series of letters and articles for Keble's Gazette, a publication based in his home town. In these, he described Margate with great familiarity (and tremendous powers of recall), while at the same time introducing his English readers to the "latitudinarian democracy" of a new, "young Britain".

Viney's interests covered a huge range of topics, from Thanet folk customs such as Hoodening, through diatribes on the perils of assigning intelligence to dogs, to geological theories including suggestions for the removal of sandbanks off the English coast "in obedience to the sovereign will and intelligence of man".

His writing is clearly that of a well-educated man, albeit with certain Victorian prejudices about the colonies that may make those with modern sensibilities wince a little. Yet above all, it is interesting because of the light it throws on life in a British seaside town some 180 years ago.

This book also contains numerous contemporary illustrations.

"profusely illustrated... draws together a series of interesting articles and letters... recommended" (Margate Civic Society)

ISBN: 978-0-9559219-2-6

The Margate Tales
Stephen Channing

Chaucer's Canterbury Tales is without doubt one of the best ways of getting a feel for what the people of England in the Middle Ages were like. In the modern world, one might instead try to learn how different people behave and think from television or the internet.

However, to get a feel for what it was like to be in Margate as it gradually changed from a small fishing village into one of Britain's most popular holiday resorts, one needs to investigate contemporary sources such as newspaper reports and journals.

Stephen Channing has saved us this work, by trawling through thousands of such documents to select the most illuminating and entertaining accounts of Thanet in the 18th and early to mid 19th centuries. With content ranging from furious battles in the letters pages, to hilarious pastiches, witty poems and astonishing factual reports, illustrated with over 70 drawings from the time, The Margate Tales brings the society of the time to life, and as with Chaucer, demonstrates how in many areas, surprisingly little has changed.

"substantial and fascinating volume... meticulously researched... an absorbing read" (Margate Civic Society)

ISBN: 978-0-9559219-5-7

A Victorian Cyclist
Rambling through Kent in 1886
Stephen & Shirley Channing

Bicycles are so much a part of everyday life nowadays, it can be surprising to realize that for the late Victorians these "velocipedes" were a novelty disparaged as being unhealthy and unsafe – and that indeed tricycles were for a time seen as the format more likely to succeed.

Some people however adopted the newfangled devices with alacrity, embarking on adventurous tours throughout the countryside. One of them documented his 'rambles' around East Kent in such detail that it is still possible to follow his routes on modern cycles, and compare the fauna and flora (and pubs!) with those he vividly described.

In addition to providing today's cyclists with new historical routes to explore, and both naturalists and social historians with plenty of material for research, this fascinating book contains a special chapter on Lady Cyclists in the era before female emancipation, and an unintentionally humorous section instructing young gentlemen how to make their cycle and then ride it.

A Victorian Cyclist features over 200 illustrations, and is complemented by a fully updated website.

"Lovely... wonderfully written... terrific" (Everything Bicycles)

"Rare and insightful" (Kent on Sunday)

"Interesting... informative... detailed historical insights" (BikeBiz)

"Unique and fascinating book... quality is very good... of considerable interest" (Veteran-Cycle Club)

"Superb... illuminating... well detailed... The easy flowing prose, which has a cadence like cycling itself, carries the reader along as if freewheeling with a hind wind" (Forty Plus Cycling Club)

"a fascinating book with both vivid descriptions and a number of hitherto-unseen photos of the area" ('Pedalling Pensioner', amazon.co.uk)

ISBN: 978-0-9559219-7-1

Lightning Source UK Ltd.
Milton Keynes UK
UKOW02f1941051215

264101UK00003B/408/P